"I'm adopting her."

"What about the baby's family? Shouldn't they have a say?"

Mack blinked at the unexpected question. "Sarah's mother gave her up."

Thea leveled pleading blue eyes at him. "Maybe she thought she didn't have a choice."

Mack straightened and crossed his arms over his chest. "Why have you been nosing around Ms. Aurora's the last two days?"

"It has to do with my sister—the last few months of her life."

"The night of the accident was the first time I'd seen her in years."

"Eileen probably kept out of sight due to her condition."

Mack turned sharply to stare at her. "She was pregnant? Where's the baby?"

"That's just it, Mack. Momma says the baby has been stolen."

"That's why you've been spying on Aurora's place." The pieces began to fall into place. "You think Sarah is Eileen's baby?"

"Sarah's the spitting image of Eileen." Sorrow along with another emotion—determination?—stared back at him. "That child you want to adopt is my niece, Mack. And I want to take her home."

Patty Smith Hall
and
Angel Moore

The Baby Barter
&
The Marriage Bargain

LOVE INSPIRED
INSPIRATIONAL ROMANCE

LOVE INSPIRED®
INSPIRATIONAL ROMANCE

ISBN-13: 978-1-335-52997-8

Recycling programs for this product may not exist in your area.

The Baby Barter and The Marriage Bargain

Copyright © 2022 by Harlequin Enterprises ULC

The Baby Barter
First published in 2016. This edition published in 2022.
Copyright © 2016 by Patty Smith Hall

The Marriage Bargain
First published in 2016. This edition published in 2022.
Copyright © 2016 by Angelissa J. Moore

For questions and comments about the quality of this book, please contact us at CustomerService@Harlequin.com.

Love Inspired
22 Adelaide St. West, 41st Floor
Toronto, Ontario M5H 4E3, Canada
www.LoveInspired.com

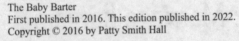

Printed in U.S.A.

CONTENTS

Patty Smith Hall has been making up stories since she was knee-high to a grasshopper. Now she's thrilled to share her love of history and her storytelling skills with everyone, including her hero of thirty-one years, Danny, two beautiful daughters and a wonderful future son-in-law. She resides in northeast Georgia. Patty loves to hear from her readers! You can contact her at pattysmithhall.com.

Books by Patty Smith Hall

Love Inspired Historical

Hearts in Flight
Hearts in Hiding
Hearts Rekindled
The Baby Barter

Visit the Author Profile page
at LoveInspired.com for more titles.

THE BABY BARTER

Patty Smith Hall

And we know that God causes all things to
work together for good to those who love God,
to those who are called according to His purpose.
—*Romans* 8:28

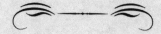

To Rose Smith. Your humble spirit
and servant heart make you a rare beauty in today's
world, sweet sister. You are a rare jewel indeed!

Chapter One

Marietta, Georgia
Fall, 1945

Sheriff Mack Worthington made it his business to notice people.

And the woman standing in the shadows of the massive oak tree at the edge of Merrilee Davenport's backyard had sent his senses on high alert. Not that he could see her all that well. The brim of her felt hat covered most of her face, leaving him at a distinct disadvantage.

But it was the little things that made him question her reasons for being there. In the tan skirt and white blouse she wore, she looked more prepared for a trip to the market than attendance at a wedding. And why did her fingers unconsciously dig into the sides of her purse as if she were holding on to it for dear life? Tension held her ramrod straight, reminding him of a soldier ready for battle.

What fight did this woman expect to face here?

"What's got you twisting around in your chair like a kite in a tornado?"

Mack glanced at the older lady to his right and felt the

knots in his stomach relax. Ms. Aurora's tone had just the right combination of chastisement and concern that came from years of caring for other people's children. He straightened in his seat. "Nothing, Ms. Aurora."

She studied him a long moment until he felt himself start to squirm again. "It don't look like nothing to me."

Billy Warner, the oldest of Aurora's current batch of foster children at twelve years old, pushed himself out of his chair, his cane anchored against his side as he stretched up to get a better look down the rows of chairs that lined the makeshift aisle. "Is Claire up to something? I knew she'd get bored with all this wishy-washy romantic stuff."

Mack's lips twitched as he put his free hand on the boy's shoulder and gently pushed him back into his seat. "Claire is on her best behavior today. That girl's been looking forward to seeing her parents get remarried since her daddy showed up back in town." John and Merrilee had a troubled past—filled with misunderstandings and manipulations by her family meant to keep them apart. But they'd triumphed over it all, as this wedding proved. And their twelve-year-old daughter couldn't be happier.

"Maybe." Billy blew out a snort. "But the ceremony's been over for a good five minutes, and we're still sitting here when we could be eating some of that spread Miss Merrilee has been cooking for the last week. I'm starving."

Mack shook his head. The boy had a lot to learn about the female of the species over the next few years, particularly when it came to things like romance and marriage. Not that Mack was any kind of expert. His few attempts at romance had been shot down in flames. Maybe women and the workings of their hearts were the only mystery he wouldn't ever solve.

A faint whimper drew his gaze, and Mack found himself staring into a pair of pale blue eyes wide with just a slight hint of irritation, plump baby fingers reaching for him, her tiny body squirming in Ms. Aurora's arms. Technically, little Sarah was in Ms. Aurora's care until the adoption was approved, but both Mack and the baby knew the truth—he was the one who had been there for her, loving her since she was dropped into his arms on the day she was born. He was her father in every way that mattered. If only he could push Judge Wakefield to make it legal.

Ms. Aurora shifted the child in her arms and held her out to Mack. "Looks like someone wants to see her daddy."

"Come here, doodlebug." Mack scooped up the baby, her warm little body instantly nestling against his chest. She reached up and Mack caught the tips of her fingers between his lips, nibbling gently, enjoying this new game Sarah had discovered in the past day or two. Her lips turned up in a gaping smile, the jagged pink line just under her nose the only evidence of her most recent surgery to fix the cleft palate she'd been born with. A wave of love like nothing he'd ever known speared through him.

"Really, Sheriff," Ms. Aurora whispered as she caught the baby's hands and wiped her tiny fingers dry with a billowy cotton cloth. "You need to teach her to keep her hands to herself."

"It's just a game we play." Mack held out a finger to the baby, who eyed it for a moment before grasping it between her palms and drawing it to her gaping mouth. "Besides, I think she's teething. At least, that's what it sounds like from all the books I've read."

The elderly woman shook her head as she extracted his finger from the little girl's grip. "You're spoiling her silly, Mack."

"I can't help it." He lifted her up, brushed a quick kiss against Sarah's silky hair, then smiled. "And what girl doesn't deserve a little bit of spoiling?"

"Not every moment of every day," the older woman scolded.

Mack silently disagreed. They'd almost lost Sarah during her last surgery to correct the disfigurement to her mouth and nose, and there was still one more surgery to come. It would be a hard trial for anyone to face, particularly a baby who had already faced too much pain and rejection in her short life.

She'd been abandoned by her young mother just hours after she'd been born. Mack had gotten the call to pick up the baby that day—Victory in Europe Day—and deliver her to the only place that would take a child with such severe anomalies. In the short half-hour drive to Ms. Aurora's, Mack had found his attention riveted to the tiny infant lying swaddled in a ragged blanket in a cardboard box fashioned into a makeshift crib. By the time they'd turned into the dirt driveway leading to the older woman's home, he'd known he wanted to adopt this child and raise her as his own daughter.

As if she had a window into his worries, Ms. Aurora laid a comforting hand on his arm. "You heard anything from Judge Wakefield about when you can finally take Sarah home?"

Mack shook his head. "Not yet."

"That's Ethan for you. Taking his ever-loving sweet time about things." The older woman gave a little huff. "I swear that man is as slow as molasses in the dead of winter."

Mack couldn't argue with her there. Judge Wakefield was known in town for his persnickety approach to his duties, but Mack had an inkling this situation was related more to the man's personal dislike of him.

"Well, what's Red doing to get the adoption finalized? I figured with all the money you're paying that boy, he would have closed this case by now."

Mack's lips twitched. Red had never grown up from being "that boy" to Ms. Aurora, not since he'd filled up the town fountain with laundry soap when he was just ten years old. She didn't seem to realize that he had become one of the leading attorneys in the state.

But Aurora did have a point. Red should have gotten everything resolved by now. Since taking this case, one thing after another had gotten in the way of finalizing the adoption. "He's supposed to be here today. I thought I'd corner him with a piece of Merrilee's juicy chocolate cake and see what the holdup is."

"The way things are going, Sarah will be a woman fully grown before you take her home." Ms. Aurora gently patted the baby's back.

Billy turned to them, his finger pressed against his lips. "Claire's giving us the eye."

Mack glanced up to where the wedding party had gathered. Claire stood beside her mother, her lips drawn into a stern line. Boy, John and Merrilee would have their hands full with that one, especially when the boys began to come courting.

Mack leaned back in his chair, a smile threatening along the corners of his mouth. What would Sarah be like at that age? Full of sass and determination? A tomboy more interested in Atlanta Crackers baseball games than school dances? Or would she love frills and lace and girly stuff Mack didn't know a thing about?

Mack's gaze fell to the bundle of ribbons and bows

perched on his lap. Was he being selfish, wanting to raise Sarah without the benefit of a mother, no feminine hand to lead her through those challenging years of becoming a woman? He shifted in his seat. It wasn't that he hadn't tried to find a wife. A number of nice women had moved into town since the bomber plant had opened. He'd even dated one or two, but things never seemed to work out.

He touched the scar just under the hairline next to his left ear. Probably for the best. If God wanted him to have a wife, He would have sent someone who could look beyond his limitations, one who would love him just as he was, deaf ear and all. Until then, he and Sarah would do just fine on their own.

A slight pressure against his right side jarred him away from his thought, and he turned to see Ms. Aurora's worried expression. Her pale eyes darkened into stormy gray as she stole a glance over her shoulder, her body rigid.

Mack lifted Sarah and nestled her against his shoulder. "What is it, Ms. Aurora?"

"I'm probably just imagining things."

Mack doubted it. Aurora Adair was one of the most sensible and down-to-earth people he knew. If she felt something was amiss, nine times out of ten she was right. "Let me be the judge of that."

She pressed her lips together as if deciding whether to tell him or not. "Remember a couple of days ago when I told you I felt like someone was watching the house?"

His heart rate kicked up a notch. "Yes."

"I didn't worry much about it. I like to think some of the families of the children who were left with me might try to get a glimpse of them, just to make sure they're all right. But this one…" The viselike grip she had on his arm put all Mack's instincts on alert. "She's been watching the house for the last two days, and now, she's here."

"Point her out to me."

Ms. Aurora gave him an annoyed look. "I can't do that. That's just plain rude."

"Then how am I—"

"She's toward the back, underneath that big old oak tree one of the children got stuck in last July. Remember?"

Yes, he remembered. Took him two hours to get that little firecracker Ellie off that high-hanging branch. "There's a crowd over there, Ms. Aurora. Which lady are you talking about?"

"The girl in the plain tan skirt with a white blouse and a brown felt hat. Doesn't look like she knew there was going to be a wedding today."

Knots began to form in the pit of Mack's stomach. He'd known the woman was trouble but just *who* was she? Mack shifted sideways to get a good long look at her. The brim of her hat still flopped over most of her face, but now he caught a glimpse of golden-brown curls clinging to the nape of her neck. She tilted her head back, casting a nervous glance at the crowd before her gaze fell on him. A dull ache settled in Mack's left jaw, and he reached for the jagged scar once again.

Thea Miller had come home.

Thea's palms grew moist inside her bleached cotton gloves, her gaze fixed on the impossibly handsome man glaring back at her. She immediately recognized Mack Worthington, football team captain, all-around good guy. And the only boy in high school she would have given a second glance. Or a third. Her heart hammered against her ribs just thinking about the crush she'd nursed for him her junior and senior years.

She didn't have time to reminisce about the good old days, not with the trouble she'd found when she'd returned home from England three days ago. Thea drew in a slow breath, then released it, her heart settling back into a normal rhythm. That silly girl with a shameful family and a hopeless crush had made something of herself, serving her country as a nurse on the front lines in Europe. If she could face those dangers, then facing down a boy she used to like should be the least of her worries.

But maybe he could help her. Someone in town had mentioned Mack had taken Sheriff Clay's place after the older man had enlisted. The news had shocked Thea at first. Knowing how protective Mack could be, she'd thought he'd enlist the day after Pearl Harbor was bombed. What had kept him in Marietta rather than serving his country overseas?

Thea shook her head. What did it matter? Mack was the town's sheriff. Maybe it was time to get the police involved if Momma's allegations were true.

Aurora Adair stole your sister's baby.

Momma's words twisted the knots in her stomach as tight as a tourniquet. The scenario sounded eerily familiar—her kid sister, Eileen, pregnant and unmarried, the child missing soon after birth, the frantic search that turned up nothing, a promise from Thea to find the baby and return it home. Her chest tightened. A promise she'd never been able to keep. Of course, she'd been little more than a child herself, barely seventeen. Eight unbearable years she'd waited to come home, thwarting the promise she'd made to her sister and had been unable to keep.

Not this time.

Besides, this was a completely different situation. Eight years ago, it had been their mother who had made the decision to give away Eileen's baby, her pride unable to handle the prospect of the town discovering that her unwed, teenage daughter had become a mother. But this time, her mother said that she'd wanted the baby—that she'd helped Eileen prepare. And Thea herself had seen the evidence: tiny sweaters and booties recently knitted, a cupboard full of washed and sterilized baby bottles and all the makings for homemade formula.

This time, they could have made things work, truly pulled together as a family in a way they hadn't done in years. But Eileen had died not long after, in a car accident. The baby had been taken from them. And Thea had returned home to find nothing left of her family but her mother—and even she was sadly changed.

All Thea could hope for now was to find her sister's baby, take her home and raise the child herself. Have a real family again.

Which might be more difficult than she'd first thought. Aurora Adair hadn't left her house once in the two days since Thea had started monitoring her movements, hoping for a chance to meet her on the street. She refused to knock on the woman's front door to deliver her accusation. It had been an answer to prayer when she'd learned Ms. Adair would be at the Daniels's place today. A public venue might give Thea her only opportunity to get this mess straightened out. She wanted badly to believe that this had all been some kind of misunderstanding, and that Ms. Aurora would be happy to return the baby to her loving family. Hopefully a quick conversation would be all it would take.

But crashing a wedding had never been part of the plan.

Thea stole back into the cool shadows of the tree and waited until the wedding guests made their way toward the house. The festive atmosphere didn't really agree with her. Not when she was still caught up in mourning for Eileen. It had been weeks since the fatal car accident, but Thea had only learned about it a few days before.

A fresh wave of sadness caught her by surprise, punching her in the midsection like a fist. It still didn't seem real, her baby sister gone. Guilt warred with grief inside Thea's heart. Maybe if she'd returned home, instead of staying away out of guilt over her broken promise, she could have kept an eye on Eileen. Maybe then she wouldn't have jumped into that car with Eddie Huffman, wouldn't have been killed when Eddie lost control.

An ache settled in the pit of Thea's stomach. She might have let Eileen down but she'd make up for it, raise her sister's baby as her own. Which meant getting the baby back.

Thea pushed away from the tree and scanned the Daniels's front yard as people lingered along the makeshift aisle, following the path the newly remarried couple had taken just moments ago. She wobbled forward and instantly yearned for the sturdy comfort of her army boots, the new heels she'd bought this morning shifting on the unlevel ground. Omaha Beach hadn't given her as much trouble as these silly shoes.

"Thea Miller?"

Thea felt her shoulders stiffen. Any hope of getting through the day unnoticed vanished. It had been a foolish hope, anyway. Nothing ever stayed hidden in Marietta. Her mother and sister had taught her that. Thea turned, her skirts whispering softly around her legs, making her long for the confidence she'd always felt in her army greens or nursing whites. An auburn-haired woman wad-dled toward her, the loose pleats of her dress floating over her swollen belly as she slowly moved down the row.

Thea's mouth turned up in an unexpected smile. "Mag-gie Daniels?"

"I thought that was you! How are you?" Maggie smiled as if she was truly happy to see her. "It's Maggie Hicks now." She caressed a loving hand against the swell of her stomach. "This here's Peanut."

"Family name?"

Maggie's smile widened. "On my husband's side."

The soft chuckles that rasped against her throat startled Thea. How long had it been since she'd truly laughed? Not since before the war, maybe even longer. "Congratulations, Maggie."

"Thank you, but what about you? Last time I talked to your mother, you were in nursing school in Memphis."

Thea nodded. So her mother hadn't told anyone in town she'd joined the Army Nurse Corps. At least she'd read Thea's letters and knew where her daughter had gone. She'd never written back, so Thea had wondered if the letters had been thrown away, her mother still hold-ing a grudge about the way Thea had left home. Though, what had her mother expected after what she'd done, giv-ing Eileen's first baby to a total stranger? "I joined the Army Nurse Corps a year after graduation."

"Where were you stationed?"

"Stateside at first, then I was sent to Sheffield, Eng-land."

"Really?" Her friend's green eyes warmed. "My hus-band's grandfather owned an airfield outside York for many years but he's been in the States for a while now."

"It must have been lovely then." Before the army barracks and field hospitals had filled the lush green fields surrounding the quaint buildings that formed the town's center. Thea closed her eyes. So much damage to that lovely land and the people who lived there. So many families torn apart, extinguished, never to be together again in this life. The need to see her own family had driven her these last few weeks, across the Atlantic then down the East Coast.

But where was home now, and who could she count as family since her baby sister was gone and her mother seemed to be a shell of herself? But then look at what Momma had lost in the past few months, her daughter and grandchild. Who could blame her for being quiet and withdrawn?

"I was so sorry to hear about Eileen."

Thea swallowed against the lump in her throat. Condolences weren't easy to hear. "Me, too."

"I didn't even know she was in town until I heard about the accident."

That little piece of news surprised Thea. "Where else would she be?"

Maggie frowned in confusion. "Didn't you know? She left for Atlanta right about the time you took off for school. This past summer was the first time she'd been back since then."

What had Eileen been doing in Atlanta? Why had she come back here to have her baby? "She must have been visiting Momma."

"Your momma must treasure that time now."

Thea drew in a deep sigh. "She doesn't talk about it much."

"I couldn't imagine, losing my child like that. It must be hard to talk about it with the pain still fresh." Maggie rubbed her hand over her swollen middle as if holding her unborn child close.

"Maybe." Or maybe not. Momma had never shown much emotion or warmth toward either her or her sister, especially after their father had died in a farming accident when she'd been only four and Eileen no more than three. Thea had taken over mothering Eileen then, rocking her back to sleep when she woke up from a bad dream, making sure Eileen was fed before she'd head off to school in the morning. As she grew older, Eileen and their mother had started to fight. When Eileen's wild ways blossomed in her early teens and proved to be embarrassing, the arguments had grown worse. Thea could only imagine how bad things had gotten after Momma had given Eileen's baby away. Maybe it wasn't that surprising that Eileen had decided to leave town. Why had she come home to deliver her second baby? Maybe she and Momma had made things right between them.

"They're ready to cut the cake!"

Both women turned to where a boy of about twelve stood on the porch at the top of the stairs, a wooden cane bearing the weight of his lean frame. Scowling, he fidgeted with his tie, leaving it slightly off center. His dark coat sat precariously on his shoulders, as if the boy hadn't decided whether to fling it off or not.

"He looks happy to be here," Thea commented.

Maggie's warm laughter coaxed another rare smile from her. "Billy's not quite sure about this wedding stuff, but give him a plate of Aunt Merrilee's cooking and he's happier than a puppy with two tails."

Thea relaxed a bit. She'd always liked Maggie, liked her plain talk and friendly way of treating everyone the same, no matter their social status. "Please tell your aunt congratulations from me."

"You can tell her yourself." Before Thea had a chance to respond, Maggie tucked her hand into Thea's arm and pulled her out of the shadows.

Thea glanced around, praying no one else would notice her. "I'm not exactly dressed for a wedding."

"You look fine, and I refuse to let a woman who served our boys overseas get away without a piece of Merrilee's wedding cake. It's the first time she's baked anything since they stopped rationing sugar and eggs."

The thought of such a sweet delight after four long years was almost too much for Thea to bear. But staying for the reception felt too awkward. She'd approach Ms. Aurora another time, maybe get up the nerve to go to her door and ask about Eileen's baby. She may not know the woman personally, but she'd heard enough about her kindness and generosity to the children she'd taken in to her home, disabled children who'd been abandoned, to hope that this had all been a simple misunderstanding. One they could resolve easily…after which, she'd be able to bring Eileen's baby home.

A screen door slapped shut in front of her, and she found herself staring into the dark wool of a man's suit coat. She lifted her gaze and admired the taut muscles of the man's broad shoulders, his tanned neck, the thick mop of dark hair that reminded Thea of walnuts ready to be shaken from the tree. He turned slightly, and a soft gasp rose in her throat, just as it had when she'd caught sight of Mack early today. The young boy she'd admired as a teenager had grown into an amazingly handsome man.

Who was more than likely married, Thea reminded herself. A faint sense of disappointment settled over her. Best if she kept her distance. No sense giving folks around here any more reason to talk about the Miller girls if she could help it.

A soft sound, something between a coo and a whimper, drew her attention to a tiny bundle of pale pink ribbons and ivory lace squirming in his arms. A baby? Well, of course, he'd have a child if he were married. Even in high school he'd talked of settling down and having a large family. But wait, she'd seen this child before—recognized the ribbons and lace of her outfit. Yet it hadn't been Mack holding the little girl when Thea had seen her before. She was certain of that. So who had it been?

There was something distinctly familiar about this child, about the sunny blond curls that hugged her head like a Sunday bonnet. Mack lifted the baby to his shoulder and the little girl staring out at the small crowd, her piercing blue eyes watchful, absorbing everything around her. Recognition caused Thea's lungs to constrict in her chest, a joy so overwhelming, it threatened to shoot out of her fingertips and her toes.

She recognized the outfit from seeing that precious baby with Aurora Adair. The baby in Mack's arms was the mirror imagine of her sister, Eileen.

Chapter Two

"Look who I found wondering around the yard."

Mack turned at Maggie's exclamation, his heart picking up tempo as he raked a glance over Thea, startled to find blue eyes the color of a summer storm staring back at him, causing the muscles in his shoulders to bunch and tighten. An uneasiness gathered in the pit of his stomach. Why was Thea here?

And why had she been nosing around Ms. Aurora's place?

"Can you believe it, Mack? Thea's finally come home!" Maggie pulled Thea closer. Had the two of them been good friends in school? He couldn't remember. Thea had pretty much kept to herself between classes. He'd only gotten to know her during her junior year when they'd both worked at the movie house in town.

Maggie was right. No one, especially not him, had ever expected Thea to come back to Marietta. What had brought her back home now? Settling his hand against the baby's back, he took a step back to put some breathing room between them. "Theodora."

Thea stiffened, her delicate chin lifting at a stubborn angle. "Sheriff Worthington."

He didn't know why but the sound of his professional title on her lips felt like more of a dig than a proper show of respect. Maybe she'd done it because he'd used her proper name rather than the nickname she preferred. He'd have to tread lightly, then. No sense starting a war with the woman, not until he had some idea as to why she'd been snooping around Aurora's. Mack forced what he hoped was a relaxed smile against his lips. "Welcome home."

She gave him a curt nod that reminded him of the pretty teacher he'd had a crush on back in fourth grade. "Thank you. I just wish I was here under better circumstances."

"That's an odd statement seeing how we're at a wedding."

Her fingers clamped down on her purse like a vise. "I mean..."

Thea still had that same little habit of nibbling at her lower lip when she was uncertain about how to act or what to say. Whatever had brought her here made her uncomfortable.

"Always suspicious, aren't you, Mack?" Maggie tilted her head slightly toward Thea as if to share a well-kept secret. "I guess that's a good trait for a sheriff to have. Probably why the town council hired him in the first place."

That, and the fact he'd been about the only man left after Pearl Harbor was bombed and men shipped out to serve in the war. Mack turned to Thea. "Sorry about that. Occupational hazard."

She nodded, then turned her attention to Sarah, the tension he'd noted in her earlier softening as the little girl reached out for the slender finger Thea held up for her. "How old is she?"

Mack studied her for a long second. Most people chose to ignore Sarah, or worse, asked questions about the bright pink scar that had connected her nose to her mouth. Why hadn't Thea fallen into that pattern? "Five months. She was born on Victory in Europe Day."

A gentle smile bloomed across Thea's face as the baby grasped her finger and gave a playful squeal. "She's so beautiful."

"Thank you." Mack narrowed his gaze. Sarah had been called many things in her short life, but never anything close to beautiful—at least, not by anyone but him.

"We were just talking about what happened to Eileen," Maggie said, patting the baby's back. "Maybe you could answer some of her questions about that night."

"You were there?"

"Yes." Mack's gut tightened at the note of sadness in Thea's voice. As the top law enforcement agent in the county, he'd seen his share of car accidents, most fender benders, others deadly. But the scene he came upon the night Eileen died had haunted him for weeks after the accident. Two people just a couple of years younger than he lost in the blink of an eye, so close to the happiness they both spent most of their lives in search of, only to lose it in one unthinkable instant.

Of all the losses the town had suffered during the war, watching Eileen Miller die was the one that had driven him to his knees.

"Why don't I take Sarah while you two talk?" Maggie slipped her hands beneath the baby's arms and lifted her away from Mack's shoulder. "I need the practice, anyway."

They stood in awkward silence as Maggie shifted the child. Oddly enough, Thea seemed to drink in even the slightest movement Sarah made until the child was nestled against Maggie's shoulder.

"Goodbye, sweet pea. See you again soon," Thea whispered as Maggie carried Sarah down the stairs and out into the yard. Soft strands of blond curls fell against Thea's shoulders as she tilted her head back to meet his gaze. "So you're a...daddy?"

The words brought a smile to Mack's face despite himself. "Not yet, but I will be soon."

A tiny line of confusion creased the smooth area between Thea's brows. "How...?"

"I'm adopting her."

Thea's pleasant chuckle felt good to his ears. "You make it sound like your wife doesn't have anything to say about it."

Was she fishing to find out if he was married? The thought sparked a warmth in his chest that he immediately tamped down. It had been years since he was a smitten teenager who cared what Thea Miller thought of him—he wouldn't make that mistake again. "Considering I don't have one, she doesn't."

Thea stared wide-eyed at him as if she were searching for answers and coming up short. How could he have forgotten the soft silver sparks that rimmed the deepest blue around her irises, turning the color from indigo to violet? He found himself noticing the tiny dimple in her right cheek, the different facets of pink that colored her bottom lip, the pale scar high on her forehead.

"What about the baby's family? Shouldn't they have a say in the matter?"

Mack blinked at the unexpected questions. Most peo-

ple had wondered why he wanted to take on the responsibility of raising a child, especially a baby with special
needs, not worried about the family who'd abandoned
her before she'd barely taken her first breath. "Sarah's
mother gave her up when she was just a few minutes old."

The mouth he'd been fascinated with just seconds before went taut. "Poor woman. Probably didn't know what
to think after what she'd gone through."

Mack's throat tightened. Was Thea implying the
woman had been coerced into letting the baby go? "Sarah's mother could have kept her."

Thea leveled pleading blue eyes at him. "Maybe she
thought she didn't have a choice."

Oh, people had choices. Mack saw it in his work all
the time. And when they got caught making the wrong
one, they had to face the consequences. Thea had never
understood that, especially where her wayward sister
was concerned. Mack straightened and crossed his arms
over his chest, his suit coat pulled uncomfortably tight.
"Why have you been nosing around Ms. Aurora's the
last two days?"

Her brows drew together slightly. "How did you know
about that?"

At least she had the good sense not to deny it. "It's my
business to know what's going on in this county."

"Ms. Adair reported me."

If he hadn't been so annoyed, he would have laughed.
Thea had always been quick to call things as they were,
except in the case of her sister. "You still haven't answered the question."

She closed her eyes, her fingers tightening around the
straps of her purse. Her words were a soft whisper, as if
in prayer. "Lord, I don't know where to begin."

Unease knotted in Mack's stomach. Thea had never been one to cry uncle, not even when the burdens her family placed on her fragile shoulders seemed to be too much to carry. What could have happened that would shake her this badly? *Lord, give me the wisdom to handle this situation with Thea. Help me treat her fairly no matter what happened in the past.* Mack rested a hand against the small of her back and gently pushed her toward a row of empty chairs. "Why don't we go over here and sit down?"

Faint color gathered in her cheeks as he held out a chair for her then took the place beside her. "The bad guys don't stand a chance with you, do they, Sheriff?"

A stall tactic, but he remained quiet, ready to listen. Thea would open up about whatever was bothering her when she was ready.

She cleared her throat. "It has to do with what was going on with my sister the last few months of her life."

"You mean the accident?"

Golden curls shimmered against the pale skin of her neck as she shook her head. "No, I mean…before the accident. When she came back to Marietta last spring."

Eileen Miller was in Marietta last spring? Not possible. Mack would have noticed. The woman had always been the type to stand out, draw attention—so different from her sister. "The night of the accident was the first time I'd seen her in years."

She drew in a deep breath as if to snap at him, then must have thought better of it. "But she was here in town last spring. In particular, around May eighth."

Sarah's birthday. The best day Mack had had in years, falling head over heels with the abandoned baby who had been placed in his arms—and deciding to adopt her. While everyone else celebrated the end of the conflict in Europe, Mack celebrated the beginning of his new role, that of Sarah's father. "Eileen had a way of making her presence felt. If she was here, Thea, I would have noticed it."

"I know she was here, Mack. She wrote in a journal she kept that she was out at the farm with Momma on VE Day."

Mack blinked. That wasn't possible. How had Eileen snuck back into town without him being aware of it? Granted, last spring had felt like a roller-coaster ride with President Roosevelt's unexpected death, then the war ending in Europe, not to mention the Bell Bomber Plant laying off some of the women workers. What else had happened right under his nose that he'd been unaware of?

"Don't beat yourself up over it, Mack. Eileen probably kept out of sight due to her condition."

Mack turned sharply to stare at her. "She was pregnant?"

The news wasn't truly a surprise. Eileen had been trouble since the moment she started powdering her nose and wearing high heels. Mrs. Miller had always been very stiff, very proper. She wasn't a warm person, not even with her daughters, but she'd been tolerably friendly, participating in community events and active in the church until the gossip surrounding her younger daughter's antics had begun. After that, she'd rarely come to town. Whenever Eileen got into trouble, it was always her big sister who came to bail her out.

But it seemed odd he hadn't heard about Eileen coming back in the spring or having a baby. Odder still that the few times he'd been called out to tend to Mrs. Miller, who had grown increasingly rattled and confused as age set in, never once had the woman mentioned a child. Mack scrubbed his jaw. "Where's the baby then?"

"That's just it, Mack. Momma says the baby has been stolen, and I need to go and bring her home."

Another mess for Thea to clean up. Hadn't that always been the way with Mrs. Miller and Eileen? Well, this was one problem he could help her clear up. Mack shoved his hand into his coat pocket and pulled out the small notebook and stubby pencil he kept on him for moments like this. "Do you know the name of the baby's father? I could check with him, see if he or his family have the child."

"No, but…" She hesitated, what color she had in her cheeks fading, though her chin still arched at a determined angle. Whatever she was about to say, Mack knew he wouldn't like it. "Momma knows who has the baby."

"Who?"

"Ms. Adair."

"Aurora?"

Thea gave him a certain nod. "Momma said she knew it the first time she saw Ms. Adair in town after the baby was born."

"That's why you've been spying on Aurora's place." The pieces began to fall into place for Mack. "You think Sarah is Eileen's baby?"

"It makes sense. Sarah looks to be about the right age, and she's the spitting image of Eileen when she was a baby. Momma said it would be like Ms. Adair to take her." Sorrow along with another emotion—determination?—stared back at him. "That child you want to adopt is my niece, Mack. And I want to take her home."

For a moment Mack's eyes went wide with shock, and he didn't seem to be breathing. Then he huffed a laugh and shook his head.

Surprise shot through Thea. He thought her claim was

so ridiculous that he was laughing at her? Not very gallant for the boy who'd protected her from the ugly whispers her sister's behavior had generated around their high school campus, who'd listened as she'd poured out her heart over her mother's indifference, who'd been more than her friend.

He was the only one who ever seemed to understand her—and he knew how much her family meant to her. Eileen was gone, but her sweet baby was here, and all Thea wanted was to give that darling girl a home with her family. Why was that so difficult to understand? Shouldn't Mack be happy that someone from Sarah's birth family wanted to claim her now? Instead, he seemed to find the very idea laughable. "Maggie would have your hide if she heard you laughing at me like that."

"Maybe," Mack replied, giving her an unrepentant smile that made her heart trip over itself. "But she'd have to catch me first."

A smile tugged at the corner of Thea's mouth, but she caught herself before she made a complete idiot out of herself and smiled back. What on earth was she doing, almost flirting with the man! She had to make him understand the situation. Otherwise, Eileen's baby would be adopted by him, and the opportunity to raise her sister's child would be forever lost to her. "I don't think what I said was that funny."

"It wasn't." A weak grin tugged at his lips. "It's just that Ms. Aurora has a hard enough time providing the necessaries for the children left in her care without going out and stealing more of them to spread her resources even thinner."

"Maybe there was a misunderstanding," Thea argued. "Maybe Eileen was upset, or overwhelmed, and considered giving up her baby. But Momma says she changed her mind. She just didn't get a chance to take her back before the car accident. This isn't an abandoned baby anymore—this is a little girl whose family wants her. Momma and I are entitled to have her."

Thea glanced into blue eyes studying her intensely as if he were staring straight into the very heart of her soul. She swallowed. No wonder the people of Marietta trusted Mack to watch over their town. He could probably drum a confession out of the most hardened criminal, let alone a young girl still haunted by the cries of her sister, years ago, longing for the first child she'd borne—a child she had held only once before the baby was whisked away in the night, never to be returned. Thea had left town to find that baby…and she had failed. This was her chance to make things right, and she wasn't going to let it go. How could she make Mack at least listen to what she had to say? "Have you ever known me to lie, Mack?"

He glanced down at her, the lines in his face taut. This was killing him. Thea knew it, but wasn't it better to learn the truth now than after the adoption had gone through? "What kind of proof do you have to back up your allegations that Sarah is Eileen's child?" Mack asked. "A birth certificate? An entry in the family Bible?"

"I haven't checked with the courthouse about a birth certificate yet." She'd never seen a family Bible around the house but that didn't mean her mother didn't have one stashed somewhere. "But I do have Eileen's journal. She wrote about delivering a little girl, just as everyone was celebrating the end of the war."

"Which will only prove she had a baby around VE Day." Mack leaned close enough so that only she could hear him. "Until you have some kind of proof that Sarah is that baby, I'd suggest you keep your claims to yourself."

"Then will you promise to hold off on the adoption until we've figured out this situation?" she countered.

A muscle in Mack's jaw jerked slightly, then he relaxed. "I'm not sure there is anything to figure out, Miss Miller. According to the courts, Sarah has been abandoned and can legally be adopted."

"Miss Miller," was she? So, he'd dug in his heels. Well, she could be just as stubborn. Thea crushed her fingers into the leather sides of her purse. She'd need a new one after the punishment this one had taken today. "You can't think I'm just going to let you adopt my niece without putting up a fight."

"We still haven't established Sarah is Eileen's child."

"It's like I told you. Sarah's the right age, and she has the same sandy-blond hair and blue eyes that Eileen did when she was a baby."

"That's all circumstantial evidence, Thea. You're going to have to do better than that."

She knew that, but the more she thought about the situation, the more convinced she was that the little girl Mack aimed to adopt was her niece, especially considering what her mother had told her of the baby's abnormalities. "According to Momma, she was born on May eighth. I'm sure the birth certificate will back that up, once I locate it."

"She probably wasn't the only kid born that day," Mack replied, though his cheeks had gone slightly pale beneath his tanned complexion, as if the news had hit a sore spot. Clearly, that was Sarah's birthdate, as well. "And finding the official record might not be as easy as you think. It can take months for a birth certificate to be filed, and I happened to know Mrs. Williams left to stay with her sick sister up in Tennessee not two days after Sarah was born."

"The preacher's wife delivered Sarah?"

Mack nodded. "Placed that precious girl in my arms no more than an hour after she was born."

It felt as if the air had been sucked out of her lungs. "You were there?"

"Mrs. Williams called me at the station. Said the girl and her family didn't want anything to do with the baby so could I come by her house and take the baby to the hospital until Dr. Adams could get someone from the state to take over her care."

Thea's world tilted slightly, a dark mist settling over her eyes. "Why didn't you do something? Did you try to talk Eileen out of giving her baby up? Or at least convince her to wait a day or two before she made such a huge decision?"

Thea didn't realize she was shaking until Mack rested his hands on her shoulders. "First—" he spoke to her in that calm way of his that had always made her feel so safe "—why would I have any reason to believe Eileen was the one giving up Sarah? I didn't even know she was back in town. I certainly didn't go back into the delivery room to see the mother—that wouldn't have been appropriate. And secondly, Mrs. Williams takes her position as midwife very seriously. She wouldn't turn a child over to the authorities without being absolutely certain the mother understood exactly what she was doing."

Mack had a very real point. The protocol Mrs. Williams had followed was the same they used in the hospital. Still, she couldn't help her suspicions, especially after what she'd seen years ago, in her dealings with

Miss Tann. Maybe Mack could answer a few questions she still had about the night Sarah was born. "How did the baby end up with Ms. Adair instead of at the hospital with Dr. Adams?"

Mack's lips flatlined. "I took her there."

"Why?"

"Because once he heard about her condition, Dr. Adams wanted to send her away." Mack glanced around. Some of the guests had begun drifting out of the house and back into the yard. Thea wondered what tales about her and the sheriff would be making the rounds about town tomorrow.

Well, if they wanted something to talk about, she'd sure enough give it to them. "He wanted to put her in an institution because she had a cleft palate."

His stony gaze sent a chill up her spine. Being on the wrong side of the law would be a hazardous business with this man in charge. "What did you say?" he asked, his voice low and dangerous.

"Whoever did her first surgery did a good job, but from the sounds she was making, I suspect she'll need more. Momma's been so worried about how the baby would survive with…a defect so severe. There are new procedures that could give Sarah a normal life."

"I know. There will be time for those later."

Thea blinked. Why was he waiting? Hadn't the surgeon explained to him that the risk of complications rose as the baby grew and the bones of the head and face fused? Did he not have the authority to arrange for the surgery since the adoption had not yet gone through?

"I think you need to go," Mack said.

She had hit a tender nerve. "I'm not just going to go away. We need to discuss this."

"Maybe, but not with all these people around." Mack thought for a moment. "I'll look at my calendar back at the office and figure out a good time to sit down together."

Sounded like a stall tactic to her. Thea would have to stand her ground. "I'm open any day this week. But I'm not giving up. I fully intend to gain custody of my niece and raise her as my own."

His steely blue-gray gaze bored into her, and Thea's heart tumbled into the pit of her stomach. "Not if I have anything to say about it."

Chapter Three

❧

The walk home took longer than Thea remembered, though whether it was the unusual warmth of the late-October day or the heavy weight on her heart that slowed her steps, she wasn't sure. A ride might have been nice, but there wasn't money for even bus fare right now, at least, not until she secured a job. Even then she'd have to be careful. Raising a child cost money, and her mother's income barely covered her own expenses.

Just another mess Eileen had left for her to clean up.

Thea shook the thought away. She shouldn't feel that way, but she did. It was one of the reasons she'd stayed away for eight long years. There had been a degree of peace in knowing she could go back to her quarters without some kind of family catastrophe waiting for her when she got home. But then, there had been no one to come home to, no one to call family, no one to reminisce with over the old days.

Mack's image flashed through her mind. Her childhood friend had grown up to be every bit the man she'd expected him to be while they were in high school. Eyes and ears peeled for any trouble, he'd always carried the responsibility of protecting those around him. She was a little surprised that he'd ended up as sheriff—going to law school had always been his dream, and he'd been full of grand plans as to how he could help people with his law degree. But it was clear to see how well his current job suited him. It was as if he had been born to the job of being sheriff, an ease about him generated confidence from the community he served, the same trust he'd earned from his classmates in high school. It was one of the qualities that had attracted Thea to him in the first place.

If only he wasn't so closed-minded where Sarah was concerned. Thea sighed. At least he'd been willing to talk to her. Most folks wouldn't have given her the time of day, not when the topic was her wayward sister. If only folks could have known Eileen as she had, confused and scared, questioning why the father she'd adored had been taken away, why her mother was never warm or affectionate the way other people's mothers were. Seeking that affection from others, especially from boys, had led to a worsening reputation and more heartache—the misery, the anger her sister had felt toward herself each time she'd fallen for another man's lies when all she'd ever wanted was to be loved.

Had she found love, at last, with Sarah's father? Thea couldn't know for sure. All she could do now was love and care for her sister's baby—the only piece she had left of Eileen.

Thea drew in a deep breath and sighed. This was not what she'd expected when she'd decided to come back to Marietta. Though what she *had* expected, she couldn't say. Her sister to be alive, for certain. Momma, the same as she'd always been, maybe more mellowed with age. Not butting heads with Mack Worthington. He'd had always been reasonable, even if it meant being proved wrong. But he was a man now, with a man's pride and the law on his side. Would he accept the truth if it meant giving up a child he obviously loved?

Thea's heart tumbled over in her chest. No matter what happened, someone was going to get hurt. *Lord, haven't I lost enough without giving up what little family I have left?*

Just ahead in the bend in the path, the familiar gables of Momma's house came into view. Thea left the dirt road and climbed the steep embankment. Dandelions whispered softly against her ankles, their cottony seeds sticking to the hem of her skirt. If only she had a wish for each one she'd sent floating across the yard over the years. Then Eileen would be dancing alongside her as she use to do as a girl, her baby in her arms, cooing at the spectacle her mother and aunt were making. Momma would be happy and loving, and Thea would have the family she'd always wanted.

A screen door slammed shut in the distance, and her stomach sank as the reality of the situation set in again. Eileen's death, Momma's sorrow and the way the years seemed to weigh on her these days. This was what her life consisted of now, her family. And that included Sarah. She'd prove that the baby Ms. Adair was caring for was her niece. It was the least she owed Eileen after failing her so miserably all those years ago.

The wooden planks squawked beneath her feet as she climbed the three steps to the porch and pulled open the screen door. "Momma?"

The sound of hurried footsteps from the back of the house clipped through the paper-thin walls until finally Mildred Miller burst out of the kitchen into the hallway, wiping her hands on her blue-and-white checkered apron.

"Where have you been? You were supposed to be home hours ago."

Thea tugged at the worn fingertips of her gloves and folded them over the top of her purse. No hello or how have you been. Then, Momma had never been one for social pleasantries at home. No, those were reserved for Sunday-morning church service or a meeting of one of her ladies' clubs in town. But wouldn't it be nice if Momma greeted her with a welcoming hello, as if she were truly glad to see her? "I went to see Ms. Adair about Eileen's baby. Remember?"

"Eileen's baby?" Dull gray eyes met Thea's in the oval hall mirror, faded blond eyebrows bunched together in confusion, a common expression on her mother's face these days. Long moments passed before Momma's face finally relaxed a bit. "Oh, yes. Your sister. She had a baby."

Thea swallowed down the slight unease she felt at her mother's behavior. True, Momma hadn't been at her best since Thea had returned to town, but that was hardly surprising. How could she expect her mother to go on unaffected after all the losses she'd suffered, first Daddy then Eileen? Did losing her daughter bring on this forgetfulness that seemed to have settled like a thick fog over her memories? Or maybe forgetting the past had made it easier for Momma to live in the present. "I'm meeting with Sheriff Worthington sometime this week to discuss it more."

"Mack Worthington?"

Her mother's response surprised her. Momma had never had much time for Thea or Eileen's friends. "You remember Mack?"

"Of course, I do, silly child. The two of you have gone to school together since you were just a little bit of a girl." Momma studied her over the rim of her glasses, a slight smile lifting the corners of her mouth. "He's that nice boy you have a little crush on."

What in the world had caused her mother to remember that particular piece of the past? And why did she talk as if Thea was still in saddle shoes and knee socks? A cold chill skated up Thea's spine. "That was a long time ago, Momma. Back before I left home to go off to nursing school, remember?"

"Oh, yes, that's right." She buried her hands in her apron pockets, her eyes fixed on a point just over Thea's shoulder, as if she'd found something more interesting to look at than her daughter. "So what did you find out about the baby?"

"Ms. Adair does have a baby girl who is the same age Eileen's baby would be."

"Then you'll be bringing her home soon?"

If only it were that easy. "There are some complications, Momma."

"What kind of complications?" Her mother pressed her lips together in that annoyed way Thea remembered well.

She'd never please her mother, would she? The muscles in Thea's shoulders bunched together, a heavy weight pressing her down into the scarred oak floors. "Well, Mack would like to see the baby's birth certificate to prove that Sarah is Eileen's child before he drags Ms. Adair into the matter."

"But that baby is ours!" Momma stepped closer to Thea. "You told him that, didn't you?"

"Yes, Momma, but a birth certificate would go a long way to proving that the baby belongs with us." Thea rested her hands on her mother's shoulders and stared into her eyes. "Do you know if Eileen filed the baby's birth certificate with the county?"

"Your sister was too busy to spend a day down at the courthouse." Momma fidgeted with the long strings of her apron. "She was always too busy for anything useful or important."

Thea ignored the implication. "What about Mrs. Williams? She delivered the baby, right? Would she have filed the paperwork?"

"I doubt it, but then again, I didn't ask her to. I figured we'd eventually get around to taking care of it ourselves."

Which meant the baby's birth certificate likely hadn't been filed. Thea turned and leaned back against the table, gripping the edges in her hands. How could she prove that Sarah was her niece if the only witness of her birth had left town for who knew how long? Where else would Eileen record the birth of her child? "Did Eileen have a Bible? Something she might have made a note in about the baby's birth?"

Momma shook her head. "Not that I know of, but you know how sneaky your sister was. Always hiding things away in her room. Secrets, she said." Her mother's thin lips flattened. "All she's ever brought home is trouble. Maybe if your father had lived..."

Thea nodded. If only Daddy had lived, Eileen wouldn't have turned wild. Thea wouldn't have been put in the middle of the violent arguments between her mother and sister. Maybe if Daddy had lived, Eileen wouldn't have had that child all those years ago, and there would have been no reason for Thea to leave home at age seventeen. Maybe she would have married some local boy, had a baby or two of her own. Thea shut her eyes on those thoughts. Daddy was gone, and wondering what might have been was just a waste of time.

This was her life. Mother, herself. Sarah. She'd best get busy living it. "I have an appointment at the hospital first thing in the morning to check on my job application but if you'd like to go, I thought maybe we could stop by the courthouse and look through some of their records just on the off chance Eileen filed a birth certificate."

"No!" Momma shook her head so hard, Thea worried she'd get whiplash. "I mean, that's all right. I've got so much to do around here, getting Eileen's old room ready for the baby and all." She gave Thea an uncertain smile. "You've always been so good at taking care of things, I'd rather leave the birth certificate up to you."

At least that hadn't changed. Momma and Eileen always left their messes for her to clean up. But her mother had never turned down a trip into town, not when the shops were open and ready for business.

"Are you sure? You haven't been out of this house since I got home. Wouldn't you like to at least go into town with me? I heard Mr. Hice has some new material just perfect for the baby clothes you've talked about making."

Momma wrinkled her nose as if the thought of a trip into town disgusted her. "The square is just so crowded with all those people from over at the bomber plant wandering around." She shook her head again. "No, I think I'd rather stay here. That's all right with you, isn't it?"

Thea blinked. Momma never asked her permission for anything, had always been too busy passing out orders or barking out commands. "That's fine, but I might be gone for most of the day. I'm going to try to catch up with Mack at his office after I spend some time looking through the county records."

"You should have been here to take care of your sister." Momma turned away from Thea and started down the hall. She'd almost reached the kitchen when she turned around and gave Thea a forced smile. "If you had been

here, you would have talked Eileen out of going with
that boy. But you weren't, and now your sister's dead."

Thea closed her eyes, her muscles weighed down with
the fatigue of the past few days as well as an equally
heavy dose of guilt. The events of the afternoon had finally caught up with her, stripped her of all her energy.
The practical part of Thea knew she shouldn't take anything her mother said personally. Momma always lashed
out when she was upset. She mourned the child she'd lost,
the grandchild she'd never held. Her mother was grieving,
that was all. Her fingers tightened around the edges of
the scarred hall table until she thought they would break.
*Lord, please let it be nothing more than that. Don't take
Momma away from me just yet.*

Maybe losing Eileen had been too much for her mother
to handle, maybe the presence of a little one in the house
was what Momma needed to find some joy in living
again. Recovering her sister's baby was the answer. Then
Momma would have a reason to fight, and it would give
Thea a chance to right a terrible wrong. To bring her sister's baby back home.

This time.

Mack usually used his morning walks before the town
came to life to meditate on the Scriptures or pray for the
men and women who would soon be filling the streets
of Marietta for another day on the job. He'd pray that no
harm would come to them and that they would make wise
choices. For the folks who visited their city, he prayed that
they would have peaceful spirits and that he would handle
those bent on making trouble with respect and honesty.

But this morning the peaceful spirit he needed in order
to meditate or pray was out of his reach. His thoughts were

scattered like the crimson-and-gold leaves gathered up by the harsh wind that had blown in late last night, yet his mind never strayed far from his conversation with Thea Miller yesterday. The bookish girl he'd known in high school had certainly changed. The way she'd stood her ground against him, her refusal to back down from her claim that Sarah was her niece and her plans to raise the child didn't make him happy but he had to respect the woman's grit. His uniform made it difficult for some folks to question his authority, but not Thea, not when it came to her family.

Was it possible Sarah was Eileen Miller's baby?

Mack absently shook his head. A juicy secret like that would be too much for someone even as close-mouthed as Mrs. Williams to resist. Surely she'd have spread the word about delivering Eileen's baby…wouldn't she? The thin letter in his shirt pocket he'd spent half the night crafting felt like a heavy weight against his chest. He'd drop it in the mailbox on his way into the office this morning. Mrs. Williams could answer any questions about Sarah's mother once and for all.

With that settled, Mack found himself thinking about Thea herself. Why had she come home after all this time? She'd missed Eileen's funeral, though to be fair, she might not have heard the news until it was too late for her to get leave. Her mother had never had much to do with her, with either of her daughters, really. It seemed odd to him, but then he'd always been close to both his parents, particularly his father. The loss of Neil Worthington four years before had been the catalyst for Mack to settle down and attempt to find a wife. Someone he could build a life with, have the kind of marriage his parents had had, raise a family.

But all his attempts at courtship had failed, and the only

female who had touched his heart was baby Sarah. Now Thea threatened to steal his hopes for the future away from him. *Just like she did when she left town eight years ago.*

"You must be praying mighty hard this morning, my friend."

Mack glanced up to see Beau Daniels, his white doctor's jacket draped over his arm, walking toward him. "Maybe I'm thinking on a certain passage of scripture. I do that sometimes."

"A far cry from the boy who used to say his favorite verse was 'Jesus wept.'" Beau gave him a crooked smile.

Mack couldn't help but notice the dark circles under Beau's eyes. "Put in the late shift last night?"

Beau nodded, stretching from one side to the other. "I want to be home when Edie wakes up. She's been having a terrible time with morning sickness."

"I hate to hear that." Edie and Beau, along with the rest of the Daniels clan, had become like family over the past few years. "Is there anything you can do?"

"Her doctor has suggested a couple of medications but everything I've read on them just makes me more worried." Beau stretched his back. "Sometimes, I think it would be better to live in ignorance than to know everything that could possibly go wrong."

"Yes," Mack agreed, his thoughts wandering toward Thea and the baby again. "Sometimes ignorance is bliss."

"I heard about your discussion with Thea Miller. Maggie told me she dropped in on the wedding yesterday."

Like most of the Daniels family, Beau was never one to beat around the bush, a quality Mack appreciated. "She claims that Sarah is Eileen's baby."

"I didn't even know Eileen was back in town until she was killed in that wreck out on Drag Strip Road." Beau thought for a moment. "Wasn't that just a couple of weeks after Sarah was born?"

"I'll have to go back and look at the accident report but I thought it was maybe a week or ten days later." Which meant Eileen *could* have been home when Sarah was born. The thought made his heart tremble. "I didn't even put the two together."

"Well, you still don't know if they're related yet. It could just be a coincidence."

Mack wasn't buying that, not when the Miller girls, particularly Thea, had caused him so much trouble. "I'd already be Sarah's father if Judge Wakefield hadn't dragged out the whole adoption process. I wouldn't have to worry about any of Thea Miller's claims then."

"You'd still worry, because you're a decent man. If you thought for a moment there might be a chance what Thea is saying is true, you'd do everything you could to set the record straight."

He might be decent, but that didn't stop him from wanting go to Ms. Aurora's and steal his daughter away. Hopefully Mrs. Williams would respond to his letter quickly and lay this matter to rest.

Beau glanced up at the pale blue sky. "I'd better get moving. Edie will be up soon."

"Tell her I hope she gets to feeling better."

"I will." Beau clapped Mack on his back as he walked by. "You want to meet for lunch later? Maybe over at Smith's Diner around one?"

"That works for me." Mack watched his friend walk to the corner, then with one last wave, head toward the parking lot. Beau had turned out to be a good man, despite his father. Though Mack had heard James Daniels had changed his ways while in prison and turned to the

Lord, much to his family's delight. Beau had even visited his dad a time or two, and Mack got a sense that the hard feelings between the two had softened. Beau had a bright future in the career he loved, a beautiful wife and a baby on the way—everything Mack had wanted for himself before Thea and the accident had robbed him of his dreams.

He may not have a wife or the law degree he'd always hoped for, but he could make a home, have a family with Sarah as his daughter.

Mack walked down Cherokee Street, past the courthouse, until he came to a row of quaint little homes just outside the main town square. Brilliant violet-and-gold pansies glistened with early-morning dew as they stretched to sun themselves, and the grass was still an emerald green, even in mid-October. A bird twittered his wake-up song overhead, drawing a reluctant smile from Mack.

He'd longed for a home in this neighborhood for as far back as he could remember. The idea of adopting Sarah had finally pushed him into putting a down payment on the small three-bedroom cottage at the end of the street. Nothing fancy, just a yard big enough for a swing set and a room where she could play with her stuffed animals and dolls in the years to come. A home where they could put down roots, where Mack could give Sarah the kind of childhood his parents had given him.

But not if Thea took her away.

He wouldn't let her, not without a fight. Sarah was his daughter, had been since the moment Mrs. Williams had placed the squirming little newborn in his arms all those months ago. One look into Sarah's inquisitive sapphire-blue eyes and he'd lost his heart.

Blue eyes, now that he thought about it, that looked very much like Thea's.

Lots of babies had blue eyes, he reminded himself. Mack shook off the thought as he turned up a side street toward his attorney's office. Maybe Red would have some good news about the adoption for him.

His footsteps echoed against the brick-paved walkway that led up to Redmond McIntyre's ranch-style home. Mack raised his fist, then hesitated. The sun had barely risen. Would Red be up yet? Well, if Mack came across as rude, so be it. The situation warranted it. His knuckles rapped against the wooden door.

A heavy bolt slid seconds before the door flew open. Red stood framed in the doorway, a coffee cup in one hand, his tie hanging loose around his unbuttoned collar. "Mack, how are you doing this morning? You don't have one of my clients waiting down at the jail, do you?"

"I'm not here on official business." Mack whipped his hat off and held it between clenched fingers. "I was hoping I could talk to you about Sarah for a moment."

"Sure, come on in," Red replied, pulling the door open wider as he stepped back. "Would you like a cup of coffee?"

Mack shook his head. Truth be told, he couldn't stomach anything right now, especially not some of Red's strong brew. He followed the man into a small sitting room just off the hallway and settled onto one side of the sofa while Red retrieved his file from his office.

"Are you sure I can't get you something? A glass of sweet tea, maybe?" Red strolled back into the room, a thick three-ringed folder neatly tucked under his arm.

"Nothing, thanks." Mack settled his elbows on the chair's arms and leaned forward. "I was hoping to talk to you yesterday at Merrliee's wedding but I never saw you."

"I had to go to Atlanta for a client at the last minute and didn't make it back in time. Did I miss anything exciting?"

Nothing Mack was ready to talk about, at least not until he did some research into Thea's claims. He shook his head. "I just want to see where we are with Judge Wakefield."

"Pretty much the same spot we've been for the last month." Red sat across from Mack, dropped the file on the coffee table and flipped it open. "As far as I've searched, there's no precedent in the State of Georgia for allowing a single person to adopt a minor child."

Red wasn't telling him anything he hadn't already heard, but Mack refused give up, not where Sarah was concerned. "But those cases didn't involve a child with the kind of health issues Sarah has."

"No, but that's because those children are usually committed to an institution."

"Or on the streets," Mack bit out. His stomach roiled at the thought of his daughter, or for that matter, any of Ms. Aurora's kids, left on the curb to fend for themselves. Who would do that to any child, flesh and blood or not? It made Mack wonder how many more children were out there on their own right now, hungry, cold and afraid. "Those kids deserve a family and a place to call home just like any other kid, Red."

Red lifted his hands up in mock surrender. "You don't have to convince me. And it appears from my discussions with Judge Wakefield that he sides with you on that point."

Mack nodded. The judge had never hidden his feelings about the need for adoptive parents for all children, even those with physical and mental disabilities, but he held fast to the notion that a child needed both a mother and a father. Mack could see his point, but no family would adopt a child with the type of medical issues Sarah had. Wasn't one loving parent better than no one at all?

"You've got a more pressing problem at the moment."

Mack settled back into the cushions. Had Red heard about Thea's claim, that Sarah was Eileen's child? "What might that be?"

Red shifted forward, resting his forearms on his thighs. "Ben Holbrook cornered me at the courthouse after I got back from Atlanta yesterday afternoon. It appears the city council is bent on restructuring the police department."

"Why haven't I heard about this?"

Red shrugged. "They just voted on it. With all these folks from the bomber factory making Marietta their home, the council wants to add more men to the force, maybe even devote entire departments to specific crimes. And there was some mention of adding more experienced men to the sheriff's department."

"What you mean is now that the boys are coming home, they want law enforcement jobs to give them." Not a bad idea. Able-bodied men with battlefield experience on the force were just what a growing town needed. "We *have* had an increase in petty crimes recently, mostly kids bored and getting into trouble. It would be good to have some additional help."

Red sat back, his lips mashed into a straight line. "From what I understand, they might be evaluating your work as sheriff."

Mack's world shifted beneath him. "Why? Are they thinking about firing me?"

"I don't think it's that dire—yet."

Mack rubbed his fingers against the raised scar high on his left cheek. "Did anybody mention where I might fit into all this restructured force?"

Red shook his head. "Not yet. I'm sure they'll take your exceptional service to the community into consideration when the decision is made."

Mack stretched out his legs and studied his old high school friend. "That sounds like lawyer talk for you've already put that information out there for them, but they didn't bother giving you an answer."

"Always looking out for my friends."

For that, Mack was grateful. "How does this affect the adoption?"

Red's smile dimmed. "With this hanging over your head, Judge Wakefield isn't likely to budge on the adoption anytime soon."

"What's the man waiting on? Does he want me to jump through hoops or something?" Mack snapped, raking his fingers through his hair.

"I don't know about him, but I'd pay good money to see you do that trick."

Mack snorted out a chuckle. "I'm sorry. I didn't mean to bite your head off like that."

"It's understandable. You love that little girl, and you're afraid you're going to lose her."

Another obvious statement but the gut-wrenching truth. Mack wouldn't give up. He couldn't. "So what do we do now?"

Red slid back in his chair. "Well, we're still going to need Sarah's birth certificate. Have you heard anything from Mrs. Williams? I figured she would have gotten back with you before now."

Mack shook his head. "From what I understand, her family lives deep in the mountains north of Knoxville. I don't think mail service is all that reliable out there. It could take some time to hear back from her." He patted his shirt pocket. "I'm sending her another letter just in case the first one was lost."

"If it were any other judge, I'd ask for the adoption to

be pushed through without a record of the birth, but Judge Wakefield is a stickler about those things."

Mack nodded. How was he going to get his next question by the lawyer without raising his suspicions? "Will Sarah's parents be listed on the birth certificate?"

"Yes, but that information will be sealed by the court once the adoption is finalized. Then a new birth certificate with your name listed as Sarah's father will be registered with the state." Red studied him for a long moment. "Why do you ask?"

No sense alerting the lawyer to another possible roadblock, at least not until he had more information. "Just thought I'd ask."

"Well, if you're planning on asking Flossie Williams who Sarah's parents are, good luck with that," Red chuckled. "That woman can be as tightlipped as a Mason jar during canning season."

Mack waited for the relief Red's answer should have given him, but felt vaguely disappointed instead. "I wonder if Mrs. Williams would respond quicker if I sent her a telegram."

"Does Western Union even deliver to the backwoods of Eastern Tennessee?"

Were lawyers paid to be killjoys, or was that just part of their nature? Maybe it was a good thing he never went to college and became an attorney as he'd planned. "It's worth looking into."

"Even if they don't, this lull gives you time to get your job situation worked out." Red hesitated, tipping the three-ringed folder shut. "Can I ask you a question?"

"Sure."

Red took a long sip of his coffee, as if to steel himself. "How far are you willing to go to adopt this child?"

An odd question, especially from a lawyer. "What do you mean?"

The distant song of birds waking up the neighborhood filled the seconds before Red answered. "There is another way to ensure the adoption goes through as planned."

Mack knew what the man was going to say. "I've told you marriage is not a possibility at the moment."

"Hear me out before you dismiss the idea, okay?"

Mack glared at the man but kept his seat. What other option did he have short of walking out on his friend and possibly the only lawyer in Marietta willing to take his case? "Go on."

"If you're so bound and determined to raise this baby, you need to consider finding a wife. It would solve the immediate problem with the judge."

"And who would I marry, Red?"

"You've got to know a woman who'd love the chance to help you raise Sarah. Someone who would love that baby as much as you do."

The image of Thea, her deep blue eyes staring up at him, drifted through his thoughts. No doubt Thea was in love with the idea of raising the baby right now, but what would happen when she learned Sarah wasn't Eileen's daughter? Would she up and leave town without a backward glance the way she'd done before? Mack couldn't risk his daughter losing her heart to the woman. Or maybe it was his own heart he was worried about getting stomped on again.

"It's just not possible, Red."

"Well, think about it," Red answered before he grabbed the folder and stood. "Because getting married might be your only hope of getting Judge Wakefield to budge on Sarah's adoption."

Chapter Four

Thea closed her eyes and relaxed into a cushioned chair in the hospital waiting room, her mind drifting aimlessly as fatigue settled into her bones. Sleep had been elusive these past few nights. She'd been on edge, too worried by thoughts of Eileen, of losing her last link with her sister, to find any rest. It didn't help that Momma had taken to pacing the halls at night. Each morning Thea got up with the same questions. Would this be the day she'd finally bring Eileen's baby home? Or would she and her mother be coping with another loss soon?

She drew a deep breath in through her nose, her body relaxing even further. Once she brought Eileen's baby home, everything would get better. Her mother would become alert and engaged again. Guilt would ease its weight off of Thea's shoulders. They'd all be happy. At least, that's what she hoped. How in the world would she take care of Sarah and work an eight-hour-a-day shift if her mother didn't snap out of this fog of sadness and confusion?

Thea forced her eyes open and glanced around the hospital's waiting area. Maybe she could work part-time for a little while, at least until they figured out a routine at home. Maybe they'd be able to hire in a teenage girl to help when Thea couldn't be at home. There might not be any extra money for a lawyer if she needed one, but she'd figure that out when it came down to it.

She would manage. She didn't have much choice. Thea's eyes slid closed again. Just a few more minutes, a cat nap, and she could face her interview with the head nurse alert and fresh.

"Thea?"

She snuggled deeper into the chair, the rumbled whisper settling over her like a comfortable blanket. What was it about this deeply masculine voice that set her mind at ease? Familiar, with warm undertones, deep, almost dreamlike. She'd clung to the thought of that dark, manly voice throughout the long nights of the war, let it lull her as bombs burst in the distance. She hadn't been able to place it at first, but then she remembered the boy who'd once been her friend. Thea drew in a deep breath, felt a smile form on her lips.

Mack.

"Do you usually take naps in the hospital waiting room?"

There was a gentle sternness to his voice that caused her eyelids to flutter open to find the man standing in front of her. Tall and broad-shouldered, this Mack was the quintessential lawman, though she'd confess she'd never met an officer quite so handsome. "What happened?"

The cockeyed grin he gave her as he pushed back his hat had her sitting up in her chair. "You fell asleep."

Thea drew in a deep breath and blew it out, her fuzzy world coming into focus. "Old habits, I guess." At his confused look, she explained. "When you work the mobile surgical unit, you either learn to grab a nap anywhere you can or never sleep. Standing up in the corner. Sitting in mess hall." She smiled. "One of the girls in my unit got caught napping in the latrine."

"That must have been…interesting." Mack's voice deepened with mirth, his lips curved up into a slight smile. Then, as if he remembered who she was, he straightened, any evidence of a smile gone. "What are you doing here?"

Needing something to do with her hands, Thea opened her purse and pulled out her compact. "Interviewing for a position."

"A job?"

For some odd reason, the way he said it irritated her. She opened the lid and studied her reflection in the tiny mirror. Anything to keep from looking at him. "I have to put food on our table and keep a roof over our heads. Momma's income is really only enough for one person."

The space between them suddenly grew smaller as he pulled off his hat and sat down next to her. "And what about Sarah?"

"What about her?"

The clean tang of his aftershave swirled around her, making her head spin in a pleasant sort of way as he leaned closer. "How do you plan on taking care of Sarah if you're working?"

She leaned back and drew in a cleansing breath. It wasn't any of his business how she handled Sarah's care. "If I'm given custody of Eileen's baby, I'll work something out."

"Sarah is going to need special care, at least until she's old enough to have her second corrective surgery." He crossed his arms over his broad chest, glaring at Thea, looking every inch the protective father, the kind of daddy any girl would have been blessed to have.

Just not Sarah's daddy. Didn't he understand the little girl was the only link she had to the sister she'd lost? Mack could make gaining custody of the child difficult, there was no doubt about it. Well, she'd lived through one war. If Mack wanted to battle it out, she was ready. "What about you?"

He blinked. "Me?"

Ah, she'd caught him by surprise. Well, good! "*You* have a job. How do you plan to care for Sarah while you're off catching the bad guys?"

His blue eyes pierced her all the way to the depths of her soul. "Ms. Aurora has volunteered to take care of her during the day, but I'll have her at night. Plus, I'm turning one of the rooms in my house into an office so I can do most of my paperwork at home."

"So it's okay for you to have someone care for Sarah while you're at work, but not me." She slammed her compact shut and cocked her head to the side. "Why is that?"

Mack glared at her for a long moment, then much to her surprise, he gave a regretful chuckle. "Stuck my foot in it, didn't I?"

Thea's heart did a sudden flip at his crooked smile. Mack had always been a charmer. It would be best if she remembered that. "I'd say so."

"Sorry." He leaned back, leaving Thea suddenly bereft of his warmth. "Just had a rotten morning."

"Please say it's not the baby. She's not sick or something, is she?"

He shook his head, twirled his hat between nervous fingers. "Doodlebug is doing fine."

Now it was her turn to gawk. "You call her doodlebug?"

He cocked an eyebrow at her. "Is something wrong with that?"

No, quite the opposite. It was endearing, the sort of sweet name a man would give his baby girl. Thea shook her head. "It suits her."

He seemed glad she agreed with him, at least on his pet name for Sarah. "The first couple of days after I took her to Ms. Aurora, the kids fought over what to call her."

"I thought she'd always been Sarah."

He shook his head, the ghost of a memory playing along his smile. "That was Merrilee's idea. Ms. Aurora generally lets the kids decide what to call any new additions to their family."

The older woman let the children name the baby? "Isn't that like the prisoners running the jailhouse?"

Her heart fluttered when he turned the full effect of his smile on her. "Ms. Aurora wants them to feel like they have a say in their family. She gave them a few suggestions, and they voted for the baby to be named Sarah, though Ellie wasn't too happy about the choice."

Was Ellie one of Ms. Aurora's children? Or had Mack adopted other children? "Ellie?"

"A little six-year-old spitfire who has lived with Ms. Aurora since she was barely two weeks old." He sat down beside Thea then leaned toward her as if to whisper a secret. "They'd just gone to see a matinee of *The Wizard of Oz* and Ellie wanted the baby to be named after one of the characters."

"But Dorothy is a nice—"

He shook his head again. "Scarecrow."

Thea choked back a giggle. "You're serious."

"I had to bribe her with a day at the park to get her to agree to the name Sarah."

Oh, dear. If Mack succeeded in his adoption plans, little Sarah would have him wrapped around her pinky finger. *Lucky kid.* "The sheriff bribing small children. Isn't there a law against that?"

"Not yet. Besides, I like pushing the kids on the swing set in the park. Takes my mind off of work."

Thea studied him as he stared out over the empty room. This was the Mack she remembered, the guy who loved being outdoors, who found joy in simple pleasures like helping his neighbor or pushing a little girl on a swing. She was glad that growing up hadn't taken that away from him. But what about all his plans for adulthood? Why hadn't he followed through on his dream of playing football in college, becoming a lawyer like his father? Why had he never left Marietta?

She swallowed the questions burning on the tip of her tongue. It would only complicate the situation more if she learned who Mack had become, what had driven him to stay here, to abandon his dreams. For some unknown reason, she felt disappointed at the loss. "I never intended to hurt you, you know."

He stiffened, the pleasure of the last few minutes fading. "What do you mean by that?"

"It's just..." She hesitated, not sure how much to reveal. Maybe if she could make him understand, make him realize how important it was to her to raise Eileen's baby, it would be easier for him to let Sarah go. "I know you love Sarah, but I love her, too."

"You don't even know her."

"She's a part of Eileen. She's my family, Mack."

"You don't know that for certain," Mack said, her words obviously falling on deaf ears. "You're going to have to produce some proof to get a judge to listen to your claim."

Thea figured as much. She'd searched through Eileen's room, through her personal mail, even the journal she kept, but had found nothing except a brief entry a few days after her baby was born. Nothing to prove Thea's claim to Sarah. "I'd planned on visiting the courthouse after I finished my interview today."

"No sense wasting your time."

She glanced up at him. "Why would you say that?"

"Because if Mrs. Williams delivered Eileen's baby like you say, it wouldn't have been filed with the county and state yet." A look of frustration clouded his expression. "As I told you before, Mrs. Williams went up to Tennessee to take care of her sister shortly after Sarah was born. Sarah's birth certificate still hasn't been filed. If you're able to find a certificate on record for Eileen's baby, then that would be proof that she's *not* Sarah."

That wasn't the news Thea had expected to hear. She'd need a birth certificate to petition the court to stop the adoption. But if she needed one to prove Sarah's parentage, wouldn't Mack need one to get final approval for her adoption? "You can't adopt Sarah without a certificate, can you?"

His jaw tightened, and for a brief moment, Thea thought she'd have to pull an answer out of him. Then just as quickly, he relaxed—though only a bit. "No," he agreed, "I can't."

So he knew her frustration. "Have you been in touch with Mrs. Williams?"

He shrugged. "I've tried. I sent a letter when I learned she hadn't filed Sarah's birth certificate but she's a ways outside of the city limits so I figured it would take a while before I heard from her. I checked on sending her a telegram this morning but they don't deliver that far up into those mountains."

"I take it her sister doesn't have a phone." Thea didn't wait for an answer. She was thinking again what it must have been like for Eileen, delivering her baby all those months ago. "Do you think Mrs. Williams tried to talk any of those girls who gave up their children into keeping them?"

She felt his gaze shift to her. Could he see the pain that had consumed her in the days since she'd returned home, the fear that her only chance at a real family had died with Eileen? Or was he too centered on what losing Sarah would mean for him? His answer was to cover her hand with his, warmth to her cool skin, and she relaxed. "This thing with Eileen has really thrown you for a loop."

"I just…" She leaned her head back against the wall, her fingers threading automatically through his as if hanging on to him for dear life. "I don't understand why my sister would do such a thing. We weren't in touch for these past few years, but I've read her journal. She talked about how much she wanted a yard full of kids, babies she could love on." And who would love Eileen back, Thea suspected. "I can't see her giving her baby away."

"Maybe she realized she wasn't ready for that kind of responsibility. Maybe she did it out of love." Mack gently squeezed her hand.

She'd like to think her sister was that unselfish, but Eileen had spent her short life desperate for the affection she never got from their mother. Thea's love had never been enough for her—she had wanted more. Giving up her baby, a child who would grow to love her unconditionally, wasn't something Thea could see her sister doing. "She could have left the baby with Momma. I could have asked for an emergency discharge and come home…"

"And cleaned up the mess your sister made just like you always did?" Mack pulled his hand away as if he'd touched his fingers to a hot furnace.

"You don't understand." How could he? Mack had always had parents who loved him, who thought the sun and the stars rose in his every movement. How could he begin to fathom what she and Eileen had endured, living with a mother who always found fault, who only made time for them when it was convenient for her? "I'm not saying Eileen didn't make mistakes. I know she did, but I did, too, and when I messed up, Eileen tried to be there for me. Sisters help each other out."

"You were too easy on her. Eileen took advantage of your sweet nature. She always did."

Thea grimaced. Yes, she probably had. But she had let Eileen down, too, at the time when her sister needed her the most. "You don't understand."

"I understand more than you think, Thea." Mack leaned a hair closer to her, just enough to see his blue eyes darken to a stormy indigo, pinning her in place.

Thea shook her head then caught herself. How could she explain her sister's behavior without Mack learning the whole truth, that this baby was not Eileen's first? That her own mother had been in cahoots with the likes of Georgia Tann, a woman who had browbeaten and threatened countless scores of women into give up their babies so that she, under the front of a charitable institution, could go on to sell those babies to the highest bidder.

To admit what her mother had done, and the circumstances leading to it, would betray the little good that was left of her sister's memory while revealing Thea's own failures. She shouldn't have taken the extra shift at work that night eight years ago, but she'd wanted to see Mack, work with him one more time before she quit to leave for college. If she had stayed home, she could have stopped her mother from ever going to the train station, before the exchange had been made with Georgia Tann.

Instead, she'd made a promise to her sister that she'd bring the baby home. And then the only option Thea'd had was to jump on that train and follow Miss Tann to the ends of the earth if need be. But it had been for nothing, and Eileen had lost whatever hope she'd held on to with the disappearance of her son, a baby boy their mother had sold to keep scandal away from their doorstep. The baby boy Thea had failed to retrieve, breaking her promise to her sister for the first time in her life—leaving her too ashamed to come home for eight long years.

Thea pushed away the awful memory. No. No matter how much Mack thought he understood her family's situation, he couldn't.

Not in a million years.

Finding Thea here at the hospital hadn't been what Mack had expected when he'd agreed to meet Beau for lunch. But these few moments he'd spent with her had given him time to get a read on her, to try to figure out what had brought her home after an eight-year absence. Only her reaction to his questions had confused him more. The woman held secrets close to the chest but her blue eyes revealed a storm of emotions that unsettled him, made him want to protect her from the pain and regret he'd found hidden in their depths. Why he felt this way, after the mess she'd left behind when she'd hopped that train out of town, after the damage she'd caused him, the loss of everything he'd ever hoped for, he couldn't explain.

No, she wasn't directly responsible for the car accident that had had such devastating consequences in his life. But he wouldn't have been out in his car that night—driving too fast to get home after dropping her off at the train station, trying to beat the curfew the coach insisted on so he'd be able to play in that weekend's big game—if she hadn't come to him, desperate, needing a ride.

If it hadn't been for her, he'd have been safely at home rather than out on the road. He'd have played in the big game instead of spending that weekend in the hospital. He'd have gone on to college, instead of losing his scholarship after the doctors said the partial deafness in one ear was permanent. He'd have lived the life he'd always planned instead of giving up his dreams.

He'd lost everything, all because he'd chosen to do a favor for a girl he'd thought was his friend. But what kind of friend would have left him behind so completely? He hadn't heard from her the entire time she was gone, even though she must have known about his accident. Not one call, or card, or even apology in eight years. Those years of silence should have been more than long enough for him to harden his heart against her.

But he couldn't deny that he still had a soft spot for Thea, maybe because he knew how tough she'd always had it at home. Probably just being overprotective, the same way he felt when he'd sworn to protect the citizens of Marietta.

And maybe President Truman plans to dance a jig in Marietta Square!

Mack stood and paced to the opposite side of the waiting room, needing to put some distance between them. Hadn't Thea taken enough from him? He touched the puckered skin just under the hairline at his ear. Nobody wanted a man who could barely hear, not even the armed services during the war, and they'd been desperate.

And now Thea was back, and this time she might cost him his child. The woman owed him a straight answer as to why she'd come home, and this time she couldn't run away.

Before he could get the question out, Thea spoke. "I'm sorry I snapped at you like that." She gave him a watery smile. "It's just…with finding out about Eileen, and well, everything, it's been a lot to deal with this last week."

Mack felt himself weaken. Poor woman. No doubt this was not quite the homecoming she'd hoped for. This situation with Eileen's baby couldn't be easy for her, either. "It's understandable. This whole thing with Sarah has got me walking around on pins and needles. I'm as grouchy as an old black bear."

"Well, maybe not that bad." Her lips twitched into a slight grin. "But almost."

He snorted out a short chuckle. That's one thing he could say for the woman. She always knew how to stop him from taking himself so seriously. But this was a serious situation. All his hopes for the future, a future that included raising Sarah, were at stake. "I love that little girl, you know."

"I know. You feel like she's your daughter."

Mack drew in a deep breath and waited. Surely she'd remind him that Sarah might be her niece and Thea intended to raise her as her own. But Thea remained quiet, as if acknowledging his love for the baby had taken what little energy she had left. He shouldn't be surprised. Thea had always been sensitive to everyone's feelings, especially her family's.

And now to his feelings, it seemed. It was a pity she couldn't have been bothered to show more care eight years ago, when he really could have used a friend. He watched her as she fidgeted with the clasp on her purse. The dark blue suit dress she wore gave her an air of dependability and professionalism while the black velvet hat turned her skin a luminous pink that matched the tiny pearls at her ears. Her brownish-blond hair had been pulled back into a loose knot at her nape, tiny tendrils caressed the smooth skin of her neck making his fingertips tingle. Would the silky strands feel as soft they looked?

Mack shook off the feeling. This was Thea, his old friend, the girl who'd robbed him of his future, and who had run away without a single glance back to the people who might need her. The woman who planned to steal his daughter.

"Why did you come back?"

Clutching tight to her purse, Thea lifted her head. "Excuse me?"

Mack took a step toward her, then stopped. He'd get no answers out of her if he intimidated her. "You've been gone for eight years, Thea. In all that time, you never came home, not once. So why now? What brought you back here after all this time?"

She gave a quick glance at her wristwatch as she bit her lower lip, pushed a tiny strand of hair behind her ear. Signs he took to mean Thea was nervous. She stood. "I must have misunderstood the head nurse about my appointment time. Or maybe she wanted to meet me in her office. That would make more sense."

The woman was going to make a run for it. How typical. Mack blocked her path to the exit. "Why is it so difficult for you to answer my question?"

"Why is it so important that you know?"

Why *was* it so important to him? For the sake of the baby, of course, but he knew that wasn't the entire reason he'd pushed her for an answer. Maybe if he opened up a little, Thea would feel comfortable enough to answer in return. "You left without a word to anyone except for maybe Eileen, and if she knew where you'd gone she didn't stick around long enough to tell anyone. I was surprised not to hear from you. I guess I thought we were friends back then."

He'd said too much, but once he'd started, the words had seemed to flow out of him before he could call a stop to them. What would Thea do now? Turn and walk away, or was she brave enough to answer his honesty with her own?

"I missed my family."

"After eight years?" All right, so that had been kind of mean, throwing that fact out there, but if Thea had wanted to see her family, why had she waited all this time to come back home? "You could have come to Marietta anytime."

"No, I couldn't," she snapped, then she jerked back as if the words had stung her. "I didn't mean…"

The guilt in her expression tugged at him. What had he expected? Even puppies snarl when you back them into a corner. But her answer had intrigued him. What was this great sin she had committed that made her think she wouldn't be welcomed back home?

The door behind Mack opened. "Miss, have you seen…" The man paused. "There you are, Mack. I've been looking all over for you."

Beau. Sparring with Thea had made Mack forget all about his lunch plans. "You must not have been looking too hard."

The man had the decency to smile at the good-humored ribbing. Beau turned to Thea. "I'm sorry about that, Miss. Mack here is a great sheriff but he's no Bob Hope."

"I don't know." Thea lifted her chin a notch higher, their gazes tangling as her eyes met his. "He can certainly hold your attention when he wants to."

The breathlessness in her response made Mack's palms sweat. This Thea was wiser, more confident. Yet, there was still a vulnerability about her that made him want to protect her, be her shelter in the storms that raged around her.

"You seem to know our sheriff rather well." Beau gave him a sly grin. "You ashamed of your old friends or did you want to keep your beautiful lady all to yourself?"

Mack rolled his eyes. Of course Beau would jump to conclusions. The man knew Mack had been searching for a wife, had even considered courting Edie Michaels until Beau had made it plain he wanted Edie for himself. But this woman? Mack had to set the record straight. "Thea is just a friend."

"Thea Miller?" Beau turned to study the woman in question with a more in-depth look. "Oh, my, it *is* you."

If Thea felt insulted, she didn't look it. "I know I didn't make much of a splash in high school, but I can't believe you don't recognize the girl who hung out with your cousin, Beau Daniels."

Beau squinted slightly then smiled, his eyes alight with recognition. "Maggie mentioned something about you being back in town. Of course, she forgot to mention how lovely you are."

Thea's cheeks turned a delicate pink. "That's mighty nice of you to say."

"I always believe in telling the truth."

Mack bit back a frown, an uncomfortable knot tightening in his gut. Beau didn't have to be quite so charming. "How's Edie doing? Still having problems this morning?"

Beau nodded, his smile dimmed somewhat, concern shadowing his eyes. "As long as we keep her in saltine crackers, she seems to be okay. I've told her to stay at home and not worry about work for right now, but my wife can be as stubborn as a mule. I'll be glad when she's a little bit further along."

Thea stepped forward and laid a hand on Beau's shoulder in a comforting gesture Mack had seen a million times from other nurses calming patients. Then why did the thought of her touching his friend, no matter how innocently, bother him to no end?

"Maggie mentioned your wife was having a rough time," Thea replied. "What is she? About two or three months along?"

"The baby's due at the end of April." Beau gave her a hesitant smile. "I just hate that I can't do anything to make her feel better right now."

"And being in medical school, you think you should be more prepared than most men?" She waited until Beau gave her a reluctant nod. "What you're feeling is what every other man with an expectant wife has felt, and it's okay. You know what you can do for her right now? Be there for her. Hug her when she's not quite sure why her emotions are all over the place. Tell her how much you love her. And pray for her, and for the family the two of you are making together."

"Thank you, Thea." The worry that had been in Beau's

expression since the day they'd announced Edie's pregnancy eased slightly. "It's easy to see that you're very good at being a nurse."

"Thank you. I appreciate that."

Mack could tell by the color deepening in her cheeks that Thea wasn't accustomed to much praise. Why was that? She'd always been one of the smartest people he'd known, her nose always in a book, her acceptance into the finest nursing school in the Southeast proof of all her hard work. Why did she seem surprised when someone complimented her?

"Would you like to join us for lunch, Thea?"

Mack blinked at the invitation. Great, he'd hoped to talk, get some information out of Beau, maybe question him about the town council's decision to beef up the police department and where the decision might leave Mack. Now, with Thea tagging along, the conversation would be limited.

"I appreciate the offer, but I'm supposed to meet with the head nurse in a few minutes, then I have a few errands to do before I go home. It was nice to see you again, Beau, and I hope your wife gets to feeling better soon." Thea's gaze shifted to Mack. "Sheriff."

Mack was grateful for Beau's silence as Thea walked across the room, the sharp clip of her heels against the tile floor receding as she proceeded down the hall. It was only after he drew in a deep breath that Mack realized Beau was watching him. "What?"

"I could ask you the same question, my friend. There was so much tension between the two of you when I came in, you could have cut it with a scalpel."

Irritation slithered up Mack's neck. "Leave it alone."

But his friend wasn't one for listening. "You've been

looking for marriage material and from what I could tell, Thea seems like a really nice girl."

Mack could hear the blood pulsing in his ears. "You're out of line."

Beau droned on. "Pretty, smart and she has a career to fall back on."

"Would you shut your pie hole?"

"And I happen to know you kind of had a thing for her back in high school."

That stopped Mack dead in his tracks. He jerked around toward his oldest friend in the world. "I never told you that."

"You didn't have to. You made it plain every time another guy thought about asking her out. How many did you threaten to pound if they so much as got near her? Five? Six?" Beau's mouth cocked up into a sly smile. "And here I thought you'd stayed friends because…well, a guy like you didn't date a girl with Thea's kind of background."

Mack had had enough. "Thea was and still is the complete opposite of what her sister was like. As you said, she's a nice girl—and I'll have words with anyone who says otherwise. I didn't date her because we were good friends, nothing more. Okay?"

"Okay. All I'm saying is she seems to be someone who would have the kind of caring nature that would be good for…say, the mother of a young girl."

Mack sighed. Almost the exact statement his lawyer had made a few days before. "You've talked to Red."

Beau nodded, his expression suddenly somber. "He did drop by. Said you might need someone to talk to about the adoption and the mess with the town council. But something else came up this morning, and I think we need to talk about it first. Back in my office."

Whatever it was had Beau worried. Mack couldn't take much more bad news, not now. "Why don't you just spit it out?"

Beau glanced around the empty room, then motioned to a group of chairs in the far corner. Once Mack sat down, Beau seemed to transform from friend to one of the white-coated med students he'd seen around the hospital. Beau gathered his thoughts for a moment, then began. "Dr. Adams got a call from Dr. Medcalf over at the children's hospital this morning."

Mack's stomach churned. Winston Medcalf? The doctor who'd performed surgery on Sarah? When she'd almost died? "What did he have to say?"

"Dr. Adams mailed copies of Sarah's medical records over to Dr. Medcalf to keep him updated on Sarah's progress."

"He's keeping tabs on her?"

Beau's mouth twitched. "It's not like one of your undercover sting operations. Doctors need to exchange information on patients under our care."

Mack guessed that made sense. "What did Dr. Medcalf have to say?"

Beau leaned forward, resting his elbows on his knees. "He feels Sarah has matured enough to give the surgery another try."

"No."

"Come on, Mack. Sarah was barely three months old the last time Medcalf had her in the operating room. She's put on some weight, her lungs have matured a little bit." He steepled his fingers together. "She needs this surgery. Putting it off will just complicate the situation later."

An ache radiated through Mack's left jaw, and he un-clenched his teeth. "She had a bad reaction to the an-esthesia last time, and we almost lost her. What makes Medcalf think things will be different now?"

"I don't know. And that's not to say Sarah couldn't have another problem. But we're racing against the clock now, Mack. If she doesn't have the corrective surgery be-fore her first birthday, the bones in her face will begin to set and make for a more complicated procedure in her future."

This was not what Mack needed to hear today. "But she's still such a tiny little thing. Couldn't we put the surgery off for at least another month or two? Give her a little bit more time to grow."

Beau dropped his chin to his chest, his fingers tighten-ing into a knot. Whatever it was he had to say was hard on him, as if he had no other choices. When he finally lifted his head, he met Mack's gaze with an honesty that came from years of friendship. "You don't have a say in the matter, Mack. You're not Sarah's guardian."

No say in matters pertaining to Sarah? "But I'm in the middle of adopting Sarah, and Ms. Aurora, she's her guardian. She won't agree to this."

Beau shook his head. "She's not officially Sarah's guardian, not in the eyes of the law, and you…" He hes-itated, as if the words hurt him to say. "We don't know how long it will be before Judge Wakefield signs those adoption papers—or if he ever will."

Mack fell back against the chair, his body numb from the news. A thought occurred to him. "Someone has to give the okay for the surgery. They can't operate with-out it."

"True, which is why the hospital got permission from Judge Wakefield this morning."

"Wakefield." Why didn't the news that the judge had gotten involved surprise him? Maybe because this mess smelled like something the judge would cook up. "Then I'll go to court. Get an injunction to stop the surgery."

"You think the judge is going to sign an injunction to stop a court order he signed himself?"

It did sound ridiculous when Beau said it like that. All Mack would do is poke the bear. And he couldn't afford to make the judge angry with him, not with the adoption still up in the air. "What am I supposed to do then? What if something happens to Sarah? How would I live with myself if I sat back and did nothing?"

"Have faith."

Why was it, when people don't have the answers, they'd tell you to fall back on your faith? *Lord, help me in my disbelief. Keep Sarah safe. Help her through this.* "What you're telling me is that there's nothing I can do to stop this."

Beau shook his head. "All you can do now is be there for your daughter. Love her through it, and pray."

Mack drew in a steadying breath. "When have they scheduled the surgery?"

"A week from tomorrow. Sarah will be in the hospital at least a month, longer if there are any complications."

Mack threw down his hat on the chair beside him and raked both hands through his hair. "You know I can't afford to pay for that long a hospital stay, and I'd rather be skinned alive than allow someone else to foot the bill for my daughter."

Beau shifted to the seat right beside him. "I've been

thinking about that. You've already paid for the surgery, right?"

Mack gave him a quick nod.

"Then the only bill you've got to worry about is for Sarah's convalescence, and that can be pretty much done at home under the right circumstances."

Home. Back to Ms. Aurora's. Why hadn't he thought of that? It was the perfect solution. Ms. Aurora could handle taking care of the baby during the day while he settled in for the night shift. But what about the other children in Ms. Aurora's care? They needed her almost as much as Sarah did now. Casting the extra work of caring for a recovering infant on the older lady wasn't fair to any of them, and Mack couldn't take time off to care for Sarah himself, not with his job already on the line.

"You're going to need help," Beau stated.

"I can't ask Ms. Aurora. She's got enough on her plate as it is."

"You couldn't take Sarah back there, anyway." Beau crossed his arms over his chest and stretched his back. "No matter how clean the woman keeps her home, those kids are walking incubators, bringing in who knows what kind of sicknesses. Even something as simple as a cold would complicate Sarah's recovery. We need to keep her well until the stitches in her mouth are somewhat healed."

Then Ms. Aurora's was out of the question. "My house, then?"

"It would be the best choice. She'd be isolated from other children there, and you can monitor who comes inside. The only problem now is finding a trained professional who can come in and take care of her during the day, while you're working."

"A trained professional? You mean like a nurse?"

"Exactly!" Beau nodded. "Sarah needs someone who can recognize any problems that could come up. Infection, busted sutures, stuff like that. A trained medical professional who would make herself available day or night."

"Her?"

"You'll have more of a chance at hiring a nurse, preferably one who's had some experience dealing with pediatric patients."

For some strange reason, Mack felt as if he'd just walked into a trap. "You have someone in mind?"

"As a matter of fact," Beau said, reaching into an interior pocket of his jacket and pulling out a folded sheet of paper. "I ran across this résumé yesterday and thought she'd be perfect for the job."

Mack unfolded the paper, glanced at the name at the top, then crumpled it into a ball. "You think I ought to consider hiring Thea as Sarah's nurse."

"Look, I know it's an uncomfortable situation, but her credentials are excellent."

Uncomfortable? Unbearable would be more like it. He tossed the wadded up sheet of paper back at Beau. "Then you know there is no way I'm letting her take care of my daughter."

"Hear me out." Beau unfolded the tight ball and pressed the paper against his thigh, rubbing out the creases with his hand. "This is a tough surgery, and Sarah already had enough problems the first time around. It would seem to me you'd want her to have the most experienced pediatric nurse available to care for her."

"And that's Thea."

Beau waved the crumpled paper at him. "She graduated near the top of her class and worked almost exclusively in pediatrics before she joined the Army Nurse Corps four years ago."

"And her references?"

Beau shook his head slowly, as if in disbelief. "She's even got one in there from General Patton."

Patton? It figured. Thea had never done anything halfway. When she'd decided to go to nursing school during her sophomore year of high school, she'd worked two jobs to stockpile money for school. But Thea living in his house? Taking care of the child they both wanted?

And it wasn't just Thea. For propriety's sake, he'd have to invite Mrs. Miller to move in, too. Though, come to think of it, it might be better to have the older woman living in town, where he and Thea could work together to keep an eye on her, and other people would be able to check on her. From what he'd heard and witnessed himself, the woman had been having trouble lately. She often seemed confused and somewhat dazed. It might just be loneliness and old age wearing at her, living alone as she had before Thea's return. Or…it could be the first signs of a more serious condition. As the sworn protector of this community, he owed it to Mrs. Miller to make sure she was taken care of.

"Look, I know it's none of my business." Beau folded up the paper. "But you're not still holding a grudge against her about the accident, are you?"

Mack's chest tightened. "What are you talking about?"

"Maggie told me about the accident. About how you were out that night taking Thea to the train station before it happened, and that's why you were out on the road so late."

"That cousin of yours sure does like to shoot off her mouth a lot."

"Now, wait a minute, don't go blaming Maggie. I pestered the truth out of her. I wondered why you didn't join up with the military like everyone else and she let it slip that you couldn't because of your ear." Beau sucked in a breath through his nostrils. "She only told me because we're friends and she thought I could help."

Phrased like that, it made Mack feel as petty and as immature as a seventeen-year-old kid. Mack glanced around the room, slightly ashamed of himself, though he wasn't sure why. He'd done a nice thing to help Thea out and ended up losing his chance at a future. Surely *he* wasn't to blame for any of that. "Help how? The doctors said there was nothing to be done to save my hearing in that ear."

"No, but I could listen. I know how much being a lawyer like your dad meant to you. It must have hurt when the college pulled your scholarship."

"Water under the bridge." At least, that's what Mack told himself. He'd made a good life since then, and though it wasn't the one he'd planned on, he didn't have a reason to complain. It didn't matter if he was arguing a case in front of a jury or making an arrest. Keeping the town a safe haven in a rapidly changing world had always been his primary goal.

"What I want to know is why are you blaming this on Thea in the first place?"

Mack's jaw tightened, dumbstruck by Beau's question. "I wouldn't have been speeding home, trying to beat curfew, if Thea hadn't asked me to take her to the train station."

"You could have told her no."

He shook his head. "Thea didn't have anybody she could depend on. That night, she was frantic. I couldn't let her go by herself, even if she could have gotten a ride from someone else."

"So you made a choice."

Mack bristled at the smug look on his friend's face. Yes, he'd made the choice to help Thea that night. It didn't mean she shouldn't take some responsibility for what happened, for the way she'd abandoned him afterward, leaving him to deal with the crumbling of his dreams without even a token of her friendship. "Just like I have a choice right now whether to hire her to take care of Sarah or not."

Disappointment flashed in Beau's eyes then, just as quickly, fled. "If it were me, I'd want the best available care for my daughter."

Mack had never felt more between a rock and a hard place in his life. Of course he wanted what was best for Sarah, but why did that have to include Thea? He took the résumé from his friend. "If Thea's so good, why isn't the hospital hiring her?"

"Every nursing position is filled at the moment." Beau hesitated. "If the town council would decide to build a new hospital that could accommodate our growth, we wouldn't have to send good nurses like Thea away."

But Thea wasn't going away. She'd as much as told Mack that during their sparring match just a few minutes ago in this very room. She had a family to care for. But how would she keep a roof over their heads and food on their table if she didn't find a job to support them?

"And there's another good reason."

"What's that?"

"You could keep an eye on her. You know the old saying, hold your friends close and your enemies closer. If she's serious about getting custody of Sarah, and you have her working for you, you'll at least know what she's up to."

Beau had a point. He'd know every move Thea made, where she went and what evidence she'd collected to solidify her claim. Guilt flushed through him and just as quickly abated. What did he have to feel guilty about? The woman threatened his family. He had to do this, for Sarah's sake.

And if he was going to muddle waist high in Thea's affairs, he might as well go completely under. "Can I keep this résumé?"

"Sure, but what for?"

"I don't hire anyone without checking out their references myself."

Beau broke into a wide smile. "So you're going to hire her?"

"Maybe." If not, at least he might finally be able to find out more about what she'd been up to in the years since she left Marietta. Mack skimmed down the page, his gaze focused on the city where Thea had landed after leaving town, a bit startled by the answer he found. *Why in the world would Thea go to Memphis when the nursing school she'd planned to attend was on the other side of the state?*

Chapter Five

W̲hat was she going to do?

Thea pushed what was left of her dessert around on her plate, her nerves too much of a jumbled mess to stomach even Miss Lucille's famous peach cobbler. It had always been her favorite item on the Smith's Diner menu but not today. She finally gave up, put her fork and napkin on the plate and set it all to the side, her thoughts firmly on the interview she'd had with Sally Eison.

It had gone so well. At least, that's what Thea had thought. The head nurse had seemed quite impressed with her battlefield experience as well as her time on the pediatric floor at Methodist Hospital. An offer of employment seemed like just a formality after the hour-long interview.

But then there'd been no offer at all.

Apparently all nursing positions were filled. Even now, the words robbed Thea of breath. There was only one hospital in Marietta for now, though Nurse Eison had shared that plans were in the works to build a larger facility in the next few years. A lot of good that would do her and her family. They'd be living on the side of the road by then.

What was she going do? The next nearest hospital was a

good hour away in Atlanta. Even if she considered taking a job there, it would mean a long commute every day, time she'd rather dedicate herself to Sarah's care, once the child was in her custody. There weren't enough hours in the day.

"Miss Lucille's cobbler not up to your likin' today?"

Exactly what I need right now. She stared up at Mack, his powerful, muscular frame blocking the sunlight, his face in shadows so she couldn't get a clear read on his expression. "Well, are you here for round three or did you just stop by to gloat?"

"I heard there weren't any openings."

There was a note of sympathy in his voice, as if he were truly sorry a position hadn't been available for her. The kind of sweet reaction Mack had always had, compassionate and caring. A good combination for a lawman.

A man who, at this moment, was staring at her. "Is there a problem, Sheriff?"

"Mind if I join you for a cup of coffee?"

Her heart gave a funny kick under her rib cage, though why, she wasn't sure. Probably because he'd already goaded her into one argument this morning and she wasn't in the mood for another one, not right now. But that didn't stop her from nodding her head toward the seat across from her.

"Thanks." Mack pulled off his hat and gently tossed it to the other end of the table before dropping down into the seat across from her. The cozy little booth she'd asked for suddenly seemed too small, his broad shoulders taking up almost the entire length of the table. The kind of shoulders a girl could lean on, the perfect pillow to rest her head after a long day of nursing sick people or caring for a growing baby.

Thea blinked. Where had those thoughts come from?

She had enough on her plate without adding inappropriate feelings for this man to the mix. Thea leaned back into the vinyl seat. "You never answered my question."

Mack gave her a quizzical look. "What was that?"

"Is there a problem?"

"Well, yes. I mean, there could be."

A problem, and Mack was coming to her? That alone was enough to keep Thea glued to her seat. "What kind of problem?"

"It's Sarah."

Her pulse quickened, her chest suddenly tight, the feeling reminiscent of those first few moments before the ambulances arrived with a fresh batch of wounded men. Now, as she always did then, she needed to assess the situation. "What's wrong?"

He must have noticed he'd unsettled her because he reached across the table and covered her hand with his. "She's okay."

"Really?"

"I promise. She's perfect."

Thank You, Lord! Thea closed her eyes and released the breath she'd been holding. If something happened to Sarah… Her eyes shot open. "Wait, if she's all right, then what's the problem?"

"Well, um…" He hesitated as if trying to find the right words and for a brief moment Thea felt herself soften at the uncertainty in Mack's expression. "I'm not really sure where to begin."

Thea motioned to the waitress who filled Mack's empty cup, then refilled Thea's. Once the girl had left, Thea reached for the creamer. "Well, I've heard the beginning is as good a place as any."

Mack watched as she poured a sizable amount of milk into her coffee. "Like a bit of coffee with your milk?"

Good, he was back to his irritatingly charming self. "It's the only way I can drink the stuff. What about you?"

"Three sugars." As if to confirm it, he reached for the sugar bowl. The spoon clicked against the side of the cup as he stirred three heaping spoonfuls into the steaming brew. "Sorry about that. It's been an interesting morning." Mack sat quietly for a long moment, studying her, as if trying to decide if he should tell her. Then, almost as if he didn't have any other choice, he gave a slight nod. "The doctor from the children's hospital has scheduled Sarah's surgery for next week."

Thea heaved out a relieved sigh. She'd been wondering why it was taking so long for the baby to get the surgery she needed. So why did Mack look at the prospect as a bad thing? "This is good news."

"Not to me, it isn't." Stormy blue eyes glared back at her from across the table.

She was confused. "You don't want Sarah to have corrective surgery?"

"Not until she's older. Stronger."

Thea pressed her lips together. She should have expected Mack to be an overprotective parent. He'd always guarded those around him he cared for, defending them as much as he could from the hurts this world inflicted. But this was going too far. The surgery and the recovery that came afterward might be hard on Sarah for a little while, but what she got in return would be worth it. Maybe if Thea could get him to talk about it, she could assure him surgery was the right thing for Sarah. "You do know this procedure will help her when she starts talking, not to mention helping now with her food intake."

"I'm not against the surgery. I'd just like to put it off for a few more months."

"Why?"

The muscles in his throat worked, as if he found the words almost impossible to say. "She could die, Thea. It almost happened last time they attempted this surgery. She had some trouble with the medicine they gave her to put her under. Dr. Medcalf had to stop before he barely got started because her heart rate dropped dangerously low."

No wonder Mack felt the way he did. The thought of sending Sarah into surgery now worried Thea more than a little bit. "Did he give you any reason as to why she could have reacted that way?"

Mack nodded. "He feels it had something to do with her weight, that maybe she was too small to handle the stress of the surgery."

The stoic sheriff was gone, replaced by a man deeply concerned about his child. Dark blond hair fell across his forehead, his brows knitted together in worry, his arms folded around himself as if protecting himself from a fatal blow. Emotions thickened in Thea's throat. She'd seen things during the war no man or woman should witness, had hardened her heart against her instinctive reactions so that she could do the job she'd been trained to do. So why did this man's pain pierce her heart like nothing she'd ever felt before?

"She could die." His voice was unsteady, as if saying the words made them so.

"I know." Thea touched his forearm, then settled her hand there when he didn't flinch. A nurse's touch, she reminded herself, unsure why the warmth of his bunched muscles beneath her fingers offered her comfort in return. "Dr. Medcalf must think that Sarah will be able to handle it now."

"But what if he's wrong?" His lips pressed into a hard line. "What if it happens to her again?"

Mack loved the little girl, thought she was perfect as she was, almost as if Sarah was already his daughter. What would happen when Thea finally found the evidence she needed to prove Sarah was her niece? She'd have to find ways to include Mack in the baby's life. But for now, he needed comforting. "You could always put off the procedure for a few more months. Give Sarah time to grow up a little bit more."

He shook his head. "I don't have a say in the matter."

Thea hadn't thought about that. "Then Ms. Aurora…"

"She doesn't have a say in it, either."

Then who? Her shoulders slumped slightly as the realization hit her. "Dr. Medcalf has gone to the judge and asked him to sign the consent forms on Sarah's behalf."

Mack sent her a hard stare. "How did you know that?"

"I've seen it done before on the pediatric floor where I worked when I was in nursing school," Thea answered, trying to quiet the painful memories. Going to the judge and having him sign off on authorizing procedures for the little ones she'd targeted for her Children Society had been a classic trick of Georgia Tann. At first, it had seemed like a godsend to desperate parents unable to pay for needed surgeries. But in return, Miss Tann took their children and sold them to the highest bidder. Of course, that wasn't the case here—but the memories were still painful.

"Thea, are you okay?"

She shook away the memory of Miss Tann and what she done with Eileen's first baby. Her concern right now was Sarah, and part of taking care of the girl meant calming Mack's fears so the necessary surgery could move forward. "I'm sure Dr. Medcalf will monitor Sarah very carefully after the last time."

But he was still focused on her. "Are you sure you're okay?"

"Of course I'm okay. Why do you ask?"

He nodded to a growing pile of torn paper in front of her. "That napkin you're holding didn't stand a chance."

"Oh." A flush of heat hit Thea's cheeks, and she dropped what was left of the napkin then brushed the lint off her hands. "I guess I'm more nervous than I thought."

Her confession brought a tender light to Mack's eyes. "Little ones have a way of changing how a person thinks about everything."

"I can't disagree with you about that." Since she'd learned about this second chance to make things right with her sister's memory, Thea had thought of nothing but getting Sarah back home. Well, she admitted to herself as she stole a glance at Mack, *almost* nothing else. Even in the mist of their disagreements over Sarah, she'd caught glimpses of the boy she'd once known, teasing her, making her smile when that was the last thing on her mind. He should have women lining up at his door, begging to start the family he so obviously wanted. So why was he still alone?

Not that it mattered to her.

Thea straightened. "Don't worry, Mack. I'm certain Dr. Medcalf isn't going to take any undue risk with Sarah."

"Good." He relaxed slightly, but Thea sensed there was something else on his mind. "But that's not the entire problem."

"It's not?"

He sunk down into the seat, his voice low enough so

that she struggled to hear him. "You know how long the recovery period is for a surgery like this."

Thea bent closer, narrowing the gap between them. "At least a month, maybe longer if there are complications. Why?"

"Can she be taken care of at home?"

"Yes, but…" Realization hit her. Corrective surgery was expensive all on its own. Adding in the cost of spending the recovery in the hospital made the price tag more than what most families made in a year's time. And Mack's case was complicated by the fact he was single. He could save money by having Sarah recuperate at home, but with no wife to care for the baby, he'd be forced to hire outside help. But how could she help? She didn't know any nurses in Marietta who were qualified to provide post-op for this procedure, and after their recent run-ins over Sarah, the man would never consider her. "If you're looking for a recommendation, I don't know any of the nurses who live around here."

"I already have a recommendation."

"You do?" Thea's midsection tightened into a painful knot. She wished she'd known Mack was looking for someone. If he'd asked her help with the search process then it would have given her a chance to interview the woman, find out if she was good with children and if she had the proper training to care for someone with Sarah's special needs.

"Nurse Eison spoke very highly of you. Said you were the most qualified person for the position."

The knot in Thea's stomach loosened slightly. She'd have to send the nurse a thank-you card for such kind words. There could be nothing as wonderful as spending each day with her sister's daughter, nursing her back to a normal life. But being recommended didn't necessarily mean Mack was on board with the decision, and he hadn't really offered her anything yet. "Are you saying you want me to take care of Sarah?"

He scrubbed an aggravated hand through his hair. "I'm not quite sure yet."

"But you're considering it."

"Yes, only because Nurse Eison says you're the best pediatric nurse in town." He leaned slightly forward, his gaze catching and holding hers, concern darkening his blue eyes. "But I don't want Sarah caught in the middle of one of our 'discussions.' She may be a baby, but it can't be good for her to hear the folks caring for her arguing."

Thea understood that. "I agree."

"For this to work, we're going to have to set aside our differences."

"A truce?"

"Yes."

Mack watched her as if he expected her to argue the point. In fact, she felt grateful. To spend time with her niece, to be a part of her daily life, to nurse her back to health. It was an answer to prayer. "I think we can work something out."

"I was hoping you'd say that." He visibly relaxed, the lopsided grin he gave her kicking her heart into high gear. "What? You look surprised."

The man could absolutely read her like an open book! "I didn't expect you to agree so easily."

His smile slid into a more serious line, and she felt a pang of disappointment at its absence. "I'd move mountains for that little girl."

Thea didn't doubt it. If fact, she felt a tad envious. How would her life have been different if she'd had someone like Mack as a constant presence to protect and watch over her? To love her unconditionally without ever expecting anything in return? She wanted to give that to Sarah. It was what Eileen would have wanted.

"Then we agree. Truce?" Mack held his hand out to her.

"Truce." She slid her hand into his, sparks racing up her arm. Once the surgery was in the past and the situation with Sarah was settled, someone would nurse a broken heart.

Please, Lord, don't let it be mine.

"We'll need to explain the situation to Ms. Aurora. Will you come with me for that?"

Oh, dear. It was a reasonable request. Thea was the one with the medical background who could answer Ms. Adair's questions. And anyway, it would make sense that she'd have to face the woman eventually. How would she feel about Mack's plan for Thea to be involved in Sarah's recovery? "Yes, of course. When's a good time for you?"

"I'm going out there this afternoon."

She blinked. So soon? Would she have time to run home and check on her mother? But she couldn't fritter away this opportunity, either. "Right now?"

"Might as well get this over with." He nodded. "Just don't expect Ms. Aurora to feel comfortable with the surgery unless Dr. Medcalf can promise Sarah will be okay."

No doctor would ever make that kind of guarantee. Maybe she could explain the procedure in a way that would give Mack and Ms. Adair peace of mind. Convince them that this was the right thing to do for the little girl they only wanted the best for.

For now, they'd be working together to take care of Sarah. And as for what would happen later…they'd deal with that then.

Chapter Six

An hour later, Mack's doubts continued to dog him as the familiar landscape along the route to Ms. Aurora's flew by. What had he been thinking, asking Thea to nurse his daughter back to health after her operation? What would stop her from taking Sarah and stealing off to parts unknown? He'd have to keep her close to keep her in line.

Which could be a problem.

Mack glanced over at Thea. He hadn't known shaking a woman's hand—or maybe it was just *this* woman's hand—could set off a firestorm of emotions inside him. Attraction, yes, but something deeper, a feeling that threatened to endanger the well-thought-out plans he'd made for his life. He couldn't trust Thea for the long term, not when she'd let him down in the past. And Thea wouldn't want someone like him, anyway. No woman had after they'd learned of his disability.

"You've got that look on your face."

Had Thea figured out what he'd been thinking? Mack coaxed his features into a neutral expression, only his knuckles, gleaming white from their tight grip on the steering wheel, betrayed the turmoil he felt. "What look?"

Her skirts rustled softly as she turned toward him. "The look that says you're wondering if you've made a huge mistake, asking me to take care of Sarah."

She'd gotten all that from his expression? He couldn't imagine what hidden truths she'd have mined out of him if he'd given her a yes or no. "It would be unwise not to wonder if you've made the right decision at times."

"But you've always been so sure of yourself, so certain of the choices you made."

"We all have to grow up sometime." Mack stared out at the road in front of him. Yes, he'd been sure of himself, almost cocky back in those days, so certain of who he was and what the life ahead of him looked like. A football scholarship, then law school and a family of his own, almost the same path his father had taken, a journey Mack had been on since birth.

Had he done the right thing in hiring Thea?

"Is Ms. Aurora expecting us?"

He glanced at her, sitting so properly, her hands folded in a neat knot in her lap. She'd freshened her lipstick, a dusty rose that reminded him of the blooms he'd planted last spring just outside his bedroom window, lovely and dewy soft.

It seemed that handling this attraction he felt toward her was going to be more difficult that he'd thought. Mack flipped the blinker on. "Ms. Aurora knows I come out and see Sarah when I get off work."

"So *you're* expected. But what about me?"

"I didn't have time to call and let her know you'd be coming, if that's what you mean." Which was the truth. Once he'd gotten back to his office after hammering out all the details with Thea, he'd had to track down paperwork for a bond hearing, then got called out for the weekly disturbance at Old Man Fletcher's house. The one time he had tried to call Ms. Aurora, she hadn't picked up. "But knowing Ms. Aurora, she'll be fine with it."

"I don't know." Thea's voice held a touch of doubt. "I mean, I can't be her favorite person. She thought I was spying on her and the kids."

"You *were* spying on her and the kids. But she is the most understanding soul I've ever met. It takes a lot to ruffle her feathers," Mack reassured her.

"She must be a saint." Thea rested back against the vinyl seat, crossing her arms over her tiny waist. "I'd be like an old momma bear if someone put my cubs at risk."

A faint memory played along the fringes of Mack's thoughts. "You always did have a soft spot for little ones. Remember how you got roped into nursery duty at church?"

"I can't believe you remember that."

Mack stole a glance at her. "Why wouldn't I? It's not everyone who can hush a room full of crying infants by just talking sweet to them."

Her cheeks turned a shade of soft pink. "I wasn't the only one who knew how to handle kids. Seems I recall you leading the boys in a raid on the toy chest more than once."

"The girls hogged all the cookies for your tea party. What other alternative did we have?" he teased, then fell quiet. "Did you always want to take care of kids?"

She nodded. "For the most part. Children are easier to handle than adults. You love them, do everything you've been taught to make them feel better and they'll trust you with their life. They're open, honest. Not like adults."

Mack didn't know how to answer, only knew that Thea's words had tightened into a knot in the pit of his stomach. Somewhere along the way, someone had abused her trust, and it had scarred her like the puckered skin hidden in his hair next to his ear. But who? And what had they done to make Thea question everyone's motives?

"How did Ms. Aurora come to take in all these children?"

Mack turned the car down the dirt road to the Adair farm. "I don't know the whole story, just that she's owned this place and brought in kids no one else wanted for as long as I've known her. Before the kids, it must have seemed like a big house without anyone else living there."

"She never married?"

Mack shook his head. "I heard she was engaged to one of the coaches at the high school for a time but it didn't work out."

"So she committed herself to the kids, instead."

The way she said it, with an air of disbelief, grated Mack's nerves. "Ms. Aurora is like that, always doing for others before thinking of herself. It's just her way."

Thea gave a noncommittal "Hmm."

"You don't seem too impressed."

"Why should I be?" There was real surprise in her voice, as if she truly didn't understand why it mattered to him.

Why did it bother him what Thea thought of Ms. Aurora? Maybe because Ms. Aurora was the most loving person he'd ever met, someone who'd truly followed God's path despite the heartache and loneliness life held. She'd be a good example to Thea on how to find contentment in her life despite all of the challenges—contentment that

Thea had never seemed to have for as long as Mack had known her.

"How many children has she adopted out?"

He shot a glance at her. Was she serious? These kids' own parents hadn't wanted them because of the physical and mental challenges they faced. Getting a stranger to agree to adopt them would be all but impossible. Was that why Thea wasn't impressed by Ms. Aurora? Because she had no idea the condition of the children the older woman cared for? "Sarah will be the first."

"Sarah will be the *first*?" she repeated.

Mack nodded. "Most of these kids were left on the streets to fend for themselves, or given to Aurora to avoid being admitted to an institution."

"I just thought…"

"What?"

Instead of giving him an answer, she went quiet, as if mulling over this new information. Was she measuring it against everything she'd seen in her years as a pediatric nurse and finding it hard to swallow? "People are cruel, aren't they," she said at last. "Abandoning their own kids like that."

The need to comfort her, to wrap her in his arms and whisper soothing words, to ease the desolation in her voice, slammed through him. Thea had never had it easy, not with her sister always in trouble, or a mother who didn't have a kind thought toward either of her children. Words would have to do for now. "I use to think of it that way, but now I look at the situation as a blessing."

He felt her staring at him and could imagine she probably thought he'd lost his mind. "How's that?"

"Maybe these kids had a rough start, but now they've got a home with someone who loves them as her very own, not to mention a family of aunts and uncles from the community." Mack maneuvered the turn into Ms. Aurora's driveway. "What someone thought of as a curse, God turned into a blessing."

"I guess that's the only way to look at it, isn't it?"

Mack frowned. Thea didn't sound convinced. Of course, she didn't know Ms. Aurora, didn't know what a Godly woman she was. Once Thea got to know her, she'd see that these children couldn't have been left in more capable hands.

"Maybe if I'd known Ms. Aurora before I left here," Thea whispered just loud enough for Mack to hear as he pulled the car to a stop near the front porch. "She might have known how to help us."

Mack's stomach lunged. What did Thea mean? What trouble could Thea have gotten into that she thought the older woman would have known how to handle?

A knock at his window surprised him out of his thoughts. Mack rolled down the glass to find Billy Warner staring at him. "Are you going to get out or were you planning to sit in the car all day?"

A smile tickled Mack's lips. The boy might have limitations but his character—and his penchant for mischief—was like that of any other kid his age. Billy glanced beyond Mack to where Thea sat. "Did you finally get a girl to go out with you, Sheriff Mack?"

Mack tried to temper the heat rising up the back of his neck. His problems with the female population of Marietta must have been the topic of one of Merrilee and Ms. Aurora's hen talks. What would Thea think? When she'd left Marietta, Mack had still been the big man on campus, still had a future ahead of him.

Mack found out soon enough. "Then I must be a lucky

woman indeed that those other girls didn't take him up on a date."

"That's what Ms. Aurora said—when the right girl came along, she'd snatch Mack up in a heartbeat." Billy grinned back at them as if he'd discovered penicillin or something.

Thea snorted softly, and the heat in Mack's cheeks flamed higher. Someone needed to have a long talk with the boy about using some tact, especially around women. He stole a glance at Thea but found no sign of pity in her expression, just a teasing warmth that melted away some of the residual anger he'd felt toward her.

Might as well face his embarrassment head-on. "As you can tell, things have changed since high school."

She gave him an understanding smile. "Truer words have never been spoken."

Mack nodded. Yes, the accident that had made him partially deaf had molded him into the man he'd become, but what of Thea? What experiences had shaped her since she had left Marietta?

And why was it suddenly so important that he know? Because he was trusting her with Sarah, that had to be it. Or, at least, that's what he told himself as he opened the car door and stepped outside.

Thea was already out of the car by the time he walked around to open her door. She studied the house, almost as if it was a specimen she was looking at under a microscope. Mack took a long look at the two-story frame. It might not be much, with the paint peeling and the torn screens, but it was the only home these kids had ever known. "It's not much to look at, but Aurora has made it into a home."

She glanced back at him. "Does a blind child live here?"

Her question surprised Mack. "How did you know that?"

Thea pointed to the clothesline that connected the front porch to the barn and various parts of the front yard. "Rather ingenious, really. Gives the child a feeling of independence when they can get from place to place in their own home. And the ramps." She motioned to the angled boards that covered every step coming off the porch. "She's made it easier for Billy and the others to move around. From what I can see, Ms. Adair has converted her house to accommodate children with special needs."

"So the peeling paint doesn't bother you?"

Her brows furrowed. "Why would it?"

He'd been prepared to defend Ms. Aurora and how much she put into making this a refuge and haven for her children. It was a little jarring to realize he didn't need to. Why had he assumed that Thea wouldn't understand? Was Beau right? Did he still blame her for the accident that night? Was that why he defaulted to assuming the worst of her? He wanted to move past it, had thought he had to a degree but could he possibly still hold her responsible for everything he had lost—and for the friendship she had abandoned on top of it all? An "I'm sorry" would go a long way to healing this gap between them, yet Thea held back. Why couldn't she at least give him that?

"Is something wrong, Sheriff Mack?"

Mack glanced down at the young boy balancing on his crutch beside him. "Why would you say that?"

"It's just you look…" Billy's gray eyes narrowed, a swatch of brownish blond falling carelessly across his forehead. "Pensive."

Pensive? Mack felt a smile form on his lips. "That's a mighty big word there, Billy."

The boy rolled his eyes. "I told Claire I'd sound like a sissy if I went around saying stuff like that, but she says if I want to go to college someday, I'd better start learning big words."

Ah, Mack should have known a woman would be involved, even if she was barely twelve and still wore pigtails. He settled his arm across the boy's lanky shoulders. "It won't do you any harm to learn a new word or two."

"Well, I think Claire is a very wise young lady."

Both he and Billy turned to look at Thea. Planting the tip of his crutch on the ground, Billy took a step toward her. "You do?"

Thea tilted her head to the side and nodded. "It's never too soon to start planning for your future. Why, I started reading biology books from the minute I realized I wanted to be a nurse, and it helped me when I entered college."

"You went to college?" The admiration in the boy's voice was undeniable.

Thea's cheeks warmed to a delightful shade of pink. "Well, nursing school."

"But that's almost the same thing," Billy argued. The boy turned slightly and glanced back at Mack. "Did you go to college, too, Sheriff Mack?"

The question still caused a band to tighten around his heart, even after all these years.

Mack stepped forward and ruffled the boy's hair. "No, Billy, college wasn't in the cards for me."

"But I thought…"

Mack glanced over at Thea. Confusion and questions clouded her blue eyes. A whole lifetime of questions. But he didn't have the time or patience to give her any answers at the moment. "We ought to get up to the house or Ms. Aurora is going to be wondering where Billy took off to."

"I wouldn't want that." Billy hobbled off at a fast pace. "Last time I took off without telling her, Ms. Aurora put me in charge of Ellie all day long. Don't want to do that again."

"Is this the Ellie who took your bribe, Sheriff?" Thea tucked her purse under her arm as Mack took her elbow.

The feel of her soft skin beneath his fingertips sent a trail of warmth up his arm. "The very same. You'll meet her soon enough."

They followed Billy across the yard, onto the front porch and into the foyer, the water-stained walls hidden behind sheet after sheet of the children's artwork. At the door, a box held wooden blocks, Tinkertoys and baby dolls with their hair matted, their clothes dirty to show how often they'd joined the children outside to play. He picked up one rat-haired doll that looked ready for the garbage can. What kind of toys were these for Sarah to play with?

"Sheriff Mack!" A small warm body crashed into his legs, throwing him slightly off balance. He reached down to steady himself, his hand landing in a bed of soft curls.

"Ellie!" Billy scolded. "You almost knocked him over!"

The girl loosened her grasp and tilted her head back to look at him, her eyes wide with concern. "I sorry."

"The infamous Ellie, I take it."

The playful grin Thea gave him made his heart tumble around in his chest. Mack crouched down in front of the child, and touched the tip of Ellie's flat nose. "It's okay, gumdrop. I'm happy to see you, too."

The girl nodded, her curls bouncing against her shoulders. "Swing?"

"Mack?"

He glanced up to see all good-natured teasing in Thea's expression replaced by a growing look of concern. "What is it?"

Thea tossed her purse on a nearby bench and bent down beside him. "Do you mind if I look at your arms, sweet pea?"

As if to answer, the child lifted her hands into the air, displaying a cluster of angry red bumps gathered under her arms spreading down to her elbows. Mack took a good look at Ellie's face, surprised to find the same red spots along her hairline and across her nose. "Did you get in a batch of poison ivy?"

Blond curls bounced when Ellie shook her head.

He pressed a hand against her forehead, then glanced up at Thea. "She's burning up."

"I thought as much." She tugged at the fingers of her gloves and pulled them off, then tossed them alongside her purse. "We need to get her upstairs and in a cool bath to get her fever down."

But Ellie had other ideas. The girl crossed her chubby arms over her chest, her expression one of mulish determination. "I want to swing."

"But you're burning up, sweetheart, and a bath will make you feel better," Mack pleaded.

"No!"

Thea kneeled down in front of the stubborn little mite. If she thought she'd convince Ellie to change her mind, she was about to get schooled in the ways of a certain six-year-old. "So you don't want to go for a swim?"

Ellie's body relaxed slightly. "But you said you were going to give me a bath."

"That's just what us big people call it." Thea leaned in closer, as if sharing a great secret with the child. "The truth is we're not small enough to go swimming in the bathtub when it gets too cold outside. But you! You can make do by swimming around in the bathtub, instead."

The small girl didn't seem convinced. "I like to jump in the water."

"I know. I do, too. And you can't jump into a bathtub in the same way. But you can float on your back and splash around just as if you're pretending it's a hot summer day." Thea nodded her head toward the toy box. "I bet one of your baby dolls would like to go swimming with you, too."

"Really?" Ellie's bright blue eyes widened with excitement. "Grandma Aurora won't mind?"

Thea gifted her with a bright smile that Mack wished was aimed his way. "I'll tell her what a big girl you're being and ask."

"I'll be right back." Ellie started for the stairs.

Mack started after the child, but Thea's delicate hand on his shoulder locked him in place. "Where are you going, gumdrop?"

"I go put on my bathing suit!" Ellie crested the top of the stairs then disappeared down the hall.

Mack would have laughed at Miss Ellie's antics, but he was too worried. Praise the Lord, Thea had a certain way with kids, though Ms. Aurora might not appreciate the soaked floors and wet towels Ellie's "swim" was sure to generate. Right now, he'd mop the floors himself. The child's fever had scorched his hand. Between that and the bumps, what could be wrong with her?

He glanced back at Thea to find her rummaging through her purse before pulling out a stubby pencil and a pad of paper. "What are you doing?"

She didn't bother to lift her head to look at him. "Making a list. We're going to need supplies."

Riddles made more sense to Mack right now than this woman. He needed to get a handle on the situation before alarming Ms. Aurora, and the best way to do that was figure out what the little girl had gotten into. "What's wrong with her?"

Thea stopped writing and looked at him then, her expression calm yet tender, her eyes the most incredible shade of pale blue. She stepped toward him then stopped, as if she'd wanted to give him comfort, maybe even hold him in her embrace, then thought better of it. Instead, she settled for a gentle smile. "Ellie's going to be okay. I promise."

"But…" He couldn't stand thinking that Ellie might be in pain or uncomfortable. And what about Sarah and the other children? Were they in danger of catching what Ellie had?

Thea's warm hand in his scattered his thoughts, her delicate fingers strong and dependable as she gently squeezed his. She'd done this once before, when he'd missed his receiver downfield and lost the state playoff game. That was the first time he'd wondered if Thea might be part of his future.

As if she'd read his thoughts, Thea released his hand and stepped back, leaving him with a faint sense of loss. "Don't worry, Mack. We may have a minor epidemic on our hands but it's only chicken pox."

Chicken pox?

"Mack, I thought that was you." Ms. Aurora hurried down the hallway toward them, Sarah fussing on her shoulder. The tiny pink spots that dotted the baby's chubby legs sent Mack's stomach tumbling into his shoes. "I'm gonna need some help. The children have come down with chicken pox."

He hoped that didn't mean what he thought it did. "What kind of help do you need?"

The older woman thought for a moment. "I think I have enough oatmeal, but I could use a bottle of aspirin."

Thea stepped forward with her pencil and paper. "I thought I'd get the pharmacist to make up a couple of bottles of calamine lotion to help soothe the itching."

Mack nodded to Thea. "You remember Thea Miller? From Merrilee and John's wedding?"

"The young lady who's been spying on us for the last week." Ms. Aurora glared at him as if he'd brought a war criminal into the house.

"And I'm sorry about that. It was never my intention to worry you." Thea's expression softened as her gaze drifted to the child in Aurora's arms. "I wanted to see Sarah so very much. She looks so much like my sister." She reached out to touch the child, then pulled her hand back. "How could Eileen give such a precious little girl up?"

Ms. Aurora glanced at Mack, confusion deepening the lines around her eyes and mouth. "Your sister? I don't understand."

"It's a long story," Mack answered. One that he'd eventually have to share with the older lady. But at the moment they had more pressing matters. "How many of the kids do you think are sick?"

"Five so far. But Billy's never had it so it's just a matter of time."

Not necessarily. Mack had been exposed to the chicken pox a number of times and never got it. Maybe Billy was immune, too. Still, five sick kids were a lot, even if Billy wasn't added to the list. Ms. Aurora couldn't handle such a load on her own. She needed help, but who? Usually, Merrilee and John would be here, but they still had a few days left on their honeymoon, and the other Daniels women who would normally pitch in were expecting and couldn't be put at risk.

He was stumped. "Got any ideas who might be able to come and give you a hand over the next few days?"

"I can."

Thea. She'd be the logical choice with her nursing background, and he'd seen for himself she had a way of dealing with children. But was it asking too much of her to care for five, maybe even six sick kids?

Seven, if Mack came down with the virus, too.

But he wouldn't.

Would he?

Chapter Seven

Mack closed his eyes and drew in a deep breath, rubbing his arms to generate some heat in his extremities, his stomach and back itching as if a nest of mosquitoes had camped out under his shirt. Though the day was warm for October, a cold chill ran up his spine as he stood in the shade of Thea's front porch.

What could be taking Mrs. Miller so long? Mack rubbed the back of his neck where a headache had settled in. Packing an overnight case for her daughter couldn't be that difficult. Toothbrush, comb, a change of clothes. But then ladies needed more than the bare basics, didn't they? Though what Thea would need, he couldn't say. She had a natural beauty about her, eyes that sparked with humor and compassion, lips the perfect shade of pink to tempt a man beyond reason.

Sucking in another breath, Mack lifted his hand to his forehead, his palm wet with moisture. Fever. No wonder his mind had wandered into this dangerous attraction he felt for Thea.

The screen door squealed open behind Mack and Mrs. Miller poked her head out, pulling Mack's thoughts back to the matter at hand. "I'm sorry it's taking so long, Sheriff, but I can't seem to find a suitcase."

Truly? He'd been standing out here for a good twenty minutes, and she hadn't even started packing? Mack pulled the door open wider and followed the woman inside. "I usually keep mine in the hall closet."

"That sounds like a place Thea would hide it."

Odd way to put it, Mack thought. Almost as if Mrs. Miller thought Thea was concealing something. He watched the older woman hurry across the foyer, pass a door Mack knew to be the closet and head back up the stairs. He frowned. Mrs. Miller had always been a little scatterbrained but since Eileen's passing, she'd seemed different, more forgetful than usual. He'd put it down to the sorrow of losing a child but what if it was something else? What if there was something seriously wrong with her?

The idea worried Mack. Thea had already lost her sister and might never be able to track down her niece. Was she now at risk of losing her mother, too? Family had always been so important to her, even with all the problems they caused. Losing her last link to her family would break Thea's heart. Maybe her staying with Ms. Aurora—leaving her mother in this house alone—wasn't such a good idea, but there was no one else to help tend to a houseful of sick kids.

Well, if he couldn't bring Thea back to the mountain, he'd have to take the mountain to Thea. Mack walked over to the bottom of the stairway. "Mrs. Miller, why don't you come with me to Ms. Aurora's? Thea is going to need all the help she can get and Ms. Aurora would love the extra company, I'm sure."

The woman turned toward him, a wrinkle worrying

her forehead. "I don't know. Thea's always done just fine on her own."

That was true, but then Thea hadn't had much choice with a younger sister running wild and an indifferent mother. She hadn't just taken care of herself—she'd taken care of them, too. Which was why Mack couldn't leave Mrs. Miller here, no matter how much she wanted to stay. "That's a lot of work, keeping all those kids from scratching themselves silly."

"What about the baby?"

Mack's heart sank. He'd hoped to get back to Ms. Aurora's without any mention of Sarah or her supposed relationship to Eileen but he didn't see any way around it. "She's covered in chicken pox, too."

Mrs. Miller's eyes went hazy, as if she was drifting in her own thoughts or memories. "So sad when babies get sick," she murmured. "And there's nothing…nothing you can do. Even when you try—but it's not my fault." She shook her head. "Not my fault that Eileen's baby passed."

Mack blinked. Had he heard her right or was it just the fever? Did Mrs. Miller almost slip up and say Eileen's child had died?

Thea leaned back against the wall, wiping off the last bits of wet oatmeal from her hands, her cuffed shirtsleeves damp around the edges. The past few hours had proved hectic as Thea examined first one child, then another, making notes—writing down each child's temperature, the extent of the blisters, the times she'd administered oatmeal baths. A second round of baths would need to start soon, and Thea had used the last of the oatmeal.

Where was Mack?

She glanced at the clock sitting on a nearby hall table.

It had been over an hour since he'd left to get supplies at Mr. Galloway's drug store. Had he ran into problems finding some of the items on her list or had he been called out on police business? Maybe at this very moment he was struggling to disarm a person with a gun. Her stomach clenched into a sick knot at the thought.

Why had he gone into such a dangerous profession when he could have gone to college and earned his law degree the way he'd planned? Being a lawyer had been his dream, at least, the one he'd shared with her the most when they studied together at the library or worked the same shift at the movie theater. What had happened? How had his dream for the future gotten sidetracked?

A noise in the front hall pulled Thea to the top of the staircase, relief cascading through her at the sight of Mack setting two large grocery bags on the front table. He'd barely put them down before he turned and walked out the door again.

Where was he going? Thea hurried down the stairs and across the hall to the door, stopping briefly to confirm what she already knew, that everything they'd need from the druggist was in the two bags. Then what, she wondered as she moved to the door, did Mack have out in the car? He walked to the passenger-side door, opened it, then leaned down.

"Momma?" Thea stepped out on the porch, the sickening knot suddenly back in the pit of her stomach as she watched Mack help her mother from the car. "What are you doing here?"

"This nice police officer thought I might like to take a ride." She tilted her head back and stared up at Mack with a look of total adoration. "Wasn't that kind of him?"

"Yes, Momma, that was very kind of him, but…" Thea

stared past her mother to where Mack extracted two suitcases from the backseat of his car. He shook his head
slightly, cutting off any further questions she might have.
He was right—that particular talk would have to wait.
The children needed them at the moment.

"Why don't we get your mother settled, then we can
make a plan of attack?"

We? Thea had figured Mack would drop off the supplies then head on home. The town couldn't do without
their sheriff while he helped her tend to a bunch of sick
kids, no matter how much she craved his presence. Ms.
Aurora, God bless her, could have handled the children
if Claire and Billy pitched in, but both of them had been
confined to their beds, their temperatures spiking in the
time Mack had been gone. Now with her mother, it was
one more person to care for.

Ms. Aurora, looking tired and worried, met the group
at the door. She perked up when she spied Thea's mother.
"Mildred Miller, why, it's been a coon's age since I've
seen you."

"Aurora Adair." Momma grasped the woman's hands
as if they were long-lost friends newly found. "It's been
forever. How have you been?"

"Why don't we go into the kitchen and have a cup of
coffee?" Ms. Aurora wrapped her skinny arm around
Momma's plump one. "It'll give us time to catch up."

"What a lovely idea! You wouldn't happen to have any
of those delicious macaroons you use to make? I never
could get you to give me the recipe."

"No macaroons, but I baked some peanut butter cookies this morning." Their voices drifted off as they made
their way down the hall and into the kitchen.

Thea spun around to face Mack. "What is she doing here?"

Mack set down the suitcases then straightened. "I went by your house on the way back from town. I figured you might need some things if you intended to stay here for the next few days. But when I got there, your mom seemed more confused than usual."

"What did you mean, more confused than *usual*? How would you know that?" Her eyes widened and her mouth fell open slightly. "You been called out to the house before, haven't you?"

Mack seemed almost reluctant to answer, as if telling her the truth would open up a new wound. "Your mother's next-door neighbor called me out there about a month ago."

"The Donohues?" They were a kind couple, Thea remembered. Always offered her a homemade biscuit every morning on her way to the school bus stop.

"Mr. Donohue came home from work and found your mother on the front porch, barefoot and in her nightgown. She was confused, Thea. Didn't have a clue where she was or how she'd gotten there."

"Oh." Thea felt like sinking into the floor. Needing something to steady her, she reached for the table and found Mack's warm arm instead. He pulled her against his broad chest, his strong arms anchoring her, keeping her safe. She buried her face in the curve of his neck. "I thought she was just rattled over losing Eileen and worried about the baby. Grief will do that to a person."

"It still could be the reason she's acting the way she is."

She felt the corners of her mouth lift slightly. Mack was being kind now, trying to ease her into the reality of her mother's situation. But Thea had always been a good diagnostician—when she didn't allow her emotions to get in the way. She knew what these lapses in memory were, what her mother's outbursts of anger and frustration meant.

I'm losing her a little at a time.

A whimper tore through her before she had a chance to react. All she had ever wanted, if she made it back from the war, was to have her family, flawed as they may be, around her again. She'd prayed about it, asked God to give her another chance to make things up to Eileen, to make her peace with Momma. It was the one hope that had gotten her through the endless line of young men that she'd sutured up and sent back out into the battle.

Who did she have now?

"You're not alone, sweetheart," Mack whispered near her ear, his hand tracing comforting circles against her shoulder blades, lulling her, making her wish she could press farther into his embrace. He'd always known how to comfort her, almost as if he had the instruction manual. If she could only have a man like Mack, someone to build a life with, and a family. She'd spend the rest of her life showing him how precious he was to her, how much she loved him.

Love? The errant thought caught her off guard. It had to be an overreaction to this crazy day. First, the job interview, then Mack's idea to have her nurse Sarah, not to mention tending a houseful of kids breaking out in various degrees of chicken pox and, of course, her mother's issues.

What man could possibly want to involve himself in that?

Thea placed her hand on his chest and gently pushed away from him. Love? How could she love a man who threatened to take the only family she had left? Besides, Mack didn't deserve to be chained to the mess her family had always been. And her problems with her mother's deteriorating health were just beginning.

"You okay?"

"I'm fine." She wasn't really, but he didn't need to know that. Walking over to the hall table, she busied herself unpacking the grocery sacks. "Did you get ahold of Dr. Medcalf's office and let him know about Sarah?"

"He wasn't too thrilled about the delay but what's he going to do? Operate on her while she's infected? Maybe he hasn't had chicken pox, either."

What did Mack mean by *either*? It wasn't possible, was it? How could a grown man Mack's age have made it through his youth without contracting the virus? She sought his reflection in the mirror hanging over the table and almost gasped. His skin was flushed, as if he ran a low-grade fever, and she couldn't be sure but a pink spot appeared to be forming high on his right cheek. Thea jerked around. "Mack, you've had the chicken pox, haven't you?"

He shook his head, then rubbed the back of his neck as if he was nursing a headache. "Never caught it. Mom wanted me to catch it." He gave her a faint smile. "Even sent me over to friends' houses when they'd come down with it, hoping they'd pass it along. The doctor said I must have a natural-born immunity to it."

Without asking, she pressed her hand against his forehead, startled by the heat radiating through her fingers. "I think whoever told you that was wrong. You're on fire."

"Probably nothing." Mack swatted her hand away. "I've been running around for the last couple of hours trying to get everything settled, that's all. Just got over-heated."

Well, she could add irritability to his symptoms. Grabbing his shirtsleeve, she tugged him into the dining room then pushed him into the nearest chair. "Be still while I check for more spots."

His dark blond brows furrowed together. "What do you mean *more*?"

"Well," she started, cupping his face with one hand and tilting it up toward the light. "You're got a small bump here." She brushed her fingertip along the outer curve of his right cheek.

Mack reached up to rub the spot but she swatted his hand away. "You're making a mountain out of an ant-hill," he complained.

"Maybe." The word came out on a shaky breath, the gentle scratch of his day-old beard against her palm sending pinpricks of awareness up her arm. Thea chided herself. She needed to focus. The man was obviously sick. "Well, I'm not taking any chances. Chicken pox can be serious business in adults. Understood?"

He gave her a reluctant nod.

That settled, Thea scanned his face, taking in every nuance: the tiny laugh lines around his eyes and mouth, the faded scar on his forehead he'd gotten when he'd taken a tumble on the fireplace when he'd been a toddler. Her gaze shifted downward, only to find him watching her.

"You have flecks of silver in your eyes."

Her heart did a funny pitter-pat in her chest. "I do?"

"Yeah." His irises turned a warmer shade of blue. "Almost like tiny bursts of starlight."

Thea felt her cheeks go warm as she ducked her head

to check his exposed neck. "I don't remember you being so poetic, Sheriff Worthington."

"It's been known to happen on occasion, especially around a pretty nurse."

Oh, my. The man must have a higher fever than she'd thought to spout such sweet words to her. But even that knowledge didn't stop her heart from beating out a wild rhythm under her rib cage. Thea dropped her hand and moved to his side, still close enough to get a good look at any spots that might have formed. "Let me check your scalp. Sometimes the lesions like to hide in the hairline."

"If you have to."

She took a deep breath, then sank her hands into his neatly trimmed strands of blond hair, her fingers gently moving. How many times had she dreamed of doing exactly this when they'd been in high school, dreamed of feeling the weight and texture of every strand against her palms as she tugged him close for a kiss? Her mouth went dry. Girlish dreams. Mack had only ever looked on her as a friend, and now, a nurse. A nurse with a houseful of sick patients.

Mack closed his eyes and slumped down farther in the chair. "Mmm, that feels good."

A soft smile turned up the corners of her mouth. "Helping your headache any?"

"How did you know?"

"I'm a nurse, remember? It's what I do." She felt along the hairline at one ear, then the other, pausing when her fingertips skimmed over a small jagged line that puckered just under his hair. "What's this?"

"What?"

Thea tilted his head slightly to one side and pushed the hair away to get a better look. She uncovered a pale, almost whitish zigzag line about an inch in length. "It looks like a surgical scar."

The muscles beneath her fingertips tightened. "It is."

"What happened?"

Mack glanced up at her, the warmth in his blue eyes suddenly chilled. "Your mother didn't tell you?"

Thea felt the air drain from her lungs. There was a note of anger in his voice, as if it was a foregone conclusion she would know what had happened to him. How could she explain that, until a week ago, she'd spoken less than ten words to her mother over the past eight years? "You know Momma. She's never been one to keep up with the news around town."

"So you don't know about the car accident I was in the night you left town?"

A hard lump formed in the pit of Thea's stomach. "How bad was it?"

He hesitated, and for a moment she thought he wouldn't answer. "I was rounding a corner on Cunningham Road and skidded. Ended up wrapped around a tree in the Deavers's front yard. I'm just thankful I didn't hit anyone else."

"What a blessing that it wasn't any worse than it was." Thea breathed a sigh of relief. "You could have been killed."

"Sometimes, it felt like I was. At least, a part of me, anyway."

Fear tightened like a fist around her heart. Whatever had happened, clearly it was much worse than Mack had told her so far. Was the accident the reason why he'd never gone to college? Had his injures kept him for going overseas to fight?

Questions whirled around in her head like a children's

top. And why had it seemed so important to him that her mother inform her about the accident? She hadn't lived in Marietta for eight years and had not kept in touch with anyone from her past.

Now was not the time for questions, not when Mack looked ready to drop any minute. Even in the short time she'd spent examining him, more spots had bloomed across his face and on his neck. She'd have to wait to get her answers.

Thea moved back, giving him room to stand. "Come on. We need to get you in bed."

Feverish eyes stared back at her. "But I can't have the chicken pox. My job…"

"Will still be there once you've recovered." Bending her knees, she lifted his arm and placed it across her shoulders, pressing herself against him to give her leverage to pull him to his feet. He tightened his hold, bringing her even closer, an odd feeling of belonging settling over her as if right here, next to him, was where she was supposed to be. Thea gave herself a mental shake. Just overwrought emotions after a long day.

"I can stand, you know."

Thea leaned her head back to glance up at him, her mouth suddenly dry again. How could the man be so adorably handsome with tiny bumps popping up all over his face? "I know, but humor me. Nurses like to feel like they're doing something to make people feel better."

"Well, then," Mack answered with a teasing note in his voice, his cheek against the top of her head, cocooning her in his warmth. "That's mighty fine with me."

Thea couldn't help the smile that formed on her lips. She'd take this minor reprieve in hostilities, might even savor it. But she wasn't fooling herself. Questions re-

mained between them, about the accident, concerning
Sarah. And the answers, Thea feared, could breach any
truce they might have reached and lead to all-out war.

With a man she was coming to care for altogether
too much.

There was a reason chicken pox was a childhood dis-
ease, Mack thought as he scooted up in the bed, the cotton
sheets sticking to him, setting off small fires around the
lesions on his back and legs. He reached down to scratch
a particularly bad patch along his thigh, first stealing a
glance at his bedroom door. Thea had threatened to wrap
his hands in a pair of socks fastened with duct tape if she
caught him scratching again, and he knew with a sinking
certainty that the woman would really do it!

Better not chance it. Mack sank deeper into his pillows. Three days now, and he still felt like the gum on
the bottom of some kid's shoe, the day hours filled with
oatmeal baths, watery broth and gallons of the calamine
lotion Mr. Galloway had mixed up. With the way Thea
dabbed the pink goo over his exposed arms and chest,
he'd begun to resemble a bag of cotton candy at the North
Georgia State Fair.

But no more. Mack pulled himself up again, resolutely
ignoring the new wave of pain slicing through him. Thea
may think he needed another day in bed, but he'd had
enough. His muscles ached from inactivity; the only daily
exercise he'd had was the short walk to the bathroom for
the oatmeal baths Thea had drawn for him.

Thea. She really was something, always patient, never
complaining, even when he'd been at his worst these past
few days. It had surprised him to find out she'd had no
idea about his accident. For years, he'd felt hurt over the

way she'd failed to live up to their friendship, never contacting him to check on his recovery. Now that he knew she'd never even been aware of his situation, he'd have to let that grudge go. As for whether he still blamed her for the accident itself…he'd need to let that go, too, after all she'd done these past few days to nurse him back to health.

Besides, it wasn't all her fault. He'd driven too fast in poor weather conditions and missed the curve. Instead of focusing on the road, his mind had been on Thea and whatever trouble her sister had cooked up.

Trouble that had caused Thea to run away and not return for eight long years. He knew she'd come back for her family…but her mother was doing poorly, and if Mrs. Miller was to be believed, Eileen's baby hadn't survived. Would Thea leave town again when she learned Sarah wasn't her niece? Maybe not at first, she'd have her mother to care for, but he could only imagine the sadness she'd carry, the guilt that she could have done more to save her family. A knot formed in Mack's throat just thinking about it.

There was a light rap on the door before it opened, and the subject of his thoughts walked in. "You're not in here scratching yourself again, are you? I don't want you to be scarred."

"With you threatening me every five minutes, I don't think so."

She chuckled, a musical sound that seemed to vibrate through to his soul. "Well, at least you're getting your sense of humor back. Sounds like you're on the mend."

Should he chance asking her if he could see Sarah? Thea had given him almost hourly updates on the infant since he'd fallen ill, but he'd feel better if he could see his daughter for himself. "Think I could get out of bed for a while? Maybe walk a bit?"

"You mean see Sarah?" She moved quietly through the room, placed a stack of freshly laundered towels on the dresser, tucked in an errant blanket at the corner of the bed before finally reaching for the glass thermometer on his bedside table. Loose curls trembled against her shoulders as she shook it, then held it up to his mouth. "Remember to put it under your tongue."

Mack grasped the thermometer between his lips while Thea continue to bustle around the room. Watching her had become his favorite pastime these past few mornings. There was an efficiency in her movements, a discipline that almost seemed as natural as breathing to her. Was that what had drawn her into nursing in the first place, this need to have some small area of her life under control?

Grasping the glass tube, she slid it out of his mouth and studied it before giving him a relieved smile. "Almost perfect."

"Good." Mack threw back the covers and sat up. He grasped the edge of the bed as the room spun around him and a dull ache started at the base of his skull.

"You tried to get up too fast. Just sit there for a minute, okay?"

He couldn't argue with her even if he wanted to. Mack closed his eyes. "Okay."

He drew in a deep breath, hoping to clear his head, but instead breathed in the heady mixture of Thea's personal scent, a combination of fresh cotton and Ivory soap that he thought smelled better than anything Mr. Hice had bottled in the perfume section of his department store. She was nearby, hovering over him as she had for the past few days, as if she were truly worried for his welfare. The thought made him feel off balance again but for an entirely different reason.

"Are you okay?"

He opened his eyes, and his heart tumbled around in his chest at the concern in her expressive face. No wonder injured soldiers fell in love with their nurses, especially if they were as beautiful as Thea was. It would be the easiest thing in the world.

If he'd let himself—which he wouldn't. She was determined to take his daughter away from him. "I'm fine."

"Good." The fabric of her cotton jumper rustled softly as she knelt down in front of him and reached for a pair of soft-soled shoes at the foot of the bed. "Let's get these on you. Don't want you to get cold."

"Are you this way with all of your patients?"

Thea chuckled as he shoved his foot into the house shoe. "Most times."

"No wonder General Patton gave you a reference letter."

She stood up and stepped back, a smile dancing along the corners of her mouth. On closer inspection, she looked pale, and the tender flesh under her eyes appeared bruised a purplish blue. She had to be tired, taking care of six children, seven if he counted himself. Exhausted was more like it, but she'd never said a word of complaint. Well, the epidemic would be all over soon.

"How's the baby?" Mack asked.

The tender smile that played along Thea's lips made his heart do a little flip in his chest. "She's fine. Not even a smidgen of fever this morning. She's still a little fussy. She tried to scratch at her spots so often, I finally had to tie a pair of socks on to her hands to keep her for tearing at her skin."

"Was that necessary? I mean, she's so little."

She stiffened. "She could scratch herself and end up with infected sores. We don't want that." Her voice wobbled a little, and he could tell she was hurt.

Guilt assailed him over his hasty words. Mack stood up, but this time when the room spun, he wasn't sure why but the only thought in his head was getting to Thea.

He cupped her chin in his hand, lifted her face until her gaze met his. Blue eyes shone with unshed tears. "Hey, it's okay."

"I'm just tired, that's all."

"Of course you are. While we've all been lying around, you've been running around taking care of us without one word of complaint." He brushed his thumb against the soft curve of her cheek, watched a rosy pink infuse her skin where his fingertips touched. "That couldn't have been easy."

"No. You were worse than the kids. At least they didn't snap at me."

There was that spark he'd grown to admire. "Maybe because I'm not use to having someone take care of me."

She seemed to think about that a moment. "I know the feeling."

He knew she did. Growing up, he'd at least had his parents to care for him, but Thea had been stuck in the role of caregiver since she was a child. Was that another reason she'd gone into nursing, because taking care of others was the only thing she'd ever known? "I still shouldn't have said what I did about how you nursed Sarah. You did what was best for her, and that's all I could have asked for."

"Really?" Her lips curved up into a tentative smile.

"Are you kidding? Nurse Eison told me you were the greatest thing since coffee beans when it came to taking care of little ones, and boy, if you didn't prove it. I'm just being an old grouch."

"Well, you have a right to be. You've been very sick." She chuckled weakly. "And I usually don't dissolve into a puddle, but I've never taken care of someone I've cared about so much before. It just about killed me to bind Sarah's tiny little hands in those socks but I've seen what an infection can do. Just the thought of what could happen to her..." She hiccuped.

"But she's fine." Thea's confession tugged at his emotions in a way he hadn't expected. Before he knew what he was doing, he pulled her close and wrapped his arms around her. "We're worrying over nothing. That's what loving a child does to you. I know not seeing Sarah these last few days has about driven me nuts."

"She's missed you, too."

Mack leaned back to look at her. "She has?"

Thea nodded. "I've noticed she watches the door in the evenings, like she's waiting on you."

Mack thought his heart would explode beneath his ribs. His baby girl missed him. "Thank you for telling me that."

"I think it would do the both of you some good if you spent a little time together today. Maybe give her her afternoon bottle and rock her to sleep?"

"You're okay with that?"

A tiny line formed between her lovely blue eyes. "You thought I wouldn't be?"

Shame sent a flash of heat up his neck. "I just figured with the both of us wanting to raise her, you'd want to keep me as far away from her as possible."

"I might have thought that way a couple of days ago," she said, moving back slightly as if she needed to put some space between them. "But you love her, and I believe she loves you, too. You're her family, and if it's proven that she's my niece, I'd want you to still be a part of her life. If that's what you want."

It was the most unselfish gift he'd ever received, the chance to be a part of Sarah's life even if Judge Wakefield denied the adoption. Filled with gratitude and wonder, he cupped her face in his hands, her skin warm beneath his fingertips. Thea breathed a soft sigh, and Mack followed the path to her slightly parted lips. For the briefest of moments, his thoughts wandered. What would it feel like to press his mouth against hers, to taste the sweetness that she lived out every day?

Her eyes widened, almost as if she'd read his thoughts, and without knowing what he intended to do, Mack lowered his head toward hers.

"Knock, knock."

Mack jerked his head around to find Beau Daniels standing in the doorway, his gaze traveling back and forth between them until he finally smiled. "If you want me to come back later..."

"A good long visit is exactly what the sheriff needs." Thea slid by Beau, She collected the dirty linens then headed for the door. "Maybe you can convince him to take it easy for another day or two."

"I'll give it my best try." They passed each other, Beau stepping toward the foot of the bed as Thea clicked the door shut behind her. He turned back to face Mack, a knowing smile plastered on his face. "Looks like Nurse Miller is taking very good care of you."

Mack didn't like the implication. "Don't say it like that. Thea isn't anything like her sister."

"I never thought she was." Beau walked over and sat

down in the rocking chair next to the bed. "But the two of you did look mighty cozy when I came in."

"All right, so I almost kissed her." Still wanted to, if the truth be told. But kissing Thea would complicate matters, especially concerning Sarah's adoption. Mack grabbed the robe at the edge of the bed and shoved his arms into the sleeves; his bumps flared back to life. He sank back to sit on the bed. "Thea's had a rough couple of days, and I didn't help things by barking at her about Sarah's care."

"So you were only trying to comfort her?"

Mack nodded. That was as good an excuse as any he could think of at the moment.

"Fine." Beau studied him for a long moment, then shook his head. "Anyway, that's not what brought me out here."

True, Beau hadn't been to Ms. Aurora's for at least four months. It must have been something important to have brought him this far out of town now. "One of the kids hasn't taken a turn for the worse, have they?"

"No, from what I can see, Thea's done an excellent job nursing everyone through the chicken pox."

Mack didn't doubt it. His own care had been superior. "Then why are you here?"

Beau's expression turned serious. "The town council met last night to discuss their plans for reorganizing the police force."

Perfect, and him laid up in his sick bed. As if he didn't have enough to worry about. "They couldn't wait a week so that I could give them my insights on what direction the county needs to take?"

"It's my understanding that's exactly the reason why they held the meeting last night, so they could feel comfortable discussing their options without your input."

Mack didn't like where this conversation was going. "Did they come to any conclusions?"

"Not really." Beau's mouth twisted to the side as if he'd bit into an unripe persimmon. "To be honest, they seemed more interested in dissecting your personal life."

His personal life! Mack jumped to his feet, the world suddenly swirling around him again. He sucked in a deep breath and grabbed hold of the iron bed railing until the room slowed to a standstill. "What personal life? All I ever do is work and spend my evenings here visiting Sarah. My big day out is going to Sunday services then having lunch with your family at Merrilee's."

"I know. Kind of sad, isn't it?"

Quite more than sad. Just like his world had become. "Do they have a problem with me adopting a child?"

"No. Everyone on the council thinks it's a fine idea, you wanting to raise Sarah." Beau hesitated, his mouth turning up at one corner in a way that had always meant trouble. "Their concerns are more about your…recent behavior."

That made Mack forget about the itching. "What exactly is it about my behavior that has everybody in an uproar?"

Beau leaned forward and rested his forearms on his thighs. "Is it true you and Thea were holding hands and making goo-goo eyes at each other in the diner the other day?"

How did folks take an act of friendly comfort and turn it into something that sounded sordid and trashy? Didn't people have better things to do with their time than spread silly rumors around town? "We were talking about Sarah's surgery and she took my hand to comfort me, that's all." Only it had felt like more, at least to him. Even now, he remembered the spark of awareness that her touch had ignited. He shook the memory away. "Whoever saw us is making a mountain out of an anthill."

"You don't have to convince me. If you say there's nothing going on between the two of you, then I believe you."

Mack drew in a steadying breath. While Beau the boy hadn't been so dependable, the man who had returned from war was as solid as the granite under Kennesaw Mountain. Mack felt honored to have such a friend. "Didn't mean to take your head off."

"I'll give you a break this time." Mack gave him a slight grin. "You've been sick."

"Anything else I should know?"

Beau shook his head. "Just like a dog with a bone, aren't you?"

He was stalling. What had those old coots on the town council cooked up now? "What is it?"

There was a slight hesitation, then Beau sighed. "Truth is, most of the council members are a little uncomfortable with the fact that you've been out here with Thea for the last few days."

Mack didn't know whether to laugh or get spitting mad. "You're kidding me, right?"

"They feel that it looks inappropriate for the two of you to be out here together, especially after the hand-holding incident in town."

"We weren't holding hands!" Mack raked his hand through his hair then instantly regretted it as the sores on his scalp caught fire. "You did tell them that there are ten people in the house, including one of the most respected ladies in town and Thea's mother, right? How many chaperons do they think I need?"

"From the looks of what I just saw, a few more might be in order, Romeo."

"Aw, be quiet," Mack grumbled when Beau chuckled. He went to scrub his jaw then changed his mind. "I don't remember Merilee and John causing this much talk when they helped out Ms. Aurora earlier this year."

"No," Beau agreed. "But neither of them is a public official like you are. People hold you to a higher moral standard. Judge Wakefield himself said this incident flies in the face of every law-abiding, church-going citizen of Marietta. A little melodramatic but it gave those busybodies in town something to chew on."

Mack's shoulders slumped. Strange as it seemed, he understood exactly what Beau meant. The citizens looked to him, as the law in this county, to be an example of moral living, a standard to which others should aspire. Even though nothing inappropriate ever happened between him and Thea in this situation, there was the appearance that broke with that standard. Without meaning to, he'd let the people of Marietta down. He glanced over at his friend. "What do I have to do to make this right?"

"Well, I thought I could take you home and follow your recuperation myself." His friend eyed the door as if half expecting someone to pop in. "But after what I witnessed today, I'm wondering if there's not another option."

Mack's brows furrowed until realization set in. "I'm not marrying her."

"Now hear me out." Beau pressed his lips together. "If I hadn't interrupted when I did, you would have kissed that woman, and if news of that ever got around town, you'd either be fired from your position or standing in front of the Justice of the Peace."

Mack pulled his fist back, then plunged it into the

mattress. The people who knew him would know the rumors of misbehavior weren't true, that he'd been isolated at Ms. Aurora's only to keep from spreading the chicken pox around town. But what could he do about those who didn't know him as well, those who would believe the rumors? What kind of standard did that set for the town if the sheriff was accused of immoral behavior?

And what of Thea? He'd witnessed the pain she'd gone through when talk centered on her sister's wild behavior, had comforted her when she'd been snubbed, watched her hold her head high even as people whispered around her. Even now, some of the old folk would have her wear a scarlet letter because of Eileen's actions. What would people say about Thea now? Would they listen to reason or brand her with the same ugly names they'd given her sister? Mack wouldn't sit by and watch her get hurt like that, not when a marriage would silence people's tongues.

That was if Thea would take him, disability and all.

"You both want to raise that little girl downstairs so why not team up? Get married and adopt her together," Beau said. "Judge Wakefield wouldn't have any reasons left for holding up the adoption then."

"You make marriage sound like I'd be joining the football team." Of course it all seemed that simple to Beau. He had the kind of marriage Mack had always wanted for himself, the kind of marriage his parents had had, a lifelong promise, a covenant between him and his bride to love, honor and cherish each other until the Lord called them home. A life with a woman who chose to be with him, to love him, to grow together in the good and bad times.

Not a woman forced into marriage because of public opinion or to skirt around the adoption laws.

He needed to talk to Thea. It was her reputation at risk.

To leave her out of the conversation about her future, about *their* possible future with Sarah, felt just plain wrong.

Besides, the other option besides proposing was letting Beau take him home—and Mack couldn't leave now. Not after he'd seen the way that exhaustion wore on Thea. Sarah and the rest of the kids needed him. One desertion in a person's life was one too many. He couldn't do that to Thea or the kids. "How long does it usually take to get over chicken pox?"

"A week, give or take a day or two," Beau said. "Why?"

"Then come back in a couple of days and we'll talk again."

Beau stared at him for a long moment. "It would be better if I monitored you at your own home."

"Better for who? The town council? If they're so worried about my reputation, have them send somebody out here to help Thea with the kids. Because that's what I intend to do the next few days."

Beau shook his head. "They're not going to like this at all."

"Maybe not, but I wouldn't like myself too much if I didn't stay and help Thea care for these kids now that I'm feeling better." Mack scoffed. "Just because a bunch of old hens got a bee in their bonnet about the situation between me and Thea doesn't mean I'm going to turn my back on doing what's right for my daughter."

Concern clouded his friend's expression. "I understand, you know I do, but you're talking about your livelihood here. If you lose your job, no court in this country would consider giving you that baby."

Beau was right. Why win the battle if it meant losing the war? Compromise seemed the only viable solution, though it left a sour taste in his mouth. "Can you get me until tomorrow? Just long enough to spend some time with Sarah and make sure she's okay?" And Thea, too. She needed sleep, and he wanted to make sure she got some rest after being run ragged these past few days.

"That shouldn't be too hard. I'll let them know that unless they want a full-blown epidemic of the chicken pox right before Thanksgiving, they'd better let you stay put."

"Thanks."

"This may give you a short reprieve," Beau started. "But don't think that the town council is just going to drop this. I talked to several of them last night about the possibility that you'd hire Thea to be Sarah's nurse after her surgery, and that didn't go over very well. I didn't know someone could raise their eyebrows so high."

If Mack hadn't been the topic of conversation, he might have liked to have seen that. Instead, it felt as if he'd jumped on the Ferris wheel at the county fair and it was spinning out of his control. Once again, Thea had entered and wreaked havoc on his life. Only this time he wasn't helpless—there was something he could do. *If* Thea was willing to agree…

Mack closed his eyes. *Father in Heaven, You're going to have to sort out this mess that's my life right now. Give me wisdom and strength to follow You in all my ways. In Christ's name, Amen.*

Chapter Eight

Thea dried the last soup bowl and set it alongside the others. Sarah's sporadic cries from across the room as Ms. Aurora walked her around the kitchen table tore Thea's heart to shreds. She wiped her palms on the skirt of the apron she'd borrowed, then turned and held out her hands. "Let me take her for a little while and give you a break."

Ms. Aurora shifted the baby's weight on her hip. "You could use a break, too. The kids have run you in circles since the rooster crowed this morning."

Sarah tilted sideways, waving her arms in the air, a signal Thea recognized. The baby wanted Thea to hold her. She scooped the baby up, the now-familiar scent of calamine lotion floating in the air between them. Sarah curled up into her, her warm body a sweet weight. "I've worked long hours before."

"On the front line over in Europe during the war," the woman said softly as she walked over to the cupboard and opened it. "Weren't you afraid you'd get killed?"

"Constantly." Thea rested her cheek against a patch of the pale blond hair that swirled around Sarah's head and held her tight. But the prospect of death wasn't as horrible as the fear of being alone, of having no one to come home to. That fear had driven Thea back to Marietta, ready to see her mother and sister again, to try and put their grievances in the past.

But there'd been no family to come home to. Eileen was gone, and Momma... The thought made her heart contract into a painful knot.

Thea glanced down at the baby nuzzled against her shoulder, her deep, steady breathing a comfort after so many sleepless nights. Watching this child suffer had torn a hole through her. Thea would have gladly borne the itching and fevers Sarah had endured to give the child relief. How in the world would she bear the weeks of pain this baby would go through recovering from the surgery to correct her mouth and nose?

Mack would be there to lean on for support.

Her heart fluttered as she remembered how close he'd come to kissing her. She'd wanted his kiss, had almost stretched up on her toes to breach the distance between them and cover his lips with hers. What would Mack have thought? Would he have branded her as wild as her sister? He'd probably laugh if he knew the truth, that in all her twenty-six years Thea had still never experienced a real kiss. Wouldn't it have been lovely if Mack had been her first?

But not with the question of Sarah's parentage hanging over their heads. No, it was best for everyone that Beau had interrupted when he had.

"You're deep in thought over there," Ms. Aurora said as she walked over to the cupboard.

Thea rocked the baby in her arms. "Just letting my mind wander. I'm too tired to think too much."

"I could do with a cup of coffee." Ms. Aurora opened

the cabinet door and took a cup and saucer down. "How about you?"

"I'd love one," Thea whispered on a shaky breath, Sarah finally asleep. "But the children…"

The older woman held up a delicate hand. "The little ones are napping while Claire and Billy keep Ellie occupied in her room."

"My mother…"

"Upstairs napping, as well." She extracted another cup and closed the cabinet. "Being around all these children has about worn the woman slap out."

"We could all use a good night's sleep." Thea yawned as the baby snuggled deeper into the crook of her neck.

Ms. Aurora chuckled as she carried the cups and laid them on the linen-covered table. "That doesn't happen much around here, even when all of the children are well."

Nights with no sleep for someone of Ms. Aurora's advancing years had to be wearing on her health. Yet Thea had seen that she loved these children with a joy and patience most parents didn't demonstrate. Shame knotted in the pit of Thea's stomach. She had severely misjudged the woman. Cradling Sarah tightly against her shoulder, Thea maneuvered herself onto a chair at the table. "I owe you an apology, Ms. Aurora."

The older woman looked at her with startled eyes. "Whatever for?"

Thea swallowed. This was harder than she'd thought it would be. "I judged you based on someone else I knew, a woman who wasn't kind to the children she took in."

"Who in the world would do something like that?"

Georgia Tann. "Just someone I knew from my nursing school days."

"I hope you reported her to the authorities."

Repeatedly, for all the good it did her. "Anyway, I'm sorry for judging you."

Ms. Aurora gave her the same sweet smile Thea had seen her give the children time and again. "It's all right. If I'd seen someone mistreating a child like you have, I'd be suspicious, too."

No wonder everyone thought so highly of Ms. Aurora. Thea sat back in her chair, the weight on her heart a little less heavy now that she had the older woman's forgiveness. "I do have a couple of questions."

"I'll answer anything you like as long as it's my story to tell."

"Well," Thea began, "what made you decide to take in all these kids?"

"If you mean did I go out looking for these children, I didn't." She opened the silverware drawer and pulled out two spoons. "God just put them in my path."

"I don't understand."

Ms. Aurora returned to the table with a coffeepot and sat it on a crocheted pot holder in front of her before taking a seat. "When I was growing up, I didn't have the opportunities to marry. I was in the hospital during the time most girls are courted. By the time I was released, I was more interested in enjoying my freedom than being chained up again."

Why had Ms. Aurora been hospitalized for such a long time? Or had she been in an institution? Thea decided not to ask. "But if you wanted your freedom…"

"I know. Silly me!" Ms. Aurora chuckled. "But God knew the real desires of my heart. He knew that I wanted a family even if that didn't include a husband."

"That must have been very difficult for your parents to understand."

Sadness blew across the woman's expressive face then just as quickly, dissipated. "They were gone from my life by then. Anyway, here I was, unmarried and yearning for a family of my own. So I did what I'd always done. I asked for God to provide me with a child if it was His will."

"You asked God for a baby, and He gave you one?"

"Well, not a baby, but two little boys." Ms. Aurora reached for the coffeepot and poured Thea a cup before pouring her own. "I was at the grocery store one day and saw a little boy stealing a loaf of bread. John, that's Claire's daddy, was about ten years old then." She shook her head. "That boy, he had my heart even before he told me he'd only taken the bread to feed his little brother. Their daddy deserted them after their mother died. John was fine, but his little brother, Matthew, was severely crippled."

The thought of those boys left to the streets to fend for themselves caused an ache to well up in Thea's soul. "Did the police ever find their father? Was he brought up on charges for abandoning them?"

"No." The woman must have sensed Thea's outrage and continued. "Taking it to the courts would have put the boys in danger of being sent to one of the state institutions, and we couldn't chance that. So Mr. Worthington and I worked out a plan. The grocer wouldn't press charges and I'd take the boys home and give them a place to live."

"Mr. Worthington?"

"Mack's daddy, and a very good man. I don't even think Mack knows this but his father used to bring us groceries every week so we wouldn't have to do without." A soft smile lit her face. "Mack's done the same thing since he became sheriff four years ago. Sometimes I wondered how that boy managed to put food on his own table when he gave most of his ration stamps to us."

Yes, Mack would do that. Even as a boy, he'd always put others' needs first. That was how they had become friends in the first place—he'd shared his lunch when there had been nothing at home for Thea to eat. "How did Sarah come to live here?"

"That was a sad situation." Ms. Aurora spooned a heaping tablespoon of sugar into her steaming cup. "Mack showed up with that little baby, only a few hours old, and it was so plain to see he was just heartbroken at the thought of her mother not wanting her. He'd fallen in love right from the start. He'd been told that the daddy was killed overseas and that her momma was all set to keep the child, until she saw Sarah's condition. Once she realized the full extent of her problems, she asked to have the baby taken away."

Thea flinched at Ms. Aurora's words. Would her sister give up her own child simply because she wasn't physically perfect? Thea feared she knew the answer, but there had been no one to tell Eileen there were medical procedures to correct her baby's misshaped mouth and nose.

"I'm so sorry. I shouldn't have spoken so harshly about Sarah's mother, not knowing if…"

"It's all right, Ms. Aurora. I know my sister wasn't a saint." Thea hesitated, shame washing over her. "I'm just going on the belief she wasn't in her right frame of mind when she gave the baby up."

"That's a possibility, as rough a time as your mother said she had."

That startled Thea, considering she'd had to drag any information out of her mother. "Momma talked to you about my sister's delivery?"

The woman nodded. "She said that Eileen was in labor for almost three days before your mother finally drove her over to Mrs. Williams to see what was taking the baby so long. Said it was the most scared she'd ever been."

Three days! Why hadn't Momma called for help sooner, or better yet, called for an ambulance to take Eileen to the hospital? Was her mother already suffering confusion and poor decision-making then that had put her sister and niece in danger? Thea held the sleeping child closer. If she'd been there, she would have taken control of the situation, comforted her sister, maybe kept Eileen from making a terrible mistake. Sarah whimpered.

"You're holding her too tight. Ease up a bit," Ms. Aurora instructed in a gentle tone.

Thea released her hold on the baby slightly. "I'm sorry, darling girl."

Sarah's answer was to stick her sock-covered fingers into her mouth and curl back into Thea's neck.

"You mind if I ask you a question?"

Thea braced herself. If there was one thing she'd learned about Aurora Adair in the last three days, it was that she was as blunt as a dull scalpel. "What would that be?"

"I can't help but wonder what's the real reason you're all fired up to raise Sarah."

Thea brushed a lock of Sarah's silky soft hair away from her face. "I believe she's my niece, so of course I want to raise her."

"Not everyone would. I mean, it's a lot of responsibility to take on, raising a child. Especially a child with special needs. Alone, for the most part." The older woman brought her coffee cup to her mouth.

Thea stared at the sleeping child resting in her arms. Yes, she'd thought about all the hardships of raising this baby with no help from anyone but Momma—and a diminishing amount of help to be expected even from her. She'd have to deal with the constant worry about money, the stigma that went along with being a single mother. But it would be worth it to have the chance to raise this precious girl. She owed it to her sister.

She wanted it for herself.

Thea looked over at the older woman, a mournful smile on her lips. "What is it?" Thea asked.

"You love that little girl," Ms. Aurora answered quietly.

"Yes, I do." Though if someone had told Thea a month ago she'd be here, back in Marietta, nursing a houseful of people with the chicken pox, falling in love with her niece, she would have thought they'd lost their marbles. But why did Ms. Aurora seem so sad at the prospect? "Don't you want me to love her?"

"Of course I do. Every child should be loved and loved abundantly." She pressed her lips together as if trying to find the right words. "But Mack loves her, too. I'd hate to see that boy lose his chance at raising Sarah if it turns out your sister is Sarah's mother."

Thea nodded. She didn't want to see Mack hurt any more than Ms. Aurora did. But regardless of what she wanted, either she or Mack was going to end up with a broken heart. "If I'm given custody, I wouldn't think of cutting Mack out of Sarah's life. She loves him and I want her to be—what was that phrase you used?—loved abundantly."

"And if she isn't your niece?"

The thought stole Thea's breath away. Maybe a week ago, it would have mattered whether or not Miller blood ran through Sarah's veins, but now that Thea had held her, had nursed her through the chicken pox, had heard her baby giggles, she couldn't imagine her life without Sarah. "I'd still love her and only want what is best for her."

"I believe you would." Ms. Aurora smiled before taking another sip. "It must have been hard, coming back here after the war, trying to pick up the pieces of your life."

"Some days, I think the war was easier."

If Thea's pronouncement spooked the older woman, she didn't show it, laughing instead. "Family can be that way sometimes. Mine cared so much for their standing in society that they sent me away rather than keep me at home." She sat the coffee cup back on its saucer. "But every once in a while, I get homesick for Momma, and I think if I could have her back for one more hour, I'd be okay."

"I know exactly how you feel." A tight knot formed at the base of Thea's throat. What she'd give to talk to Eileen, or even Momma in her right frame of mind. To tell them how sorry she was for running out on them, for not being here over the past eight years. She tasted salt and sniffled, willing herself not to cry. What was wrong with her? Grief? Exhaustion? Probably both. Or had returning home turned her into a silly old watering pot? Thankfully, the older woman was too involved in pouring herself another cup of coffee to pay much attention to Thea.

"I thought you were going to let me rock Sarah to sleep."

Thea glanced toward the kitchen door where Mack stood, leaning one muscular shoulder against the door frame, his hair pushed back as if he'd raked it into place with his hands. An uncertain smile hovered on his lips as his gaze turned to the baby resting in her arms.

Ms. Aurora was right, Thea thought. Seeing Mack lose the opportunity to raise Sarah would hurt her, as well. How could this situation be resolved without leaving either one of them with a broken heart?

Thea silently whispered a short prayer as she stood and carried Sarah across the kitchen to where Mack stood. *Dear Lord, I don't have the wisdom of Solomon but You do. Help us find a way so that neither Mack and I come away from this broken. Please, Lord, help us.*

Mack followed Thea down the hallway, marveling at the way she looked so natural holding Sarah in her arms, dropping a kiss on the baby's brow every now and then, pushing a loose curl out of Sarah's eyes. How would Thea be with Sarah as she grew older? Loving, yes. Strict, after her experience with Eileen, that was a given. And completely devoted to her, as she had always been to her family.

To be loved abundantly. Guilt rippled through Mack. He shouldn't have listened in on their conversation, but when Thea had spoken of her love for Sarah, her desire to include him in the baby's life even if she was the one given custody, so that Sarah would have a life filled with love, he hadn't been able to turn away. It didn't matter that Sarah might not be Eileen's child. Thea would love her abundantly regardless. He'd seen it in the way she cared for her mother and sister, giving of herself without any expectations. And now with Sarah. What would it be like to be the object of such a love? Would his scars, his shortcomings keep him from ever finding that kind of devotion and affection? Or would love, real love, true love, make his physical deficiencies seem insignificant even to himself?

"Mack?"

His thoughts evaporated as he focused on Thea. "Sorry, must have been woolgathering."

She studied him for a long moment, her brows furrowed in concern. "Don't push yourself. If you need to go back to bed for another day or two, there's nothing wrong with that."

Mack smiled at her concern. A man could get use to that kind of attentiveness coming from a woman like Thea. "I'm fine, really. Just thinking, that's all."

He followed her into the deserted living room. The large faded rug on the floor had frayed edges, and an irregular-shaped hole marred the wool near the coffee table, but the material was thick enough to ease a child's fall. A scarred cedar chest in need of a good sanding and a coat of varnish sat in the corner. Odds and ends of furniture, most likely donated, filled up the room. Nothing was shiny or new, but everything was comfortable and welcoming. A homey place to raise children.

"You want to sit down here?" Thea nodded toward a frilly concoction of eyelet lace that cushioned Ms. Aurora's rocking chair. "Once you get comfortable, I'll hand you the baby."

"It's kind of hard for a man to be at ease with all this girly stuff hanging off the chair."

She gave a throaty chuckle, the sparkle in her eyes rivaling the most beautiful sapphires in Mr. Friedman's jewelry display. "There's nothing wrong with a woman liking to pretty up her house a bit." She motioned again for him to take a seat, and he dropped down into the chair. The cushions proved more comfortable than he'd thought, and soon he was sinking back, his eyes closed in peaceful rest.

"You look better than you have in days." The warmth in her voice soothed him, like warm honey sliding down a parched throat. He opened his eyes, surprised to find Thea barely a breath away, watching him. The memory of their almost-kiss fluttered though his mind. What would she do if he rocked forward, breached the space between them and covered her lips with his own?

Sarah squealed.

Mack pressed his feet against the floor and rocked backward while the squirming baby jumped up and down in Thea's arms. Mack couldn't help but smile. "I always feel good when I get to see my doodlebug here."

"Well, she's happy to see you, too."

Sarah showed her agreement by bouncing with excitement, her bright blue eyes watching Mack like a hawk. She had a few remaining spots but nothing compared to what his imagination had drummed up in the last few days. Her arms and legs fluttered, but Thea kept a firm hold on her until she was safe in his embrace.

Sarah stared up into his face, her gaze darting from one scab to the next as if in concern. Then, as if deciding he was okay, she stuck her tiny sock-covered fingers into his mouth and he nibbled on them lightly. "I missed you, doodlebug."

"She missed you, too," Thea said as she dropped down on the couch and stretched her long legs out in front of her. "I've never seen her this animated. Almost like she got her favorite playmate back," she teased.

Mack gently tugged the baby's fingers out of his mouth. "I hate that I haven't been here for you, baby girl."

"Baby girl?"

He brushed a kiss against Sarah's brow. "My other nickname for her."

"My daddy used to call me that."

Mack glanced over the baby's head to where Thea sat. In all the years he'd known her, she'd never once mentioned her father. Back then, he'd thought she might have been too young when he died to have many memories of him, but now, knowing Thea's love for her family, he wondered if it simply hurt too much to talk about him. Mack turned the baby around so that she sat up in his lap, his chest against her back giving her the stability she needed. "What was your dad like?"

She shrugged. "I don't remember much. He died when I was only four." A sad, sweet smile graced her lips. "But I do know he always carried around lemon drops in his pants pockets and played guitar as well as some of those folks on the radio did."

"And he called you his baby girl," Mack added. "What did he do for a living?"

"He was a farmer. Momma said he loved working outside in the dirt, had a knack for growing things. She said it was like he never grew up from being a little boy playing in the mud."

A thread of sadness laced her voice, and Mack found himself wishing he could find a way to ease her pain, obvious even now, years later. So much loss in Thea's life, and if Mrs. Miller was telling the truth about Eileen's baby, another disappointment hung on the horizon. "Do you have a favorite memory of him?"

She sat quietly for several long moments. Had it been

wrong to ask? Did Thea even have a good memory of her father to hang on to?

"When I was a little girl, I loved to follow Daddy out into the fields." She smiled more to herself than for him. Her eyes had a dreamy faraway look to them as she got caught up in the distant memory. "In the spring when he had to plow the fields to get them ready for the planting, he'd hitch our old mule to the plow then let me ride up on Bessie's back. Each row we'd dig, he'd sing a song with these silly lyrics that he'd made up just for me and Eileen. Momma thought it was vulgar for a little girl to straddle a mule but Daddy never paid her any mind. I loved every second of it."

"Sounds like your father was a good man."

She nodded. "He was. I just hate the fact that Eileen never got the chance to know Daddy the way I did. A father is so important to a little girl."

Had Thea realized what she had said? Was she conceding that Sarah needed a daddy? *And what about a momma?* Would he give too much away if he conceded, as well? "A girl needs her mother, too."

Thea fell back into the cushions and crossed her arms around her waist as if to protect herself. "What are we going to do about the baby, Mack?"

Now was the time to tell her about his conversation with Beau, but he wasn't ready quite yet. Instead, he shrugged. "That's the question that's been keeping me up at night."

"Me, too." She drew in a deep breath and sighed. "Either way, one of us misses out on raising Sarah. It just doesn't seem right, does it? Not when we both love her so much."

Mack pressed the baby close to his chest. He hadn't

been certain when he'd overheard her talking to Ms. Aurora about allowing him to play an important part in Sarah's upbringing, but now Thea had confirmed it herself. "You almost sound like you're worried about my feelings."

Pain flashed across her features before her mouth flattened into a straight line, her eyes suddenly dull. "Of course I have to consider your feelings. You obviously love Sarah a great deal, just as she loves you."

Mack kissed the top of Sarah's head. It said a lot about the woman Thea had become, her understanding of his feelings for the little girl. Could he be as generous to her? He prayed so. "You know, Sarah loves you, too."

Thea snorted a short humorless chuckle. "She's only known me for a few days."

"That's the beauty of children. A week feels like a lifetime to them."

"She's a baby, not a puppy."

"Yes, but to her, you've been here for as long as she can remember."

Thea didn't look convinced. "Okay, I get that. But what makes you think she loves me?"

Mack smiled. He had her now. "Haven't you noticed how her attention follows you around the room, always watching your every move? I noticed it the first second you gave her to me. And she doesn't usually like to cuddle, but she'll curl into your neck and fall asleep just like she's found a home."

"Really?" A tremulous smile lit up Thea's face. "You think she loves me?"

The woman was so beautiful, especially when she looked at Sarah with eyes full of love and devotion. What would it feel like to have that smile turned on him? Mack cleared his throat. "Yes, I do."

"Thank you." It was almost a prayer, whispered to Sarah or to the Lord, Mack didn't know. Thea leaned forward, extending her hand to the baby, her eyes widening as Sarah grabbed one finger and drew it into her mouth.

"You think she's hungry?"

Thea didn't answer right away, instead remaining quiet, her focus completely on Sarah. "Maybe, but I think she could be teething."

Mack tilted his head to the side and glanced down at Sarah. "I thought so, too, but isn't she a little young to be doing that?"

"No." Thea lowered her face until she was level with the baby. "She's perfectly in line with what's normal."

Mack remained skeptical. All the books he'd read said baby teeth didn't come in until later in infancy. But Thea was a pediatric nurse. Surely she would know. "Are you sure?"

She straightened and held her hand out to him, palm up. "Here, I'll show you."

Her hand felt soft and delicate against his as she guided him to the spot, his finger gliding over the wet, bony section of Sarah's gums once, twice. On the third time, he felt it, the tiny ridges erupting through the skin. "I feel it, a little tooth right up front."

"I know." Thea's smile almost blinded him with its excitement. "Soon our little doodlebug is going to be able to grin at us with her own set of pearly whites."

Our little doodlebug. It shouldn't sound right to Mack's ears, but it did, just the way it felt right for them to be sharing this moment. What about the other milestones in his little girl's life, when she took her first steps, her first day of school, her first homecoming dance? Time was slipping away. Sarah was growing up, and he was missing it every minute the adoption papers remained unsigned.

Mack refused to miss anything else. There was one way to make sure Sarah became his daughter and to give the woman beside him the family she longed for. "Thea?"

"Hmm." Her attention was still focused on the baby. She loved Sarah, more than he'd ever imagined. At least that played in his favor.

"I think I've come up with a way for us both to raise Sarah."

Blond curls bounced lightly against her shoulders as she lifted her head, her clear blue eyes fully focused on him. Boy, a man could die happy staring into those eyes every day. "You have?"

Mack nodded. He might live to regret this, but as he glanced from Thea to the little girl who would be their daughter, he wondered if this could possibly be the best decision he'd ever made in his life.

"We could get married."

Thea blinked, as though the words had stunned her. Well, she wasn't the only one stunned by his proposal. "What did you say?"

He swallowed, suddenly nervous she'd say no. At least she hadn't rejected him outright, and as surprised as she might be, her question had also held a note of interest. Mack clung to that thought as he worked up his nerve to ask the question that would secure their daughter's future.

"Thea Miller, will you marry me?"

Chapter Nine

~❧~

Thea's thoughts went all fuzzy. Mack couldn't have said what she thought he'd said. "Could you repeat that, please?"

"I asked you to marry me."

This was a joke. It had to be. Though she'd never known Mack to be unkind. But this—offering her a chance to be his wife, to raise Sarah as their child—was just too cruel for him to kid her about. And yet, the determined set of his jaw, the intent expression on his too-handsome face told her he was altogether serious. "Why would you want to do that?"

"Think about it." He leaned closer, and she felt the air go out of her lungs. "If we got married, Judge Wakefield would let us adopt Sarah without a second thought."

Marriage with no mention of love. For some reason she was afraid to ask herself, the thought left her depressed. "I thought you wanted to raise Sarah on your own."

"I did." Mack hesitated for a moment. "Or, at least, I thought I did. But the more I think about it, the more I know Judge Wakefield was right. Sarah needs both a mother and father who love her very much. Who better than the two of us?"

She couldn't fault his reasoning. Still…

"If you're worried you won't get to see enough of Sarah, I've already told you I'd give you time. I want you to be part of her life."

"And I want you to be a part of her life, too, Thea. What better way to do that than become a family?"

A family of her very own! Her heart fluttered, her fingers and toes numb with joy, the future unfurling before her. She could see them chasing lightning bugs and reading stories together before bedtime, sharing Christmases and Easters and all the other holidays in between, curling up on the couch together in front of the fireplace after the children had gone off to bed and sharing about their days.

Whoa! Where had that thought come from? The man proposed marriage, not love. A means to an end to raise only *one* child. A way to secure Sarah's future while assuring their positions in her life.

To secure a family for herself.

She needed to think. Thea stood up and paced across the room, rolling her bottom lip between her teeth. Marry Mack? There was a rightness to it, but was that because marrying him offered her what could be her only chance to raise her niece? Or had the crush she'd nursed for him so many years ago matured into more than a childish fancy? "What makes you think the court will automatically agree to us adopting Sarah?"

Mack stood, Sarah braced against his chest, and walked across the room to stand by her. "Judge Wakefield has never kept it a secret that he would give my adoption file more consideration if I were married. In fact, he said more than once that he would sign the papers the minute I presented my wife to him in his chambers."

The old coot sounded pushy to her, forcing a man to

choose between the baby girl he clearly adored and his possible future happiness with a wife. Mack deserved more; he deserved to find someone who would treasure his kindness and determination, a woman who could make him proud, not bring shame upon him because of who she was, who her family was. Not that she wouldn't cherish being Mack's wife, but he could do better than someone like her. *So much better.*

"There's something else you should know."

A sister gone, a mother ill, a chicken pox epidemic. A marriage proposal from a wonderful man. How much more could she take?

"What is it?"

Sarah wiggled her fingers at Thea and, without much thought, she dropped tiny kisses along the baby's arm. She glanced up from the baby's shoulder and caught Mack watching her, his blue eyes dark with longing. Did he want the same thing she did, a family to call his own? Mack had to, didn't he? Why try to adopt Sarah if he didn't?

"There's been talk…about us."

"Us?" Thea straightened, a familiar knot of dread tightening in her throat. "Why would anyone be talking about us?"

"The town council is considering expanding the police force in Marietta, so of course there's been some discussion about what role I might play. Apparently, there were some who—" he hesitated for a moment as if searching for just the right phrase "—voiced concern over the amount of time you and I have been spending together lately."

"What are they—?" *Oh, no,* Thea thought. *They couldn't mean...*

"Are they talking about our time here? Don't they

know there's an outbreak of chicken pox? That there are six—" she glanced over at him "—seven people who are sick. Not to mention, my mother's staying here, too. There's nothing inappropriate about that."

"Well, yes, but we were also seen together at the diner. And in the hospital waiting room. And at the wedding."

When Mack put it like that, no wonder rumors were flying around town about them. Thea dropped down into a wingback chair close to the window. How had this happened? A couple of innocent meetings, an offer of help to a poor woman, and her name and Mack's were being dragged through the mud all over town. Were they calling her the same names they'd used to describe her sister? How would she find a job now? How would she take care of her mother?

She glanced at Sarah. What judge would give her custody with rumors like this floating around?

What about Mack? He was the sheriff in this town—and apparently his position was currently under review. What kind of repercussions would there be for him if they didn't marry? Thea pushed a loose strand of hair behind her ear, her stomach tied in painful knots, her heart beating out a pained rhythm. "Can I ask you something?"

"Anything you like. We need to be honest if we want this to work."

She sucked in a deep breath. "Why aren't you married already? I mean, there's got to be someone you're interested in, maybe a girl you've been dating?"

He shrugged in that self-deprecating sort of way that Thea found endearing. "I hate to tell you this, but I'm not considered much of a catch."

Mack not a catch? Where in the world had the man gotten such an idea? Any woman would be blessed to have someone as kind and considerate, someone who loved the child in his arms so abundantly. Had he been hurt by a woman in the past? Or had she bruised his ego by dismissing the notion of marriage so quickly? "What I'm trying to say is there has to be someone else you want to marry besides me. Isn't there?"

"No." He hesitated. "I'm not even sure I'm the marrying type."

From the way he said it, she was now certain that Mack had been hurt deeply. The thought caused an ache in her chest. Thea swallowed hard. "I don't know that I am, either."

"Marrying kind or not, we have to consider this for Sarah's sake." His expression turned sober.

But what about them? What about their future? Sarah would one day grow up and make her own life. Had he thought what the next forty or fifty years might hold for them? Would a loveless marriage be fair to Sarah? To either of them? "Then I guess the next question I have is, why me?"

"You make it sound like there's some reason I *shouldn't* ask you."

"It's not that." She hesitated. As he had said, they owed it to each other to be truthful with their concerns. "Well, maybe there is. I mean, you know my family's reputation. Not the kind of people that the sheriff would usually want to associate with, at least, not without an arrest warrant."

The corner of his mouth lifted in a wry smile. "Everybody's got an uncle or a cousin who makes them shake their head. That's what makes life interesting."

"And what keeps the local gossips' tongues wagging," Thea muttered.

"Sweetheart."

She lifted her head at the endearment until her gaze met

his, and almost sighed. What made this man holding this darling baby girl in his muscular arms so utterly irresistible?

"I know your family," Mack started. "But more important than that is that I know you. You love Sarah as much as I do. I've always admired the way you're so devoted to your family, loving them unconditionally even when they don't deserve it. It's what I want for Sarah. What she needs from her mother."

Thea's heart lifted slightly, but there were so many other questions that needed answers before she'd even consider something so drastic as marriage. "What about you, Mack? Don't you want to fall in love?"

He shrugged, adjusting the napping baby to a more comfortable position. "After four years of being one of the only marriage-aged men in town without any takers, I figure love isn't in God's plan for me."

Love not in God's plan for Mack? If anyone deserved that kind of happiness, it was this man. Irritation threatened to clog her throat. "Who are these silly women not to know a good man when they see one?"

His lips twisted as if he thought her question funny. "There've been a few."

She swallowed the sudden pang of jealousy. "Then they don't have the sense the good Lord gave them."

"I don't know. They may have thought it was a lucky escape."

The uncertainty Thea heard in his voice didn't sound like the confident boy with all the big dreams she'd known in high school. What had changed him? Why was he settling when he could still find love, have children of his own?

"I don't expect for this to be a marriage in the real sense of the word. Sarah needs our full attention for right now, at least until we get her through the surgery."

Thea wasn't sure why, but his statement disappointed her. "So, a marriage in name only." She sank back into the couch. "I didn't know people did that anymore."

"I'm sure they do. You just don't hear folks talking about it much."

Thea certainly never thought she'd be having this conversation. Of course, if they agreed, it would be a marriage of convenience. It wasn't as if they loved each other. Friendship, yes. Attraction, most definitely. But what was a marriage without love?

"What are you thinking?"

Thea felt a slight smile curve her lips. "You've always done that. Even when we were kids, you'd ask me what I was thinking."

"That's because I like to know what's going on in that beautiful head of yours."

Her heart fluttered, though from nerves or at his compliment, she wasn't sure. "I can't pinpoint one thought right now. They seem to be scattered all over the place."

He nodded as if he understood. "Just know this. If you marry me, I'll be there to protect you, to help shoulder whatever the future may hold, to partner with you in raising this child, to be your friend and helpmate for as long as I live."

A vow, but still no mention of love. And yet she knew that marriages have been built on much less. If she turned him down, it was almost a certainty she would lose whatever chance she had at raising Eileen's child. But if she agreed, what did Thea risk losing then? The promise she made to Eileen so long ago roared through her. She'd let her sister down then, had never brought Eileen's first child home. She refused to fail her again. It didn't matter what she lost as long as she played a part in raising Sarah.

"Mack, could you ask me again?"

"Ask you? Sure." He stood, then bent down and placed Sarah in her lap.

Thea shook her head. He really was the most handsome man she'd ever known, spots and all. But when Mack straightened, then knelt down at her feet, Thea almost forgot to breathe.

Mack took her free hand in both of his, his thumb making tiny circles on the inside of her wrist that sent delightful sparks shimmering up her arm. He lifted his head, his blue eyes gentle and with a touch of vulnerability that made Thea's heart ache. "Thea Miller, will you do me the honor of marrying me?"

Someone's heart will be broken, and I fear it will be mine.

Sarah whimpered. For now, Thea would settle for the chance to help raise this child she loved more than life itself. Eileen's child. Her family.

Thea lifted her chin a notch and with a steadiness she didn't feel, gave Mack his answer. "Yes, Mack. I will marry you."

Mack packed his razor and aftershave into his leather bag and dropped it in his suitcase, the tangy lemony-lime scent of his shaving cream refreshing after days of lying around in bed. He scraped his hand against his clean-cut jaw and relaxed. No beard or itchy spots for the first time in a week.

Beau had given him, along with the rest of Thea's patients, the all clear this morning, right before he'd packed Mack's bride-to-be and her mother into his car for a ride back to the Millers' place. Mack hadn't been keen on the idea. He'd wanted to escort Thea home himself, just to make sure she got her mother settled in without any problems. Wasn't that his duty as Thea's future husband, to make sure she was safe and got the rest she so desperately needed?

But Beau didn't see the situation in quite the same way. Tongues were already wagging all over town about his and Thea's quick engagement. No sense giving folks more ammunition than they already had.

Mack shoved his pajamas into the case. Most of them could hang for all he cared. Rumors were easier to believe than the truth. But it was Thea he worried about. She'd gone through years of shrugging off gossip about her sister, buried beneath the weight of Eileen's sins. If Beau driving Thea and her mother home protected them from being at the blunt end of someone's tongue, Mack would step aside.

But it didn't mean it sat well with him. Maybe it would be better for both their sakes to marry sooner rather than later. When he got back into town this afternoon, he'd work out a plan. If Thea agreed, they could be married by the end of the week.

"Almost ready to go?"

Mack glanced up from his packing to find Ms. Aurora hovering in the doorway, a bundle of clean clothes loading down her arms. Her hair had turned a shade grayer and her wrinkles were more pronounced since her heart scare last spring, but there was still a vivid spark in her tired eyes, as if she knew the work she'd started with these children wasn't quite finished. Still, tending a houseful of sick children couldn't have helped her any. *Thank You, Lord, for Thea.*

"Ready to be rid of me?"

A faint smile graced her face. "You know you're welcome here anytime."

It was true. Since his mother's death a few years ago, Mack had found himself at Ms. Aurora's door more and more often, like a stray dog looking for food scraps. She'd befriended him, allowed him to mourn his loss, given him a sounding board when something troubled him and always spoke her mind, even when it was something he didn't want to hear.

Like now.

Mack dropped his robe on the bed and turned to her, crossing his arms over his chest. "You've got something to say, Ms. Aurora?"

She didn't even pretend she didn't know what he was talking about. "You're going to marry Thea?"

Mack drew in a deep breath. This morning before Beau arrived they had told Ms. Aurora their plans to marry and adopt Sarah. She'd appeared to understand the reasons behind the match, had even seemed thrilled as she offered them congratulations on their impending nuptials. But obviously the older woman had reservations. "I thought you were happy for us."

"I am. I think outside of knowing the Lord as your Savior, Thea might just be the best thing that's ever happened to you."

That surprised him. Considering Thea had been spying on Ms. Aurora, Mack would have guessed the old woman wouldn't have thought so highly of his future bride. But then, Ms. Aurora had always had a soft spot for those folks who cared about her children. "Then what's bothering you?"

Her pale gray eyes turned almost sorrowful. "I know

the two of you love Sarah, but don't you both deserve something better than a marriage in name only?"

"Maybe." He turned back to his suitcase, picked up his robe and bunched it into a ball. "But neither of us can bear the thought of losing Sarah. If we marry, we stand a very good chance of the adoption going through."

"And what about love?"

Thea had asked him almost the same question. What *about* love? It wasn't as if he'd never opened himself up to the possibility; he had, more times than he cared to admit. But no woman had ever indicated any hint of love toward him. They wanted a soldier, a man ready to die for his country. A whole man, not someone carrying around a physical disability. His lack of military service was considered a flaw in his character, and his refusal to give any kind of explanation simply fueled that belief. "I haven't exactly had women lining up for a chance to marry me, now have I?"

"And whose fault is that?" She took the wrinkled mess that was his spare uniform shirt out of his hand and smoothed it to fold it properly. "There were a couple of lovely ladies who showed an interest in you at church but you were too involved in your work."

"If you're referring to that Mason woman, I caught her selling ration stamps she'd lifted off of some of the girls at the bomber plant. And Susan Bailey told me right from the first she didn't want any kids."

Ms. Aurora pressed her lips together. "I didn't say they were perfect, just that there were ladies in town you've known for a while, someone you might have fallen in love with."

Oddly enough, Thea's face came into focus. Other women had never fascinated him the way she did. Never talked straight to him instead of sugar-coating every word. He respected Thea's opinion, admired that she gave as good as she got. But was that enough to build a marriage on? Could it eventually lead to love, or would she be like all the others when he didn't come up to scratch? Maybe he was asking too much from God to even hope for love in his marriage. He'd have his daughter, a job that he liked, his renewed friendship with Thea. That would have to be enough. "Love just muddies the waters. Better for us to have a straightforward understanding."

"That's not the only thing that muddies the waters in a relationship." Her voice hinted at sarcasm.

"What are you talking about?"

She put the neatly folded uniform on the dresser then joined him in folding his remaining clothes. "When were you planning to tell Thea about the night you got that scar?"

"I already told her about the car accident."

"And the extent of your injuries? Have you told her that?"

Mack's stomach fell into his shoes. "Did she ask you about them?"

"No." Ms. Aurora spared him a glance then went back to folding. "I wouldn't have told her, anyway. It's not my story to tell."

He breathed a sigh of relief. "You're making a mountain out of an anthill."

She took his uniform pants and shook them out. "That night changed the way you looked at yourself."

"No, it didn't." Mack grimaced. "Everyone else changed the way they looked at me."

"Mack, no one can take away what we believe about ourselves unless we give them the power to do so."

Sounded like something his mother might have cross-stitched into a sample. Only there wasn't any truth to it. "They can when they cancel my college scholarship or tell me I'm not good enough to fight for my country overseas."

"I know you were disappointed when the military turned you down, but look what you did. You kept our town safe for the people who stayed behind to build the equipment our boys needed to win the war." She rolled the pants into a neat little bundle. "As far as school goes, you could have gone to college without your scholarship. It might have been a tougher row to hoe to pay your way through, but you would have had your degree."

"And do what? Who would have hired a partially deaf lawyer?"

Ms. Aurora's mouth quirked up into a sweet smile. "Marietta hired a partially deaf sheriff, and I hear he's doing an outstanding job."

When he wasn't fighting the town's rumor mill. Mack stuffed another pair of socks into the suitcase. "They hired me out of pity after the military declared me a 4-F."

"Those old coots? They don't do anything unless they feel it's the right thing for the city." She cupped his face in the palm of her hand the way his mother used to when he was a small boy. "You're the right man to police our town, Mack Worthington."

He wanted to believe her, but how could he? How would he measure up against men who'd experienced battle firsthand? He couldn't. All he'd done during the war was hand out parking citations and mediate neighbor disputes. No, now that war heroes were back in Marietta, his days as sheriff were numbered. Disappointment settled over him. For a job he'd never wanted, Mack was going to miss it. "Maybe I'll look for a job in a smaller town. I hear Hiram is looking for a sheriff. Or Rockmart."

"Then you'll have to talk to Thea. You can't expect her to move that far away without some reason as to why."

Mack hadn't thought about that. Leaving Mrs. Miller behind in her fragile mental state was out of the question, but how could he expect Thea to balance motherhood and being her mother's caregiver in a new town without any friends to support her? "I'll figure out something."

"Hmm." The older woman moved to the bed and started stripping the sheets. "Have you ever asked Thea why she left town that night?"

"At the time, she said it was a family emergency, but she didn't explain beyond that." And for years he hadn't cared, too busy dealing with the consequences of the accident to think too much about Thea and her family's problems. But since her return, the question of what could have sent her running that night had stayed on his mind. And what had kept her away in all the years since.

The more he thought, the more questions he came up with. How would Thea feel when she learned the whole truth behind his scar? Sympathetic for his loss? Angry he'd kept the truth from her? Hurt that, until the past few days, he'd held her at least partially responsible for what happened to him that night?

"Are you going to talk to her, Mack?"

He didn't know that he could, but if he wanted answers he'd have to try. Eventually. "I'll think about it."

"Well, when you do, think about this." Ms. Aurora bundled the soiled sheets up and headed for the door. "It's not your deafness that's holding you back. It's your attitude."

Chapter Ten

"We're here."

Thea could barely keep her eyes open, her body heavy with exhaustion from the past week of caring for a houseful of sick kids. She drew in a deep breath and willed herself awake as she glanced over to the driver's seat and found Beau Daniels pushing the gearshift into Park. She struggled to sit up. "Sorry, I wasn't very talkative. I guess the week's caught up with me."

His mouth curled into a slight smile. "I'm used to it. Edie's at that stage in her pregnancy where if she's not sick to her stomach, she's asleep on the couch."

Thea smoothed her wrinkled skirt down over her knees. "So what you're saying is everything is absolutely normal."

"Yes." His smile widened. "And don't worry. You weren't the only one who fell asleep on me." He nodded toward the backseat.

Thea turned slightly to see that Momma's hat had fallen down over her eyes and her mouth was pursed as she released small, almost ladylike, snorts of air. Her features were relaxed, not tensed into the frantic stiffness

Thea had seen in her mother in recent days. Once she got them some lunch, maybe she could convince her mother to take a nap. Thea knew she could use one herself.

Beau got out of the car and walked around to open her mother's door, then Thea's, before stepping to the trunk to retrieve their suitcases. Both she and her mother were waiting by the time Beau joined them, a bag in each hand.

"That was so kind of you to bring us all the way out here." Momma snapped open the clip of her patent-leather purse and dug out her wallet. "How much do I owe you?"

Oh, no! Thea stepped forward, her arm coming around her mother's shoulders. "Momma, I don't think that's—"

Beau interrupted, bowing slightly. "Mrs. Miller, just the pleasure of your company is all the payment I need."

Momma blinked, then broke out into a wide smile. "Well, aren't you a sweet boy! Though your boss might not be too happy with you, passing up a fare and all."

"Momma, why don't you go on up to the house while I settle things with Beau?"

Her mother nodded and shot another smile at Beau before turning toward the house.

"I don't think anyone's used *sweet* or *boy* in the same sentence to describe me since I was in diapers," Beau said, as they watched her mother struggle with the door for a moment before disappearing into the house.

Thea chuckled. "No, but then you've been teasing little girls almost from the moment you could walk. Remember how you use to pull my ponytail in Mr. Miley's science class?"

"Only because I knew it would get a rise out of Mack." Beau laughed. "He's always been an easy target where you were concerned."

Mack was protective of her even then? "You must have

read too much into the situation. Mack and I, we were just friends back then."

"Really?" Beau's smile widened as if he had a multitude of secrets he'd like to share. "You remember Todd Armstrong?"

Thea went completely still. Of course she remembered Todd. Junior year, she'd been almost certain the boy was going to ask her to the Junior/Senior Prom. But just as suddenly as he'd started paying attention to her, he stopped. Next thing she heard, Todd had asked Barbara Emerson. Thea had ended up taking another girl's shift at the movie theater and working that night. "What about him?"

"Word got back to Mack that Todd was bragging about how he was going to take you up to Kennesaw Mountain on prom night. I'd never seen Mack so mad. He took that kid out behind the boy's gym and told him if he even looked at you funny, Mack would knock him into next week." Beau chuckled. "Now that I think about it, he did that to every guy who thought about taking you out."

No wonder she'd never had a date in high school. All this time, she'd thought it was her, or her family's reputation that had scared the boys off. To think it had been Mack! She would wring the man's neck the next she saw him. Protective, huh! More like overbearing, butting into her business. She snorted out a breath. "I should…"

"Come on, Thea. Mack did you a favor. You didn't want to go out with a jerk like Todd."

Maybe, but it didn't take the sting out of missing the prom that night, of watching the other girls walk by in confections of satiny blue or silky white from the ticket counter at the movie theater, the boys she'd grown up with dressed in suits and ties. She'd been in her silly uniform, working that night at the movies. Her heart skipped a beat.

Alongside Mack.

His father had taken ill by then, so Mack had taken the job to earn extra money to help his mom out with the bills. It said a lot about him, about the kind of person he was, working so hard to take care of his parents while he worked on his grades to get into college. But then he hadn't gone to college after all. Did his accident keep him from accepting the scholarship he'd gotten from the University of Georgia?

"You know, you're doing the right thing marrying Mack." Beau's voice drew her out of her thoughts. "He's always been sweet on you, and it'll just be better for all of you in the long run."

When had Mack had the time to confide in his friend about their situation? "At least it will give Sarah the stability she needs."

"And quiet all the talk going on in town."

Thea felt her jaw tighten. "Let's see how that goes."

Beau pushed his hat farther down on his head. "I wasn't sure Mack would tell you."

"Mack's honest with me, Beau, just like I have to be honest with him. It's the only way this marriage is going to work." She crossed her arms over her waist. "But I do believe Mack would try to protect me from the worst of the gossip."

"You're right. It's why he didn't drive you home himself. He didn't want to generate more rumors."

She'd wondered why Beau had brought them home. "So, how bad is it?"

He grimaced. Yes, she'd put him in an awkward position, but she needed to know what they were dealing with. "You know how folks are," he finally answered. "A pretty nurse and the town's sheriff holed up in a house for almost a week. It gets people to talking."

When he said it that way, it sounded so...*scandalous*! Like something her sister would do. The kind of thing Thea had worked hard all her life to avoid. "They did know we had a chicken pox outbreak on our hands, didn't they?"

"Yes, but you know how people are. Take a couple of nice people, throw in a few unfortunate incidents and add some busybodies with nothing better to do with their day than gossip, and they'll cook up a scandal that'll travel faster than a jackrabbit during hunting season."

Her breath hitched. She'd hoped it wasn't as bad as Mack had made it out to be, that with time the rumors would die down and this marriage he'd proposed wouldn't be necessary. But from the way Beau described it, it was even worse than she'd thought.

Mack was right. Even if they could get the judge to allow someone unmarried to have custody of a child, neither of them would be considered a good candidate to adopt Sarah with these rumors hanging over their heads. Marriage seemed their only choice to quiet people's tongues and bring Sarah home. And even with a marriage, there would still be some who would never forget. If Judge Wakefield allowed them to adopt Sarah, she might have to live with the rumors, the kids from school who'd taunt her, tell her how her real mother had abandoned her. How her adoptive parents were forced to marry.

And what about Mack? He'd built a solid reputation in this town. Not only could he lose Sarah, the town council might decide he wasn't fit to be their sheriff. She couldn't live with herself if she caused him trouble. "Mack's not going to get fired, is he?"

Beau shook his head, oblivious to the turmoil going on inside her. "The news of your engagement has stemmed any talk of relieving him of his duties for now."

She nodded, but found no relief in his words. Because of her, because of her family's reputation, Mack had become the focal point of shameful gossip that could even now cost him his job and steal any hopes he had of adopting Sarah.

And now he was stuck marrying her.

Thea swallowed hard against the knot in her throat. She should never have come home, should have built a new life as far away from Marietta as she could, where she couldn't hurt or disappoint the people she cared for. Like Eileen, and now Mack.

If there'd been any other way around this mess, she'd have taken it, but she'd do whatever it took to save Mack's sterling reputation, to save his job.

Even marry the man.

"Have faith, Thea. This situation hasn't taken God by surprise," Beau said.

Thea gave a humorless chuckle. "No, but it sure has thrown me for a loop."

Beau studied her for a long moment, then sent her a slight smile. "The more I think about it, the more I'm convinced you are the perfect person for Mack. You don't mind saying what you think. Mack needs that in the people closest to him. He admires it."

"Then he'll be admiring me a lot."

Beau laughed. "It wouldn't surprise me at all if the two of you fell head over heels in love."

Thea snorted softly. "Spoken like a man who's hopelessly in love with his wife."

"Guilty as charged." He bent the brim of his hat toward her. "See you later."

Thea waited until the car engine revved up before waving one last time, then turning toward the house. Edie Daniels was a very blessed woman to have someone like Beau to love her as deeply as he obviously did.

A sense of disappointment settled over her like a heavy quilt at the memory of Mack's response to her questions about love. He'd once believed in falling in love. She'd heard him talk countless times about finding that special girl, someone he could settle down with and raise a family. What had changed his mind? Who had hurt him so badly that he'd lost faith in his own happily-ever-after?

Thea picked up the suitcases Beau had left at the front door and walked inside, her shoulders heavy, the weight of the emotional roller coaster she'd been on this last week or so pushing in at all sides. What she wouldn't give for a long hot bath and a good book to read. She eyed the stairwell that led up to the bathroom where the claw-footed tub beckoned her.

But there were bags that needed to be unpacked, laundry sorted, lunch made. Thea gave one last wistful glance up the stairs before turning toward the kitchen.

"Thea, is that you? I thought I heard the front door."

Her heart sank. Momma had done so well at Ms. Aurora's, had even been a help with the children at times. Had she already forgotten that they'd driven home together? "Yes, Momma. It's me."

"Is that nice Worthington boy with you?" Pots and pans clanged together as she dug through the cabinets, her best hat lopsided on her head. "I saw the way he was smiling at you across the breakfast table this morning, like you were the sweetest thing since sugar was invented."

Momma was more than confused, she was hallucinating. Mack had barely glanced at her over his bowl of oatmeal this morning, too busy answering questions from Ellie and the twin boys to pay her much mind. Meanwhile, Thea had had her hands full, feeding Sarah watered-down oatmeal that ended up on her blouse rather than in the baby's mouth. "Mack was more than likely watching me because Sarah was in my lap. If he was smiling, it must have been at her."

Her mother sat back on the kitchen floor. "No, this was when you were at the sink, getting cleaned up. Reminded me of how your father used to look at me, as if he couldn't get enough of me."

Had Momma, in her confusion, seen something in Mack's glance, tenderness or affection maybe? Wishful thinking on Thea's part. But perhaps she could use this chance to ease her mother into their marriage plans rather than springing it on her all at once. She'd discussed it with Mack and he'd agreed, even told her to take as much time as she needed to get her mother used to the idea. Who knew how much her mother absorbed these days? But Thea had resolved to try to explain.

She picked up the dish towel that had fallen from the stove and threw it on the countertop. "You remember Mack and I told you we're courting, don't you, Momma?"

"Of course I do, which is why I thought he might come by this afternoon. Gentlemen who are interested usually call around suppertime so they'll be invited to stay." She glanced up, her hands going to her hat and plucking it off her head. "Do you think I should make some chocolate chip cookies, just in case? Your daddy just loves my cookies."

Momma baking cookies? She'd barely known where the kitchen was when Thea was growing up. Thea walked over to where her mother sat and helped her to her feet. "Mack's got a lot to do at his office today. Why don't I make us grilled cheese sandwiches, then maybe we could take a little nap. I know I could use one."

"Well, I am a bit tired." Momma pulled out a chair from under the table and dropped down into it before glancing up at Thea, a confused look crossing her expression. "Where's the baby?"

For the fifth time today. "Sarah's back at Ms. Aurora's, remember? She's going to stay there until Mack and I can bring her home."

"Why?" Momma's salt-and-pepper brows crinkled together. "I don't understand."

Thea walked over to the counter and snatched a stale loaf out of the bread box before carrying it back to the table. "Sarah doesn't have a birth certificate, remember? Without one, I can't prove she's Eileen's little girl, so I can't take custody of her without the court's approval. A judge won't allow a single woman to adopt a baby so Mack and I are going to adopt Sarah together."

"Adopt?" Momma straightened in her chair. "But that's our baby!"

Thea settled a hand on her mother's shoulder. "Momma, Mack and I have it all worked out. Sarah's going to be okay, and we'll be able to bring her home soon. Everything will be fine." Thea wasn't sure if she said that for her mother's benefit or her own. This whole "marriage in name only" had thrown her usual orderly world off-kilter.

Maybe a grilled cheese sandwich and a long nap would

put things into perspective. She walked over to the ice-box, opened it, pulled out butter and cheese, and set them on the table.

But she couldn't find a frying pan. She crawled further inside the cupboard, picking through the pots and pans until she finally found a small one in the back corner under some cookie sheets.

"Do you always climb around inside the cupboard?"

Thea jerked up and yelped as the crown of her head met a low-hanging plank. Stars exploded behind her closed eyelids as a sharp pain echoed through her head, then dulled into an ache.

The inside of the cupboard went dark as Mack sat in the cabinet doorway. "Are you okay, sweetheart?"

Something—either the endearment or the hint of concern in his voice—made her heart flutter so hard she thought it might stop. Somewhere along the way, her feelings for Mack had changed. Or maybe they had laid dormant all these years, waiting for the right moment to bud and bloom into the love she'd always dreamed of while she was growing up.

"Thea?"

"I'm fine," she whispered. But she wasn't. She was falling in love with a man who didn't think himself worthy of being loved.

"You want me to come in there and get you?"

The thought made her smile. "And have us both get stuck? I don't think so. Just give a minute to brace myself."

"Okay, but if you take too long, I'm coming in there."

And he would, Thea had no doubt of that. Because Mack had a soft spot for her. He worried about her. He would do anything in his power to protect her, even marry her if need be. But was that enough to build a life with this man on?

Maybe.

She backed out of the cupboard slowly. Before she could stand on her own, Mack pulled her free of the cabinet, his hands gently clasping her arms, his gaze locked on her. "Are you sure you're all right?"

Thea nodded, despite the ache knocking around in her head. "I may have a small knot on top of my head, but it will serve me right for scrounging around in the cabinets like that."

"Let me see." Without any warning, Mack cradled her face in his hands and tilted her head down. Sharp needles of awareness lanced through her as he gently massaged his fingers against her scalp, tenderly working his way back until his fingertips closed over the knot. "You didn't cut yourself, so you won't need stitches, but you could use some ice for that bump."

Mack lifted her head up, studying her eyes. "Look at me."

Common procedure to check for concussion, but it felt like much more. Thea couldn't breathe, could barely think as Mack's fingers slid through her hair, catching her behind her neck and holding her still. His eyes studied hers, their vivid blue depths a warm indigo.

"Thea? Are you all right?"

Momma. Thea took a step backward and banged into the cupboard. Mack put out a hand to steady her, then stepped away to put some distance between them. "I'm fine, Momma. Just a little clumsy today, that's all."

"You've always been something of a klutz," her mother answered in that sharp tone Thea recognized from her childhood. "Let's hope the baby doesn't pick up your bad habits."

Thea leaned back against the cabinet as if struck. *This* was the woman she remembered from her youth, sharp-tongued, always finding fault in everything she did.

She couldn't look at Mack, couldn't bear to see the pity in his eyes. She'd never wanted him to know this about her mother, never wanted him to look at her any differently because she couldn't live up to her mother's expectations. No one could.

"Thea…"

Before she could finish, Mack interrupted. "Mrs. Miller, why don't you go upstairs and lie down for a little while? You look like you could use a nap."

Momma rested her chin in the palm of her hand as if giving it serious thought. "I am tired."

Thea hurried around the table to where her mother had started to stand up. "Let me help you upstairs, okay?"

"That's very sweet of you, dear," she said as she leaned her full weight against Thea. "Everything will be all right once we get the baby back. Then my daughter will come home and take care of everything for me."

Dread tightened like a steel band around Thea's chest. "Who are you taking about?"

"My daughter, silly girl! Eileen Miller."

Pain exploded through her, as if her mother had reared back and slapped her as hard as she could. Momma didn't know the pain she'd inflicted when, for the briefest of moments, she couldn't remember who Thea was.

Thea straightened on wobbly legs. War had not broken her, the years of endless shifts and dying children might have taken some part of her, but she'd held fast, stayed strong. But the weight of this loss, of losing her mother slowly, of watching her fade away second by agonizing second, fell heavy against her soul. "Let's get you to bed."

Minutes later, the scent of lilacs—her mother's favorite—faintly hung in the cool air of her mother's room as Thea sat Momma in a chair, then pulled back the handmade quilt that had graced her mother's bed since Thea was a little girl. By now it was worn and frayed along the edges, and for the life of her, Thea couldn't understand why her mother hung on to it after all these years. A question never to be answered, perhaps.

Downstairs, Mack had peeled back the wax paper from the bread and was pushing a knife through the stale crust as Thea walked back into the kitchen. She lit the stove, took one slice he'd already cut, slathered it with butter, then placed thinly sliced pieces of cheese on the bread and sat it in the frying pan.

Mack handed her a spatula. "You want to talk about it?"

"Not right now."

"Okay, but you know I'm here when you need me."

She buttered another piece of bread and sat it on top of the other one, then took the spatula and turned it over, the butter sizzling against the hot pan. "You've always been a good listener."

Thea couldn't be sure but she thought she saw him grimace. He ducked his head and went to work on another piece of bread. "Mind if I have a sandwich, too? I've been busy since I left Ms. Aurora's."

"Sure." Thea opened the cabinet and pulled down two plates before flipping the finished sandwich onto one. "Trying to get caught up with work?"

"Nope." He handed her a slice of bread and started

sawing off the next piece. "Busy making plans for our wedding."

Their what? "That was quick."

He gave her a lopsided grin that could have melted the butter without the pan. "I figure the sooner, the better."

The sooner, the better. Maybe he thought he was doing her a favor, but shouldn't she have a say in her own wedding? She planted her fist on a hip and glared at him. "And what do I do during all this, just show up?"

She almost smacked him with the spatula when he laughed. "No, that's why I'm here. I wanted to get your opinion and make the decisions together."

"But your plans…"

"Aren't carved into granite. This is your wedding, too, Thea. I wouldn't do anything without asking you first."

Thea smacked the flat end of the spatula nervously against her skirt. Mack's rush to the altar had thrown her for another loop, but she should have heard him out before she barked at him. "I'm sorry. I just wasn't expecting you to want to get married so fast."

"I know, but I think it's best for everyone." He handed her the last slice of bread then rewrapped the leftover loaf in the wax paper. "This way, we put an end to the rumors going around and get our adoption petition into the court before Medcalf sets another surgery date."

Mack had been doing a lot of thinking since she'd left this morning. Thea slid the spatula under the sandwich and moved it on to the other plate. "When were you thinking we could get married?"

"In two days."

Two days! "Have you lost your mind? Two days!"

"Is that too soon for you?"

She'd marry him this moment if she thought there

was even the slimmest chance Mack could love her. But never once in all their discussions about getting married and adopting Sarah together had love been mentioned.

Sarah. Mack was right about one thing. Now that Sarah had recovered from the chicken pox, Doctor Medcalf would waste no time rescheduling the surgery. If they wanted a say in her care, they would have to act quickly.

If only there was a hope that Mack loved her—or even that he would come to love her in time. It would make everything so perfect. But life never fell neatly into place that way, at least it never had for her. Raising Sarah and her friendship with Mack would have to be enough. Thea handed Mack his plate and picked up her own. "If we're getting married in two days, we'd better get to work."

Chapter Eleven

Thea glanced at the bedside clock and bolted upright in her bed. Nine o'clock! She had an appointment to meet Mack in the hallway outside of Judge Wakefield's chambers at two. There, the judge would marry them and sign the reworked adoption papers, which Red would file with the court this afternoon. In a few short weeks, Sarah would legally be their daughter. She lay back on the mattress, her heart bursting from the joy of it.

A family of her own!

But not if she didn't get moving. Thea pushed back the heavy quilts, her toes curling up against the cold as she sat up on the side of the bed. *Mrs. Thea Worthington.* Mack's wife. A tiny thrill ran through her.

In name only, remember?

The thought tempered the excitement she felt. Okay, so maybe she and Mack wouldn't have a full and complete marriage, but the past couple of days, working on their makeshift wedding, they'd drawn closer, rebuilt the relationship that had cracked under the strain of Thea's desertion all those years ago. And she'd be Sarah's mother in every way that mattered. That would be enough to make her happy. A heavy knot tightened in Thea's midsection. It would have to be, wouldn't it?

A soft rap drew Thea's attention to the door as Maggie peeked her head around the corner. "Oh, good. You're awake." She nudged the door open with her elbow, a small tray in her hands. The scent of fresh coffee, warm blueberry muffins and shortbread cookies filled the small space as she crossed the room and sat the tray down on the nightstand next to Thea's bed. "I thought you could use a little pampering this morning. It's not every day a girl gets married."

"That's so sweet of you to do this." Thea grabbed her robe off the end of the bad and threw it around her shoulders. "I don't know how I can ever thank you enough."

"You haven't tasted the muffins yet. Mine aren't as moist as Merrilee's and I can't for the life of me figure out why." As if to demonstrate, Maggie picked up one of the small muffins and peeled back the paper, bringing bits of blueberries and crumbs along with it.

"You've still got me beat, though I do make a killer grilled cheese sandwich." Thea pulled a coffee cup toward her, splashed a small amount of milk into it, then reached for the coffeepot.

"If you want more milk, don't mind me. Most everyone around here drinks it black. I only brought some up because Mack said you liked a lot in your coffee."

"Well, thank you." Thea poured in a generous splash then filled her cup. The porcelain cup warmed her fingers as she took a long sip. How sweet of Mack to remember such a small, insignificant thing as how she took her coffee. What other little habits of hers had he remembered? Just the thought that he'd made a note of it made her feel unique and special.

"Thinking about Mack?"

Thea's cheeks grew heated as she glanced over the rim of her cup. "Just wondering how he talked you into letting me stay with you on such short notice."

"Mack thought you wouldn't have to rush trying to get to the courthouse if you were staying in town." Maggie grabbed a shortbread cookie from the plate and broke it in two. "A wise man knows a woman needs a little bit more time to get herself ready on her wedding day."

"That was kind of him."

"He's a sweet man, just as good as they come." Her friend gave her a smile before popping a small portion of cookie into her mouth. She covered her mouth as she spoke. "But a two-day engagement! What's the rush?"

"That's exactly what I said," Thea muttered over the rim of her cup. "But Mack was determined."

A giggle escaped Maggie's covered mouth. "I'll say he was. Planning the whole wedding. Arranging for your mother to stay with Ms. Aurora until after you're able to take Sarah home. I guess when Mack met you again, he didn't want to wait longer than he absolutely had to."

It would have been nice to carry that thought around in her heart, but it was nowhere near the truth. "Is that how it was for you and Wesley?"

Maggie pushed a crumb at the corner of her lips into her mouth and chuckled. "Oh, no. When I first met Wesley, I thought he was this hotshot pilot who couldn't bear the thought of a woman flying one of his precious planes. But as I got to know him—" her voice softened, her hand resting against the soft curve of her swollen belly "—I couldn't help falling in love with him."

Thea smiled against the rim of her cup. It was wonderful that Maggie had found contentment and happiness with her husband. In fact, it appeared most of the Danielses had made marriages based on love and trust. A tiny pang of envy sobered Thea's mood. This marriage she was about to enter into may not be the kind she'd dreamed of when she'd been a little girl. But dreams changed, didn't they? The opportunity to raise Sarah alongside Mack, to grow as a family, to put down roots, was far more than she deserved.

"You'd better get moving if you want any hot water for your bath." Maggie stood, brushed a stray crumb or two off her skirt then arched her back, resting a fist near the base of her spine. "Grandpa mentioned the weather being warm enough to wash the windows today, though why he'd want to do that right before winter sets in is beyond me."

Thea replaced her cup on the tray, then stood, belting her robe at her waist. "From everything I've heard about Wesley's grandfather, he's always been an active man. Maybe he's bored."

"I hadn't thought about that. I wonder if he'd want to help me work on the nursery. The room could use a new coat of paint, and we haven't put up any decorations. Wesley won't let me near a ladder to hang curtains, much less paint."

"Of course the man won't," Thea teased. "He adores you too much to see you get hurt."

"There's adoring, then there's annoying." Maggie flashed Thea a knowing smile as she picked up the service and headed for the door. "But you'll find that out soon enough."

Would she ever know that feeling, of being so loved it was annoying? Both she and Mack had agreed Sarah would be their focus, at least for the foreseeable future, but what about later? Mack had always wanted a large family. If they could find their way to loving each other, there might be a chance at more children. To have his child nestled right under her heart started an ache deep in the pit of her stomach.

"There's bath salts and body cream in the bathroom in case you want to use them. I also put some extra towels out, just in case."

How sweet of Maggie! "That's really very nice of you."

Her friend opened the door before turning and looking back at Thea. "Mack deserves all the happiness the world has to offer this side of heaven. You do, too." She gave Thea a watery smile. "I've always thought the two of you belonged together, even back in high school. You're going to make each other very happy."

How could Maggie be so certain? Thea almost asked but the door had already clicked shut before she could get the question out. The mattress sank beneath her as she sat at the foot of the bed. Marrying Mack might make her happy, but what about him? Didn't someone so good and decent deserve more than a bride thrust on him because of cruel gossip? A woman whose family carried more baggage than the Union Pacific railroad? She vowed never to give him a chance to regret this decision. Because at this moment, Thea knew what choice she'd make.

She chose Mack.

Excitement thrummed through her veins as she rushed over to the dressing table, grabbed her vanity case and headed down the hall to the bathroom. Warm, moist air perfumed with the scent of ginger filled the tiny room, swirls of stream rising from the tub, a trickle of water coming from the faucet. Another gift from Maggie. Setting her case on the vanity, Thea slipped out of her night-clothes and into the fragrant water.

Less than an hour later, Thea emerged from her room, powdered and primped, feeling more like a woman than she had since shipping out to Sheffield four years ago. Looping the strap of her purse up her arm, she tugged on her chocolate-brown gloves, the perfect match for the pale gold dress she'd splurged on for the ceremony. She was still chasing the last button on her glove when she became aware of someone watching her. Thea glanced up to find Maggie and Beau waiting at the bottom of the stairs.

"My word! Mack won't know what hit him when he gets a look at you!" Maggie exclaimed as she took hold of Thea's hands and held them slightly out to her sides to get a better look at her dress. "You're absolutely gorgeous!"

Thea knew her friend was exaggerating a bit but couldn't deny the compliments helped boost her confidence. "Thank you."

Beau nodded. "My friend is a very blessed man."

Thea hoped Mack viewed their marriage that way. "You don't know how much Mack and I appreciate your help with this."

Beau glanced down at his wristwatch. "He won't be so grateful if I don't get you to the courthouse on time. We need to get going."

"Hold on just a second." Maggie gave her cousin a look of mild annoyance. "A bride is supposed to keep her groom waiting for a few extra minutes, at least long enough for us to say a quick blessing for the new couple."

Both Danielses looked at Thea. She nodded. "Mack and I could use all the help we can get."

They each lowered their heads, clasping hands as Maggie began. "Dear Lord, we're coming to You today to ask for Your blessings on Mack and Thea as they begin their lives together. Guide them as they become parents to little Sarah, and take their hearts and shape them into one guided solely by You. In Christ's name, Amen."

As Thea lifted her head, a peace that wouldn't have been possible even five minutes ago flowed through her. Now she felt certain that God would bless this marriage and this new family they were forming today. A bubble of happiness lifted the corners of her mouth as she glanced at Maggie and Beau. "I guess it's time to go and get me married."

"One more thing." Maggie waddled across the foyer to the hall table and came back with a small bouquet of deep burgundy-and-gold mums, sunny daisies and baby's breath. "Mack brought these by this morning. Said he wanted his bride to have flowers on their wedding day."

"He did?" Thea whispered into the bouquet as she took it from Maggie, a slight dampness seeping through her gloves. Mack had thought of even the smallest detail, almost as though this was a real marriage.

Maybe it would be, Thea thought, following Maggie out the front door. In time.

Mack read over the first page of the case file for what seemed like the fourteenth time, then tossed it to the side, unable to concentrate on the finer details of Officer Sydney's report. His recent bout of chicken pox had left him with a mountain of paperwork and correspondence that needed to be addressed. A good way to pass the time until the nerves he'd been outrunning all morning finally caught up with him.

He was getting married today.

He glanced up at the wall clock that hung over his door

and smiled. Maggie would have given Thea the flowers by now. Had she noticed, as he had, how the gold mums matched the color of her hair in the sunlight? Or that the ribbon holding her flowers was the same vivid shade of blue as her eyes? Red had thought it nonsense standing in Wilson's Flower Shop as Mack picked out the blooms. Said his brain must have been attacked by chicken pox for Mack to throw money away on flowers for a marriage in name only. But to Mack's way of thinking, this wedding needed flowers to let Thea know that what they had was special, no matter the circumstances of their marriage.

A rap on the door lifted Mack's head just as his secretary, Nell Jamierson, peeked inside. "Judge Wakefield is expecting you in twenty minutes."

"Thank you, Nell."

"Have you got the ring?"

Leave it to a woman to remember that kind of detail. Mack opened his desk drawer, took out the small box he'd picked up at Mr. Friedman's just this morning and opened it. A slender and delicate band of gold, decorated with a light blue stone, it had instantly reminded him of Thea, as if it had been made especially with her in mind. He held it out to his secretary. "What do you think?"

Nell stepped forward. "I don't know any women who'd turn that rock down. Your Thea is a very lucky girl."

His Thea. Something about the phrase pleased him, maybe because after today they'd be bound to each other, as friends, as parents raising Sarah. *As husband and wife.* Mack gave himself a mental shake. Maybe Red was right, maybe the chicken pox had muddled his brain, though truth be told, he'd been in a tangled mess since he'd spied Thea peeking out from underneath that oak at Merrilee's wedding. At first, it had been only because she'd threatened the hopes he'd built around raising Sarah as his own, but that had all changed. Lately, he'd found himself thinking about her all the time—wondering what she'd done during her day, whether she'd had a good day with her mother. Not to mention the time he spent thinking about kissing her, holding her close. The need to comfort and protect her from the crazy world they lived in just about drove him mad.

"Now, you don't worry about anything. I'll hold down the fort while you're gone. Don't want to keep your bride waiting."

"Right." Mack stood, straightened his tie, then grabbed his suit coat off the back of his chair and put it on. Once he had the coat buttoned, he reached for the ring box and, with one last look, closed and dropped it into the safety of his coat pocket. He came around the desk and headed for the door.

The walk to Judge Wakefield's office usually took five minutes, but the news of his impending marriage had traveled around town as if Betty, the operator at Marietta Telephone Company, had made it her personal job to be the town crier. Folks all along the square stopped him with congratulations and well wishes, so the short trek from his office took three times as long as usual. As Mack rounded the corner on Main Street and hurried up the courthouse stairs, a horn honked behind him, and he turned to see Beau pull up to the curb with his cousin Maggie riding shotgun in the front seat.

Where was Thea?

Mack's heart jumped into his throat. Had she changed her mind? Had she decided marrying him wasn't worth the opportunity to raise Sarah?

Beau waved to him as he rounded the front of the car

and opened the door for Maggie. She stood, then, seeing him, hurried across the brick sidewalk toward him, her green eyes flashing with happiness, her wide smile as big as the skies she loved. She playfully pointed her finger at him. "You, Mack Worthington, are a very blessed man."

He was? Being blessed wasn't something he'd felt much over the years, at least not since the accident. "Why do you say that?"

"Just wait. You'll understand in a minute." She turned back toward the car and Mack followed her gaze.

And felt as if all the oxygen had suddenly been sucked out of the atmosphere.

Thea stood next to the car, her full skirts swirling around her legs, a tiny bow belted at her trim waist and another at the neckline of her bodice. Her blue eyes were hidden by a wisp of a veil, her hair restrained by a band of dark chocolate brown. A cloud of curls gathered about her delicate shoulders, giving him a tempting glimpse of her long, elegant neck.

"Breathe," Maggie whispered to him.

Easy for her to say. Her heart wasn't racing a million beats a minute. Thea had to be the most beautiful woman he'd ever seen, and she was about to become his wife.

In name only.

Disappointment lanced through him, and he sucked in a much-needed breath. Mack couldn't expect their union to be anything but a way to adopt Sarah, to share in raising the little girl, not with the baggage he carried. He still hadn't told Thea about his bad ear, or the part she'd played in the accident that caused it, but he would. Ms. Aurora was right; Thea needed to know the entire story about the night she left town. Just not today.

Mack started toward her, but Thea met him halfway, her skirts brushing against his legs. "Hi."

"Hi."

"You look…so beautiful." The words tumbled out in a husky whisper.

"You think so?" Thea glanced up then, her gaze meeting his, a faint hint of skepticism clouding their blue depths. Did the woman have any doubt as to how lovely she truly was? Had no one ever bothered to tell her?

Mack took her free hand and held it in his. "You're the most beautiful woman I've ever seen."

A ghost of a smile danced in the corners of her full lips. "You clean up right nice yourself, Sheriff."

The simple compliment warmed his heart. "Well, thank you. I try."

"And thank you for my flowers." She lifted the buds to her nose and drew in a deep breath. "It was very sweet of you to think of it."

Heat crawled up the back of his neck as if he were some schoolboy going to his very first dance. "Couldn't have my girl walking down the aisle without her bouquet."

"Still, it was sweet of you." Her cheeks turned a lovely shade of pink that matched the mums in her hand.

He threaded her gloved hand through his, his heart crashing against his breastbone at the touch of her slender fingers against his forearm. "Ready to do this?"

Silky curls fluttered against her shoulders as she nodded. "How about you? Any second thoughts?"

Oh, yes. Second, and third, and fourth and…but looking at Thea now, feeling the warmth of her hand against his arm, all the reasons they shouldn't marry dissipated like the morning mist on Sweetwater Creek. "Not a one."

"I don't mean to interrupt," Beau broke in. "But it's warm out here. Mind if we move this indoors?"

"I didn't even notice," Thea whispered to her flowers, almost as if she hadn't meant to be heard.

So she'd felt the same thing he had, as if the world had faded away, leaving them completely alone. Her eyes widened when she finally looked up and met his gaze. She lifted her hand from his arm as if to retreat, but he gently kept her there, pressing his fingers against hers. Mack leaned closer, the faint scent of ginger and tea imprinting itself on his memory, growing stronger as her hair brushed against his cheek. "I'd forgotten Beau and Maggie were even standing there."

She pursed her lips into an impish grin, and he had to force himself not to focus on the temptation of her mouth, instead holding her close as they started up the stairs. "Let's get inside."

Not more than a minute or two later, the group stood outside the massive doors that led to Judge Wakefield's chambers. Mack knocked on the door, then waited until it opened slightly, a young man Mack recognized as Wakefield's clerk lodging himself in the opening as if guarding the gates of the city of Oz. "Mr. Lemmon, we're here to see the judge on a private matter."

The young man nodded. "I'll let him know you're here. It will be just a few minutes." He gave Thea a long look, then smiled. "I'll come and escort you into his chambers when he's ready."

Mack's stomach twisted. Little runt had a lot of nerve, eyeing Thea like that. He tightened his fingers over hers. Didn't the man know she was about to become Mack's wife? Just proved he had more brains than common sense.

Why am I getting so worked up over this, anyway?

The steady clip-clop of work boots against the marble floor drew Mack's attention to the stairwell where a tall, lanky man stood, the leather bag on his back almost as brown as his weather-worn face. Judson Marsh was the town's mailman. He was tall and lean, and some folks thought he looked the spitting image of Jimmy Stewart, but Mack didn't see the resemblance.

Maybe a string bean, but nothing like the Hollywood actor who had fought in the Army Air Force, and risen to the rank of Colonel.

"Well, howdy folks. Miss Maggie, Dr. Daniels, Sheriff." He gave Thea a speculative glance. "Don't reckon I know you, Miss."

"This is my fiancée, Thea Miller. Thea, Mr. Marsh, our mailman."

Mack felt slightly deprived when Thea let go of his arm and held out her hand to the older man. "Nice to meet you, Mr. Marsh."

The older man took her hand in his and shook it. "Getting married, are ya? I've heard what people are saying around town, about the two of you being out at Ms. Aurora's, and I've got to tell you, I find the whole situation shameful, just shameful."

Thea tensed beside him, but the expression on her face was resigned. It infuriated Mack. Was this what she'd dealt with when people use to talk about Eileen? Or had she heard some of the rumors that swirled about her, guilt by association? Well, government employee or not, he'd deck the postman before he'd let him bad-mouth his future wife. "Mr. Marsh…"

"I know how bad it can be, taking care of a houseful of youngsters who're sick." He leaned close to Thea as if he wanted to share a secret only with her. "Me and my wife had eight girls and a boy, and when they were down with the measles or the chicken pox…" He shuddered. "Besides, anyone with eyes in their head can see why the sheriff decided to marry this little lady." A toothy grin split his weathered face. "Married my Edna just so I've have someone that pretty waiting at home for me." Marsh slapped Mack on the back. "You've done good picking this one, Sheriff."

"I think so," Mack answered. Thea relaxed against his side, and without even thinking, he dropped a kiss against her hair. For Marsh's benefit, and for Thea's, he told himself.

The man swung his bag around, lifted the leather flap and rifled through the contents. "Seeing as how you're here, Sheriff, mind if I give you your mail now? It'll save me a trip to your office this afternoon." Marsh gave them a cockeyed grin. "My daughter-in-law is bringing our grandbaby home from the hospital today, and I sure would like to be there when they get home."

"Of course you would." Thea glanced up at Mack. "We both understand how you feel."

Mack felt for the man. He'd lost his only son in the liberation of Paris and his grandchild was his last link to the lanky boy Mack remembered from church. The stack of letters needing to be stamped and sent from his desk could wait until tomorrow. "Sure, Mr. Marsh. I can take them back to the office."

The door opened. "The judge can see you now."

Mr. Marsh handed a small pack of envelopes tied with string to Mack, then closed the flap on his bag. "Well, good day to you, Miss Thea. Miss Maggie. Doc." The older man gave Mack a sly smile. "And congratulations to you, Sheriff. You've got yourself a mighty sweet lady here."

For once, Mack agreed with the old coot. "Thank you, Mr. Marsh."

"Mr. Marsh," Thea added. "You have a good visit with that grandbaby of yours this afternoon."

"I'm going to try, ma'am. Thank you." He tipped his hat, then turned and headed back toward the stairs, giving them one last look before walking down the hallway.

"Sheriff Worthington." The impatient edge in Mr. Lemmon's voice grated on Mack's nerves. "Judge Wakefield doesn't have all day."

This scrawny kid was just begging for a lesson in manners. But Mack pushed back his temper. "Would you please tell the judge I'd like to have a few minutes alone with my bride before the wedding?"

Lemmon pursed his lips as if he'd been sucking on an unripe persimmon, then nodded. "Please be advised that the judge has another appointment on the hour."

Mack glanced down at the woman beside him, then back at their friends. "Could you give us a moment?"

"Sure." Maggie reached out and hugged him as best as she could, turning to one side to accommodate her growing midsection. "Be happy, my friend," she whispered on a sniff.

She turned then and hugged Thea while Beau walked over and shook Mack's hand. "You're doing the right thing by Sarah, giving her a mom and a dad. Remember that."

Mack nodded. Yes, he needed to remember that every time he thought of Thea, of the tumble of emotions she caused just being near him, of the attraction that made him wish this was something more than a marriage in name only. He waited until his friends had stepped into the judge's chambers before turning back to his bride.

She looked so lovely, standing there in her dress made of gold, nibbling on her bottom lip in that nervous way he found endearing, the little bouquet he'd brought her this morning clutched between her hands.

She pushed a loose curl behind her ear, another nervous habit that he found equally appealing. "Is everything okay?" she asked.

No, but then he hadn't been okay in almost two weeks, not since he'd seen her at Merrilee's wedding. His mind felt muddled, his feelings tangled up in knots all because of this woman. But that night eight years ago still remained unresolved between them, and until Mack had laid all of that to rest, he had to keep his feelings in check.

Mack reached out and pried one of her hands free of the bouquet. "I thought I'd give you a minute. Figured you might need a breather before all the excitement."

She tilted her head to the side. "Maybe you wanted to take a breather yourself?"

Thea always did know how to read him. Mack chuckled softly. "Things *have* been going at a record speed."

"Mack, if you've changed your mind, I'll understand."

"No," he barked, then cleared his throat. "I mean, no. What about you? I just sprang all this on you a few days ago. Any misgivings?"

Her smile widened, her blue eyes taking on a glow that enveloped him in its warmth, made him feel as if he'd finally come home. She slipped her hand into his and gave it a reassuring squeeze. "None."

His heart collided with his ribcage, his senses punch-drunk. That Thea—wonderfully smart, assertive Thea—

had no qualms about marrying him gave him hope. "Beau's going to be crowing about this for years."

"Beau?"

"He's the one who thought it would be a good idea if we got married."

Thea tilted her head slightly to the side, her eyes glittering with mischief beneath the lacy veil. "So we should thank Beau for this mess we're in now?"

"Yeah, let's blame Beau," he answered, pulling her arm through his. Mack glanced down at her once more, his heart quivering like a jar of Merrilee's apple jelly. "Ready to get married, Miss Miller?"

For a brief instant, all her lingering doubts clouded those expressive eyes of hers, but then a smile that seemed to come from the very depths of her heart bloomed across her face as she pressed into his side. "I'm ready."

In fifteen short minutes, he'd have everything he'd dreamed of most of his life: a wife and child, a family to come home to in the evenings. Everything he'd searched for over the last eight years.

Well, almost everything.

Becoming Sarah's father, being Thea's husband in name only would have to do for now. Mack turned the knob and opened the door, standing to one side, waiting, watching as she walked into the judge's chambers.

Chapter Twelve

"If you'll take her left hand in yours, Sheriff."

Thea swallowed, the bravado she'd felt just a few minutes before gone, nerves choking the very air out of her lungs. They were really going to do this, get married and raise Sarah together. Thea would have the family she'd been longing for over the past eight years, people she could pour out all her love on, devote herself to, love and be loved by in return.

Only Mack didn't love her.

She didn't realized she'd lifted her hand until Mack's warm palm closed over her fingers, his hand like its owner—sturdy yet infinitely tender, strong yet unbelievably kind. His thumb swept over the top of her knuckles, grazing the gentle peaks and valleys as if memorizing each one.

"Do you, Marcus Fletcher, take Theodora Grace to be your lawfully wedded wife?"

Thea's breath hitched, the steel band around her chest tightening with each second as she waited for his answer. What if he'd changed his mind? What if he realized she wasn't nearly good enough to be his wife? To raise the child he'd claimed as his own? What if she made the same mistakes with Sarah as she'd made with Eileen? Then she would be all alone. *Not alone, Lord, never alone. But so very lonely without an earthly family to cherish.*

She glanced up and found herself lost in the inky blue depths of his gaze, the sparks in his eyes lighting a way through the darkness. His fingers tightened slightly around hers as if he never intended to let her go, then he gave her the most tender of smiles.

"I do."

Her heart fluttered in a wild rhythm beneath her breast. Was this what love felt like, this indescribable joy at just being near him, of hearing him pledge his life to hers, anxious for the moment when she could do the same?

And then the moment was upon her.

"Do you, Theodora Grace, take this man, Marcus Fletcher, to be your lawfully wedded husband?"

"I do."

His irises darkened, light flaring to a brilliant glow in his eyes. Could it be possible he felt some of the same emotions she was experiencing at the moment? Or was he simply counting on her to hold up her end of their bargain, a marriage in name only for a chance to raise Sarah?

"The ring, please."

A ring? Thea hadn't thought of that. Had Mack? Would they still be married if…? Reaching his right hand into his pocket, Mack fished around until he pulled out a slender golden band and slid it into place on her finger, then, without warning, bent and press his lips against the cool metal.

Her knees wobbled, and she feared there was a very real chance she'd melt into a puddle at his feet. The ceremony needed to end as quickly as possible or Mack would realize what she'd wrestled with these past few days.

That she'd fallen in love with him. Completely, totally in love with a man who only wanted a marriage in name only.

"I now pronounce you husband and wife. You may kiss the bride."

Thea sucked in a breath and butterflies fluttered in her midsection as if freed from their cocoons for the first time. For years she had developed a sterling reputation, holding herself in check, holding fast to the hard lessons she'd learned from her sister's behavior. Only now she found herself completely unprepared.

Mack's warm breath sent a sweet shiver down her spine. When had he moved to stand so close? Or was she the one who'd moved to be near him? His lips brushed softly against the sensitive shell of her ear, his voice barely a whisper. "Is this your first kiss?"

Heat flooded her cheeks. How had he known? Of course Mack would know. Mack, to whom she'd confided her girlish disappointments, who understood how much her sister's behavior had influenced her own. "Yes."

"Then trust me, Thea."

He stepped back slightly, just enough for him to lift the lacy veil and push it back away from her face. Yes, she trusted him as she'd trusted no one else in her life. All other thoughts splintered as Mack lifted his hands to cradle her face, his thumbs tracing the line of her cheekbones, his eyes dark and unreadable as his gaze floated over her eyes, her cheeks and nose, before settling on her mouth. His handsome face blurred as he moved closer, lowering his head to hers as her eyelids fluttered shut.

Mack brushed his lips against hers, and Thea forgot

to breathe. When he finally settled his mouth over hers, she looped her arms around his neck and drew him even closer. This was the man she'd married, the man she'd raise a family with. The man who'd stolen her heart.

Somebody cleared their throat. "I hope you two don't plan on acting like that in front of an impressionable child."

The judge's words sank in. *Sarah.* The only reason Mack had asked her to marry him in the first place. That, and a feeble effort to save her reputation, as if that could ever be repaired. Thea broke off the kiss and pressed her lips together. How long would they tingle like this? When had the room grown so warm? Did kissing always drive every thought from your mind, or was it just kissing Mack?

She stole a glance at him through thick lashes. He looked as shell-shocked as she felt. Did that mean he'd felt something, too, that the vows they'd made, the kiss they'd shared had forged an unbreakable bond between them? Or was she reading more into his feelings because her own were such a tender mess?

A hand at her shoulder turned Thea around to where Maggie stood, happiness lighting her eyes. "Congratulations."

"Thank you."

The women watched as Beau gave Mack a hearty slap on the back.

"And bravo!" The redhead waved a hand in front of her face as if she was warm. "I'm going to have to go home and kiss my husband after watching that."

Thea had never blushed as much as she had this morning. "I made an idiot out of myself, didn't I?"

"An idiot, for kissing your husband? If so, then there's a lot of us idiots who enjoy kissing our husbands."

Thea didn't have time to respond before Beau swooped over and gave her a kiss on her cheek. She absently accepted his congratulations, her thoughts still in a tangle. After the way she'd returned his kiss, did Mack think she was anything like her sister? Would her behavior ruin their chances of adopting Sarah?

A loud pop echoed in the room as Judge Wakefield slammed a book shut, shaking Thea out of her thoughts. "If you all are finished pawing at each other, we've got other business to attend to before my next appointment."

She risked a glance at Mack. He looked as if he held himself on a tight leash, the muscles across his back and arms stretched with tension like a lion ready to jump its prey. What good would it do to strike out at Wakefield when the man had already made up his mind? She pressed a hand to his arm, steeling herself against the anger she knew would be reflected in his eyes.

Mack turned, his eyes flashing as his hand covered hers, all the protectiveness he'd shown toward Sarah now focused on her. "I won't let him talk about you like that."

If possible, Thea's heart melted a little bit more. She curled up against his side. "Let's just sign whatever papers he needs and get this over with."

Mack nodded, then turned back to face the judge. "What is there left for us to do?"

The older man glanced past them to where Maggie and Beau stood. "As this is a private matter, you're free to go. Thank you for your participation."

The judge continued to shuffle papers as Mack and Thea said goodbye to their friends. Maggie pulled Thea close for a hug. "If you need someone to talk to, I'm here. Just know there's a whole bunch of us praying for you."

People prayed for them? The thought touched a place in her heart that had been numb for years. "Thank you," she managed.

After their friends had been escorted outside, she and Mack returned to their place in front of Judge Wakefield's desk. "Again, I ask you," Mack started. "What is there left for us to do?"

"Nothing, really." The older man shucked off his robes, hung them on a nearby coatrack then pulled his chair away from his massive cherrywood desk and sat down. He shuffled through some folders before finally pulling one out and opening it. "I've already approved the two of you to act as Sarah's guardians until the final decree comes through. Until then, the state will monitor the child's progress, so they'll be sending out a social worker in the next few weeks."

"No!" The word burst out of Thea without warning. She didn't want anyone from the state near Sarah, not after what she'd witnessed Georgia Tann and her political cronies do to countless children and their families during her time in Memphis. Stealing children away, never to be seen by their parents again for trumped-up legal reasons, signed off on by Miss Tann's pet judge.

Judge Wakefield studied her over his wire-rimmed glasses. "Do you have a problem, Mrs. Worthington?"

"Thea?"

She glanced up at Mack. Questions clouded his expression, questions she'd have to answer sooner rather than later. But not now, not in front of the judge. How could she convince Judge Wakefield to change his mind without going into the sordid details?

"It's just…" The hairs on the back of her neck rose. What could she offer as a perfectly reasonable explanation for her outburst? "Your honor, Sarah has just recovered from the chicken pox and is due to have major surgery in a matter of days. Her immune system has already been compromised, and the more people she's in contact with, the more likely she'll contract something else."

"Which will delay the surgery even longer," Mack interjected.

God bless Mack! He may not understand her reasons, but he was backing up her explanation as any good husband would. "So you see, sir, I'm thinking about Sarah's well-being."

"I see." The man fell back into his chair, his fingers steepled over his waist. "I know it seems as if I've given you a difficult time with this adoption, Sheriff, but I only want to do what's right by the child." He shook his head. "So many judges don't take their responsibility as seriously as they should and the child is always the one who suffers for it." He leaned forward and rested his forearms on his desk, studying them for a long moment. "While I can waive most of the social worker's visits, she will need to visit your home at least once to check out the child's living conditions. Maybe that can be arranged before you bring the baby home from Ms. Aurora's. That should satisfy the state requirements."

Thea didn't know what to say. Everything she'd ever heard about Judge Wakefield had left her with the impression he was a stickler for the law. An old coot, she'd once called him. Maybe the man had a heart after all.

Mack recovered before she did. "That's kind of you, sir."

"'Thank you' will do just fine."

Mack's face broke into an extraordinary smile. "Thank you. I can't begin to tell you how much this means to us."

"You're welcome." The man closed the file in his hand, pushed it to the side, then grabbed another one. "Now, get out of here before I change my mind."

"Yes, sir." Mack caught Thea's hand in his and tugged her toward the door.

Thea felt as if she were floating. Married and with a new daughter all in one day. A real live family of her own. Maybe not the way she'd always dreamed, but she didn't care. She had Mack and Sarah. At the door, she turned back toward the judge. "Thank you again, sir."

Judge Wakefield glanced up at her, a glimmer of a smile playing along his lips. "Wait until you've been married to that one for a while. Then let's see just how grateful you are."

The evening sky had turned a bruised purple by the time Mack turned the squad car onto Cheatham Hill Road. The chill of the late-fall evening nipped at Thea's fingers through the thin cloth of her gloves. A comfortable silence had fallen over them since they left Maggie and Beau back at the diner, an array of tin cans and old shoes tied to the back of the squad car, announcing their marriage to the folks in Marietta.

Thea stole a quick glance at her husband. In the fading light, she could barely make out the pink edges of the scar that peeked out from under his hair. The ache she felt at the hurt and confusion he had to have suffered was almost overwhelming. But had that accident been enough to make him give up his dreams?

Mack could still go to college and do all the things he'd planned. Be a lawyer, settle down and have the family he'd dreamed of having. An image of him, dressed in a well-cut wool suit, briefcase in hand, coming through the door to her and Sarah popped into her thoughts. Her putting the last touches on dinner while Mack played with their daughter. Him wrapping his arms around her waist, his lips brushing a gentle kiss behind her ear right before he whispered *I*...

A sharp turn onto an unfamiliar dirt road jerked Thea out of her daydream. She whipped around to face Mack. "Where are we going?"

"We need to talk somewhere where no one is likely to bother us."

"What's so important that we can't talk about it at home?"

A smile played along the corner of his lips. "I like how you said that, as if you already consider my house your home."

Anywhere Mack was would be home to her, but he didn't need to hear that right now. "So why can't we talk there?"

"My sources tell me that some of the guys are planning an old-fashioned shivaree at our place this evening."

Thea laughed. "I thought that kind of thing went out with hooped skirts and parasols."

"There are some in our community who still live by the old ways. So while they're trying to figure out where we are, I thought we'd talk about what happened with Judge Wakefield today. I want to know what you have against social workers."

Thea straightened, her hands clasped in a tight knot in her lap. She wanted to let the topic drop, but she knew that wasn't fair. If she had the opportunity to pry the facts out of him about his injury, she wouldn't let him back away from the truth, no matter how painful it was. Why should she expect any less from him now?

They bumped along for several minutes until they reached a small clearing shadowed by a circle of tall trees. Long stems of wild grass swished against the metal doors as Mack maneuvered the car into a patch of fading light.

Recognition dawned as she glanced around, then back at Mack. "This is Lover's Pass."

"You've been here before?" he growled as he shoved the car into Park.

His question felt more like an accusation. "Petey Henderson brought me here after a basketball game my junior year. But we didn't stay long once he found out I was nothing like Eileen."

"And that was the only time you've been here?"

"I figure the answer to that question would be obvious, seeing how I'd never been kissed until..." Her words faded into the waning light. *Until you kissed me.*

She thought she heard him mutter "Good" as he turned off the engine.

The keys jangled in the ignition as Mack turned to face her, propping one knee on the seat beside her. "All right. Now, I want you to explain to me why you have this problem with a social worker coming to evaluate us."

Thea swallowed. How could she ever explain everything that had happened without making her sister sound worse than she was? There wasn't any way, and Mack deserved the truth. All of it.

But that didn't mean it would be easy for her.

"Eileen spent most of her life looking for love, wherever she could find it. When she got into her teens, she started looking for anyone who could make her feel special. Most of the boys were willing to give her lots of attention, but only in exchange for a good time, and after it ended Eileen would be heartsick about what she'd done. But that didn't stop her from searching. Midway through her sophomore year, Eileen realized she was pregnant."

Mack shifted back slightly in his seat. "She never looked…you know, while we were in school."

It was kind of sweet, his awkwardness with discussing such a delicate matter. If only the topic didn't involve her sister. "Eileen didn't start to show until she was six months along, and by then, school was out. That summer she stayed close to home. She talked about keeping the baby and becoming the kind of mother we never got to have." Thea drew in a steadying breath. "I really believed she was going to turn over a new leaf."

"But in the end, she gave her baby away."

If only it had been that simple. Thea shook her head. "No, Eileen wanted to keep her baby. She told me as much. But Momma…" She swallowed against the thick knot forming in her throat. "The shame of having a pregnant teenage daughter was just too much for her, so the thought of an illegitimate grandchild was unbearable. Weeks before Eileen's delivery, Momma got in touch with someone she'd grown up with in Memphis—a woman named Mrs. Cook who knew how to handle adoptions."

"Your mother thought she could change Eileen's mind?"

Disgust for what her mother had done almost cut off her breath. "Momma didn't plan to give Eileen much of a choice. She had heard about a woman up in Memphis who'd had a lot of success getting children adopted to wealthy people, like movie stars and such. Mrs. Cook promised to deliver the baby to that woman. She arranged to be in town, and met Momma that night at the train station, just hours after Eileen gave birth."

"That was why I drove you to the train station that night."

She nodded, sorry she'd had to involve him in her family's sordid problems. "Eileen called me at work, half out of her mind with grief. She'd overheard Momma on the telephone with Mrs. Cook." Thea hesitated. "I would have told you what was going on that night, but I was so ashamed. What kind of person would give her grandchild away?"

In the fading light, she could make out the sharp angle of his jaw. "Is that why you left that night like you did?"

There was a harshness to his voice she couldn't decipher. "Eileen was so desperate for her baby. She wanted to go after him herself, but she was in no fit state to travel. I couldn't sit back and do nothing. I knew if I didn't follow Mrs. Cook, my chance at recovering the baby would be less than zero. I had my savings for college in my pocket so I bought a ticket and followed her."

"You went after the child," Mack whispered.

She nodded. "I promised Eileen I'd bring him home. But it wasn't as easy as I thought it would be. The first couple of times I went to see Mrs. Cook, she denied knowing what I was talking about. I finally got in touch with the woman who ran the children's home where the baby had been placed, a Miss Georgia Tann. She told me the baby had died."

Mack shifted forward, his particular scent of lemon-lime aftershave and something purely him comforting her frazzled nerves. "There have been rumors floating around about Miss Tann for years."

"You mean the rumors of her stealing babies from their families and then selling them to the highest bidder?"

"I didn't want…"

He'd tried to spare her feelings. "Thank you. But I've faced the truth of the situation many times over the last eight years and it still didn't bring Eileen's child home."

Mack's hand covered hers. When had he moved so close to her, his shoulder brushing up against her own? "It's not your fault, sweetheart."

The endearment wound its way around her heart until she thought it would burst, but the joy quickly faded. He just wanted to comfort her, that was all. "That's not how Momma and Eileen saw it. When I called to tell them what had happened, Eileen refused to speak to me and Momma, she told me not to bother coming back home."

"That's why you're so sure Eileen wouldn't give up her baby girl? Why you thought Ms. Aurora stole Sarah away? Because you thought she was like Georgia Tann?"

Thea gave a shaky shrug. "I only knew what my mother was telling me, and from what I'd seen of Miss Tann and her allies, I thought it was a possibility. But not now. I was so wrong about Ms. Aurora. I told her as much when I apologized to her. She adores those kids and they love her to death." She sighed. "I guess I just wanted my family back, that's all."

"But Thea, you *have* a family, one with you and me and Sarah." Mack took her hand in his, warmth running up the length of her arm at his touch.

Yes, Thea thought. She did have the family she'd always wanted. Why, with all she had, did she still feel all alone?

Chapter Thirteen

"Got some news from Judge Wakefield's office this morning I thought you'd like to hear." Red burst through Mack's office door a week later without so much as a knock.

"Good afternoon to you, too." Mack finished the thought he'd been writing on an upcoming case, then lifted his head to see his friend had made himself comfortable in the leather wingback chair in front of his desk. "Did it ever occur to you that I might be busy?"

"Still trying to catch up from your bout with the chicken pox?

"Yes." But that wasn't altogether the truth. Since marrying Thea he'd been keeping shorter hours. Work hadn't held the same appeal as going home to find his lovely bride poring over cookbooks or covered in paint from decorating the nursery. Their drives out to Ms. Aurora's to see the baby and Mrs. Miller included interesting discussions of the news around town as well as updates on their friends. It was a vast improvement over what his life had been, yet he craved more. More time with Thea, more laughter. He smiled to himself. And lots more kisses.

"Well, I figured this news would be worth taking you away from reports on parking tickets and petty theft."

Mack filed the report in his desk drawer, then turned and grabbed the next one off the stack. "One of your clients get caught doing something illegal?"

Red leaned back into the chair and stretched his long legs out in front of him. "If you don't want to hear about Sarah's birth certificate, I certainly won't tell you."

That news brought Mack up short. "What do you mean? Mrs. Williams hasn't come back home, has she?"

"No, but she did send Judge Wakefield all the particulars of the baby's birth so the necessary documents could be filed. Wrote in her letter that she'd sent you a copy, too, seeing how there was a dispute over the identity of the baby's mother."

He hadn't received any correspondence from Mrs. Williams. Reaching for a stack of mail Nell had brought in earlier, Mack shuffled through the envelopes, then went through them slowly in case he'd missed something. When he'd completed his search, he turned back to Red. "She must be mistaken. I haven't gotten anything from her."

"It's possible it arrived last week. It didn't get filed with the court until today, according to Mr. Lemmon."

Last week. Could it be in the stack of mail Judson Marsh had given him the day of the wedding? He'd been so occupied with Thea and the baby, he'd plumb forgot. Mack pushed back his chair and hurried over to the small closet where he stored his coat. Shuffling through the hangers, he came across the jacket he'd worn the day of the wedding and reached into the pocket, coming out with a stack of envelopes along with bits of rice and confetti from the wedding lunch he and Thea had shared with their friends.

"Well, did you find it?" Red asked.

Mack untied the string binding the letters and shifted quickly through the stack. Second from the bottom, a small envelope in Mrs. Williams's nondescript handwriting stared up at him. "It's here."

All the answers he'd been looking for in the last month sat at his fingertips. Sarah's parentage. Thea's claim. But now, instead of being evidence he sought, Mack felt a stab of the pain at the possibilities the answers might reveal. If Thea lost her certainty that Sarah was her niece, she lost her last hope of making peace with the memory of her sister. Not that it mattered to him. In his heart, Sarah was as much Thea's child as if she'd given birth to her. Burdening Thea with a new loss would hurt her too much, and her pain had become his own.

I'm in love with Thea.

Mack let the admission settle over him, amazed it had taken him this long to admit what his heart had been trying to tell him from the first. Of course he loved her, had loved her ever since she'd worn her hair up in those adorable pigtails while they were still in high school; admired the generous, loving woman she had become despite the sorrows she'd borne.

"Well, what are you waiting for? Open it."

Mack glanced over at his attorney. Red would never understand his reasoning, but then he wasn't paid to understand Mack's every move, now was he? "I'm not going to open it."

Red sat up. "But you've been waiting for a month to find out the truth, and now that you have it, you're not going to read it?"

What Mack felt for Thea, for Sarah, the relationship he shared with his Savior. Those were the only truths he needed to know. Mrs. Williams's letter could only deliver news that either wouldn't matter, or would cause pain.

What about Thea? Shouldn't she have a voice in this matter? Shouldn't she make her own decision about knowing the contents of the letter? Of course she should. They had promised to base their marriage on trust.

Mack scraped a hand across his jaw, shame rising inside. A hollow vow, considering he hadn't confessed the anger he'd felt toward her since the night she'd left. If he wanted a chance at making this marriage real, he had to bring it out into the open, lance this old wound once and for all.

Mack threw the rest of the mail on his desk, grabbed his coat off the back of his chair and rounded his desk, heading toward the door.

Red jumped to his feet, his expression one of bewilderment. "Mack, what are you doing?"

"I need to talk to Thea."

"Don't you think you need to make a decision before bringing her into this?"

"You can find your own way out." Mack took one last look at his lawyer, then hurried across the room and walked out the door. It didn't matter who had given birth to Sarah, only that Thea was her mother now and always would be.

He'd made his decision.

He was going to follow his heart.

Thea stepped out onto the sidewalk in front of the white marbled bank, the soft fall sunlight doing nothing to ward off the chill that had taken up residence in her bones over the course of the past two days. Tending to her mother's scant finances had led to another dead end. The latest one was a safety deposit box. Momma had kept the key to it in her dresser drawer since before

Daddy died. If Thea had hoped to find a life insurance policy or jewelry inside to help fund her mother's care, she'd been disappointed.

Another worry for Mack to deal with, Thea thought as she tugged on her black gloves, their color matching her mood. Her mother was her responsibility, not his. She'd find a way to cover Momma's bills. Maybe the hospital knew of a doctor who needed a nurse. Of course, she'd have to consider Sarah's needs, and she wouldn't do anything until she talked to Mack.

Thea tucked her purse against her side and glanced out over the square. The trees in the park had been shaken bare, a happy occurrence if the children running and jumping into the piles of red-and-gold leaves had anything to say about it. Two women sat together on a bench, each rocking a stroller, deep in conversation as if comparing notes on motherhood. The earthy fragrance of pumpkins from the corner market next door lightly scented the air.

The perfect place to raise a family.

"If only that was all I wanted," Thea muttered as she shoved her purse under her arm.

"You always talk to yourself like that?"

Thea's heart did a funny little flip, her standard response to her husband's voice. She lifted her chin a notch. "Sometimes, when I get lonely and don't have anyone else to talk to."

Her blunt honesty caught him off guard, and even left her feeling a little flustered. What had possessed her to confess that she got lonely at times? Mack, Marietta's golden-haired boy, would have no idea what it was like to feel all alone in a world full of people with no one to talk to or confide in.

But when she lifted her gaze to his, a shock ran through

her at the hint of vulnerability in his eyes. Was it possible Mack felt the same loneliness? His parents were gone, and though he had dozens of friends, it wasn't the same as having someone to count on, someone who cared enough about you to tell you when you were making a mistake, someone who loved you despite your flaws.

They'd been friends once, and this past week had seemed to erase all the years they'd been apart. She was his wife, his partner. He'd never be alone again, not if she could help it. Thea slipped her arm through his and gave him what she hoped to be a flirtatious smile. "You're looking mighty good for a man who just got over chicken pox not that long ago."

"Well, I owe that to the good care I received. In fact, the nurse who took care of me was so wonderful, I married her." He leaned down and whispered as if they were sharing a secret. "And I finally got the last of the oatmeal out of my hair this morning."

"I'm glad to hear that, Sheriff." Thea brought her gloved hand up to stifle the giggles. "I wasn't expecting to see you until tonight. Have you heard from Ms. Aurora today?"

"Sarah is fine, as always." Mack pushed the brim of his hat back on his head, revealing more of his handsome face. "John and Merrilee are back from their honeymoon and stopped by Ms. Aurora's to check on everyone. John even dropped your mother back at your house to pick up some things. He'll go and check on her throughout the day, then take her back to Ms. Aurora's this evening."

Worry flashed through her, then slowly dissipated. Ms. Aurora wouldn't have agreed to this unless she felt Momma would be all right. "Has Momma been giving her any trouble?"

He shook his head. "Not any that she mentioned. She seems to think your mother does better when she's kept occupied, so she's been helping with the twins."

"Ms. Aurora's a wonderful woman to take Momma in for a few days but it's got to be exhausting. Maybe I should go stay with her? Let Ms. Aurora get some rest."

Mack gave her an approving smile that warmed Thea to the tips of her toes. "That's sweet of you, but John and Merrilee are staying with Ms. Aurora until their house is ready. They'll help her."

"That's good to know."

"Besides, we have other things we need to take care of."

"What exactly is it we need to do?"

"I figure with Sarah recovered, Judge Wakefield will be pushing for the surgery again very soon."

There was a tone in his voice she hadn't heard often. Irritation? Annoyance? "You're not a big fan of the judge."

Mack glanced over her head, his eyes trained on a building behind her. Thea glanced over her shoulder to where the county's courthouse stood. "He made this whole adoption situation more difficult that it had to be."

An interesting admission from this man. The Mack she'd grown up with never had a bad word to say about anyone. What had changed him? Something about Judge Wakefield bothered Mack more than a little bit. He needed to talk this problem out. Maybe she could be his sounding board. "There's something more to it, isn't there?"

"More to what?"

Now the man was just being evasive. "Why you don't like the judge."

The muscles in Mac's jaw tightened, and she could feel the sudden tension in the air. "I guess it just bothers me the way Judge Wakefield stonewalled me about adopting

Sarah almost since the moment I filed the paperwork. As if he thought I wasn't good enough."

"Why would you think that?"

His humorless chuckle caused a pang of pain near her heart. "Because he gave me one reason after another why I wasn't capable of raising a child, the biggest reason being that I'm a single man." Mack's lips flattened into a grimace. "He felt that a little girl needed a mother in order to be brought up properly. The judge thought I'd be cheating Sarah out of the family she deserves."

"But having a mother doesn't guarantee you're going to raise the perfect child. I mean, look at my sister." Thea felt Mack watching her and glanced up at him. He'd stopped glaring at the courthouse and was watching her with that same stubborn protectiveness he always showed toward her when her sister was mentioned. Her heart overflowed with affection and tenderness. If only he could find a way to love her. "Still, the judge did apologize."

"When?"

She playfully swatted Mack's arm. "At our wedding, silly man."

"He did?" His blue eyes turned almost black, a pale light rimming the irises drew her deeper into his gaze. "I was kind of preoccupied at that moment."

Her heart fluttered to a wild beat in her chest. It almost sounded as if he didn't regret this marriage to her, as if he was open to the possibilities a life with her could bring. Could Mack ever care more for her than the friendship they'd rekindled between them after all these years? Was it possible Mack might love her someday?

No, her mother's voice whispered through her. Why would a man like Mack, so good and decent, someone who could have anyone he wanted, pledge his life to someone like her?

Thea walked slowly toward the crosswalk, not sure if Mack would follow, only knowing she needed to move. She had to make this marriage work for his sake as well as Sarah's. Mack deserved so much more than being forced into a marriage with her.

"Did I say something wrong?" Mack asked as he caught up with her.

She should have expected he would follow her. Mack had never liked seeing her upset, even back in school. He'd always managed to tease a smile out of her or make her laugh after a rough night at her house. He was the only reason she'd made it through some pretty bad days back then. Thea shook her head. "No, it was kind of sweet, really. Like something Cary Grant might say."

One blond eyebrow quirked high on his forehead. "I'm betting that if Mr. Grant had said that, you wouldn't have taken off as if your life depended on it."

"Probably not," she teased, pressing a gloved finger to her cheek. "But then, he is quite handsome."

His face collapsed into a sorrowful expression but his eyes twinkled with playfulness. "You wound me, dear lady."

The laughter she'd worked so hard to suppress bubbled up in her throat. "I'm so sorry. That was rude of me to walk away from you like that." She struggled to find the right words. "You don't have to sweet-talk me."

"I didn't know I was." The laughter slowly drained from his eyes. "There was a lot going on that day. It was more an honest observation than anything."

"Oh." Disappointment flooded through her. She was

just being a romantic idiot, twisting Mack's words to mean something they obviously didn't.

Thea had to contain the light shiver that ran the length of her spine when Mack gently touched the small of her back and guided her across the street. "We've already stood through two lights. Folks are beginning to notice."

They'd been standing there that long? Thea glanced around and noticed a couple of older ladies on the other side of the street stealing looks at them. The same kind of looks she'd gotten whenever she'd come to town with Eileen. Had they heard the false rumors going around town about her and Mack? Had they already tried her and found her guilty before she'd even been given a chance to clear his name?

"Good afternoon." Mack tipped his hat toward the ladies. "Nice day to get your errands done."

The darker-haired woman looked as though she'd swallowed her gum, but the silvery blonde gave them a friendly smile. "Yes, it is, Sheriff, and not too cold just yet. I can't handle the cold. My arthritis, you know."

"Yes, ma'am. I remember."

The woman took a cautious step forward as though she thought Thea might bite. "It's good to see you back on your feet. Zelda was just telling me you were under the weather a couple of weeks."

I bet that wasn't all Miss Zelda was saying. Thea shouldn't feel like this, but she'd had enough experience with people to know better. Thea shifted away from Mack but his hand remained firmly at her waist, almost possessive, as if he was staking his claim.

"That's true, Miss Helen. I was in bed with the chicken pox, as were all of Ms. Aurora's children. Fortunately, we had a wonderful nurse to care for us while we recovered."

Mack gave her a grateful grin that made her stomach do little flips. "Ladies, I'd like you to meet my wife, Thea. Thea, this is Helen and Zelda Shirley. They moved down from Chattanooga to work over at the bomber plant."

"We *did* work at the bomber plant until the war department cut our shift," Miss Zelda muttered.

"Now, sister," Miss Helen cajoled, then she turned back to Thea and Mack, an apologetic smile on her face. "We should be counting our blessings that this horrible war is finally over and that our boys are coming home."

"And our girls," Mack added. "Thea here was an army nurse. Followed the troops onshore at Normandy."

That bit of information sent Miss Helen to twittering. "How exciting, and oh, how brave you must be! I guess a chicken pox epidemic is boring compared to what you must have seen."

"Both can be challenging." Thea slid Mack a teasing glance. "It all depends on who your patient is."

Miss Helen glanced from one to the other so fast, Thea was sure her eyes must hurt from the exertion. "Well, it must have been exciting, seeing how the two of you are married now."

So, word of their nuptials had gotten around. How fast would word get around town if anyone ever learned the truth, that Mack had married Thea to adopt baby Sarah? What would folks say then? *One more thing I have to leave up to You, Lord.*

"All I have to say," Miss Zelda started, glaring at Thea, "is marry in haste, repent at leisure."

"Sister!"

"Well, it's true."

Miss Helen's cheeks flushed a deep red. "You'll have to ignore Zelda. She's got the manners of a billy goat."

Thea could think of another barnyard animal the older woman emulated more. "That's all right, Miss Helen. I believe in complete honesty." Thea gave Miss Zelda her sweetest smile. "That way, I know exactly where I stand."

Mack choked on a chuckle beside her. Miss Helen gasped while Miss Zelda studied Thea for a long moment, then nodded, something close to respect glimmering in her eyes.

"Ladies," Mack said. "I hate to break this up but Thea and I still have an errand to run before we need to get home, so if you'll excuse us."

Miss Helen nodded. "Of course, Sheriff. It was nice to meet you, Thea."

Thea smiled. "Nice to meet you, too."

As her younger sister walked away, Miss Zelda lingered, finally holding out her hand to Thea. "Pleasure to meet you, young lady. And thank you for serving your country the way you did. We appreciate it."

Thea took her hand and gave it a firm shake. "Thank you."

She and Mack watched as Miss Zelda limped over toward her sister, then turned and headed down the sidewalk. Mack gave a low whistle and shook his head. "Thought I was going to have to break up a tussle there for a moment."

Oh, dear. Thea hadn't thought how this episode might embarrass him. "I'm so sorry, Mack. I wasn't thinking how this might look for you."

"Are you kidding? That woman's been a burr in everyone's side since the second she and her sister got off the train." Her skin tingled when he pushed a dislodged curl behind her ear. "But you, you had her tamed in a matter of seconds."

"I'm not so sure she's tamed. All I did was be honest with her."

"Well, that was enough to earn her respect." Mack took her elbow and leaned closer, his breath a soft rustle against her ear. "I was mighty proud of the way you handled yourself."

Mack was proud of her? How was that even possible? Her presence at Ms. Aurora's house, as innocent as it was, had caused a scandal that could have robbed him of his livelihood and his one chance to adopt Sarah. Of course, this marriage gave him what he wanted most, the opportunity to raise Sarah. But children grew up. One day in the not so distant future, Sarah would leave home and build a life of her own. What would become of their marriage then?

"I can hear that brain of yours working all the way over here."

She shook her head slightly. "Just thinking."

"Want to talk about it?"

"It's nothing." Thea pushed the thoughts away and focused on the present. "What exactly is this errand we're supposed to be on?"

"We kind of got sidetracked, didn't we?" He maneuvered her around a parked car and across a deserted side street. "Anyway, Sarah's not going back to Ms. Aurora's after the surgery, not if we want to keep her from catching something else. I know you've been painting the nursery but if we want to get the social worker's approval we really do need to look at buying a baby bed and stuff."

"You're right." And here she'd been thinking of something of a more romantic nature, like another trip out to Lover's Pass. She should have known better. Thea unclenched her hands. "You know, we've already got that dresser in the guest bedroom that's not being used. I thought I'd sew some padding together and make the top of it into a changing table so we wouldn't have to go out and spend money on one."

"I hadn't thought of that. I'd picked out a crib for her before we got married, but it's up to you. I know you'll want to make it perfect for Sarah." He hesitated, and for a moment Thea thought she caught a glimpse of color in his cheeks. "I'm not real good at this decorating stuff. I only bought the house right off the town square because I wanted Sarah close by to where I work so I can drop in on her during the day, maybe take her to the park in the evenings."

Thea tried to drum up some degree of annoyance, but how could she? Mack not only wanted to be a part of Sarah's life, he'd planned his life around her. What a blessed little girl she was, to have that certainty of Mack's love. What must that feel like, to be loved so completely, so unconditionally by this man? Maybe, one day, she might have that kind of love, the kind of family she'd always wanted with this man who was so good and kind, better than she deserved. If he offered her a chance at love, she'd embrace it with her whole being.

And if he couldn't love her? She'd take whatever he was willing to offer as long as she could stay with him and Sarah.

Thea cleared her throat. "Well, if you want me to, I could stop by Mr. Hice's department store and make a list of the items I think we'll need. Then we could talk it over at dinner tonight."

"I was kind of wanting to do the shopping together. Maybe pick out something that we both liked."

It was such a sweet gesture, the kind of thing a real married couple would do together as a way of welcoming their new baby into their home. Thea could almost envision Mack sitting cross-legged on the floor, wrestling with the directions for the crib while she folded each diaper and nightgown, all the tiny bibs and playsuits, and arranged them lovingly in the dresser, anticipating the arrival of their little one.

Oh, dear! She really needed to stop daydreaming like that before Mack figured it out.

"I took the afternoon off so that we could do this together."

An entire afternoon with Mack! Thea intended to savor every moment. "I was in Hice's Department Store the other day and noticed they had a nice selection of baby things. Why don't we go there and have a look first, then decide where else we might like to go?"

Mack gave her an easy smile. "Sounds like a plan to me."

"Good." Thea took a step in the direction of the store but Mack's hand at her elbow stayed her. She tilted her head back to look at him. "What is it?"

"I just wanted you to know."

Her pulse quickened. "Yes?"

"When I decide to sweet-talk you," he whispered, his blue eyes pinning her, robbing her of what little breath she had, "you'll definitely know it."

"What would you like to look at first?"

Mack glanced around the baby department of the store and suddenly felt overwhelmed. Along one high wall was every conceivable item a baby would ever need—diapers, washcloths, soaps and blankets in a rainbow of pastel shades, decorated with tiny stitched emblems of ducks, frogs and rabbits. Racks of tiny clothes filled out the area, making him feel like a giant out of one of those fairy tales he read in the evenings to Sarah. Along the other wall, a row of cribs stood at attention, ready for their inspection.

He glanced down at Thea, her expression bright with anticipation and excitement. "It's a lot to take in."

Thea leaned into his arm and gave him a playful shove that sent his senses reeling. "We're not buying out the entire store, silly man. Just the necessities."

That was a relief. He wasn't sure his bank account could take another hit so soon after buying a house. "Do babies really need all this stuff?"

Thea shook her head. "Babies just need to eat, sleep and be kept warm and clean. And, of course, be loved."

"And this?" Mack swept his arm out to take in the entire section.

"For the parents. Makes them feel like they know what they're doing."

Mack gave a bark of laughter. It was nice to hear a woman say exactly what she thought. "Then what would you suggest we look at first?"

"The crib you picked out would be a good start."

"This way." He held out his elbow to her, the air crackling between them as she looped her arm through his, her hand a warm weight. It felt so natural to be with her like this. But he couldn't help worrying that the fragile relationship they were building might crumble at any moment.

The letter from Mrs. Williams burned a hole in his pocket. What would Thea do with the letter? Would it change how she looked at Sarah, at their marriage? Mack knew how he felt. Thea was the only mother Sarah needed, and the only woman he wanted as his wife.

"What do you think of this one?"

Mack jerked himself out of his thoughts and glanced at

the cherrywood baby bed Thea was examining. "Looks like one of the jail cells down at the county lockup."

She shot him a quelling look. "This is important."

Goodness gracious, but she was taking this much too seriously. "It's a crib, Thea."

"Where Sarah will sleep for a third of her day, every day for the next two years or so."

A third of her day? How had she come up with that number? Eight hours in a twenty-four hour day is... Mack studied her with new appreciation. "I'd never thought of it that way."

Thea pushed up on the railing then gently slid it down to the floor. "It's something my nursing professor told me right before she began scheduling our class for thirty-six hour shifts." Her lips turned up in an impish grin. "Guess she didn't figure nursing students fit into that category."

"Understaffed sheriffs don't, either." Mack walked over to the other side of the crib and stretched his arms across the top of the railing. "Did you like nursing school?"

"It was all right. A means to an end." She pressed her hand into the mattress as if to test it, then nodded. "My clinicals were particularly tough because the staff at the hospital where I studied relied on nursing students to pick up the slack. I don't think I slept for the entire two years I was in school."

"Then you joined the army and didn't sleep for four more."

"That's about the gist of it." Her eyes sparkled with humor as she turned and walked over to the crib behind him.

Mack twisted around, the fragrance of ginger and sweet tea floating around him as she moved closer, the urge to take her hand, tug her into his arms and kiss her almost unbearable. But common sense stopped him.

Their marriage was an arrangement, a "means to an end" as she put it. The thought of the years ahead, married yet not truly in a marriage with Thea, left him feeling more alone than he thought possible. At least he'd be Sarah's father, but even that wasn't enough, not when he loved Thea more than he ever could have believed.

"What about you? Do you like being the sheriff?

He shrugged. "I guess. It pays the bills."

Thea glanced back at him. "That doesn't sound like you."

Of all the things she could have said, he wasn't expecting that one. "How would you know that? You haven't been around for the last eight years."

"Maybe, but I know you used to pore over law books when you didn't think anyone was watching. And you interned during the summer with Judge Huffman your junior and senior year so he'd write you a recommendation for college." Thea turned and leaned back against the crib's railing. "You were always so passionate about going to college and then to law school. What happened?"

Mack's gut tightened. Wasn't this the opening he'd wanted, to come clean and be honest about that night? If he wanted a future with Thea, he needed to tell her what had happened to put his life on a different course. Discussing it in the baby section of the town's department store just hadn't been his plan.

"I shouldn't have asked you that. It's none of my business."

Mack reached out and took her hand, her cool tapered fingers a balm to emotions roiling around inside him.

Mack cleared his throat. "I didn't go to college because I couldn't afford it."

A tiny line of confusion formed between her perfectly

arched brows. "But you had a full scholarship to play football."

He'd hoped she wouldn't remember that part. "After my car accident, the doctors wouldn't sign a medical release. So the university rescinded their offer."

Her face paled. "You were that badly injured? A doctor would only do that if you had a long-term medical issue or if there was a risk of doing further injury to yourself."

Mack gave a humorless snort. "Yeah, that's what the doctors told me, too."

Thea's gaze shifted to the area where the scar lay hidden under his hair. "From the placement of the injury, they must have thought you'd lose your eyesight or your hearing."

Mack couldn't help the slight smile. Thea always had been sharp as a knife. "Cochlear concussion, they called it. I'm partially deaf."

Thea's eyes widened, her creamy skin a ghostly white, concern etched in her expression. She nibbled at her lip as if to keep it from trembling. "That must have been a horrible accident."

"It didn't look too bad at the time. The doctors were more concerned with my broken jaw than anything." He hesitated. "Then I noticed I couldn't hear what was going on right beside me. That's when the doctors sent me for a hearing test and discovered the problem. They felt that there was a chance another blow to my head would make me completely deaf in that ear."

And there it was. That look on her face was the reason he hated telling anyone what had happened to him. Who wanted to be pitied? To have their lives defined by one random moment? Pity colored how people viewed him, how he saw himself.

As if he were less of a person. Sometimes it felt as if he'd never been that boy Thea had known back in high school. The accident had taken more than his hearing and his dreams of being a lawyer. It had taken a part of his very soul.

Consider it all joy, My brethren, when you encounter various trials.

Okay, God, I get it. You never promised life would be a rose garden. But when does this trial end so that I can experience the joy?

"You could still go to college."

Mack grimaced. *He* was the one with the bad ear, not her. Had she not listened to a word he'd said? "That's not possible."

"Why not?"

"You're not serious." Mack jerked his head around toward her. Everything from her earnest gaze to the determined set of her jaw spoke of her sincerity. "I'm almost completely deaf in my right ear."

"Someone once told me that nothing worth having ever comes easily." Her blue-gray eyes challenged him.

Leave it to Thea to remember some motto he'd tossed out at her when things were tough back in high school. But, as much as he hated to admit it, there was a grain of truth to what she said. "I thought nurses were supposed to have the gift of mercy."

"Sometimes it's more merciful to be honest than to allow someone to drown in self-pity."

Ouch! Mack stepped back as her words sank in. Was that what he'd been doing, wallowing in self-pity? He thought for a moment. Why hadn't he found another way to go to school when the scholarship fell through? Had it been easier to not try rather than face his limitations every day in the classroom?

But it was too late for him. He'd missed his chance. He had a house payment, a job, and a wife and daughter. Or was he just using them as more excuses not to try?

Pinpricks of awareness raced up his arm as she joined him, her warm hand closing over his. "I'm sorry, Mack. Sorry that you had to go through all of that. But I believe in you, and if you want to go to school, we'll find a way."

Thea wanted to give him his dream. Before he knew what he was doing, Mack grasped her hand and tugged her into his arms, all the hurt and anger over the past few years that had borne down on him finally, blessedly, lifting. She fit neatly under his chin, her feminine curves a perfect match for the hard plains of his body, the scent of ginger and tea invading his senses as she nestled closer. "Aw, Thea. I can always count on you to tell me what you think about things, even when it's hard for me to hear."

The brim of her hat softly bumped his chin as she tilted her head back. "Then, can I tell you something?"

Mack braced himself. No telling what the woman might say this time. "What's that?"

Thea tilted her head back, that impish grin he was coming to adore flashing at him. She nodded toward the crib behind her. "I love this baby bed."

A bark of laughter erupted from Mack's throat. The next hour flew by as they looked through bedding and blankets, diapers and safety pins, bottles and bibs. A seemingly endless pile of baby items awaited them as they followed the sales clerk to the register. As the order was being rung up, Mack turned to ask Thea a question but she wasn't there. He scoured the clothing racks before finally finding her in a small selection of rocking chairs at the corner of the department.

Mark turned back to the clerk. "Can you wait just a moment? I may need to add something to the bill."

The young woman's smile brightened. "Of course. Take all the time you need."

Mack skirted around the racks until he stood just a few feet from Thea, sitting in one of the rocking chairs lining the wall. Sooty lashes rested gently against the curve of her cheek, several strands of silky blond hair fell free from their place behind her ear, giving her a mussed look that was in perfect contrast to the orderly woman Mack knew her to be. Life and experiences had changed her, molded her into the strong, capable woman she'd become. Yet Mack sensed a vulnerability beneath her strength, and a heart for others that risked being hurt. A surge of protectiveness welled up inside him. He would do whatever it took to keep her heart from being broken.

Even at the risk of my own.

Her eyelids fluttered open, the soft dreamy look in her eyes tugging at his heart. "Did I fall asleep again?"

"Looks like it." Mack slipped down into a chair next to her. "Maybe you need to have Beau check you out."

She drew in a deep breath through her nose and stretched her back into a slight arch before resting back against the chair. "Got to grab some shuteye whenever you can."

Mack glanced around. "Even in a department store?"

She gave him a gentle smile. "Even in a hedgerow outside of Caen during a forty-seven hour bombing raid and nonstop surgery."

His respect for her grew even more, if that was possible. "Sarah's a lucky little girl to have you for a mother."

Thea tilted her head toward him, the soft glow in her eyes snatching what breath he had. What would it be like to make Thea light up like that for him? "That's a sweet thing to say."

"It's true. You're going to be a wonderful mother."

"I just hope I'm better at it than I was at being a sister."

She'd always done that, beaten herself up over how Eileen had turned out. Maybe Thea was ready to hear a few truths of her own. "You were a great sister, Thea. It was Eileen who had a problem."

"I know. She was hurting so much." Thea drew in a defeated breath. "Maybe if I'd been here when Sarah was born, things would have turned out differently."

"You don't know that." He couldn't stand to see her blame herself for Eileen's decisions. Mack reached out and covered her hand, surprised when her fingers threaded through his as if by habit. "Your sister probably would have given up her baby, anyway."

"Maybe, but I'd like to think that eventually she would have learned from her mistakes. That she'd grow up and find love, real love, with somebody who wouldn't ever think to let her go."

"She did."

Thea glanced over at him. "What?"

Mack couldn't believe no one had told her. Not even him. Customarily, he wouldn't give out information on other victims in a car accident. But it was important Thea knew the truth of the night her sister died. "Eileen didn't die by herself in the accident. Gene Allgood was with her that night. His parents said they were on their way to the justice of the peace."

Thea's eyes glittered. "Eileen was getting married?" Her fingers felt cool against his as he squeezed her hand. "I never found a marriage license at the scene of the accident, but Mr. Allgood said his son had been seeing Eileen since he'd come back from the war. They'd been dating about a year when they died." They rocked in silence for long moments before Mack spoke again. "I really thought someone had already let you know. I'm so sorry I didn't tell you."

"You have nothing to be sorry about."

It didn't seem like that to him, not when he could feel the pain she bore. "But…"

She interrupted. "You just told me my sister had found love, was on her way to get married to the man she loved. I remember Gene from Sunday school. He was a good guy who loved the Lord. Maybe he took Eileen to church. Maybe she had a chance to meet the One who loved her most of all."

Thea would look at the situation that way, with a hope and optimism no one else who'd gone through what she had would lay claim to. It was one of the many reasons he loved her. Mack reached into his pocket. Maybe now was the time to give her Mrs. Williams's letter and resolve Eileen's memory once and for all—so they could move on from it together.

"Mack, would you mind if we checked on Momma? I don't like the idea of her being out there in that house all alone."

"We can run her back over to Ms. Aurora's." Leaving the envelope in his pocket, Mack pushed to his feet. Then they would go home, and he'd lay his heart out to her. Tell her he wanted their marriage to be real.

Mack could only pray she wanted that, too.

Chapter Fourteen

Thea straightened in the passenger seat and stared out over the inky blackness yawning before her. "I sure did have a good time with you today."

Mack glanced over at her as he turned the squad car out of the square. "Are you saying you usually have a bad time with me?"

She laughed. "You're fishing for a compliment."

"No, I'm not." But there was a teasing quality to his voice, a playfulness that almost made her think she was back in high school. "I just like to know I can still show a lady a good time."

"Taking her shopping for a crib. That's always a good first date."

"Hey, don't forget the rocker."

"Sarah is going to love that rocking chair, especially when she doesn't feel so well and she wants to cuddle."

They fell into spurts of conversation followed by moments of companionable silence that felt so easy. Within minutes, they were working their way through the shadows until they reached the smooth surface of the paved road.

Mack broke the awkward silence. "Do you smell that?"

Thea sniffed, the taste of salt and something acrid coating her throat. "Is that smoke?"

In the dim light of the dashboard, Mack reached down and unhooked the receiver from its place next to the radio and brought it to his mouth. "Myrtle, this is Mack. I'm out on Cheathem Hill, and there's a distinct smell of smoke in the air. Has anyone called in to report a fire out here?"

The radio cracked and hissed for what seemed like an eternity before Myrtle replied. "Just got a call in. Sent the fire crew to number twelve Cheathem Hill Road."

Number twelve! The air shot out of Thea's lungs as if she'd been struck by a baseball bat. Frantic, she pushed herself up to the edge of the seat and dug her nails into the leather dashboard as she searched the darkening sky for signs of smoke. "Momma."

The radio receiver dropped to the floor at her feet, then Mack's strong arm pushed her back into the seat as he gunned the engine. "Hang on, sweetheart. We're almost there."

Time slowed to a crawl as the world narrowed, her heart pounding out a frantic beat in her ears, her palms moist beneath her gloves. A glimmer of light sparked through the trees up ahead, growing as they drew nearer. When Mack pulled into the front yard, Thea opened the door and jumped out even before the car slowed to a stop. Reddish-gold flames shot high above the treetops in the rear of the house, casting an eerie silhouette against the night sky. Embers floated in the air like the lightning bugs she and Eileen used to chase across the front yard as children. A loud crack to her right caught her attention and she watched as the awning crashed into the front porch railings, sending sparks high into the air.

"Momma!" Thea dashed from one end of the house to the other, then surged forward.

A familiar pair of arms caught her around the waist and pulled her back against his chest. "You can't go in there."

"But Momma's in there, Mack."

"I know, sweetheart," he whispered against her ear. "But let's look at this a moment and see if there's a way we can get your mother out without getting either of us killed."

Mack was thinking of going into that inferno? No! What if something happened to him? How could she live if he walked into the flames and never returned? Thea looped her arms around his waist and hung on for dear life. "You can't go in there."

"Listen to me." Mack gave her a gentle shake that caught her attention. "I have to do this, you know that. But you're going to have to let me go if we want any chance at saving your mom."

Thea knew what he said was true. No matter how hard she fought him, eventually he'd go in after her mother. It was his nature, to protect those under his care even unto death. It didn't make it any easier for her to let him go.

Mack studied the house for a long moment. "It looks like the fire started in the back right-hand corner, near the kitchen."

Thea nodded, her eyes burning from the smoke. "But Momma doesn't stay in there much. At night, she usually sits in the front parlor and listens to the radio while she knits. Maybe that's what she was doing instead of packing." Thea didn't know the woman her mother had become in her absence.

Mack eased his hold just a bit as if he didn't trust her not to bolt. "Do you have a rain barrel?"

"Over there, under the downspout, but…" She grasped the arms that held her. "Let's check around first. Maybe she got out on her own."

"I don't have time to argue with you about this." He circled her wrists in one hand and gently pulled her toward the back of the car and opened the trunk. In the distance, the sound of sirens filled the night air. After a brief search, Mack pulled two snowy-white cloth diapers from their recent purchases and wadded them up in his hand. "Rain barrel?"

She pointed to the far corner of the house. "Mack, please."

"Stay here, Thea or I'll handcuff you to the car."

Of all the… "Fine, go get yourself burnt to a crisp."

Mack cut her next words short as he trapped her chin between his thumb and forefinger and stepped closer, the lines of his handsome face blurring into a pleasant haze. Her breath caught as he lowered his head, his lips a gentle brush against his own before settling over her mouth in a too-brief kiss.

She felt disoriented by the time he lifted his head and pressed something into her hand. "This is for you, sweetheart, with all my love."

Before she could react, he ran across the yard to the rain barrel then, with wet cloths in hand, Mack disappeared into the fiery inferno.

Mack pressed the wet cloth against his nose and mouth, and sucked in a heavy breath, the heat pressing at him from all sides, as if he'd stepped inside a raging furnace. A watery film formed over his stinging eyes. The smoky fog that settled in the front hallway grew thick and dark toward the back of the house, tiny flames licking the doorway to the kitchen.

He didn't have much time. When lit, these old houses went up like seasoned kindling. He only had a few minutes, maybe less, to find Mrs. Miller and get them to safety.

Father God, help me find her.

He turned left, took a quick look around the dining room then headed to the room across the hall. Dust motes stirred in the murky air, a cloud of whitish gray smoke billowing from the lit fireplace, piles of folded paper crinkled like an accordion into black ash. With one corner of the wet cloth, he wiped soot out of his eyes and glanced around. In a wingback chair near the hearth sat Mrs. Miller, her head slumped to one side, her mouth gaping open, the irregular rise and fall of her chest a sign she was breathing, but just barely.

Mack hurried across the room, knelt down in front of the woman and folded the other wet cloth he'd been holding against her face as he tied it into place. "Hang on, Mrs. Miller. I'm going to get you out of here."

A loud crack beside him split the opposite wall into two sections, fiery fingers burning a path along the seam up to the ceiling. Time was running out. Grabbing her hands, Mack dragged the woman to the edge of the chair, planted his shoulder against her midsection and lifted her onto his shoulder. He shifted her weight to get a firmer grip on her then turned.

The smoke had thickened, leaving the room obscured in shades of black and gray. He moved forward until his knee connected with the blunt end of a table, and then he retreated. Without a clear path, there was no way he could get them to the hall and out the front door. Mack's lungs tightened, his nose and throat on fire despite the make-shift mask plastered to his face. Watery tears blurred his vision, and his legs wobbled underneath him.

The imagine of Thea, the devastation he'd seen in her expression as they'd pulled up to the house, pushed to the front of his thoughts. She'd lost so much already—her father, her sister. Mack would do everything in his power to help save the only person in this world she had left.

Please, God, for Thea's sake.

A glimmer of light from a nearby window caught his eye. Heat closed in around them, the struggle to put one foot in front of the other becoming more difficult as he pushed toward the exit. Mack punched the elbow of his free arm through the glass, felt a sharp sting against his back as he stepped across the window sill. Drops of water sizzled against his skin, his lungs bursting for air. Just a few more steps…

"Mack!"

Thea! He opened his mouth to speak but the words caught in his parched throat. His legs buckled and he collapsed to his knees. A weight lifted from his shoulders as the darkness he'd tried so hard to evade overwhelmed him.

Thea pushed back a matted lock of hair from Mack's face, her fingers lingering a moment longer than was necessary. Reassured by the steady rise and fall of his chest, she felt his skull, telling herself she was checking for any lumps or cuts the medics might have missed. Though she couldn't deny the comfort she found in touching him, in knowing he'd survived.

Crazy man! What had he been thinking, running into

the growing flames like that? Didn't he know how close he'd come to being killed? How close she'd come to losing him without ever telling him how much she loved him? How much she wanted him in her life? The thought sent a cold shiver down her spine.

"Here's some water for when he comes to." The fireman who had introduced himself as Bobby handed her a glass jug. "The medic just finished checking out your mother. She's fine, though little confused. I do have to ask. Was there a child in the house we didn't know about?"

Thea shook her head. "Why would you ask that?"

"It's just that…" Bobby stopped, as if searching for the right words. "Your mother keeps talking about someone called Eileen and how it's her fault the baby died."

Thea shook her head, the sudden pain that tore through her being almost physical. She remembered what Ms. Aurora had said about the three days Eileen had been in labor. Had Eileen's baby not survived her traumatic delivery? Had her mother buried the loss so deep that she'd latched on to the idea of Sarah as Eileen's baby, even though it wasn't true?

"The medic is giving her some water. Sometimes dehydration can cause confusion, too."

"Thank you, Bobby." Thea swallowed. "I appreciate all you guys have done."

A set of white teeth smiled sympathetically from a soot-stained face. "I just wished we could have saved the house, but these old places go up so fast. It was a wonder Mack was able to get your mother out like he did."

Mack! How would he respond when she told him that Sarah might not be her niece? She drew some measure of comfort watching his chest continue to rise and fall. "Why hasn't he come to yet?"

"Probably got a little smoke inhalation. What he did, going in after your mother, takes a lot out of a person. Give it some time," Bobby said before heading back toward what was left of the house.

All things she knew as a nurse, but knowing it didn't calm the unsettling fear she had. If only Mack would wake up. Thea unbuttoned her coat, tugged it off then folded it and gently lifted Mack's shoulders slightly to angle it under his head as a pillow. She grabbed one of the clean cotton diapers she'd brought from the car and soaked it with water, wringing out the extra fluid before gently wiping away the patches of soot on Mack's face.

Even wearing grit and cinders, he was still the most handsome man she'd ever known. Smoky lines of soot marred the intelligent slash of his brow as well as the high cheekbones that were a throwback to some Cherokee ancestor. She skimmed the cloth down the ridge of his nose and detected a small knot unnoticeable to the eye. When had Mack broken his nose? As a boy in a playground scuffle? Or maybe later in his duties as sheriff? Thea shivered at the other dangers Mack might have faced.

She stilled as she came to his mouth, the memory of that brief kiss before he ran into the flames making her lips tingle even now. Well, maybe it was more of a brush of his lips against hers but she'd felt it down to the deepest depths of her soul. Her pulse picked up speed. What would it be like if she never had the chance to kiss him again? Never had the opportunity to bask in the warmth of his smile again? Her heart would never recover.

"Like what you see?"

Thea lifted her gaze and met Mack's dark blue eyes. There was a playful gleam in them, as if the past two hours had never happened, but she also found something that hinted her answer mattered to him. The thought sent a tiny thrill up her spine. She sniffled and leaned close, pushing her hands through his hair. "Are you fishing for a compliment?"

"Would that be so bad?"

Thea shook her head. "After what you've done, I don't think there would be enough words to tell you…" The thought of what could have happened, of all that had changed in the course of the last hour, clogged her throat.

"Come on, you can do better than that."

"I know what you're doing, trying to get my mind off of…" She waved her hand toward the burning structure. "That."

"Thea, you can do this."

His way was probably better than her making a fool over herself. Thea sat back on her heels as if she needed to get a better look. If the man was fishing for a compliment, she'd certainly give him one. "You're…passable."

"That's it? Just passable?" He leaned up on his elbows, his face within a whisper of hers.

Maybe she should lean forward just a hair and kiss him. Her heart stepped up a beat at the thought. "You know you're terribly handsome."

Her breath caught as he came even closer, his handsome features blurred. "I'm glad you think so."

Her eyelids fluttered shut, his warm breath a soft caress against her cheek. The fear she'd felt as he'd run into the burning house seized her again. She could have just as easily lost him. *Thank You, Lord, for this man.*

"How's he doing?"

Thea pulled away, heat rushing up her neck and into her cheeks as she glanced up at the fireman. She sat back, her hands pressed into the folds of her skirt. "The patient is doing fine."

"Patient, huh?" Mack whispered with a hint of laughter in his voice.

"Good," Bobby answered, then addressed Mack. "You gave the little lady here quite a scare. She was worried sick."

"Nice quality for a man's *wife* to have, don't you think, Bobby?"

The man glanced at Thea, then looked at Mack and gave him a crooked grin. "I thought I heard something about you getting married. Congratulations." He turned and headed back toward the men near the house.

"You were a little worried about me?"

"Maybe," she conceded. She'd been more than a little worried. She'd been frantic. Why wouldn't she be? She loved him, more than she'd ever believed it was possible to love another person. The man had been willing to risk his life to save her mother, knowing the kind of person the woman was. Knowing what she had done with Eileen's first child.

If Mack did ever come to love her, he wouldn't care what other people thought about her family, only how he felt about her. That was why she loved him so completely. Is that why she'd gone through with this marriage? Because she knew at her very core that there would never be another man she could make her wedding vows to?

"How's your mother?"

Thea cleared her throat. "Fine. The medics checked her out but want to take her to the hospital as a precautionary measure."

"Good." Mack took a deep breath to Thea's relief.

"She was breathing kind of shallow when I found her. I wondered if she had some smoke inflation."

"No, just mad she's got to go to the hospital." She glanced toward the ambulance. "I'm surprised they haven't been over here to get you ready for the ride back into town."

Mack tried to chuckle but it came out as a cough. "I'm not bottling up the ER on the count of my sorry hide when there are others in the community who need to be seen."

That's what he thought. Didn't he realize he'd been unconscious for a spell? Smoke inhalation, concussion, each possibility worse than the last, shuffled through Thea's mind. Whether Mack liked it or not, he needed to be checked out by a doctor. "You're going, and that's it."

A stubborn glint flared in Mack's eyes. "It'll just be a waste of time."

Well, bullying only made him dig in his heels even deeper. Maybe there was a more persuasive way to convince him. Thea leaned forward and pressed her cheek against his, the stark smell of smoke a reminder of what she could have lost. She whispered softly into his good ear. "Please, Mack. I couldn't live with myself if something happened to you. Do it for me. And for Sarah. She's lost so much already. Don't take a chance of her losing you, too."

His jaw loosened slightly against hers. "All right, Thea. I'll do it. For you both."

Chapter Fifteen

In the end, Mack got Thea to compromise. No hospital but Beau agreed to meet them at their place after Thea got her mother settled in at the hospital for the night.

"The Lord was watching out for you this evening, Mack," Beau said a couple of hours later as he tossed his stethoscope around his neck and made notes on a piece of paper resting on the coffee table. "What possessed you to run into that house in the first place? From what I hear, it was almost fully engulfed by the time the fire department got there."

"Mrs. Miller was in there."

He'd like to think he would have done the same for any of the folks in his county, hoped he'd respond in the same way as he had tonight. But he wouldn't be honest with himself if he didn't admit the prospect of Thea losing her mother had played a very definite role in his response tonight. The look of absolute devastation that marred her expression in those first few moments after their arrival, the look of complete and total loss haunted him even now. She had borne so much in her life—

losing her father, then her sister. Her nephew and niece. If she'd lost her mother, too…

Mack grimaced. But wasn't that what was happening already? Mrs. Miller hadn't been herself in months, even before Eileen had died. The confusion only seemed to grow worse with each passing day. What if Thea had been at home in bed asleep when the fire broke out? Would Mrs. Miller even have remembered her daughter? The thought sent a shudder through him. No wonder Thea clung to the hope Sarah was her niece. The child would be the only family she had left.

I will never leave you or forsake you.

Mack had held fast to that verse in the days after his father and his mother had died. Still, he remembered the deafening silence of his parents' house in the months after Mom's death, the feeling of being totally alone. No one who shared your history. No one to call your own.

Well, he was Thea's family now, and he'd be there for her. All the days of their lives, if she'd let him. She wouldn't have to bear her mother's illness alone.

"How's our patient doing?"

The men glanced up to see Edie Daniels walking quietly toward them, a tray of sandwiches and sugar cookies along with a pot of coffee in her hands. Mack had once fancied himself in love with the beautiful engineer, but what he felt for Thea filled up parts of his heart he hadn't known existed until she'd come back into his life. If tonight had taught him anything, it was that whatever time he had left on this Earth he wanted to spend it loving Thea.

Beau moved the papers to a side table, then stood and hurried to take the tray from his wife. "You shouldn't be carrying something that heavy."

"Really, Beau." Edie flashed her husband a teasing smile. "I'm not going to break."

"Maybe," he answered as he dropped a kiss on her brow. "But you're the only wife I want so I'm not going to take any chances."

The tender look they exchanged made Mack duck his head. Beau's life had not been an easy one. An abusive father and time in a Germany POW camp had seen to that. But the love he'd found with Edie Michaels and his newfound faith in Christ had changed him, set him on a solid path.

How would Thea's love transform Mack? She'd already brought him through the pain of his disappointment, showed him how to serve others with a glad heart. What other lessons would they learn together as the years passed? Could she ever learn to love him?

Mack glanced toward the doorway that led to the hall. "How's Thea doing?"

"Better than I would have been." Edie filled one cup with coffee and handed it to him. "She wanted to get out of those smoky clothes and freshen up a bit before she joined us."

It felt as if she'd been gone forever. Probably a reaction to this evening, but he wanted to be close in case she needed him. "Could you go and check on her? She's had a rough night and I'd feel better if I knew she was okay."

Edie studied him as if he were one of those building plans she used to draw for the War Department, then nodded to her husband before standing and heading down the hall.

Mack glanced over at Beau. "I might have breathed in my share of smoke tonight, but what was that look all about?"

His friend chuckled as he reached for the coffeepot.

"We had a friendly argument going, and my darling wife thinks she's won."

Mack wasn't sure he wanted to know, but curiosity got the better of him. "What was the argument?"

Beau glanced down the hall, then settled back, taking his cup with him. "Edie said you would fall in love with Thea."

Mack raked a hand through his hair and chuckled. And he thought he'd played it so smooth. That made him laugh even harder. "How did she figure that out?"

"She recognizes that dog-eared look a man gets when he's pining after a woman." A cloud of steam rose as Beau blew across the hot liquid before taking it to his lips. "Met, matched and married, all within a month. That's pretty quick."

"Eight years and a month, but then who was counting?"

"I told Thea you had a thing for her back in high school, but she said it was my imagination." He took another sip. "I have to say, since she's been back, I've seen more of that guy who didn't have a huge chip on his shoulder."

Mack rubbed his eye. Had he really been that awful? Probably, yeah. "I didn't know how to handle what had happened to me. The accident, losing my chance to go to school. It was a lot for me to lose."

"You blamed Thea."

He was ashamed to admit he had. It had been easier than facing the truth, that he'd caused the wreck that cost him any hopes he'd had for the future. "I realized I was wrong. The accident was all my fault."

"I'm glad you figured that out. Maybe now, you'll consider going to school and becoming a lawyer just like you always talked about doing." Beau nodded slowly as if mulling over that particular piece of information. "Though, after tonight, you may have a hard time convincing the town council to let you out of your contract."

"So now they want to keep me on as sheriff?"

"Are you kidding? You're a hero." Beau laughed. "What do you want to do?"

Mack knew what he wanted. He wanted everyone gone so he could finally tell his wife how much he loved her. Kiss her the way he'd been dreaming of since the day they got married. Try to convince her to make their marriage a real one with children and laughter and love. Years and years of love.

Mack glanced over at his friend. "Thea thinks I should go back to school, too."

"So you told her about the accident?"

"Ms. Aurora convinced me I should." Mack set his cup back on the tray. "But the more I talked to Thea about it, the more I realized I'd blamed her because life hadn't turned out exactly as I'd planned."

"It never does. But I've learned the hard way that God takes whatever mess we make out of things and works it to our good and His glory."

Boy, wasn't that the truth, Mack thought, though even a few weeks ago, he couldn't possibly have seen the good in the past eight years. Looking back, he would only wonder at God's faithfulness in the face of his anger. Maybe it was past time he talked to the Lord about it.

"So, what are you going to do?"

Mack's shoulder ached when he shrugged. "It depends on what Thea wants."

"And if Thea wants you?"

"Then I'll spend the rest of my life making sure she never regrets it."

The Baby Barter

Beau reached for a sandwich. "Yep, I'd say you're in love."

"And if Thea doesn't want that?"

Beau chuckled. "Do you know what my part of the argument with Edie was?"

Hadn't his friend heard him? "Well, if you disagreed with her then that must mean you thought that I wouldn't fall in love with Thea."

"No." He leaned back into the sofa. "I thought that Thea would fall in love with you first."

"You thought that Thea would…" The memory of those first seconds after he'd woken up, the tiny worry lines that were etched in her forehead, the shimmer of tears laced within the dark fullness of her lashes played out in his mind. She'd been more than a little concerned.

Thea cared about him?

Even now, the thought that she might somehow have feelings for him radiated warmth though his veins. It didn't matter how deep her feelings went. They'd have something to build on, caring and trust, a base to work from as partners, friends, someone who was committed to him and to their family.

Thea.

Beau and Edie couldn't leave soon enough for Mack.

Thea glanced around the living room thirty minutes later, her robe pulled tightly around her, the letter Mack had given her in the moments before he'd run into the flames in her pocket. Only after they had returned home and she had escaped to the quiet solitude of her bedroom had she looked at the envelope, the return address reaching out and grabbing her attention.

Mrs. Williams. The woman who'd delivered Sarah. Why had Mack given it to her? What did the letter mean?

As if sensing her presence, Mack opened his eyes, exhaustion and worry lining the area around his forehead. "You okay?"

A slight smile lifted the corners of her mouth as she studied him for any signs of distress that warranted medical attention. "You're the one who ran into a burning building tonight."

"All in a day's work," he quipped.

She glanced down at the two cups stacked neatly on the coffee tray then at Mack. "Did Beau and Edie leave already? I wanted to thank them."

Mack nodded. "They needed to get home, but they wanted me to tell you good-night and that they'll see you in the morning."

"Of course. Edie must have been tired." Instead of coming farther into the room, she stepped behind the rocking chair. It was the only thing keeping her from making a complete fool out of herself by throwing herself into his arms.

Telling him she'd fallen in love with him, that she wanted a real marriage might be more difficult than she'd thought. "How are you feeling? Headache, nausea?"

"I'm okay, sweetheart, really I am." Thea's heart skipped a beat at the endearment. "If Beau had had any reason to worry, he wouldn't have thought twice about admitting me to the hospital."

Thea relaxed for the first time in hours. "Good, but I'm still going to keep my eye on you."

Mack gave her a lopsided grin. "I certainly hope so."

Thea's fingers dug into the rocker's headrest. How could Mack be flirtatious after what he'd gone through tonight? Hadn't he lost enough—his dreams, then tonight, almost losing his life—all because of her family?

"How's your mom?"

Thea drew in a deep breath to steady herself. The reality of her mother's illness had finally sunk in. "The nurse said she's sound asleep from that sedative the doctor gave her. He's going to arrange an appointment with a doctor who specializes in diseases in the elderly. She can't stay by herself anymore."

Mack stood and crossed the short distance to her, wrapping his arm around her waist and drawing her close. "I'd like to go with you to talk to the doctor, if you don't mind."

Thea glanced up at him, startled by the sincerity in his expression. How would Mack feel about her mother when he learned she might have lied about Eileen's child? "Why would you want to do that?"

Mack dropped a gentle kiss on her brow. "We're in this together, aren't we? Come on." He guided her over to the couch, then—still holding her close—sat down beside her.

Mack smoothed her hair away from her face. "Let's think about that tomorrow. There's something else we need to talk about right now."

He wanted to talk about the letter now? Thea pushed a few inches away, anything to put some distance between them. Might as well get this over with.

"Is this about the letter from Mrs. Williams?"

"Yes."

Her heart galloped in her chest. "All right, but first there's something I need to tell you." She wet her lips. "Sarah can't be Eileen's baby. Momma told the paramedic that Eileen's baby died."

"We don't know that that's the truth." Mack pushed a stray curl behind her ear. "All we have is your mother's word, and that's not very reliable."

"You knew?" The question came out strangled and high-pitched. Thea cleared her throat. "When?"

"The day the kids came down with the chicken pox and I went by your house so your mother could pack you a bag. Her thoughts were scattered all over the place so I didn't take her talk about Eileen's child too seriously."

Mack had suspected Sarah wasn't Eileen's since before the wedding, before his proposal? "Why didn't you tell me?"

His thumb feathered lightly over her chin before he cupped her cheek in his hand. "Because we didn't have any real proof and until we had some kind of confirmation, I didn't want to risk hurting you."

That must mean something, but what?

"Do you know why I gave you that letter?"

A sheen of tears sprang to her eyes as she bit her lower lip. "To let me know you knew who Sarah's mother was?"

He shook his head. "I already know who Sarah's mother is." Mack tapped the tip of her nose. "You."

Thea hadn't expected that answer. "Me?"

"Sweetheart, you may not have given birth to her, but Sarah doesn't have any other mother than you."

She was confused. "Then why did you give me the letter?"

"Did you look at it?"

Thea refused to tell him she'd stared at it for the last half hour. "Yes."

"Did you notice anything about it?"

What was there to notice? It was a plain, unopened...

She lifted her eyes to meet his, a spark of hope flaring up inside her. "You didn't open it."

"And I don't plan to. I don't care what it says." Mack reached over and pulled her onto his lap, rocking her back and forth, brushing comforting kisses against her brow. "You poor sweetheart. I really mucked this up, didn't I?"

She sniffed. "I don't know. I think you're doing okay so far."

Mack's laughter rumbled beneath her ear. "When I sent that letter off, I wanted answers about Sarah's mother. And if Sarah was your niece, you needed to know that, too. By the time Mrs. Williams replied, I knew it didn't matter who had given birth to Sarah, only that you were Sarah's mother and that I had fallen very much in love with you."

"Oh, Mack!"

She threw her arms around his neck, her body pressed against his, her tears wet against her cheeks. Mack cradled her head in his hands as he tilted her head back and lowered his mouth to hers.

Several minutes went by before they broke apart, breathless and gasping for air. Thea was still trying to regain her voice when Mack spoke. "I love you, Thea. I love your sweet spirit, and the way you boss me around when I'm sick. I love the way you love our little girl, the way you've always loved your family, so unconditionally."

She buried her face in his shoulder. "I could have lost you tonight."

"But you didn't." He dropped another kiss on her hair.

She lifted her head and met his gaze, his blue eyes dark with longing and just a touch of uncertainty. "I can't stand the thought that you could have died without my telling you how very much I love you."

Mack cradled her cheek, his thumb tracing the path of her tears. "You do?"

Thea leaned into his hand. "I think I've been in love with you since we were in high school. I just didn't know it until now."

All in God's timing. Just like Ms. Aurora said. He kissed her cheeks and the tip of her nose before brushing a soft kiss against her lips. "I sure hope you do, sweetheart, because I love you so much. I want this to be a real marriage."

A brilliant smile graced her lips. "I want that, too, Mack. I want to be your wife."

"Sweetheart, you're more than just my wife. You're the mother of my child. You're my family. And I'll love you forever."

Epilogue

❧

Thea straightened the flat sheet on the baby crib stationed in the hospital room, every corner pulled into a crisp wrinkle-free line, then grabbed the cloth doll from the bedside table and sat it against the railing.

Two muscular arms circled her waist and pulled her back into the familiar warmth of her husband's chest. "You really think she needs the doll?"

"It's her favorite, Mack. She's already going to be in a strange place. I thought it might help."

He dropped a soft kiss on her cheek. "If you think that it will make her feel better, then I'm all for it. I just can't stand to see you so worried."

Thea turned toward him, relaxing against him, her hand pressed to his chest, the sure, steady beat of his heart a comfort to her rattled nerves. "I just need to keep busy. Anything to get my mind off of all the things that could go wrong."

"I've got an idea to help with that." Mack cupped her cheek in his hand, tilted her head back until his lips caught hers.

In the three months since they'd made their marriage

into a real one, Thea had found she never grew tired of Mack's kisses. Or the shoulder he gave her to lean on, or the talks they shared after they'd returned from visiting Sarah every night. If possible, she'd fallen even more in love with him as she watched him tenderly care for their daughter and her mother.

Thea broke off the kiss, slightly thrilled by the disappointment registered on her husband's face, and laid her head back on his chest. "Do you know how much I love you?"

She felt his soft kiss against the top of her head. "Almost as much as I love you?"

Thea started to respond, but a knock on the door interrupted them. A young nurse—Corrine—poked her head around the door. "Mr. and Mrs. Worthington, there's someone here to see you."

Thea lifted her head to look up at Mack. They'd both agreed that until Sarah was further along in her recovery, they would limit her visitors. Besides, the Danielses, Hickses and Davenports were camped outside the delivery room, waiting for Maggie to give birth while Ms. Aurora kept busy with Mrs. Miller and the kids.

"Did they give a name?" Mack asked.

"A Judge Wakefield."

Mack threw Thea a quick look before turning back to the door. "Send him in, please."

"Yes, sir," the young nurse answered.

Thea glanced up at Mack, her knees wobbly beneath her, her hands suddenly cold. "What do you think he's doing here? The last time we talked with him, a couple of weeks ago, he said it might take a few months before we heard anything about finalizing the adoption."

Mack gently backed her into a nearby chair, his hands

on her shoulders as he stood behind her. Almost immediately, she leaned her head back against his midsection, drawing strength from him for whatever news Judge Wakefield brought.

Another knock on the door, and the judge walked in, his overcoat thrown over one arm while in his hand he held his gray felt hat. He bowed his head slightly. "Sheriff, Mrs. Worthington. How's the baby doing?"

"She's in recovery right now," Mack answered. "Dr. Medcalf says the surgery went very well. We should be able to take her home in a few days."

"Good, good." The judge smiled. "I'm glad to hear that."

The knots in Thea's stomach pulled tighter. Why couldn't the man simply tell them whatever news it was he had and be done with it? Why was he drawing this out? Unless he had bad news and didn't know how to tell them.

Mack squeezed her shoulder. The man had to be on pins and needles, yet his first thought was always of her. She reached up, took his hand in hers and gave it a reassuring squeeze. No matter what happened, no matter what life threw at them, Mack was her family, the man of her dreams, her love. They would get through this together.

"I was down this way on another case and thought I'd drop by to give you the news myself."

Thea's chest tightened and she could barely breathe. "What news would that be, Your Honor?"

The judge reached into his coat pocket, pulled out a thick envelope and handed it to Mack. "This came in the mail this morning. I thought you might like to have it."

Thea felt Mack tremble and stood, linking her arm

through his, wanting to give him a small portion of the strength he always gave to her. He pulled out a set of thick papers and unfolded them, skimming over the first page.

"What does it say?" Thea managed to squeak out.

Before she knew what was happening, she was in Mack's arms, rocking side to side as if in a slow dance. "She's ours, sweetheart," Mack whispered in her ear. "She's really ours."

Tears sprang to her eyes, but she refused to cry. She'd wept enough over the past few years to fill the seven seas, now was a time of unbelievable joy!

"We'll still have a more formal signing of the papers once the baby has recovered," the judge said with a smile in his voice. "But as far as the State of Georgia is concerned, you are legally the parents of Sarah Eileen Worthington."

Sarah Eileen Worthington. Thea smiled. Mack had been the one to suggest the baby's middle name, a tribute to the sister she had loved, a way to start healing from the loss. She might never learn the truth about what had happened to Eileen's baby, but Thea had forgiven herself for the mistakes she'd made with her sister.

Still holding Thea close to his side, Mack held out his hand to the judge. "Thank you, sir. We can't begin to tell you how much we appreciate you coming all this way to give us the news."

"No problem at all." The man glanced down at his watch. "I'd better get going if I hope to make my next appointment." He slipped his hat on, then touched the brim. "Sheriff. Mrs. Worthington."

Before the door had even closed, Mack swung her up in his arms again, his blue eyes bright with untethered happiness, his smile the most beautiful she'd ever seen. "You're a momma, sweetheart."

"And you're a daddy." Thea's heart soared as she dropped a quick kiss to his lips.

They stood wrapped in each other's embrace, an unimaginable joy passing between them, drawing them ever closer, twining around them, forging them together.

"If someone would have told me this time last year I'd be a happily married man, completely in love with my wife and father to a beautiful little girl, I would have thought they were nuts," Mack whispered. "But God had another plan."

"I wondered at times. But then He gave me you and Sarah." She chuckled. "What have I ever done to deserve this much joy?"

"You haven't done anything. None of us have." Mack dropped a kiss on her head. "It's only through God's goodness to us that He gives us our heart's desires."

"I'm glad he gave you to me."

A knock on the door was followed by the door being held opened wide by Nurse Corinne. "Mr. and Mrs. Worthington, we're bringing your baby back from recovery."

Our baby. Thea and Mack glanced at each other, the smile they shared full of love and hope for the future. Fingers entwined, they walked to the door to greet their sleeping daughter.

* * * * *

Angel Moore fell in love with romance in elementary school when she read the story of Robin Hood and Maid Marian. Inspired by her husband, who taught her everything she knows about living happily ever after, Angel writes stories of faith and a hope she knows is real because of God's goodness to her. When not writing, she's probably reading a book or watching way too much television. After all, every love story is research, right? Find her at angelmoorebooks.com.

Books by Angel Moore

Love Inspired

Their Family Arrangement

Love Inspired Historical

Conveniently Wed
The Marriage Bargain
The Rightful Heir
Husband by Arrangement
A Ready-Made Texas Family

Visit the Author Profile page
at LoveInspired.com for more titles.

THE MARRIAGE BARGAIN

Angel Moore

Let nothing be done through strife or vainglory;
but in lowliness of mind let each esteem other
better than themselves.
Look not every man on his own things,
but every man also on the things of others.
—*Philippians* 2:3–4

To my editor, Emily Krupin.
Your encouragement makes me work harder.

To my mother, Mary Ellen, for sharing her love of reading. Thank you for celebrating with me at every step along the way and for teaching me to be brave.

To Lisa, for the love only true sisters know.

To Austin, my first editor and reader.
Your insight and knowledge are priceless.

To Jason, for understanding when Mama has to work.

To Bob, who taught me everything I know about happily-ever-after.

And, as always, to God, Who makes it all possible.

Chapter One

Pine Haven, Texas
January 1881

The sound of shattering glass snatched Lily Warren awake. She bolted upright in bed with a gasp, only to feel her lungs fill with acrid smoke. Coughing uncontrollably, she threw the quilt back and tugged on her dressing gown.

Unfamiliar with her surroundings, she fumbled about in the darkness, searching for the doorway to the stairs that led to her new shop.

Heavy footsteps pounded on the staircase outside her room. Lily turned toward the sound, desperate for fresh air. The coughing racked her chest, and she was getting dizzy.

She cried out between coughs. "Help!"

The door burst open, and the orange glow of flames gave her enough light to stumble toward her rescuer.

Her landlord, Edward Stone, came into the room with an arm across his face in an apparent effort to keep from breathing in the smoke. "Do you have something to wrap up in? A blanket?" His voice was intense.

She reached for her mother's quilt on the bed, though the coughing hindered her movements.

He snatched it up and, before she knew what he was going to do, wrapped it around her shoulders and picked her up like a child.

She stiffened and argued, "I can walk."

"Try to keep your mouth closed until I get you out-side." He kicked the doorway open wider and started down the stairs.

"What?" Pressed against his chest, she couldn't hear over the roar of the growing fire.

"Quiet! The smoke." He reached the bottom of the stairs and turned toward the back door.

She could see the flames licking up the side of the back wall and climbing across her workbench. All the beautiful hats she'd made for her shop were being con-sumed by the hungry fire.

Kicking and squirming against Edward, she screamed, "My stock!"

He tightened his hold on her and reversed his direc-tion to take her out the front door. He turned back to face the building and lowered her to stand in front of him.

The church bell rang from the opposite end of the street.

She tried to move away from him, but her hair was tangled in the buckle on his suspenders. She cried out in pain as it pulled.

"Hold still." He spoke close to her ear. "I'll try not to hurt you, but I've got to put the fire out." He tugged at the knotted curls.

A voice barked behind them. "Stone! Is anyone still inside?" The sheriff came running up the street.

With a final and painful pull, Lily was free of him.

She turned to see what must be most of the town's population coming from every direction.

Edward shot around her and hollered his answer to the sheriff as he went back through the front door of her shop. "No one else was here. I think it's contained in the workroom in the back. There's a rain barrel in the alley behind the back door." The sheriff ran toward the rear of the shop.

Lily stumbled on the ends of her mother's quilt when she started up the steps. A man she hadn't met in the two days since her arrival in Pine Haven restrained her. "You can't go in there, miss," he said.

"My stock is inside!" She turned to plead with him to let her go. He wasn't tall or large, but was strong for his size, and she couldn't break free. "Everything I own is in there."

The lady from the general store came up beside them. "Miss Warren, you mustn't resist. The men need to put out the fire so it doesn't spread to the rest of town." Mrs. Croft put an arm around her shoulders. "Doc Willis, I've got her. Help them! Please!"

Smoke boiled through the open front door now. Lily could see Edward's shape through the haze as he swung his coat to beat back the flames. Every available man and woman scurried to form a line and pass buckets filled from the water troughs and barrels near the surrounding buildings.

Lily shrugged off Mrs. Croft's confining arm. "I've got to help at least." She let the quilt drop to the dirt and ran to fill a wide place in the line of townsfolk fighting to help their newest resident.

It had only been minutes, but seemed like hours, when

Edward appeared in the front doorway with his charred coat lifted high in one hand. "It's out! We did it!"

Cheers went up from the crowd, and the line fell away. Everyone gathered near the steps of her shop.

Lily pushed her way through the people and stopped at the open front door. Water covered the floors she'd polished on her first day. Mud tracked through to the workroom. She leaned against the jamb.

She turned to look at Edward. "How bad is it?" Water ran in tiny rivulets through the soot on his face.

"I'm afraid your stock is ruined. What didn't burn will be damaged by the smoke and water." He dragged an arm across his forehead and smeared the soot away from his eyes.

Mrs. Croft came through the crowd at the bottom of the steps. "Miss Warren, please." The woman held Lily's quilt up by the corners. She lowered her voice to a conspiratorial whisper, and her eyes darted toward the people gathered behind her. "You need to cover yourself."

Lily gasped and looked down at herself. The tie to her dressing gown had loosened while she passed one bucket of water after another. The lace of her nightgown peeked out where the robe gaped open. She snatched the quilt from Mrs. Croft and wrapped it around her shoulders, clenching it tight, high against her neck. The heat climbing up her throat let her know she was turning as pink as the nightgown everyone in town had just seen.

"Thank you, Mrs. Croft." The mortification she experienced at the woman's condemning stare almost dwarfed the loss of her belongings. Almost.

She turned back to Edward. "Thank you for saving me." She remembered the feel of his arms around her as he carried her from the building. Strong, determined, protecting.

"You don't owe me any thanks. I'm just sorry we couldn't save your merchandise." As her landlord, he'd want Lily's Millinery and Finery to be a success. How could it be now, with nothing to sell?

Mrs. Croft's tinny voice broke into their conversation. "How did you see the fire, Mr. Stone?" Her lips were pinched tight, and her eyes narrowed.

"I was on my porch and saw the glow through the shop windows." He seemed at ease explaining what happened, but Lily's stomach sank and pressure built behind her eyes when she looked at Mrs. Croft and knew the woman was making an accusation.

The busybody confirmed Lily's suspicions with her next words. "But your porch faces in the opposite direction." A hum of low conversations ran through the people who'd only just put out the fire. Now the woman from the general store was trying to start another one. The kind that could destroy Lily's reputation. The potential damage could forever ruin her business before it opened.

Several of the people gathered looked over their shoulders in the direction of the blacksmith's shop and home. His porch faced a lane that ran perpendicular to Main Street. Lily held her breath.

Edward's tone was clipped. "I was leaning on the corner post and watching the night sky. The view of the moon is best from there."

"I see." Doubt hung on each syllable from Mrs. Croft. "It's just that when we came out to help, you were holding Miss Warren in your arms."

Mr. Croft interrupted. "Liza, he just pulled the woman from a burning building." He put a hand on his wife's shoulder. "Let's go home and get some rest. The whole town will be tired tomorrow after the excitement of tonight."

People murmured around them. Some were in agreement with Mr. Croft, but Lily knew in her soul that others were siding with Mrs. Croft. Only two days in her new town and something beyond her control had drawn her character into question. She couldn't let them all disperse without an attempt to protect herself.

"Mrs. Croft, I assure you nothing improper went on here tonight. Mr. Stone was merely rescuing me. If he hadn't come, I'd never have found my way out of my bedroom."

A light gasp escaped some of the ladies.

"I see." Mrs. Croft's eyes swept across Lily from top to bottom and then landed on Edward. "I guess it's okay where you come from to entertain gentlemen in your home after dark, but you'll soon learn that in Pine Haven we hold to a higher standard of propriety."

Edward took a step closer to the edge of the porch. "Miss Warren has told you there was no impropriety here." He looked at Mr. Croft and then the others standing in the street. "Thank you all for your help. By saving my building, you very likely saved many others from certain disaster."

Dr. Willis spoke up then. "And at least one life."

Lily let her gaze move over the crowd then. "Thank you all so much." She turned to Edward. "Especially you, Mr. Stone."

People began to walk away a few at a time, the rumble of voices fading into the night.

She pulled up the bottom of the quilt so she wouldn't stumble and stepped inside the shop.

"Miss Warren, I don't think you should stay here tonight." Edward's voice was kind.

Lily stilled for a moment. "Is the building sound?"

"Yes. And tonight when I say my prayers, I will thank God that the fire didn't spread to your private rooms. But the smoke and water damage are serious." He gestured toward the floor and the workroom.

She stepped inside and took in the magnitude of the destruction. There was a trail of muddy water from the front door to the workroom where water had sloshed from the buckets as they were passed from the porch and through the shop to put out the fire in the back room. She picked her way slowly to keep from slipping and stood in the entry to the workroom. Water dripped from the workbench. The stench of the smoke hung thick in the air. And everywhere she looked, the remains of all her hard work lay soaked and covered in soot. Now she had to begin anew. Not from the beginning, but from a new beginning much further behind any point she'd imagined.

She squared her tired shoulders and spoke. "All the more reason for me to stay and get to work." She nodded in dismissal. "Thank you again for all you've done. I'm certain it would have been a lot worse if you hadn't seen the fire." She looked down at the quilt her mother had made. "I'm grateful you saved my mother's quilt. I don't have many of her things. This one is important to me." As much as she'd tried to keep her emotions in check, she couldn't stop the tears from spilling over her lashes now. With a sniff she stood straight and moved to the front door.

Edward followed her and stepped onto the porch. His hand came up to keep her from closing the door on him. "Cleanup can wait until morning. It's only a few hours."

She shook her head. "The water will damage the floors if I don't mop it up now."

"Then let me stay and help you."

She'd come to Pine Haven for independence. Her recent failed engagement had driven her to create a new life for herself. The first two days now seemed like a distant dream. Making hats and polishing the furniture her father had sent with her to use in her new shop had filled her hours. The memory of humming while she cleaned the floors and set up the private rooms to suit her needs faded behind a cloud of dense smoke.

This was a major setback, but she wouldn't become dependent on her landlord. Now. Or ever. "No. You best get home to your niece. I'll be fine." She'd met his young charge on the first day and knew the child would be home alone.

He chuckled a bit. "Ellen can sleep through anything. That child wouldn't hear the church bell or commotion unless it was in the room with her."

"It's good she has such peace. Sound sleep is often a sign of contentment."

Edward looked over his shoulder toward his house. "In all her seven years, I've never known her sleep to be disturbed. Not since she was a baby. For her, it's more about how she wears herself out when she's awake. The child has more worries than a body ought."

"All the more reason for you to go home now. In case she awakens and you aren't there." When Lily was five, her mother had died. Being young and frightened was something Lily had experienced firsthand.

He dipped his head in agreement. "Please get some rest. I'll be back in the morning so we can assess the damage and begin repairs."

Lily stood in the doorway to her workroom after he left. The hats she'd made yesterday were scorched and ruined. What wasn't blackened by fire was covered in ash or wilted from the water that had doused the flames. She thought about crying, until her bare feet reminded her of the floors and all the work she needed to do.

She shrugged off the quilt, bundled it into a ball and tossed it onto a crate in the corner of the front shop. Lighting a lantern, she went through the workroom into the alley behind her shop and retrieved the mop she'd used to clean the floors. Bucket in hand, she determined to prevent as much damage as possible. Repairing the building would take more skill than she possessed, but she could clean up the mess. Then Edward could get started as soon as he arrived in the morning.

Could she undo the damage done by Mrs. Croft's words in the aftermath of the fire? Why had the woman so blatantly accused her and Mr. Stone of poor behavior?

Losing a night's sleep did not compare to what she stood to lose if she didn't get her shop open before her father arrived in a few weeks' time. Now she not only needed to get Lily's Millinery and Finery open for business, she also had to repair the damage done to her reputation in front of the townsfolk by Mrs. Croft's words. Her own lapse in decorum when she was unaware of her appearance in her dressing gown in front of the entire town added to her problems.

The water on the floor was the least of her worries, but it was the only thing she could control at the moment.

Edward urged Ellen out of the front door the next morning.

"I want to see what happened." Ellen protested by dragging her feet.

"You can't go inside the building until I make sure it's safe for you to be there." He stooped to be eye level with her. "Promise me you won't try to sneak in."

Her reluctant nod came after a long pause. "What did she do to set Momma's shop on fire?" This was the reaction Edward had been afraid of. He knew his niece might blame Lily for the fire and use it as an excuse to spew the frustration and fear she was warring with against his tenant. "I said it was bad to let someone in Momma's shop." Her face turned into a pout.

"I'm not sure what caused the fire. That's one of the things I need to find out today." He pulled her into a quick hug. "Now you need to head off to school so I can get to work."

"I don't see why I got to hurry 'cause you got to work." He reminded himself to be patient. She was at the age where she often wanted an explanation for things. Knowing that was how she learned, he complied.

He put a hand on top of her head and pointed her in the direction of the school. "Because you are one of the reasons I work, ma'am."

Ellen went a few steps, swinging her lunch pail in one hand and holding her slate close to her chest in the other. Then she pivoted and looked at the shop across the street from their cabin. He watched her study the building, which showed no outward signs of the fire last night except for the film of smoke on the windows. She bolted back to wrap her arms around his middle. "I know you can fix it like new, Uncle Edward. You're the best uncle a girl could have."

"I'm going to do my best, Ellen." He kissed the top of her head. "You know you're my favorite niece."

She leaned back and scrunched her face at him. "I'm your only niece."

Edward peeled her arms from around him. "Just like I'm your only uncle." He chuckled and turned her toward the school again. "Now get to school, or I'll be the only uncle at school today being scolded by the teacher for letting you be late."

The school bell rang, announcing the time, and she kicked up the dust around the hem of her skirt as she ran. "Bye, Uncle Edward," she hollered over her shoulder.

He laughed as she stumbled and caught herself. The child was fun and loving. He wished he could make her as happy as she deserved to be.

When he'd come back home after the fire, just as he expected, she was curled up in the middle of her bed. The quilt had slid to the floor, so he'd pulled it back over her. He'd marveled that the commotion in the street hadn't awakened her. Oh, to be so carefree.

Only she wasn't carefree. She waited every day with him for news from her mother. When his sister had insisted on leaving town with her husband to start a new business in Santa Fe, he'd begged her to reconsider. Ellen needed her mother. Jane and Wesley had wanted to get their business started and come back for Ellen in a few weeks. Edward wished they'd been contented with running the local hotel, but Wesley had lost interest in Pine Haven when he'd heard of the growing economy in Santa Fe. Edward had purchased the building he now leased to Lily in hopes that Jane could convince Wesley to stay and let her open a bakery to add to their business interests in Pine Haven.

In the end, nothing Edward said had changed their minds. And now the weeks had turned to months. No word from them for the past several weeks was causing him to worry. He tried to dampen the fear that pulled at his heart and caused him to wonder if something dreadful had happened. Ellen's future was his responsibility. He'd have to give her a proper home if his sister didn't return soon. He said another prayer for Jane and Wesley and went into his blacksmith shop to gather some tools.

He needed to start the cleanup and repairs on his building. Having Lily's father lease the shop from him had eased the strain to make the mortgage payments. But he couldn't in all good conscience take money from her while the building was damaged.

He'd stop in at the post office first and see if there was a letter from Jane.

"Quite a night we had, Stone," Jerry Winters, the postmaster, greeted him. "Glad you saw the flames. Hate to think what could have happened to my family, it being right next door and all."

Winston Ledford walked into the post office as Jerry was speaking. "It's a good thing for all of us that you had your eye on Miss Warren. I'll admit she's worthy of a second look." A smirk Edward didn't like crept across the saloon owner's face.

Edward's gut roiled. This was exactly the kind of gossip he worried about after Liza Croft made such a scene in front of most of the town. He refused to rise to Ledford's goading.

Instead, he nodded at Jerry Winters. "I think we were all blessed by God's mercy."

Mrs. Winters came from the private quarters behind the post office and joined her husband. "We all owe you a debt of gratitude, Mr. Stone."

"I doubt he'll be missing much of what goes on at the

new hat shop, Mrs. Winters." Winston Ledford came to stand beside Edward at the counter. "Do you have any mail for me?"

The disapproval on Mrs. Winter's face almost made Edward chuckle. If it wasn't such a serious subject, he'd laugh at how soundly Ledford's comments were dismissed. She turned to search the cubbyholes behind her and handed several letters to the man.

Winston shuffled through the small stack, tipped his hat and said, "Good morning to you all." He opened the door to leave. "I think I'll stop by and see how our newest resident is this morning. Must have been quite a shock to her."

Edward's back tightened, and he drew a deep breath. "That won't be necessary, Ledford. I'm on my way there now to begin the repairs."

A cantankerous laugh burst from Winston. "As I suspected. You've already staked a claim on our new merchant." He stepped onto the sidewalk and turned to close the door. "Don't be surprised if you find yourself engaged in some friendly competition over the likes of Miss Warren." The door closed, and his grinning face filled the pane of glass before he turned in the direction of the building next door.

Edward followed him at a brisk pace.

"Stone, don't you want to know if you have any mail?" Mr. Winters called.

"I'll check back later." He was through the front door. "It's not fitting for Miss Warren to be subjected to the likes of Mr. Ledford without warning."

It was one thing for Mrs. Croft to make unfounded accusations, but for Winston Ledford to think that a fine, upstanding lady like Miss Lily Warren was open to his attentions was another matter. Edward wouldn't leave her unprotected from the saloon owner's lack of good manners.

Serving as an unsolicited chaperone was the only right thing to do. It was more about protecting Lily's reputation in the community, and thus his income from her rental, than anything else.

Edward opened the door to Lily's shop and found Winston Ledford leaning on the glass display case Lily had brought with her when she'd arrived only two days earlier. She caught sight of him over Ledford's shoulder. Was that relief in her gaze?

"Thank you for checking on me, Mr. Ledford, but I assure you it isn't necessary. I'm quite all right." She stepped from behind the case and walked toward Edward.

Once again he was struck by her beauty. When she'd first come to Pine Haven and stepped from the train, he couldn't help but notice her. Everyone noticed her. But within moments, her independence had become clear to him. She was lovely, but she wasn't the kind of woman who wanted to settle down and care for a home and family. Not the kind of woman he'd begun to think he might need for Ellen. After a childhood of being neglected and mistreated by his stepmother, he'd replaced any yearning for love with a mistrust of women years ago. If he did marry for Ellen's sake, he'd choose carefully.

"Good morning, Miss Warren." Edward set the wooden box he'd filled with tools on a crate near the front door and removed his hat. "I've come to get started on the repairs."

She lifted a handkerchief to her face and coughed. "That's very good of you."

Winston Ledford turned to face them. "If you're certain there's nothing I can do for you, Miss Warren, I'll leave you in the care of Mr. Stone." He sauntered toward the door. "He seems determined to watch over you." He tipped his hat at Lily and walked through the door Edward held open for him.

Edward closed the door with a snap. "I hope you aren't taken in by the likes of Mr. Ledford." He picked up his toolbox.

"I'm a big girl, Mr. Stone. You don't have to worry about me." Lily went back toward the workroom behind the shop. Perhaps the relief he'd seen in her face earlier was imagined. Nothing she'd done since he'd met her upon her arrival in town Monday had suggested she was anything other than a woman determined to make her own way in the world. Her single-minded focus might be the very thing that protected her from people like the saloon owner.

"That's good to know. Some women are swayed by fancy talk and refined appearances."

"I assure you, I appreciate fine things. I also look for quality. In people and things."

She directed him toward the workroom. "Thank you for coming so early. I've done what I could about getting everything dry and removing the rubbish."

Her movements were swift and fluid, like a bird on air. She'd brushed her hair into a loose bun and changed her clothes, but the fatigue of her ordeal showed in eyes. Another coughing spell wrenched her breath.

"You didn't need to do all that by yourself, Miss Warren. I assured you I'd be here this morning."

She lifted a hand and waved it in dismissal of his words. "I couldn't sleep anyway. My schedule was tight before the fire. Now I'll need to work at a quicker pace than I'd planned."

He entered the workroom behind her. The back door

stood open, and he could see the pile of rubble she'd created in the alley beyond. "You stayed up all night?"

"It's a matter of no consequence." She indicated the shelving on the left of the storeroom. "Do you think any of this can be salvaged?"

Obviously she'd moved beyond the fire and had set her mind on repairs. Most women would be wallowing in a pool of pity, bemoaning their misfortune. Her determination was admirable.

"First things first," he said. "I need to discover how the fire started, so we can make certain we don't have another incident." He turned to see her blush and lift a hand to her forehead. She rubbed her fingers across her brow in a smoothing motion.

"We won't have to worry about it again." A deep breath caused more coughing. "Please forgive me." She tucked the handkerchief back in the pocket of her apron.

"How are you feeling?"

"I'm fine. Just frustrated with the amount of work I've caused us both."

"You caused?"

Could Ellen be right? Had his tenant been the reason for the fire? The last thing he needed was for his niece to discover Lily had put the building in jeopardy. The child already resented her presence in the shop. Edward didn't have the energy to deal with more trouble in their lives— especially not from a woman he'd just met.

Chapter Two

Edward prayed he'd misunderstood Lily. "What do you mean, 'you caused'?"

"It seems the fire was my fault." Lily pointed to the wall near the back door where the most damage appeared to be. "I was working late, trying to make a few extra hats. I had set a lantern on this workbench."

She didn't seem the irresponsible type. "Surely you didn't leave a lantern burning when you went to bed. You'd have noticed the light."

"No." She jerked her head to stare at him. "Of course not! I took the lantern with me."

She pointed to a small stack of charred kindling near the stove. It was considerably smaller than the amount he'd cut and placed there before her arrival. Normal circumstances wouldn't have caused her to use so much kindling.

"Right before I went upstairs, I swept up the trimmings from around the workbench. Bits of ribbon and feathers. Things like that. I swept them into a pile near the door, intending to dispose of it this morning. Then I checked the stove. Some embers must have blown out and landed among the trash. It must have smoldered and caught when it got near the kindling. I don't know how else it could have started. I'm so sorry." Another cough stopped her from speaking. "I'll pay for the damages."

Edward stirred the kindling with the toe of his boot and studied the scorched wood and the wall in the corner of the room between the stove and the door.

"It's possible a gust of wind blew under the door and carried the embers back to the kindling." He turned to Lily, who was coughing again. "No one was hurt. That's the most important thing."

"Please forgive me. I never meant to start the fire." She covered her mouth again to cough.

"You took in a lot of smoke. Have you been to see the doc?"

"No. I'm fine. There's too much work to do to stop for a minor cough."

He knew how much smoke had been in her rooms. The stairwell had acted like a chimney and drawn the smoke upward. No doubt a draft around the windows had pulled the dangerous fumes under the door at the top of the landing.

"I'm taking you to see Doc Willis." He headed for the front of the shop. "Where's your coat?"

When she didn't follow, he turned and waited.

"You are not taking me—" a cough interrupted her words "—anywhere."

He raised his eyebrows. Would she be so stubborn as to refuse medical treatment? "Then I'll have to ask Doc Willis to come here." He opened the door and stepped onto the sidewalk. "We need to get this place ready for you to open your business. The sooner you get that cough taken care of, the sooner that will happen."

"Wait, please." She coughed again. "If it will set your mind at ease so we can get to work on the repairs, I'll go." She shrugged her arms into the sleeves of her coat and turned up the collar.

The January wind whipped around him, and he rubbed his arms against the cold. They walked briskly in the direction of the doctor's office. "I'll feel better knowing you aren't making yourself worse by not resting."

Lily turned to look at him. "You must be freezing."

"I'm fine." He dropped his hands to his sides.

"Your coat was ruined when you put out the fire."

"It was time for a new coat anyway. I'll go by the general store after lunch and get one." She walked beside him across the main intersection in town. He hoped she didn't notice the curious glances being sent their way. It was obvious to him that the events of the night before were on everyone's mind this morning.

"You must allow me to pay for it." She seemed too focused to notice the people who turned their heads to whisper when they passed. He wasn't sure that was a good thing. It might be better if she were more aware of what went on around her. If she were, they wouldn't be the object of town gossip. He knew it wasn't fair to blame her, but he didn't like the idea of anyone gossiping about him. Ellen would be harmed if he was cast in a poor light. And it wouldn't do Lily's new business any favors to open the shop in the midst of swirling lies smearing her name.

"I'll pay for my coat. And the repairs." He opened the door to the doctor's office.

She opened her mouth as she entered the building, most likely to argue the point with him, but quickly succumbed to another coughing spell.

* * *

Lily continued to cough while Edward called out, "Doc. I brought you a new patient."

Lily sank unceremoniously into a chair near the door. The smell of camphor and dust assaulted her senses. A curtain rustled and parted. The man who'd kept her from running back into her shop during the fire came into the room.

"Hello, Edward. Finally find yourself a wife?" The short man with spectacles looked from the blacksmith to Lily.

"A wife?" What was this man thinking?

"No, Doc. She's my new tenant. You probably saw her last night. I went by to start the repairs this morning." He pointed to Lily as she interrupted them with a cough. "This is how I found her. I think the smoke got to her. She's been hacking away."

"I saw her. Actually had to restrain her to keep her from following you into the burning building." The doctor motioned for her to have a seat on the table in the center of the room.

"I'm not injured, Dr. Willis." She moved to the table and sat stiff with her hands in her lap.

He seemed to ignore her. "Are you light-headed?" He peered into her eyes and checked the pulse at the base of her neck.

"I am not." She glared at Edward, who had retreated to stand near the door. "I told Mr. Stone this trip was unnecessary, but he insisted." She slid toward the edge of the table, but the doctor prevented her from getting up.

"Just the coughing?" He assembled his stethoscope and pressed the bell against her back. "Take a deep breath."

She drew in a breath, and the coughing began again.

He moved to the opposite side of her back. "Again." The results were the same.

"I don't think you've done any major damage to your lungs, but it's probably going to take a few days for you to recover from taking in so much smoke." He paused to look at her. "Your color is good. I think it's just a matter of getting some rest."

"I don't have time to rest. I've got a business to open." She coughed into her handkerchief again, hating that her body was betraying her so. She needed to work. There would be time for rest later.

"A hard worker, are you?" The doctor tilted his head to one side and studied her.

Lily straightened her shoulders. "I am. It's how I was raised. We Warrens don't cotton to laziness or excuses."

He turned to Edward and nodded his head in Lily's direction. "She looks as good as any other lady around here. You oughta think about this one."

"I don't think so, Doc." Edward seemed to be laughing at her from his place in the corner of the room. First he'd insisted on bringing her here, and now he was a party to her ridicule. She wouldn't stand for it.

"I don't need a doctor." Anger gave her fresh strength, and she turned her eyes to the blacksmith. "Or a husband."

"As you wish." Dr. Willis backed away from the table. He turned toward the curtains where he'd made his entrance.

Another coughing spell overtook her. Between coughs Lily said, "Wait a minute, Doctor."

The doctor stopped with a hand on the curtain and raised an eyebrow. "Don't got all day, missy."

"I'm sorry. Can you give me something for the cough?" She hated to submit to the man but had no time for setbacks. Her father and sister would arrive in a few short weeks. She needed to have her shop open and bringing in business before then.

The doctor went to a glass cabinet against the back wall. Lily caught Edward looking at her with a grin of satisfaction. He was enjoying having been right about insisting she see the doctor.

"I want you to use this flaxseed to make a tea." The doctor handed her a bottle. "You can do it several times a day. It will help with the cough and clearing your lungs."

She took the bottle reluctantly. "Thank you."

Dr. Willis nodded. "Sensible, too, Edward. You need to reconsider this one."

Lily might submit to his ministrations but not to his attitude. "Really, Doctor, I don't think it's appropriate for you to discuss me as if I'm a prize horse."

"I didn't say you were a prize. Just worth a second consideration." He looked at Edward standing with his back to the door. "But only if she's given to moments of quiet."

The blacksmith laughed then. "I haven't seen one yet, Doc."

Lily scowled. "If you'll tell me your fee, Doctor, we'll be on our way." She hoped this ordeal was drawing to an end. How was it possible for her to be at the mercy of not one, but two belligerent men?

Edward waited while Lily paid the doctor, then held the door open for her to walk through before him.

"I'm coming back to the shop to get started on the repairs."

"Thank you for being so eager. I'm going to have to work harder than ever to get ready to open."

"Just don't try burning the candle at both ends."

"Very funny." She gave a tiny giggle. Then, in a fashion he could only imagine a cactus flower able to perform, her prickly expression transformed into beauty with a smile like none he'd ever seen. Golden hair framed her face. Vibrant blue eyes sought him out. His heart jolted. Nothing could lessen the power of her grace.

He shook his head. What was he thinking? She was beautiful all right. A rare beauty. But gentle and graceful? Not with the sharp tongue and feisty resistance he'd witnessed in the short time he'd known her.

Lily Warren might be named after a gentle spring flower, but her cactus-like thorns could prove dangerous, if not deadly, to a man not on his guard.

And Edward Stone was a man who would not let his guard down. Ever again.

"Possum run over your grave?"

"What?" He had to pay better attention.

"You're shaking your head and shivering." Lily's expression teased him, but he wouldn't tease back.

"No. Just a bad thought." He turned away from her and continued down the sidewalk. "Nothing to worry about." He'd make certain of that.

Lily picked up her pace and left him to follow. When they arrived at the shop, she opened the door, and the bell announcing their arrival clanged to the floor and bounced.

She sighed. "Great. Something else to be fixed."

"Be careful not to break anything else."

Her eyes widened in question. "Oh, so that's my fault? I see. Looks like our relationship will be one of blame and accusation." The smile was there again, but Edward was determined to thwart its power.

"Our relationship will be landlord and tenant." He stooped to retrieve the broken bell from just inside the doorway. "And the fault of this was mine, so I'll be responsible for the repair."

"You think it can be fixed?" Her uncertain gaze met his.

"Sure. It's a simple repair." He turned the bell over in his hand. "I should have made it stronger in the first place."

Blond brows lifted. "You made it?" Disbelief crossed her face.

"Don't look so surprised. I am a blacksmith."

"I'm sorry. The blacksmith in East River made horseshoes and wagon wheels. Not art."

Was she complimenting him? Did she realize it?

"I make horseshoes and wagon wheels, too. And iron gates, and farm tools…"

"I understand. Sort of a jack-of-all-trades, are you?"

"Are you suggesting I'm master of none?"

"Well, the bell did break…" Her smile was the only clue she was teasing him. Tormenting might be a better word, given the tightening of his gut when she looked at him.

"I wouldn't call myself an artisan. But I do enjoy creating unique things." He drifted into the past looking at the bell. It had been a gift for his sister, Jane. One she'd never taken the time to enjoy.

A swift movement had the bell in his pocket. Hidden with the memories it evoked.

When he raised his eyes, he found Lily staring with open curiosity.

"I best get to work, Miss Warren." He stepped into the center of the room. The late-morning sun lit the street beyond the deep windows. Windows Jane had dreamed of filling with pastries and cakes.

Lily breezed through the opening, which led from the large front room into a work area, with a lightness he'd never seen in any woman. If he'd had to describe it, he'd say her steps floated across the floor.

He followed her, and together they came up with a plan for the repairs. He would tear out anything damaged beyond repair. She proved a strong helper by toting all the charred boards out to the alley behind the shop.

They stopped at midday, and he made a list of the supplies he'd need to get the shop back in good shape.

He prepared to leave. "I'll stop by the lumber mill and order what I need before I go to the general store. I'll get a quick bite of lunch and come back."

"What about your coat?" she asked.

"That's why I'm going to the general store."

"Let me come with you so I can pay for it. You wouldn't need a coat if there hadn't been a fire."

He shook his head. "No."

"I insist."

Edward turned to look her full in the face. "Miss Warren, what do you think Mrs. Croft would think of that? After all she insinuated last night?"

Lily's cheeks went pink.

He looked over his shoulder out the front window. "I'll bring my wagon when I come back. We can use it to haul away the debris."

"I can help with that." She was unlike any other woman of her type, and Edward was impressed by how determined she was to help. At first glance, she gave the appearance of a lady accustomed to fine things. But she hadn't shied away from any of the work brought on by the damage from the fire.

"No, ma'am." He still wouldn't let her help load the rubble piled in the alley.

Lily smiled. "You must be as strong as an ox." Shock covered her face almost before the words left her mouth.

"I can haul my share of a load." He couldn't resist teasing her. As hard as he tried, his reserve kept slipping. "Most people don't call me an ox."

"Maybe not to your face, Mr. Stone." At least she had the decency to blush when she said it.

Edward heard the rumble of laughter in his chest. It had been a long time since he'd laughed out loud. "I'll be back after lunch." He tipped his hat and escaped through the front door.

He sobered immediately on seeing Mrs. Croft exit the post office next door. Her scowl spoke louder than anything she could have said before she turned and walked in the direction of her store.

Dust stirred in the street as his boots beat a path away from Lily Warren and her shop. He'd only rented it to her father out of desperation. The mortgage on the shop needed to be paid, not to mention the cost of providing for Ellen. He couldn't afford to let the shop stand empty any longer. When Jane came back, they'd make new arrangements. Until—or unless—she did, he needed the money.

He had to protect Lily's reputation, because if her shop failed, he could lose the building to the bank. He turned the corner and headed to the general store. His hands were shoved deep into his pockets, but the cold of the day was biting at him. Or maybe it wasn't the cold of the day, but the cold realizations storming his thoughts.

Life was complicated now. More than he'd ever wanted it to be.

In the back of his mind was a growing dread crying out for his attention. As a single man, if something tragic had happened to his sister and her husband, he'd need to marry. A young girl shouldn't be raised by her lone uncle. Ellen would need a woman's hand. Someone who was strong and gentle at the same time.

Someone like Lily.

Lily opened the door and wrapped her older sister in a hug. Could it be eleven years since Daisy had married and moved away from East River, their childhood home? When they'd reunited on her arrival in Pine Haven, Lily understood why their father had come home after his recent visit to Daisy's family wanting to sell everything in East River and move here. When he and Jasmine arrived in the spring, he'd have all his daughters together again. They'd been apart too long.

One look at Daisy's face and Lily prepared herself to be scolded. Even at twenty-four years old, her sisters still treated her like the baby of the family.

"What happened?" Daisy shifted baby Rose onto her shoulder and looked around at the destruction left by the fire.

"It was an accident." Lily knew Daisy wouldn't be satisfied without some explanation.

"How did it happen?"

She pointed to the chair she'd set up in front of the hall tree so her customers could view their hat selections in the mirror. "Have a seat, and I'll explain." She pulled up a stool and told her sister all that had happened.

"So Edward Stone saved you?" Daisy pushed Rose's

bonnet away from her face and handed the child to Lily. "Handsome, isn't he?"

Lily lifted the baby and took in the sight of her chubby face. "She's so like Momma. I'm glad you named her after her." She pulled Rose close and breathed in the sweet baby smell. Rose twined her fingers into Lily's hair and gave a firm yank.

"Ow... She's a strong one, too." Lily loosed the tiny hand and nestled the babe in the crook of her arm.

"That she is." Daisy's face shone with love for her daughter. "You didn't answer my question about Edward Stone."

"Did you ask a question?" She hoped to avoid this kind of question about any man, let alone one who was already being accused of paying her too much attention. She couldn't risk feeding those rumors. Not even to her sister, who obviously hadn't heard them yet.

She jostled the baby. "Where are the twins?"

"They're in school."

"I can't believe they're nine years old. Seems life has begun to move at such a rapid pace."

"It comes from growing older, I suppose." Daisy looked her square in the face. "Lily, what do you think of your landlord?"

Lily stilled and answered. "He's my landlord. Yes, he saved me, but he also saved his building. That's all there was to it."

Daisy turned first one way then another and surveyed the shop. "If you say so."

"I do." Lily swept her free arm toward the open space. "I wanted to have it in better shape, but I wasn't planning on a fire. What do you think?"

Daisy reached for Rose as the child started to whimper. "Don't worry. I'm sure Edward will have the repairs done in no time."

"I hope so. I've got to make this place work, or Papa will insist I live with him and Jasmine when they come." Lily fought back the fear of being isolated again. She'd spent too many years taking care of her sick father at home while all her friends had married and started families.

Daisy paced the floor, gently rocking the baby. "That wouldn't be so bad, would it? You've always lived with Papa. Why is this shop so important to you now?"

"It just is. You wouldn't understand. You have your life. A family. A farm. I didn't have anything." Anxiety sent her voice up a notch. "Until now."

She put a hand on Daisy's arm and stopped her motion. "Daisy, you have to pray for me. Papa isn't convinced a woman my age should be on her own. But I've just got to do this. I can't live in the shadows anymore. I want my own life."

"You talk as if you've been locked away as a slave. I know that isn't true. I lived there, too, you remember."

"It's not that at all. It's just…well." Lily wasn't certain she could articulate her thoughts. "I love Papa, and I'm so pleased he's well now. We weren't sure for so long that he'd ever get better. I'd do it all again in a heartbeat." She willed Daisy to understand. "But I need this for me."

"Of course, I'll pray for you, sweetie. I'll even make sure all my friends come see you as soon as you open."

That was encouraging. She could almost see the unknown ladies milling around the shop, fingering the lace on a handkerchief or smiling at their reflection wearing a new hat. "Are the ladies of Pine Haven ready for fancy hats and parasols?"

Daisy chuckled. "What ladies aren't?"

Lily was grateful for the support she saw in Daisy's expression. "Thank you. I promise I'll make you proud. Papa, too."

"The thought of having all of you here in Pine Haven is more than I ever dreamed. Your shop is like an extra blessing on top of that."

"I've got a lot of work to do to replace the things that were ruined. Thankfully, I hadn't opened all of the crates I brought." She indicated the crates stacked around the front of the shop. "These things are undamaged."

After lunch she'd gone over everything in her mind. Hopefully a couple of days would see the shop repaired. Maybe two more days after that and she'd be back on schedule for her new life.

She prayed the insinuations made by Mrs. Croft had been forgotten by those who heard them last night. That was the one detail she hadn't told her sister. If God answered as Lily wanted, she'd never hear of those accusations again.

She shook off the doubts that threatened from the recesses of her soul. A new life full of promise. She would do everything in her power to make it happen.

Chapter Three

Edward pulled his wagon behind the building and loaded the debris. He came to the front of the shop to enter, so anyone watching from the nearby businesses would see him. He was determined to do his part to squelch the rumors. Going in the back way would only feed the gossipers.

Lily was kneeling in front of an open crate rummaging through its contents and didn't hear the door when he opened it.

"Think I'll have to stop by Doc Willis's office and let him know how you're taking it easy."

Startled, Lily jerked up straight. "I'm perfectly fine."

He watched her frustration as the coughing overtook her again. "As long as—" she coughed "—no one tries to scare the breath out of me."

He closed the door. "Have you rested at all?" Everywhere he turned he saw evidence that she'd been busy.

"I stopped working and visited with Daisy. She came by to check on me."

Did he dare bring up the subject that he'd heard being discussed everywhere he'd gone in the two hours since he'd left her? "I saw her when I was leaving the lumber mill."

"Were you able to get the lumber ordered?" She didn't seem the least bit curious about anything other than the progress of the repairs.

"I did. Will Thomas said he'll have the order ready for me after I haul off the debris behind the shop."

She stood and brushed her hands together. "Let me help you load it."

"It's done." Knowing she'd be stubborn, he hadn't let her know he had returned until after he loaded the rubble into the wagon.

"I told you I would help."

"Doc Willis said you need to rest. I only came inside to see if you have anything else that needs to go."

"No." She rubbed her hands down the front of her skirt to smooth it. "At least let me go with you to unload it." She stepped toward the workroom. "Where are you taking it?"

"I've got a small burn pit behind my shop. What can't be salvaged, I'll burn later."

She came back into the front of the shop tugging on work gloves. "Are you ready?"

"Miss Warren, you can't come with me."

"Why ever not? The sooner you unload, the sooner you can get the lumber order and start on the repairs."

He cast a glance out the front window. "Have you been anywhere today? Besides the doctor's office?"

Her brow furrowed. She was cute with her face scrunched in confusion. "No. There's been too much to do here to go visiting."

Was it possible she had no clue? "Did your sister go anywhere before she came to see you?"

"No. She stopped by on her way into town." She looked at him. "Why?"

He didn't know the best way to tell her, so he just said it straight out. "We seem to be the topic of conversation all over town today."

"We? You mean about the fire?"

"No," he said. Her face had relaxed, and he didn't think she understood what he was trying to tell her. "I mean you and me."

Her shoulders lifted, and she gave a small snort. "That's silly." With one hand she gestured between the two of them. "There is no 'we.'"

"I know that." He paused. "But…"

She rose up a bit taller now and drew in a slow breath. "But what?" She angled her head away from him as if it would prevent the full onslaught of something she didn't want to hear.

"It seems that Mrs. Croft's assumptions from last evening have captured the fancy of some of the townsfolk."

Her eyes closed, and she drew her pretty lips inward. He watched her sigh as the implications sank in.

"Everywhere I went, someone brought it up."

Lily dropped onto a crate and wrung her hands together. "Oh, my. I hoped it would be forgotten in the light of day. No one knows me here. Why would they think I'd be so bold as to entertain a man in my home—unchaperoned—late at night?" Her gaze snapped to his. "Unless…what kind of reputation do you have, Mr. Stone?"

How dare she imply that his name in town was without respect! "Me?"

"Yes, you! In East River no one would ever suspect me of any behavior other than that of a Christian lady."

"I had hoped because you're Daisy's sister these rumors would not take hold." He shrugged his shoulders. "But they have."

The front door opened, and Daisy entered the shop. "Oh, Lily! I've just come from the general store." She put a hand on Lily's arm. "Why didn't you tell me what happened?"

Lily must not have expected it to be a problem, or surely she would have told her sister what had been said the night before.

Edward could see the panic filling her eyes when she answered. "Nothing happened! Except a fire!" She lowered her voice and asked, "What are they saying?"

Daisy hesitated. "I'm embarrassed to say." She glanced at Edward, then took Lily by the hand. "Mrs. Croft has given details about you being held in Mr. Stone's arms." She seemed to choose her words with great care. "In your dressing gown."

He needed Daisy to understand the truth. "I pulled her from a burning building. Her hair caught in my suspenders. There was no embrace. I carried her outside because she was overcome by the smoke."

Daisy shook her head. "That's not how Mrs. Croft portrayed it." She looked at Lily. "And because so many people were coming to see what was happening, they witnessed just enough to lend a hint of truth to her tale."

Lily stiffened her arms at her side and clinched her fists. "Truth? We'll tell them the truth! You tell them, Daisy. They'll believe you."

Daisy's husband, Tucker Barlow, came into the shop. Edward knew from his expression that this situation was not going to fade away.

Tucker removed his hat. "I see the news has made its way to all of you."

Lily almost begged for an answer from them. "What am I going to do?"

Edward didn't know what she was going to do. All he knew for sure was that his situation had become more desperate after he'd left Lily just before noon. He'd stopped in at the post office, and there was still no word from his sister, Jane.

He'd gone by the telegraph office and discovered the query he'd sent to the sheriff in Santa Fe had been answered. An outbreak of influenza had hit the community where Jane and Wesley lived, and they'd become gravely ill. The local doctor had sent them to a hospital in another community. No word on the name of the community or their condition.

If Jane and Wesley had passed, he was Ellen's only living relative. He'd do anything necessary to take care of her. He wouldn't risk losing this building. Talking of opening a bakery here would be one of the last things Ellen had shared with her mother. He'd keep the shop for Ellen to have when she was grown. A legacy in Jane's memory.

He cringed when the answer entered his mind, but he knew it was for the best. "What are *we* going to do?" He had to protect Ellen from the gossip that would surely swirl around the shop—and Lily if they didn't act quickly.

"We?" Lily countered.

They were standing in the workroom. The ravages of the fire all around them.

Edward pointed to a small frame Lily had hung on the wall over the workbench. "Are these the verses you live by?" The edges of the frame were scorched, but the intricate needlepoint was intact.

Lily followed his gaze. "Yes. Philippians is one of my favorite books in the Bible."

He read the words aloud. "'Let nothing be done through strife or vainglory; but in lowliness of mind let each esteem other better than themselves. Look not every man on his own things, but every man also on the things of others.'" He looked at her, hoping she'd agree. "That's what we need to do now."

"What do you mean? I'm not at strife with anyone in Pine Haven. I'm not out for vanity. But I do need a good name to run a successful business. What man will want his wife to patronize my shop if he thinks poorly of my character?"

"I'm afraid that's already happened. People assumed the worst when they saw us together last night."

"But we weren't together."

He shook his head. "That's not what they saw. I don't think we'll be able to convince them otherwise."

Lily put her hands to her face and closed her eyes. After a moment she opened them and held her hands out, palms up. "I came here to be independent. How can I do that without the goodwill of the townsfolk? You've ruined everything!"

"Would you rather I'd let you die in the fire? I couldn't stand by and watch the building burn to the ground, knowing you were inside."

Her shoulders slumped. "You're right, of course. But what are we going to do?"

Daisy and Tucker stood quietly while he and Lily tried to sort out this conundrum.

What he had to say next was private. He didn't know Lily well, but he was most certain no lady would want witnesses for what he was about to say. "Will you excuse us, please?"

Daisy looked at Lily. Sisterly sympathy emanated from her.

Tucker took his wife by the arm. "We'll go for a slice of pie at the hotel and come back after you've had time to talk."

When the door closed behind them, Edward turned to Lily. "You know you're going to have to marry me now."

Lily's jaw dropped. To his surprise, words seemed to fail her.

"There is more to consider here than just you and me. I received word today that it's very possible my sister and her husband may have died of influenza."

She closed her mouth. "I'm so sorry. Poor Ellen." She'd gone from incredulous when he spoke of marriage to compassion for his niece in an instant. He hoped it would help her understand why he was making this proposition.

"I won't allow gossip to cause an innocent little girl to lose the only family she may have left. If my name is smeared with yours, I could lose her. A judge could say I'm not fit to be a guardian as an unmarried man—especially if I'm purported to have committed unseemly behavior."

"But we're innocent."

"I know that, and you know that." He put a hand on her sleeve and turned her so she could see through the entry of the workroom to the windows in the front of the shop. Two women had stopped to peer in the glass. When they caught sight of Edward and Lily, they frowned and hurried away. "But we'll never convince them. Or the people who are like them."

"Did the doctor put this notion in your head?"

He shook his head. Never would he have imagined himself offering marriage to someone he'd just met. If it weren't for Ellen, he might not have offered.

Then he looked into those blue eyes, churning to violet with emotion, and knew he was doing this for Lily and himself, too. No one deserved to be destroyed by gossip and rumors. "Believe me, I was just as resistant as you. Until I spent part of the day trying to convince people that nothing happened. Now it looks like we don't have a choice."

He willed her to understand. "If you don't open your shop, I don't know how I can pay the mortgage. I can't lose this building. I need to be able to give it to Ellen when she's grown. Maybe it will help her remember her mother."

"But why would you want to marry me? I'm not your responsibility."

"It's not just about you." He drew in a breath. "Ellen needs a mother. It's something I started pondering lately, and this must be God's way of answering."

"I can't mother her. My own mother passed when I was younger than Ellen. I won't know what to do."

"I think you will. You're strong. She'll need to be strong." He hesitated. This was not the way he ever imagined proposing to someone. For that matter, he hadn't really imagined proposing to anyone. His solitary life had suited him just fine before Jane left Ellen in his care. "But you're also gentle. She needs a woman's hand."

"How did this ever happen?" Lily's head sank into her hands.

"It seems that it was out of our control from the beginning."

She looked up at him. "Do you think we can do it?

Raise Ellen and protect my reputation so the shop will be successful?"

"From what I've seen of you, I don't think the shop's success is in question, as long as we take care of your honor." He prayed he was doing the right thing. "As for Ellen, it looks like the good Lord left her in my care. I don't think He orchestrated your problems, but I'd say as His children, He's giving us a way to make the best of it."

"I can't think why you'd do this for me." Lily bit her bottom lip.

"It's like the verse." He pointed to her needlework. "We're taking care of the needs of others. Ellen needs us both."

Lily's face turned pink, and she met his gaze. "What kind of relationship do you expect the two of us to have?"

He could tell it cost her a great deal to form the words. Then he felt the same heat rushing into his face. "Miss Warren, I'd expect for you to care for Ellen as a mother. This arrangement will be strictly for the sake of my niece."

Edward watched her as the breath she'd been holding seeped out of her to be replaced by relief.

"For the sake of Ellen?"

"Yes. And you."

"I didn't come to Pine Haven to find a husband. I'll never forget what you've done here today, Mr. Stone. You're giving up an awful lot to take on a wife you didn't want."

"I want Ellen to have a mother."

"In that case, I accept." She offered her hand for him to shake. Did she really see this as a business arrangement like the one he had with her father for the lease on his building?

It was a relief she seemed to accept his reasons so quickly, but the reality of how much his life was about to change threatened to overwhelm him at any moment.

"I do." Lily stood in front of Reverend Dismuke and repeated the marriage vows.

Daisy and Tucker had agreed with Edward, and it had only been a matter of hours before they'd arrived at the church. Long enough for Lily to change to her best dress. The lingering hint of smoke in its fibers reminded her of the reason she was doing this. When she'd prepared for bed the night before, she'd never have dreamed today would be her wedding day.

Edward took her hand and slid a small gold band onto her finger. She'd told him she didn't need a ring, but he'd insisted, saying it was another way to reinforce their union in the eyes of the community. He'd escorted her into the general store and asked her to choose from the tray of rings. She'd been relieved when he'd asked Mr. Croft to assist them, leaving Mrs. Croft sputtering and mumbling as she'd moved on to help another customer.

Lily looked at the delicate, plain ring. Edward didn't release her hand for the rest of the short ceremony. His hands were large but gentle. And strangely comforting, as if he was trying to reassure her they were doing the right thing.

"You may kiss the bride." Reverend Dismuke's words rang out in the nearly empty church. Only Daisy and Tucker, with their twin sons and baby daughter, sat on the bench opposite the reverend's wife, who kept an arm around the shoulders of Edward's niece. Lily wasn't sure if it was an effort on the woman's part to comfort Ellen or an attempt to keep the child from fleeing. The young girl had refused to attend until Edward told her she had no choice.

Edward took his other hand and turned Lily's chin to face him. A small smile played on his lips. He'd said they'd have an easier time overcoming the gossip if everyone was convinced their marriage was born of affection and not shame. But did he honestly intend to kiss her?

"Relax," he whispered. Then he grazed her cheek with the briefest of contact.

In an instant Lily found herself wrapped in her sister's hug while the preacher clapped Edward on the back and congratulated him.

Why was everyone so merry? They all knew she and Edward, given the choice, would never have married. Well, maybe the Dismukes didn't know that, but her family did.

Daisy held her hands and spoke, "We're taking Ellen home with us for the night." She gave a nod in the direction of the bench where Edward's niece still sat clinging to her handkerchief doll. Lily had never seen the child without that doll.

Lily watched as Edward accepted Tucker's welcome into their family. Lily hadn't thought about being alone with Edward. No, she needed Ellen to be at the cabin tonight. And every night.

"That's not necessary."

Daisy smiled and patted her hand. "We insist. I've already told her she can sleep in Rose's room."

"But…" Lily felt her life spinning like a toy top. She had to maintain some form of control.

Edward turned and met her gaze. He must have sensed her desperation, because he came to stand beside her. He was close enough for her to feel the warmth of him, but he didn't touch her. "Tucker just told me they've invited Ellen to their place."

"She can stay with us. There's no need." Better to face Ellen's reluctance than to face alone a husband she hadn't expected to have.

He leaned in to speak near her ear. His breath ran across her neck, leaving a chill with each word. "We've got a lot of things to sort out. I'd like to do it without Ellen's eager ears close by."

What did he want to sort out? She straightened her shoulders. There were a myriad of things. How they would handle finances, daily chores, the rebuilding of the work-room in her shop, and how to protect Ellen.

She agreed.

"Thank you, Daisy. That's very kind of you." Lily smiled at her sister but knew the smile didn't reach her eyes. Numbness was the only sensation she experienced at the moment, and she feared it would fade into regret.

Ellen plodded over to Edward. "Do I gotta go to the Barlows' farm?" Her bottom lip protruded, and the doll hung from her crossed arms.

He lifted the little girl's chin with one knuckle. "You know you love to go visit the Barlows. You can play with baby Rose." He smiled at her and patted her shoulder. "You'll have a good time, I promise. You can come say hello in the morning on your way into town for school."

Daisy moved to stand behind Ellen and put a hand on her shoulder. "Why don't we go by your cabin and get some clothes? Then we'll head out to the farm, and you can help John and James feed the animals."

Ellen's eyes aimed a dart of resentment at Lily before she agreed to Daisy's suggestion. "Bye, Uncle Edward."

"Goodbye, Ellen." As she started to tromp away, Edward called to her again. "Ellen, you forgot to tell your aunt Lily goodbye."

"Aunt Lily? I gotta call her 'aunt'?"

"You are permitted to call her Aunt Lily." He tilted his head to one side. "It's a privilege."

A long sigh came from her little body. "Bye, *Aunt* Lily."

"Goodbye, Ellen." She smiled at the girl, wondering how she must feel. Without warning, her home had changed today, and there was nothing she could do about it. In a way, Lily understood her childish frustration. She was almost tempted to cross her arms and pout, too.

Edward offered Lily his arm. She knew he was merely keeping up appearances. It was comforting and unsettling at the same time. Their marriage was the only way to remove themselves from the whirlwind of tortuous rumors they'd been caught up in for the past twenty-four hours.

Lily wanted to protect their good names. Individually. Hooking her hand on his arm and leaving the church felt as false as the lies Mrs. Croft had spread about them. Were they perpetrating one lie to negate the effects of another lie? Would God honor them for trying to save Ellen? She hoped so.

They rode in silence to her shop. Edward set the brake on the wagon.

"Do you need a few minutes to put your things together?" he asked.

Most of her clothes and personal belongings were still in trunks and crates. There would be little to pack.

She looked across the street to the cabin she would now share with Edward. Her husband.

Her husband? She had come here to escape a marriage to a man who only wanted a companion for his ailing mother. Now she sat in a wagon between the shop she was opening to start a new independent life and a cabin where her primary role would be to care for a young girl she'd only known a few days. A girl who'd made it plain that Lily was an intruder in her turbulent young life.

Lily had heard stories of people who disappeared in the night, leaving only a note for their loved ones, striking out on their own, hoping for a fresh start. She'd come here for that reason—with the blessing and help of her family. Had it only taken two days for her world to turn upside down?

Edward's touch on her sleeve drew her attention. "Are you all right?"

It was tempting to write a note and steal away in the night. But she could never leave her sisters and father like that. Not after all her father had done to give her a new life. Somehow she'd make this work. Edward had noble intentions, which was more than she could say for her former fiancé, Luther Aarens.

She shook off her thoughts and accepted her fate. "Fine, thank you."

Edward nodded toward her shop. "You'll want to get your clothes and such."

"Yes." She scooted to the edge of the wagon seat away from him and prepared to step down. "I'll need a little while to put some things back into the trunks."

"Wait a minute. I'll help you down." He climbed from the wagon and came around to assist her. With the briefest of contact, he lifted her and set her on the ground. "You go in and take care of that. I'll make space in the cabin for you."

She looked at him when he spoke, but his gaze went over her shoulder. When he did focus on her, she turned away. "I won't need much space." She twisted her hands together.

"I remember you had a couple of pieces of large furniture upstairs." He pointed to the window of her front room above the shop. "From when I helped carry it in."

Awkward held new meaning as they stood talking about her things. Things she hadn't thought she'd share with anyone. Things she'd brought to make her comfortable in her new home. Nothing was turning out as she'd planned.

She remembered a verse in Proverbs. "In all thy ways acknowledge Him, and He shall direct thy paths." Her faith in God would have to sustain her now. There was no course except to move forward as she'd agreed.

"We can move those things another day. If you don't mind, we can just get my clothes and personal items today. Perhaps Tucker can help with the furniture later."

Edward shuffled from one foot to another. He must be as nervous as she was. "That's good." He dipped his head and looked over his shoulder at the cabin. "I'll just be on my way, then."

He turned and took a step. Not knowing she was going to do it before it happened, Lily reached for his arm. He stilled and turned back to her.

"I know this isn't what either of us thought we'd be doing today." When he looked at her hand on his arm, she dropped it. "I hope we can make this work without everything being uncomfortable or awkward."

His thin lips curled into a half smile. He really was a giant of a man. Tall and broad with all the strength she imagined a blacksmith would need to do his job. But the softness of the smile and the way his almost-black eyes twinkled was a pleasant surprise. "No promises about not feeling awkward for a while. I haven't shared my home with another living soul until Ellen came to live with me a few months ago. I'm not quite sure you and I will see eye to eye on everything. It's a big adjustment to get to know someone new. I'm guessing we complicated it more than a little bit by getting married before we could do that."

She felt herself smiling in return. "That's a wise observation, Mr. Stone. I'm sure you're right."

"That's what I mean."

The smile faded and she asked, "What?"

"Mr. Stone? Really? Is that how you intend to address me?"

She gave a small chuckle. "I see. No. I don't think that will do any longer." She drew back her shoulders and took hold of her future with all her strength. "Edward, I'll be about a half hour preparing my things to move into our home. If you'd be so good as to meet me in the shop after you've finished preparing a space for me, I'll be most grateful."

She gave a little giggle. "How was that?"

He laughed in a deep tone. "That's just fine." He nodded. "Just fine, indeed."

When he headed for the cabin, she entered the shop. As she climbed the stairs to the home she'd only spent two nights in, she marveled that it would be the only two nights of her life spent as an independent woman.

Her dream of a shop wasn't dead. She wouldn't let it die. But her independence was over. She prayed for God to help her as she packed away the things she'd so carefully placed in her new home. When she'd asked for a new life, she wasn't prepared for this twist. God would have to light her path, because it was one she'd never dreamed would be hers.

In one major event, she'd gone from Lily Warren, milliner and shop owner, to Lily Stone, milliner, shop owner, wife and mother.

Chapter Four

Edward tossed his dirty clothes into a pile by the bedroom door. His cabin wasn't grand, but it wasn't small. If he'd built it himself, it would not have had two bedrooms, but the house was part of the deal when he'd bought his blacksmith shop from the previous owner. As soon as he was old enough, he'd moved out on his own to escape the stepmother his father had brought home shortly after his dear mother had died. She'd given no affection to him or Jane. Time and again he'd wished his father had never married her. Finding work as an apprentice to the town blacksmith had given him a purpose and place in life.

Eventually he'd nurtured a vague hope of one day having a family of his own. But over the years, he'd found it safer to retreat alone at night into the sanctuary of his home. His mistrust of women in general was based on years of watching his father's wife take advantage of his father. Her sweet facade had quickly faded after she'd convinced his father to marry her. She'd never truly loved him and had been horrid to Edward and Jane. Nothing they did was ever good enough for her. She'd settled into their home as mistress and ordered them about in her aloof manner, as though she felt them beneath her care or attention. Jane had been too young when she married, but until Wesley had whisked her away to Santa Fe, Edward had thought it was for the best.

Edward stripped the linens from the bed and added them to the pile by the door. A small crate from the back porch would suffice for his personal items. He put his shaving cup and brush in and then tossed in the small mirror from the top of his chest of drawers. He pulled a rag from his back pocket and took a swipe at the dust on top of the furniture.

Backing up in the doorway, he took a last look around. Not what he'd have done in normal circumstances for bringing home a wife, but it was the best he could manage in the half hour she'd allotted him. He stowed the small crate in a corner near the stove and gathered up the laundry. He tossed it onto the workbench on the back porch and headed back into the front room.

A light rapping sounded on the door, and his breath caught. He was doing this for Ellen. She needed a mother. Life might be upside down, but that little girl would always have a home with him.

He lifted the latch on the door and pulled it open. Lily stood in the street at the bottom of the porch steps. She must have knocked and backed as far away as she could.

He dragged his palms down the sides of his pants. "Hi."

Pink color soaked into Lily's cheeks. She really was a beautiful lady. At this moment, she must be just as nervous as he was. "Hello."

Edward stepped through the doorway. "Did you get everything packed?"

"Everything I'll need until we can move the furniture." She didn't look at him.

He reached inside the cabin and took his hat from the peg by the door. "Okay. I'll go get everything, then." He pushed the hat onto his head and walked down the porch steps.

She hesitated. "Would you mind if I took a look inside first?"

"Inside the cabin?"

"Yes. I want to see how much space there is, so I can decide what to bring and what to leave behind."

"Oh." He took the hat off again. "That makes sense." He shrugged his shoulders and lifted an arm to invite her up the steps. He heard a thump and turned to see the door of the livery open. Jim Robbins stood in front of his place and made no effort to hide his interest in the goings-on at Edward's house. Edward turned and looked up the street. Mrs. Winters was sweeping the sidewalk in front of the post office. He pivoted and saw Will Thomas in the doorway of the lumber mill.

Edward put his hat back on and took Lily by the elbow. "It seems we're being watched."

She followed his gaze and saw the obvious interest their neighbors were showing. She giggled like a schoolgirl. It was a light sound, like water over rocks in a stream in summertime. "You'd think there was a fire or something."

He chuckled. "One would think so."

"What should we do? Wave? Or ignore them."

He drew in a breath. "Do you trust me?"

"I believe I've proved that already. After all, I did marry you less than an hour ago."

Mr. Croft walked by on the street and tipped his hat.

He made a show of greeting Mr. Robbins when he arrived at the livery.

Edward leaned in close. "What goes on here will affect us all. How well your business does, and how well our marriage is accepted. All of it could have consequences for us and for Ellen."

Lily looked over his shoulder and nodded. "I'd say this town is very interested in us at the moment. I hope it will fade in time. Quickly, would be my preference."

"Then I say we do our part to keep the busybodies from having anything to talk about."

"How do you propose to do that?"

"By living the part of a normal married couple."

Lily's eyes grew wide.

He gave her elbow a slight squeeze. "What I meant to say is if we give every indication of being a normal married couple, when we're outside the cabin, no one looking will have any reason to question our relationship. The best way for them to concentrate on someone else is for there to be nothing to see here."

"I think I see what you mean." Her face relaxed.

"Good. So we're agreed?"

She nodded.

"Here we go, then." Edward leaned close and, with one hand behind her back and another behind her knees, he scooped her off her feet.

Caught unawares, she gave a tiny yelp and wrapped her arms around his neck. She whispered close to his ear. "What are you doing?"

"I'm carrying you across the threshold." He climbed the steps and walked into the cabin. He turned in the doorway and kicked the door closed with his foot.

Lily laughed. "I think I may have married a deranged man."

Edward laughed and set her on her feet. He put the distance of the room between them. "Not deranged." He closed the shutters across one of the front windows. "But never happy to be the center of attention." He closed the other shutters and dropped into a chair at the table.

Lily stepped to the cabinet next to the stove and looked out of the window that faced Main Street. "Then why did you make such a scene? Mr. Winters has joined his wife on the sidewalk, and they're talking to Mr. Croft. Mrs. Winters is smiling and looking in our direction."

"Close the shutters." Edward leaned back in the chair and stretched his legs out in front of him.

"It's the middle of the afternoon."

"I know. But if you don't want them walking by on this side of the street and trying to peek in the window, you'll close the shutters."

Lily swung the shutters closed. The dim interior of the room was lit only by the fire. He marveled again at how gracefully she moved.

He went to the stove and set the coffee to warm. "Why don't you sit by the fire? You've got to be bone tired."

A slight shrug of her shoulders was the only response.

"It's not the day either of us planned." He opened a tin of cookies Mrs. Dismuke had brought for Ellen. His niece might not want him to share her treats, but he'd deal with her later.

Lily sat on the edge of a chair facing the fire. "Nothing has gone like I planned for most of my life." He watched the back of her head as she shook it slowly back and forth. "I'd so hoped things would be different in Pine Haven."

Edward poured two cups of coffee. "Do you drink coffee?"

"Yes." She didn't turn away from the fire. Her shoulders slumped forward.

He brought a cup to her and set the tin of cookies on the table by her chair. "This might help you." He retrieved his cup and sat on the bench in front of the fire facing her.

She sipped the brew, and her face twisted. "Oh, my."

"Not to your taste?"

"Is it to yours?" She looked up at him.

"Not really. But it's the best I've been able to do."

She sat up straight and set the cup on the table. "Did you bake the cookies?" A wary eye told him she was being cautious when it came to his efforts at cooking.

"No. The preacher's wife brought them for Ellen. They're quite good."

"Do you think Ellen will be upset with you for sharing them with me?"

He grinned. She'd only been in town a couple of days, but she'd already figured out Ellen's personality. "Probably. So consider it her wedding gift to you."

She took a cookie and nibbled at it. Then she took another bite and picked up a second cookie.

"Have you eaten today, Lily?"

"I don't remember. Everything has happened so fast." She stared into the fire again. "I think I had some lunch."

"Eat another cookie, then, and we'll get some things figured out before we go get your trunks from the shop. I've got to take care of the wagon, too."

She put the half-eaten cookie down and stood. "I'm sorry. I forgot about the wagon."

"Relax." She was like a frightened colt, jumping at every noise. "We need to wait a bit before we go outside again. If it's all the same to you, I'd like to talk for a few minutes."

She paced to the fireplace and back to the chair. "What are we doing?"

Edward stood and set his coffee on the table. "We're making life better. For you. And for Ellen."

Blue eyes looked up then. "We are, aren't we?" She seemed to calm a bit.

"Yes." He'd have to guard against those eyes. They were the kind of blue that could pull a man in against his will. Like a gorgeous sky that demanded attention. He took a step back. "Would you like to look around? Ellen's room is through that door." He gestured to the door closest to the fireplace. "I've cleared some space for you in my room." He pointed to the other door on the back wall of the room.

Lily stiffened. He didn't see it, but as soon as he said the words he knew it happened.

"Your room?"

"What I meant to say is, you'll have the other room." He nodded toward the fire. "I'll be sleeping out here."

"But I couldn't take your room."

"If you don't mind, I'd like to keep my clothes and such in there, but I brought out my shaving things and stripped the bed. I thought you might have fresh linens you'd like to put on it."

"Really, we can bring the settee from my rooms at the shop. I can sleep there." She wrung her hands. "You'd never fit on it." She lifted one hand to indicate his height. "You're much too tall." She pointed to the center of the room. "We could move the chairs back and…"

She was talking so fast he had to break in. "That won't be necessary." He pointed to the floor. "This is where

I slept when I came here as an apprentice. The former owner took me in."

"But now you're the owner, and a man ought to sleep in his own bed." Her voice became higher, and she was wringing her hands again.

He reached out and caught her hands in his. "Lily. Stop." He kept his tone calm. If she maintained this pace, she'd work herself into a frenzy. "It's going to be fine. I'll sleep out here. Ellen goes to bed early. She'll never know. You will take my bed. It's the best I could do with the time I had."

She withdrew her hands and put them to her cheeks. "It is all happening rather quickly, isn't it?" She lowered her hands and met his eye. "I'm sorry. I'm not usually the sort of person to panic."

"Anyone would be unsettled under the circumstances."

"You don't seem to be." She tilted her head to one side and drew her brows together. "Why is that?"

"I told you. I've been considering marriage for the sake of Ellen." He smiled at her. "Granted, I had thought to have more time for making the decision, but I was pondering it." He moved to the bedroom door and opened it. "If you'd like to take a look around, I'll see what I have that we could eat for supper."

"Thank you." She walked by him, and he went to see how much bread was left.

He had planned on making pancakes for Ellen and himself. It hardly seemed a fitting wedding supper. Even if they weren't in the throes of young love, they were married today. His bride deserved a fine meal.

Something banged on the floor in his bedroom.

Lily called out. "Sorry. I tripped on the broom."

He walked over and stood in the doorway of the room.

"I shouldn't have left it there. It's usually on the back porch." He'd never hesitated about going into his own room before. But it wasn't just his anymore.

"Thank you for doing such a nice job of preparing for me." She stood in the center of his room with her hands clasped in front of her. "It's very nice."

"I'm sure it's not what you're accustomed to." He backed away from the door.

"Really, it's fine." She stepped into the front room again. "Let's go get my things. I'd like to close up the shop. There's a lot to do this evening." She had walked to the front door while she talked. "Did you find anything to eat?"

Edward grabbed his hat from its peg. "Nothing fit for a wedding supper." He opened the door. "I think we've earned a treat. Let's get your things and go to the hotel for supper."

Lily laid her hairbrush between the comb and mirror in the satin-lined box her father had given her for her last birthday and closed the lid. She ran her hand across the wooden box and marveled at its uniqueness. The beauty of the ornate dresser set made her smile every time she used it. It reminded her of her father's love.

Every woman deserved to feel special. She'd come to Pine Haven to bring beautiful things to the ladies in town. It was one thing she could do well. She knew what ladies liked and how the smallest treasure could brighten even the most menial life.

Now, three days into her new adventure and she was preparing for bed in a home she shared with a husband she just met.

Dinner had been delicious. The thick slices of ham

served with the fluffiest potatoes were as fine as any she'd eaten. They'd dined at the hotel her father was buying and would run with her sister Jasmine, when he arrived in a few weeks' time. If it hadn't been her wedding supper, she knew she'd have been able to enjoy it more. Never had she dreamed her wedding would be a hasty affair orchestrated to prevent the demise of her good name in a town of strangers.

Lord, I don't know why all this happened. Help me to handle it in a way that pleases You. Please bless and protect Edward and Ellen.

She lowered the wick, and the lamp went out. Lying in bed and staring at the moonlight that shone around the shutters brought no calm to her rattled soul.

A rap at the door startled her. "Lily? Are you awake?"

Lily sat up in bed and pulled her mother's quilt under her chin. "Yes." Her voice was so low she wasn't sure Edward could hear her.

"I hate to disturb you, but I left my Bible by the bed."

"Just a minute." She climbed out of the bed and slid into her dressing gown. This time she cinched it securely. A loose robe would never happen to her again. Of course, the only time it mattered had already passed.

She barely opened the door. "Do you have a lamp? I put mine out and don't know where the matches are."

"Yes." Edward retrieved a lamp from the table by his chair near the fireplace and handed it to her. "I'm sorry to bother you. I'm having a bit of trouble getting to sleep. I usually read the Bible at night."

"I understand." She turned into the room and found the well-worn book. "I was just saying my prayers."

A smile lit his eyes. "I hope you said one for me."

Glad for the relative darkness, she passed the lamp

back to him as her cheeks flamed warm. "I did. And for Ellen, too." She handed him the Bible and backed away from the door.

"Thank you."

"You're welcome." She looked over her shoulder into the room. "I guess I'll turn in now."

He nodded. "Well, good night, then. I'll see you in the morning. We've got a lot of work to do."

"Yes. I'll be ready." She closed the door and leaned against it. How would she ever get to sleep tonight? An exciting adventure into independence had turned into the journey that would last her lifetime. She prayed God would give her the strength to make it.

When she awoke the next morning, the cabin was quiet. She dressed without delay, grateful she'd thought to bring her pitcher and bowl with her. The privacy of Edward's bedroom shielded her from having to face her new life before she was alert. She opened the shutters over the window to be greeted by a sun much higher in the sky than she'd expected. How had she slept so late?

Opening the door into the front room, she braced for her first encounter with her husband. Her husband.

God, give me strength.

This was quickly becoming her constant prayer. God must be showing His sense of humor today, because Edward was nowhere to be seen. She took a peek into Ellen's room. Everything was just as it had been the night before.

Sunlight streamed through the windows in the front room. No time for breakfast now. She went back to her room and snatched up her hat and coat. This was no way to begin her new life. What would Edward think of her shirking her responsibilities on their first day of working to repair the shop?

Lily walked across the street without seeing anyone. She found the shop empty, too. Where was Edward? She hung her hat and coat on the hall tree and got to work. A full hour later the front door opened. Edward came in carrying a package wrapped in brown paper. He propped it in the windowsill and shrugged out of his coat.

"Oh, good. You're here." He hung his coat next to hers. "Did you sleep well?"

"Where were you?" Lily's stomach growled in hunger.

"Excuse me?" Edward went to the front door and started to remove the wooden trim from around the window he'd broken so he could get into the shop on the night of the fire.

"I've been here for over an hour. I thought we were going to work together this morning." Why didn't he look at her? Was he as uncomfortable as she was?

"I've been working for several hours, Lily." He dropped the trim pieces into a pile at his feet and scrubbed the end of the hammer along the edge of the frame to remove the remaining bits of broken glass.

"I wish you'd awakened me." Lily had established a comfortable working relationship with Edward as her landlord. But today he was also her husband. She didn't know how to behave toward him.

"I knocked on the door."

"I didn't hear you. You could have made certain I was awake."

He dropped the hammer into the small box of tools near his feet and turned to her. "Really?"

"Of course." She backed up a step from him. "I wanted to be here early. I don't know when I've slept so late."

"How was I supposed to respect your privacy and wake you without coming into the room?"

Lily looked at her feet. "Oh. I see." She walked to the glass display case and picked up the rag she'd been using to wipe the soot from the furniture. Edward must be as off balance by their situation as she was.

She heard him tearing the paper from the package he'd brought with him.

"Will you hold this glass steady while I nail the trim work back into place?"

She dropped the rag and brushed her hands together. "Certainly."

Edward set the pane on the lip of the frame and held it steady. "Put your hands here and here."

Lily followed his instructions. He stooped to pick up the first piece of trim and slid it between her and the door. She stretched as far as possible to one side, so he could hammer without hitting her. He worked with several small nails between his lips. Each time he hammered one into place he retrieved another.

Talking around the nails, he admitted, "I knew you hadn't slept the night before. You needed the rest."

"I'm sorry." She shifted so he could put the next piece of trim on the opposite side of her, all while holding the pane of glass. "I wanted to help you."

"There was nothing you could do this morning. I was picking up the supplies we need." He tapped the last piece into place, and she backed away. It was difficult to be so close to him working, knowing neither of them had intended to be working together at all, much less as husband and wife.

"Well, all the same, I'd have been here if I were awake." Her stomach rumbled again.

"Let me guess." He picked up the box of tools and headed for the workroom. "You didn't eat breakfast."

She followed to retrieve the broom and dustpan. She might not have gone with him to buy the supplies, but she would clean up the mess. "No. I wasn't sure where you were. I was late enough as it was."

He dropped the box onto the workbench. "Lily, we need to establish some kind of expectations for our relationship and act accordingly."

She stilled, broom in hand, and leaned against the doorway between the shop and the workroom.

Edward exhaled as if he were gathering his nerve. "We were able to work together in a friendly manner before the fire. I'd like for us to continue to do that. We've both been on pins and needles since we decided to get married. We both did it for noble reasons. Do you think you can relax? I declare, the more nervous you are around me, the more nervous it makes me." He stopped and drew in a deep breath.

A rumbling laugh bubbled up in her throat. She tried to swallow it but couldn't. "You're so right. We're no different than we were two days ago."

His eyebrows shot up. "Maybe a little different."

She did laugh then. "Yes, but we're the same people. With the same goals."

"Some of the goals are different, too." He scrunched up his face a bit.

"You know what I mean." She stepped forward and put a hand on his arm. "I agree with you. Let's continue as the friends we were becoming before the fire."

"Good." He looked at her and then at her hand on his arm.

She dropped her hand. "I'm glad we got that settled." She turned to go back into the shop and sweep up the glass.

Edward followed her. "Would you like some lunch?"

"Yes, I would. As soon as I sweep up this mess, I'll go upstairs and put something together for us. All my food stores are still here."

"All right." He nodded toward the workroom. "Then I'll get to work in here."

"Okay, then." She swept up the glass, wondering what her life would be like now. Everything she'd envisioned was like the glass at her feet. Shattered. Beyond repair. Replaced by something new. The new glass served the same purpose, but the old glass would soon be forgotten. Could she forget her dreams of independence? Would her new life afford her the same fulfillment? Establishing her shop would make her financially independent. That would be a comfort to her as she watched the rest of her dreams disappear. Tonight Ellen would return, and Lily's new role as mother to the young girl would begin.

Lily knew opening a new business would be a great challenge. She was certain winning Ellen's trust would be greater.

Chapter Five

Edward stepped into the front of the shop and heard Lily cry, "Oh, no!"

She let out a yelp, and he was at the workroom door as she stumbled backward. The highest shelf in the storeroom was just beyond reach from her stool. She'd climbed onto the workbench, overreaching to push the extra hatboxes out of the way.

Seeing her arms flailing, he crossed the shop floor as she lost her struggle to right herself. The breath whooshed out of her as she landed against his chest.

"Wonderful." Edward set her to her feet. "I see you're still following Doc's orders."

Disapproval, not surprise, covered her face.

"I was just trying to make room to work." She brushed her hands together to remove the dust. "I'm perfectly fine."

"Just how fine would you be if I hadn't come along?"

"How do you know I wasn't startled by you coming into the shop unannounced?"

"Because I heard your screech while I was outside."

"Never you mind. I'm not hurt, and I've more work to do." Lily twirled and marched to the front of the shop.

"You're welcome." He followed her.

Lily hung her head but smirked. "Thank you so much for helping me catch my balance."

"Catch your balance? You'd be lying on the floor broken if I hadn't come in here when I did! You might want to be more careful if you intend to open your shop next week. Or at all."

"You're right. I have a tendency to lessen the intensity of things after the fact." She smiled. "Thank you for saving my life."

"Catching your balance? Saving your life?" Edward laughed. "Is there no middle ground with you, Lily?"

Her eyebrows shot up when he spoke her name. Would she be able to relax and accept a modicum of familiarity from him?

He grimaced and indicated the bell he'd dropped on the table when he'd rushed to help her. "I came to mount this."

She reached for the bell. "It's lovely." She studied his handiwork. It hadn't taken long to repair, but it was intricate work. He was glad she approved.

"I brought a new bracket to make sure it doesn't fall again." Their fingers brushed when she handed the bell to him. A tingling sensation caught him off guard. He didn't know if he was more surprised by how the touch of her fingers stirred his skin or how her words of kindness and approval brushed against his wary heart.

"Thank you. I've work to do in the back room. I'll leave you to it." Her quick steps confirmed her hurry to escape his presence. "If you need me, just give a shout." She darted a glance over her shoulder.

"It's a bit more likely you'll be calling out for help from me," Edward muttered as he turned to work on the bell.

"I heard that." She laughed. "You're probably right, but allow me the opportunity to think I might be safe on my own."

He'd replaced the burned shelves in the workroom by midafternoon, then left her to get her supplies set up as she pleased. That had given him time to go across the street to his shop and repair the bell. He hoped it was the last thing she'd need. After two days away from his shop, he was behind on his work.

Edward dropped the bell, and it clanged on the wooden floor.

"Are you all right out there, or do you need my help?" Lily's sarcasm danced into the room on her words.

"Got it." He inspected the bell for damage. "Thankfully, my foot broke its fall."

"Good thing it didn't hit you in the head. You'd have to make a new one." Lily snickered from the opening to the workroom.

He stood with his hands holding the bell above the door and angled his face to see her. Just as he suspected. A wide grin.

"Very funny." He chuckled before turning back to his work. He gave the nail one final rap and released the bell and bracket.

"Good as new." He started gathering his tools and putting them back in the box.

"Great."

He picked up his toolbox. "Is that everything?" He watched as she looked around the shop.

"I think so. The rest will be up to me. I've got to make new stock. I'm hoping it will only take a few days."

"Provided you don't sleep the mornings away?" He dipped his hat and stepped out the door. "I'll see you at home in a little while."

Edward heard her stamp her small foot on the floorboards as he closed the door, and a grin tugged at his mouth.

Standing on the steps of the building—his building— he marveled at the life one small creature could bring to a place. Not since his sister left town had he sparred with a woman. He found it invigorating.

A shudder ran up his back, and he tromped off the porch. That was not a healthy path to travel. Following the excitement of conversation with a young woman was not where he was headed in life. Not at all.

Their marriage was about Ellen. He'd serve himself well to remember that.

Edward opened the door to Ellen's room. "Come to the table, young lady. Aunt Lily called you several minutes ago."

His niece sat in the middle of the bed with her arms folded around the doll his sister had made for her. "I don't like carrots." Her bottom lip protruded.

He sat on the side of the bed. "You're saying you'd rather have pancakes again?" He tousled her hair, hoping to improve her disposition.

"I'm saying I don't like carrots." She kept her arms crossed, but lifted them and flopped them back down across her chest. "I don't know why you married her, anyway. First she took Momma's shop. Now she's taking you."

"She's not taking anything. She's cooked us a fine supper, and we are going to eat it with the gratitude she deserves."

"I don't like her."

Edward stood. "I don't like your attitude. Lily is here because I asked her to be. You will be kind to her." He moved to the door. "You've got two minutes to be at the table with a respectful attitude."

He closed the door and turned to see Lily standing at the table watching him.

"You heard?"

She nodded.

"She'll adjust."

Lily turned back to the stove and put food on a plate. She placed it on the table with two others. She took her seat at the foot of the table and folded her hands in her lap.

The clock on the mantel chimed seven times.

Edward sat at the head of the table.

Lily looked to Ellen's door. Nothing.

Edward bowed his head and said grace over the food. When he opened his eyes, Ellen was standing at his elbow.

"Take your seat and apologize to Aunt Lily for delaying the meal."

Ellen shuffled her feet and plopped into her chair. "Sorry."

"Ellen." He would not let her win what he was certain would be the first of many battles of wills.

The child narrowed her eyes at him and turned to Lily. The sugary sweetness of her words belied her true feelings. "I'm so sorry, Aunt Lily, for delaying this meal. I know it can't taste better if it gets cold."

He watched Lily draw in her bottom lip and chew it.

How had he managed to find himself at the table with not one, but two reluctant females? Both would rather be anywhere than here with him.

Lord, I think I'm gonna need the wisdom of Solomon to bring these two together.

"You may find a cooling supper preferable to a chunk of bread and a cup of milk in your room before bed."

Edward wasn't sure who was more surprised by Lily's words. Ellen or him.

"You can't do that!" Ellen jumped up. "Uncle Edward won't let you!"

Lily looked at him. He had no doubt this moment would define how his new family would be from this night on.

"Sit down and be silent, Ellen. You may stay at the table only if you eat quietly. If you show any disrespect, you will do as your aunt has said."

Ellen opened her mouth, and he raised a finger in caution. She closed her mouth and looked at Lily and then him.

"Would anyone like a biscuit?" Lily passed the bowl of bread to Ellen, who took one and handed the bowl to him.

Ellen's attitude had degenerated to rudeness in the previous weeks, while they'd waited for word from her parents. He'd overlooked it because he was sorry for her. Watching Lily require good behavior or promise consequences confirmed he'd made the right choice for Ellen by marrying her.

He took a bite of the fluffy biscuit and closed his eyes. It was delicious.

"Well?" He opened his eyes at Lily's question.

"It's wonderful. I had no idea you were such a fine cook."

Lily spoke to Ellen. "Do you like it?"

Ellen looked to Edward for permission to speak. At his nod, she said, "Yes, ma'am."

Lily gave the child a small smile. "I'm glad. Now try your carrots. I think you'll find the brown sugar makes them taste a bit like candy."

By the end of the meal, Edward wondered if Lily was not just the right choice for Ellen but for him, as well.

Something was missing. On Friday after lunch, Lily stood in the middle of her shop and spun in a circle, taking in everything she'd arranged with such care. One hand came to her mouth, and she tapped a finger against her lips as she contemplated what it needed.

The clanging bell drew her attention. Edward's mouth lifted for a split second before settling into a bland expression. "I was passing by and saw you through the glass. How's everything coming along?"

She turned to the display case and back to the front windows.

"If you must know, something isn't right."

Edward took in the shop and shrugged his broad shoulders. "It all looks fine."

Lily drew her brows together. "Of course, it looks fine to you. You're a man."

His blank response caught her eye.

"That's not an insult, just an observation."

She spun again to the windows. "If I could just put my finger on what it is." She tapped one finger against her lips again.

"Not sure I can help you, but…"

"Aha! Oh, yes, you can! Wait right here." She dashed into the workroom and plundered through the crates she'd emptied. A lid fell to the floor, revealing what she searched for. "Eureka!"

She rushed back to the front room with a fashion magazine she'd received from Paris. Flipping through the pages, she found the picture she needed.

"Can you make this?" She pointed to a drawing of hat stands advertised for sale. They were different heights with a metal base anchoring a post that was capped with a metal cup inverted to hold a hat. They would be perfect in the front windows. She could order stands, but they wouldn't arrive before she opened.

"Of course, you can make these! You're an artist. The bell proves that." She was becoming overexcited, but this would set her apart from the other shops in town. The only other place that carried hats was the general store. Their hats were stored in boxes on a high shelf, and the owner had to open every one for any customer who showed an interest.

Edward studied the drawing. "Seems simple enough. How many do you want?"

"At least a dozen, in different heights and sizes." She pointed to the windows. "This was the best I could do, but stands will be so much better." She'd arranged small crates upside down and draped them with a length of fabric before placing the hats at various angles. Gloves hung over the edges of the boxes, and an open parasol was propped in the corner of one window.

"A dozen? Sure you need so many?"

"Yes. At least. I'll put some in the windows, a couple on the sideboard, and some on this table." She indicated the center of the room. "The hall tree has hooks, so I won't need any on that side of the room."

Lily smiled at the thought of the finished displays. "Can you have them by Monday?"

Edward chuckled. "Monday? You do realize this is Friday?"

"Yes. I'll pay for them. I really need them before I open." She looked out the front window into the street beyond. "As a matter of fact, I'm going to keep the shades down so the display will be a complete surprise when I open on Monday."

She pushed the magazine into his grip and started to dismantle the window display.

"I won't be able to finish by then." Edward came to stand close behind her.

Lily straightened to her full height. "Why ever not? They seem simple enough to me." She went back to her task, the matter settled in her mind.

"May I suggest you stick to making hats—" he waved a hand at the various displays "—and whatever else it is you do? Let me handle the blacksmith work."

She stopped her work as quickly as she'd started. "Hmm… I'm much too busy to argue with you today. And it would only serve to slow you down. Not a risk I'm willing to take." She pursed her mouth in a small show of triumph.

"I doubt you'd ever pass on an opportunity for a good argument, Lily."

She refused to give him the satisfaction of a retort. "Do as many as you can. I'll put them in the window and make do inside the shop until you finish the rest. I think six will be a good start."

At his lifted brow, she added, "You can have six for me, can't you?"

He stood without a word and watched her face. She

didn't know what it was, but something made him decide to help her. In an instant his eyes shone with determination.

"I can do six, but I won't promise more."

Lily put a hand on his. "Thank you so much."

"They won't be ready until Monday morning. I'll bring them over first thing. You may have to delay the opening for a little while that morning to do your setup, but I can't do anything faster than that."

"Perfect." A new excitement filled her. She was going to make this work. Her days of toiling away in the background of her father's life were over. A bright future was in reach. And reach for it, she would.

Edward pulled his hand from hers.

"Oh, my. I did get a bit carried away. Sorry." She put a hand to her hair and pushed the blond curls behind her ears. Keeping the unruly tresses in a bun was a never-ending struggle.

"I'll be on my way, then." He slapped the magazine against the palm of his hand. "I just got a large order from a new customer. Mustn't keep her waiting." He gave a nod and slipped out the door. "But I won't accept payment for them."

"Why ever not?"

"You're my wife now. My responsibility is to provide for you."

Lily stiffened. "If you refuse payment, I'll rescind the order."

"Why? It's proper for a husband to provide for his wife."

"We both know this is not an ordinary marriage. You've done me a great favor by protecting my good name. The least I can do is make the most of this shop to help provide for our family and save this property."

She watched his eyes as he processed it all. "You may pay me for the materials. Nothing more."

"But your time. If you're making these, you won't be doing other projects that will pay for your time and materials."

Edward put up a hand. "I'll work in the evenings. That's my final word on the matter."

Lily knew pushing him further would insult his dignity as a man. She followed him onto the sidewalk. "Thank you, Edward."

"Uncle Edward? What are you doing?" Ellen sidled up next to Edward's far side. She tucked herself behind his leg and peered up at Lily. Her hair was mussed and her dress dirty.

He put a hand on the girl's shoulder. "I was checking on Aunt Lily."

"Hello," Lily said to Ellen.

"Uncle Edward told me you wouldn't take up his time."

"Ellen. Be kind." His cheeks flamed. Was that guilt in his eyes?

"Did he, now? Well, I'll let him get back to his work, then."

"You best. He's got lots of work to do and don't got time to waste on you."

Lily took a half step back. This was a strong-minded child. At only seven, she possessed the directness of someone much older without the wisdom to hold her tongue.

"Ellen, apologize this minute." Edward looked into the child's upturned face. She seemed to hold her own against her uncle. He dwarfed her in size but not spirit.

"Didn't say nothin' wrong."

"Ellen, say you're sorry."

A small foot scuffed the boards on the sidewalk. Ellen looked at Lily and then back at Edward in what appeared to be an effort to discern his seriousness.

"Sorry." Ellen's hands had been behind her back, but now she pulled the tattered and dirty handkerchief doll into the circle of the arms she folded across her chest.

"For?" Edward prompted his niece.

"For speaking when I should be quiet."

"I accept your apology."

"Can I go home now?" Ellen's words were quiet but resolute.

"Run on back to the shop. I'll be there in a bit." Edward gave Ellen a nudge and turned to Lily.

"I'm sorry. She can be difficult sometimes, but I'm doing the best I can."

God, forgive me for judging him so narrowly. Of course, there's more to this man than what I've seen in just a few days.

"I'm sure it's been hard for her since her parents left."

"No girl should be without her momma," Edward said.

Lily knew the pain of growing up without a mother. When hers passed away, she had been five years old. It was the hardest part of childhood. Her father had tried to fill the void of maternal nurturing in their home with a housekeeper. Beverly Norton had done her best. Lily and her sisters loved Beverly, but there was still something missing.

Lily had taken to mothering others in an effort to fill the hole in her young heart. First her doll, then her favorite dog and, finally, her father during his long illness. She'd been swallowed up in her efforts to replace her mother. Lily's Millinery and Finery was her attempt at finding herself again.

"I've been praying for them to return." It sounded feeble, but what else could she say?

He nodded his head with no outward sign of hope. "That's what we pray for. Every night. Can't say my hope isn't all but gone."

"Ellen is quite a handful."

He met her frank statement with a cold stare. "That's why I need your help."

"I didn't mean anything by that, Edward."

"Yes, you did, Lily. You might wish you didn't, but you did." He stepped off the sidewalk.

"Please, I wasn't trying to say you aren't doing a fine job with her."

Edward turned for a brief moment. "I'm doing my best. That's all my sister asked." He nodded his head in dismissal of further argument. "I'll be home late. Don't wait supper for me."

And he was gone, his shoulders not quite as square as before but still very much a man in charge of his world.

Would she ever learn to hold her tongue? There she stood moments ago thinking the child didn't know when to be silent, and she'd committed the same sin.

Lord, help me to be swift to hear and slow to speak. It's such a challenge for me.

"Duck." Edward stepped onto the porch of the general store with Ellen on his back. Tiny arms encircled his neck. She was getting so big he thought she might bump her head when he entered.

Giggles filled his ear when she leaned in close. "Can

I have candy?" She asked the same question every Saturday morning.

He slid the child to stand on her feet. "Two pieces. Go pick out what you want, but wait until Mrs. Croft isn't busy to ask for it. I've got to get a few supplies." Little feet tapped a happy rhythm as they left him near the doorway.

Edward picked up a box of matches and went in search of shaving soap. He reached for the bar he usually bought and caught sight of Lily as she came through the front door. Moving behind a barrel of brooms, he was able to study her unnoticed. Her hat was set at an angle, her hair swept low over her forehead.

Lily looked in the opposite direction from where he stood. Her coat was buttoned against the gray morning, and she wore fine gloves. The hat was fancier than any he'd seen in Pine Haven. She was like a wave of beauty and all things fine coming into their midst.

Before he'd left the house, she'd told him she was going to change clothes and run errands. Then she planned to work in her shop afterward.

He still hadn't adjusted to having her in his life. The pancakes she'd made for breakfast had surpassed his meager cooking skills. Everything about her had improved his life.

She pivoted on the heel of a small boot and caught a glimpse of him. He feigned interest in a broom before acknowledging her with a tip of his hat. She came toward him with a purpose that pinned him to the spot.

"I didn't realize you'd be here." Her smile lit the dark corner of the store.

"Just needed a few things." He held up the box of matches.

Lily raised a delicate hand to touch her hair. "I need to replace some things that were damaged in the fire."

"I was about to speak to Mr. Croft about adding you to my account. You can charge your purchases."

Lily shook her head. "I told you I'm prepared to care for all of my needs. It was never my intent to be a burden on you."

Did she know how her words cut him? Or how he wished he could say he didn't need her money? How he hated the loan on the shop. If he'd never borrowed the money, he'd never have been in a position to need to have a tenant.

But then he might not have had reason to spend time with Lily. And she wouldn't have agreed to care for Ellen. Even with the good he saw in knowing her, he despised being beholden to her financially. One day he'd pay for everything she needed. He'd pay off the mortgage and free himself of that burden as quickly as possible. Then he'd be able to take care of his wife without the shame of needing her money.

She changed the subject. "How is my order coming along?" Directness was definitely one of her character traits. Not common in a young lady, but nice to see for a change.

"I'm making progress."

"Oh, I hoped seeing you out on the town meant you'd finished." Her pert response almost made him laugh. Until he realized she wasn't teasing.

"I have things to tend to. Your order will be ready as, and when, promised." He tipped his hat to her and went to gather Ellen.

"Did you pick your candy?" His niece waited at the

counter with her chin resting on fingers that clutched the edge of the glass case.

"Mrs. Croft made me wait while she helps another lady. Said I could wait till you were ready." The little face went from longing for the anticipated treat to scrunched with disapproval over being pushed aside.

Edward placed his items on the counter and gave her a wink. "Mr. Croft can help us." He lifted a hand to signal the owner. Mr. Croft added Lily to his account and tallied his purchases.

He couldn't help but notice Lily out of the corner of his eye as he paid. She held a blue fabric to the light in the front window. Without turning, he knew it matched her eyes perfectly—something he scolded himself for knowing. Mrs. Croft busied herself trying to convince Lily to make a purchase.

"Can we go to Mrs. Milly's today? I wanna play with Reilly." Ellen yanked on the end of his coat. "I hadn't got to go nowhere after school in too many days. All you do is work. I ain't havin' no fun."

"Lick that sugar off your lips, little missy." He watched the valiant effort to catch every speck of her weekly treat with her tongue. "You should know better than to complain when your mouth is full of candy."

A tiny hand went against her forehead. "I forgot. Thanks for the candy. Can I go play with Reilly now? He gots a new marble, and I wanna see it."

Edward put a hand on her shoulder and directed her to the door. "I don't see why not, since you asked so nice and all."

"Thanks for coming in, Mr. Stone," Liza Croft called to him as he opened the door.

Her next words were addressed to Lily but followed

him for the rest of the day. "I'm surprised you and your husband aren't shopping together."

Lily's sharp intake of breath brought him to a stop in the open doorway.

"My husband is a very busy man. I don't think a woman should drain the life out of her husband by demanding his constant attention."

Edward walked out and let the door close behind him. A smile crossed his face at the thought of Lily's words of rebuke searing Mrs. Croft's nosy ears. In the time since he and Lily met, he'd learned she could stand her ground. They might not exactly be friends, but in this situation he knew they were allies.

Chapter Six

Sunday morning dawned clear and cool. After breakfast Lily dressed in her favorite blue dress, added a wool coat and walked the short distance to the church with Edward. Ellen had gone ahead to attend a children's class taught by Mrs. Winters before the service.

She cast a glance at Edward, who was stretching his neck to one side. "Did you sleep well?"

He straightened and said, "Yes."

"Really? And your neck isn't bothering you?"

"Just a little stiff."

"I'd feel better if you let me sleep on the settee and you took the bed. We could ask Tucker to come tomorrow and help you move my furniture from the rooms above the shop to your home." She paused, wondering what he would think of her next suggestion. "We could set up my bed in Ellen's room. There's ample space there. I could share with her."

Edward stopped, forcing her to wait on him. "We talked about this. Ellen needs things to be as normal as possible. That doesn't mean for her aunt to sleep in one room, while her uncle sleeps in another."

Lily tilted her head to one side and met his gaze. "That's exactly what we are doing."

"But Ellen doesn't know it." He started to walk again.

"Not yet, but the way you snore, it's only a matter of time."

"The way I snore?" He turned toward her. "I don't snore."

"Loud enough to wake me in the middle of the night." She laughed. "I thought a wild animal had gone under the house to keep warm and found itself caught."

"That can't be true."

"Oh, yes. Like wild dogs growling a warning to anyone who dares to come near."

"Well, if Ellen asks, I'll tell her I was disturbing you and moved to the front room so you could rest."

Lily's laughter ended. It wasn't right for him to work hard all day and sleep on the floor at night. There had to be a better solution. She'd think of something.

The muted sounds of singing reached her as they approached the church door. She closed her eyes in silent prayer.

Lord, please give me friends here. Help me make a good impression on the people of Pine Haven.

No sooner had she settled on the bench next to Edward than the door creaked open again and clanged to a close. Ellen clomped up the middle aisle to her uncle's side. Lily glimpsed his disapproval in the glance he shot the little girl. Ellen shrugged her shoulders and began to sing with utter joy.

Lily shook her head and smiled at the girl's oblivion to the distraction her entrance caused. The wet bodice of Ellen's dress suggested she'd been to the well for a drink of water. The braids Lily had carefully fashioned after much disagreement that morning were loose. She looked as though she'd been playing tag instead of attending a Bible lesson.

Lily spotted her sister, Daisy, a few rows in front of her. Daisy held baby Rose in her lap and sat between her sons. Tucker sat on the end of the bench. She wasn't jealous of Daisy. Not really. Lily had a family now. She'd chosen to marry Edward. But the fact that he didn't love her was clear from the start. She stuffed the dreams of having children of her own back into her heart and forced her attention on the service.

At least, that was her intention. Every time she shifted in the seat, she brushed against Edward's arm. She felt like a restless child trying, without success, to sit through the service without moving. The third time she bumped his shoulder, he looked down and captured her gaze with his. And there in that moment she stilled. The calm in his eyes poured peace into hers. At his discreet smile, she focused toward the front of the church and sedately took in the rest of the minister's sermon.

When the service ended, Lily and Edward were among the first of the congregation to make their way to the door. Reverend Dismuke shook her hand and welcomed her. His wife, Peggy, invited Lily to visit when she had time. Lily thanked them, complimented the minister on his message and descended the steps to stand in the churchyard while Edward excused himself to speak to someone about a job he was working on.

As the people came out of the small church, she looked down Main Street, taking in the sights of the new town that was now her home. Preparing the shop to open had kept her too busy to explore Pine Haven. During her first week, she'd only visited the doctor's office, the bank and the general store.

Of course, she'd been to the church and the hotel on her wedding day. Pleasure at the memory surprised her. Why would she smile at the thought of how her life had changed that day? Now her plans were gone. Replaced with their plans. Plans so vague they were yet to be made clear.

The vision of a handsome man in a leather apron manifested before her eyes. Only, instead of an apron, he wore his Sunday best.

Lily had been so lost in thought, she didn't notice Edward's approach. Even at midday the man cast a shadow over her small frame.

He tipped his hat. "Having pleasant thoughts?"

Her smile had betrayed her. "Just enjoying the day and surveying the town." Lily grabbed for any excuse to keep from letting him know her thoughts were of him. He couldn't know that. "It was a lovely service."

He smiled in agreement. This handsome churchgoer wasn't the same man who had carried her across the threshold. In midair, with strong arms. Against a broad chest. The man she'd seen this week was as strong as his stature. This Edward had a softness in his eyes.

Ellen stood beside him, holding his hand and frowning up at Lily.

"What did you learn in class today, Ellen?" Lily twisted the cords of her reticule around the fingers of her gloves as she spoke.

"Stuff about God."

Edward gave Ellen a telling look.

Lily tried again. "What exactly did you learn? About God's love? Or a particular Bible story?"

The girl pointed at Lily's reticule. "You tied your hands in a knot."

"Oh, my." Lily pulled the cords in vain. The knots grew tighter as she tugged.

"May I?" Edward reached a tentative hand toward her.

"No, thank you. I'll get it." She continued to struggle with the cords.

Ellen blurted out, "I want to go play."

"Do not interrupt, Ellen." Edward reached for Lily's hands. "Please."

She relented and held out her hands. The cords had tied her gloves together. "I do seem to be making it worse."

Dust flew up and scattered on Lily's shoes and skirt as Ellen kicked the ground at her feet.

"Ellen, be still. You'll soil Aunt Lily's dress." Edward didn't look up as he worked with the mass of tangles. His large hands made the heavy cords of the reticule seem tiny.

"There you go." He released the last of the knots and backed away, slipping his hands into the pockets of his trousers. He stared over her shoulder and asked, "Tell me. Did you get everything set up so you can open tomorrow?"

Was he as uncomfortable as she? When they worked together, they kept busy. This was the first occasion for them to be together as a family in the community. Their first day of rest and worship.

Ellen was clearly not enjoying herself. She stood close to Edward, arms folded, pouting while she waited for permission to leave them.

"I'm almost ready. There are a couple of things to do before you bring the hat stands in the morning." Lily studied Edward's profile. Today he was clean shaven.

His brown hair curled behind his ears a bit. His shirt was not new, but it was clean. The brim of his well-worn hat shaded his face.

Daisy and Tucker approached them with their growing family. The twins asked to go run and play with the other children while the adults talked.

"Okay, boys, but don't go far. Your momma's got lunch ready for us at home." Tucker waved the boys away.

"We'll stay close!" James, the older twin, answered for both boys and tugged on his brother's arm. "Come on, John. They won't think we're coming if you don't hurry up." John took long, awkward strides to stay upright as James dragged him away.

"Can I go?" Ellen pulled on Edward's elbow.

"Just for a few minutes."

"Thanks!" She pivoted on one heel and lifted the other leg to run.

"Not so fast, young lady." Edward put a hand on her shoulder and turned her to face Lily. "You haven't answered the question about your Bible lesson."

"It was about family." Ellen jerked to look at him.

"What about family?" Edward's voice was deep and even.

Ellen twisted her face to Lily and drew in a deep sigh.

"Answer the question or go to the wagon without playing," Edward prodded.

"Okay, okay. Just let me think a minute." Ellen chewed her bottom lip and her eyebrows twisted toward one another. Lily could almost see the wheels of her mind turning.

In an instant Ellen's eyes opened wide, and she held up one finger to touch the corner of her mouth. "It was about honoring your momma and papa. And since I don't get to see mine, I didn't want to hear it. I went outside and played by the water till it was time for church." A curt nod of her head, and Ellen flew away so fast Edward couldn't catch her.

Lily met Edward's unhappy gaze. "She's really hurting." She watched Ellen catch up to the boys.

"This is what I was afraid would happen. She's lashing out in pain because she doesn't know how to handle not knowing where her folks are."

"We'll get her through it." Lily put her left hand on his sleeve. Then she saw Daisy slip a thoughtful glance at Tucker. Oddly, Edward hadn't seemed to mind. He actually turned toward her when she put her hand on his sleeve. She jerked it away and held the offending reticule with both hands.

A smile turned up one corner of his thin lips. His dark eyes danced. She could see her embarrassment reflecting in their depths. He was enjoying her discomfort. Too much.

Daisy chimed in then. "Edward, will you and Ellen join us for the afternoon? Lily promised when she arrived on Monday that she'd spend her first Sunday with us at the farm. We'd love to have you."

"Thank you for the invite, but I think Ellen needs my attention today. It's been a busy week. That will probably explain part of her poor behavior earlier." He nodded at the group. "Y'all have a nice afternoon."

"Well, you and Ellen are welcome anytime. We'd love to have you out real soon." Daisy handed baby Rose to Tucker.

Tucker smiled at his daughter. "I'll bring Lily back to town this evening, Edward." He put an arm around his wife, and they walked toward their wagon.

Lily had looked forward to spending time with Daisy and her family, but it didn't seem right to leave Edward to deal with Ellen alone. Not when that was their agreement.

"Are you certain? I can stay."

"You go. I'm going to try to help her come around to understanding our new arrangement. A little resistance at first was to be expected." He looked across the church yard to where the children played. "It's time for her to accept things now."

"Are you going to talk to her about her parents?" Lily knew it would be difficult.

Edward shook his head. "I won't tell her anything unless I know for certain it's true." He looked into her eyes. "Thank you for offering to stay with us. You go enjoy your family. Maybe Ellen will be in a better mood by the time you return."

"I'll pray for you. She's a strong-willed soul. It won't be easy for her to accept me as long as she's holding out hope for her parents to return."

"She'll adjust. It'll take time, but she will."

Lily watched him walk away with a heart heavy with thoughts of his sister. She wished she could do something to mend the pain he and Ellen shared. Braiding hair and cooking meals wasn't enough to make up for the loss the two of them were bearing. She prayed that somehow his sister and brother-in-law would return.

If they did, would Edward still want her to be his wife?

Edward sat on his porch and whittled. Ellen played with her handkerchief doll in the cabin behind him. Through the barely open window, he could hear her cooing and pretending to coax the doll to sleep. She hummed the song her mother had sung to her as a babe.

The afternoon sun had settled low on the horizon when he saw Tucker's wagon coming up the road. At a distance he recognized Lily by the hat she'd worn to church.

He was glad she had family in the area. He couldn't fathom why her father had sent her to Pine Haven alone. Lily's reputation wouldn't have been compromised if her father had been here. But would he have been able to convince her to marry him and care for Ellen if she hadn't been concerned about what people thought of her?

Tucker slowed his wagon as he neared Edward's cabin. It was built to face a lane that ran beside his shop. The back of the cabin butted up close to the side of his shop, leaving just enough space to prevent the cabin from catching fire if there was ever an accident with the forge. The porch lined the front of the cabin and sat perpendicular to the main road. He enjoyed sitting outside in the evening after being closed in all day with the fire and metal of his work. It wasn't always possible in the winter, but sunshine had warmed the mild day.

"Evening, Tucker. Lily." Edward stood and dropped the small horse he was whittling onto the table by his chair. He stepped off the porch to help Lily from the wagon.

"Good evening to you." Tucker pulled the brake as the wagon came to a stop. "Not as cold as I thought it'd be. I need to get Mack shoed if you've got time this week."

"Be glad to. Just let me know when." Edward answered Tucker, but his gaze went beyond his friend to rest on Lily. She sat with her back straight. Her coat was buttoned all the way up, and she tugged at the wide ribbon of her hat. He smiled at how the color matched her eyes. He was certain it was intentional.

Tucker spoke and drew his attention. "I'm coming to

town late tomorrow morning with Daisy. She wants to visit the shop on Lily's first day. Can I bring him by on the way in and leave him with you?"

"That'll be good." Edward watched as Lily continued to avoid looking at him. Was she uncomfortable with all men, or just him?

"First thing in the morning I've got some business to handle for Lily." He offered his hand to her as she moved to the edge of the wagon seat.

"Thank you." Lily gave him little more than a glance as she spoke. "I trust you were able to complete my order." Her eyes challenged him.

"Remember I promised you six stands tomorrow. The rest will be done by the end of the week." He released her hand, and they backed away from the wagon.

"Please don't be late. The windows will have to be dressed before I can open."

"I won't be. You just make sure you're ready. In my experience, it's not usually a woman waiting on a man, but rather the exact opposite." He tried not to grin at her, but the temptation to taunt her was irresistible. Her cheeks brightened at his words. He could almost see the wheels turning in her mind for something to say. No doubt, she'd thought of several things but was weighing the right choice.

"Perhaps your experiences have been with the wrong sort of woman."

Yes, she'd chosen well. Not the nicest statement, but the one that brought the most reaction. Probably her first thought.

"I'm not in the habit of associating with the wrong sort of woman."

"So you do admit you are in the habit of associating with women." She was smirking now. How had she gotten the upper hand in a conversation about when he would deliver an order?

"Uncle Edward? Can you come inside? I need you." Ellen's voice broke into the conversation through the window.

"In a minute, honey," he said over his shoulder without looking back.

Ellen tugged the window until it opened wide. "It's important. I can't do it by myself." There was no real emergency, but a childish urgency in her words. He watched her stare at Lily. Did Lily threaten his niece's peace of mind? He'd hoped his talk with her after lunch would ease the tension between Ellen and Lily, but it seemed to have had the opposite effect.

"I'm coming, Ellen. Just as soon as I finish my business with Mr. Barlow."

The distant sound of hammering came from the direction of the main intersection in town.

Tucker indicated the noise with a nod of his head. "Have they been at that all afternoon?"

"Pretty much." Edward's distaste for working on Sunday was surpassed only by his disappointment that the town council was permitting a saloon to be built in the center of the growing town. "I wish they weren't building the place at all, much less working on the Lord's Day."

"Everything that comes to town because of the railroad isn't good for us." Tucker shook his head. "We'll have to pray for God to keep our community safe."

"That, and make sure Sheriff Collins stays on top of any riffraff who try to settle here," Edward agreed.

"Surely, the good people of Pine Haven will outnumber any new folks who try to change the community."

Lily's pinched expression showed her reluctance to believe evil could find a home in her new town.

"We do now. But it'll take prayer and courage to keep the sort of evil that comes with a saloon from pollutin' the town." Edward wished he could be as naive as Lily. Life had taught him hard lessons. Sadly, they were lessons she, too, would learn in time.

"Uncle Edward? Are you coming?" Ellen's voice rang through the open window, her tone impatient.

"I'll see you in the morning, Edward." Tucker released the brake.

"If I'm not here, just leave Mack. I'll get right on it when I get back."

"Good night, Edward. Good night, Lily. Ellen." Tucker tipped his hat at the ladies.

"Bye, Mr. Barlow." Ellen stood framed in the open window, her hands on the sill. She sent a look to Lily that Edward was sure she hadn't intended for him to see.

Tucker steered the horses forward and pulled the wagon away from Edward's porch. Edward didn't move to go inside until Lily and the pretty hat disappeared through the front door. The last thing Ellen needed was to feel that he'd overlooked her by allowing himself to be distracted by Lily.

Lord, help me not to focus on what's not good for me. You know I get in more trouble than I can handle that way.

He pulled the front door open to find Ellen back at play with her doll, whatever assistance she'd needed earlier forgotten. Something about Lily didn't sit right with his niece. Over the past few months, he'd determined that nothing—and no one—would put Ellen at risk. She was his responsibility until her parents returned. No amount of curiosity or intrigue surrounding a petite blonde lady would move him to violate the promises he'd made to his sister and himself—not even if that lady was his wife.

Lily came into the front room, her hat and coat gone. "Have you two eaten supper?"

Ellen pretended she didn't hear the question, but Edward saw her cut her eyes at Lily. He put a hand on the girl's head and ruffled her hair. "No. We had a big lunch today. I was just about to see what I could round up for a light supper."

Lily was already tying on an apron. "How about some scrambled eggs and toast?"

"Sounds good to me." He turned to Ellen. "How about you, Ellen?"

She didn't look up. "I don't care." Her voice was rife with tension.

"Okay, then." Lily turned her back to them and put the cast iron skillet on the stove. "Eggs and toast for Edward, bread and milk in her room for Ellen." She pulled a bowl off the shelf and began to crack eggs into it.

Ellen's mouth dropped open. She looked at him and then at Lily. "But…"

"No buts." Lily didn't look away from her task. "We warned you that your manners would be polite or you would eat bread and milk in your room." She pulled the bread to her and began to slice thick pieces of toast.

"Uncle Edward." Ellen came to tug on his sleeve. "Don't make me go to my room. It's too early. I want to play some more."

He could feel Lily's gaze on him when she retrieved the butter from the table. He couldn't risk siding with Ellen and undermining Lily's new authority. Parenting was hard. Being fair and wise wasn't easy. There weren't always absolute answers. He would do the best he could. "It's your choice, Ellen. You know the rules. If you are disrespectful, you choose to go to your room."

The little girl stood, palms up, eyes wide. "I can't believe this."

Lily turned then. "If you do not change your tone, you will have water with your bread. Disrespect for your elders will not be tolerated in our home."

Ellen stamped her foot. "It's not your home! It's my home!" She turned, ran into her room and slammed the door.

"Ellen, come back here." Edward called after her, but there was no response.

"I think we best give her time to calm down." Lily stood, wiping her hands on the apron. "Did something happen today that I'm unaware of?"

"I had a talk with her. I hoped it would make things better. She feels threatened by you." He shook his head. "I'm not sure what to think of it."

"Did she ask about her parents?" Lily's voice was barely more than a whisper.

"Yes. I tried to be vague, but she kept pressing."

The butter in the skillet started to crackle on the stove. Lily whipped the eggs with a fork and poured them into the pan. "How did you handle that?"

He came close to keep Ellen from overhearing their conversation. "I told her we have to pray for them, that they were sick and had been to the doctor. I didn't have the heart to tell her no one knows what happened after that."

"Poor child." She stirred the eggs. "If I'd known, I wouldn't have been so firm."

"You had no way to know. And, even so, she must be respectful."

"Yes, but we've got to show mercy in her situation. She'll never listen to me if she thinks I'm unkind."

"You were not unkind. You were trying to teach her."

"There's a time and place for everything. And when you're worried about your parents being far away and sick, it's not a time to go to bed with bread and water." Lily scooped the eggs out of the pan and onto a plate of toast.

"You go comfort her." Lily cracked more eggs and dropped them into the bowl. "I'll fix her something to eat. Tell her you'll read to her after supper. That always calmed me when I was a girl missing my mother."

He left her at the stove and went into Ellen's room, marveling that Lily would dismiss the poor treatment his niece had thrust on her and then cook a meal and offer comfort. Even so, he'd see that Ellen apologized before the meal.

Lily was exactly what Ellen needed. If only he could convince Ellen to let Lily care for her.

Chapter Seven

~❧~

Lily admired the row of newly made hats lined up on her workbench. This might be Texas, a land known for hard work and strength, but Lily didn't believe there was a woman alive who didn't want to be feminine and look pretty. Even her sister Jasmine, who loved to ride the range and tend cattle, liked a fancy hat now and again. Lily would soon see if the women of Pine Haven would appreciate her offerings.

Concern for how to reach Ellen had combined with excitement over opening her shop and kept her from sleeping the night before. She'd awakened early and left breakfast for Edward and Ellen. She had to get everything just as she wanted in the shop. In her best dress she watched the hands of the clock creep slowly toward the hour of opening. Except for the windows—their shades pulled low waiting for Edward's arrival—she was ready.

No one coming today would see any evidence of last week's fire. Edward had worked quickly on the structure, and she'd worked long hours to make new stock.

Hoping the normalcy of the activity would calm her nerves, Lily decided to busy herself by creating another hat. She pinned two long feathers above the brim. Turning it from side to side, she decided to follow her first instincts and add a small tuft of silk net organza. She reached for her scissors just as the front bell announced a visitor.

"I'm coming." She set the hat on her workbench and brushed bits of thread and ribbon from her skirt. They floated to the floor to join the kaleidoscope of colors she'd used to make her inventory.

Lily stepped through the doorway into the front of the shop. "I thought you'd never get here." She stopped behind the glass case. With the windows covered, the dim room cast the face of her giant visitor in shadow.

"Hello to you, too." Edward approached her. He carried a display stand in one hand. He set it on the case and watched her face. "I finished."

Lily's mouth dropped open. She lifted a hand and traced the base of the delicate stand with her fingers. It was fashioned into a leaf. From the center of the leaf rose a stem. On each side of the stem, at different heights, additional leaves arched outward. Lily's hand followed the stem to touch the top of the stand. Thin metal curled to form a calla lily. The pistil in the center, perfectly shaped, completed the work of art.

"I can't believe it." The words came out like a soft breeze. "This is nothing like the picture I showed you."

"If you don't like it, you don't have to use them." Edward's response snapped Lily from her bewilderment.

"It's amazing! I've never seen anything so beautiful."

"Are you sure you like it?" Doubt played in his eyes.

"I'm positive. I just don't know what to say." Lily put up a hand to her cheek and felt the warmth of her blush. She was moved almost to tears by the beauty of his work.

"I never imagined this. I don't know how to thank you." She moved her fingers to cover her lips and shook her head slowly back and forth. After several moments she tore her gaze from the beautiful display and lowered her hand.

"I was worried you wouldn't be able to finish."

"I had a slow couple of days." Edward backed up and nodded his head in the direction of the door. "Do you want to see the others?"

Lily eyed the stand again. "Of course." She crossed the boarded floor and went through the door he held open for her. They approached the back of his wagon, and he threw back the edge of a heavy canvas to reveal more of the beautiful stands, each nestled in the bed of straw. Varied heights and length of leaves, balanced on unique bases.

"I thought you might want the stands to reflect the concept of Lily's Millinery and Finery, even when you removed a hat to show a customer." Edward spoke from beside her as Lily took in the sight of his craftsmanship. "You can hang gloves or hankies on the leaves. I thought you might get more use of your shop space that way."

"What a wonderful idea." She was touched by his thoughtfulness. He may have been overworked and stressed to the limit by raising his niece alone, but his creativity wasn't diminished.

A sudden movement and high-pitched sneeze drew their attention to the far edge of the canvas near the seat of the wagon. The sound of metal snapping accompanied the sneeze.

"Ellen?" Edward spoke the child's name slowly and deliberately. His eyes narrowed in on the exact spot that now stirred beneath the canvas.

A whisper was his only answer. "Yes, Uncle Edward?"

He pulled the canvas from the wagon and exposed Ellen's hiding place behind his seat. "Get up, child."

"I'd rather not, if it's all the same to you." Ellen met his gaze without cowering. Lily could see the bravery to stand her ground was a show of spirit and not outright defiance.

"It's not the same to me." Edward lowered his chin and pinned her with his stare.

Lily watched the struggle between the two strong-minded people. Even though she'd only met them days before, she had seen firsthand the contest of wills that took place daily in their home. She was certain her marriage to Edward was the source of much of their recent conflict.

Ellen stood without moving from her spot. The hem of her calico dress almost hid the broken display stand at her feet. The edge of a leaf stuck through the hay that lined the wagon and hung on the lace of her small boot. She frowned at the offending leaf.

"It wouldn'a broke if you'd let me come with you in the first place." Her already full lower lip protruded farther.

"I didn't want you to come because I didn't want anything to get broken." Edward stepped around the lowered gate on the back of the wagon and retrieved the broken stand. He pulled the leaf free from her laces. "Tell Aunt Lily you're sorry."

Ellen jerked her head in Lily's direction. The pouting mouth became a snarl. "It ain't hers yet. She ain't paid for it. I'll tell *you* I'm sorry, but it ain't got nothin' to do with *her*."

Lily almost expected the child to spit as a way to punctuate her distaste at the idea.

"Ellen. Apologize this minute." Edward's voice brooked no argument, but Lily saw a challenge fly through Ellen's eyes before she turned back to Lily.

"I am so very sorry to have broken my uncle Edward's work." Ellen twisted up her mouth and cocked her head to one side. The saccharine in her voice spoke of bitterness Lily understood now. Having lost her own mother at the age of five, she had known the importance of her father's attention and the mounting jealousy from even a hint that someone would take it away. She imagined Ellen must feel the same way about her treasured uncle.

"I'm sure he can repair it, Ellen." Lily watched the girl's pride swell at Lily's words.

"You bet he can. He's the best blacksmith in Texas. Probably in the whole United States." Ellen gave a curt nod to emphasize her opinion. "I ain't never seen him turn down a job 'cause it was hard. He can make or fix anything."

"I imagine you're right." Lily smiled at the little girl standing like a statue in the back of the wagon. "These stands are beautiful and much fancier than what I ordered." Lily was beginning to realize Ellen's gruffness came from a place of deep pain. A pain Lily understood. "Would you like to come inside and have a look around?"

The little girl's brown eyes looked to Edward. "What do you think? Do you need help toting all this in?" There was an apparent reluctance to respond to Lily, but a child's curiosity about what was happening inside the shop must have prompted Ellen to stow away in the wagon in the first place.

"That depends on you, Ellen. Will you be careful?" Edward's tone warned that she would be held accountable for her actions.

"Yes, sir." Ellen's confidence and determination didn't waver. She stepped toward the edge of the wagon closest to Edward.

"You will help me repair this after school today." He held the pieces of the broken stand for Ellen to see, then put them under the seat to protect them from further damage.

"That'll be easy." Ellen grinned and wrapped her arms around his neck. "Now help me down, so I can see what she's done to Momma's shop."

Edward hoisted Ellen to the ground. "It's Aunt Lily's shop now."

"She's gonna have a hat store here, but it's still Momma's shop." A frown clouded her dark eyes. Ellen spoke to Edward but turned her head to Lily. "In my heart it always will be."

Recognizing the challenge, Lily said, "Your mother picked a wonderful building for a business. Come inside and see what I've done so far."

Edward called Ellen out of her reverie as she stood, hands on her hips, eyes drawn together, watching Lily's back disappear inside the shop.

"Take a stand with you. If you're going to help, you can start by helping me unload the wagon." He handed her one of the smaller stands and turned to pick up two of the largest ones. "And mind your manners. Lily has worked hard here, and we need to respect her efforts."

"She better not mess up Momma's shop. One day, Momma's coming back, and we're gonna open a bakery here." Ellen stepped onto the porch. "That's all I got to say about it."

"That's all you better say about it, or you'll be having

a long conversation with me later. Now go inside and be nice." Edward winked at her to soften his words. He took a deep breath and braced himself before they entered the shop together.

He had no idea what had just transpired at the wagon, but he had a feeling Ellen may have met her match with Lily. He was training Ellen to be strong. He wanted her to stand up for what she believed in. He didn't want her to be weak in any way. But, given her attitude toward Lily, he needed to work on finding a balance to include teaching her to be kind.

Edward and Ellen stopped just inside the door and took in everything. Lily had arranged her wares with care. A large round table stood in the center of the room. The wood was polished down to the ornately carved pedestal. Against one side wall stood a hall tree with a large mirror. Lily had placed a chair in front of it. He assumed she'd seat her guests there while they tried on her hats. A long chest stood against the opposite wall.

Ellen broke the silence. "Where do you want me to put this? It's kinda heavy."

"You can put them all on the floor by the windows. I'll arrange them in a few minutes." Lily spread her arms wide. "What do you think, Ellen?"

Ellen set the small stand down with a thud and went to look in the mirror.

"Remember to be careful, Ellen." Edward set his load near the opposite window.

"I didn't break nothin'." Ellen turned to Lily. "Why you got such a big mirror? Don't you know what you look like?"

"Ellen." Edward sent her a warning glare.

"It's for my customers." Lily approached the mirror

and met Ellen's gaze in the reflection. "Seeing how a new hat looks on you is important before you buy it. Sometimes a lady wants to see how the color looks with her eyes. Or she may want it to match her hair or dress."

"Can't see why you don't just put on something to keep your head warm in the winter and be done with it." Ellen stared at herself and tugged on the ribbons of her worn bonnet.

Lily seemed to hesitate a moment at Ellen's logic. Edward could see both of their faces in the mirror as he walked to the door to bring in more of the stands.

"You are right about a hat helping to keep you warm. But isn't it nice to have something to make you feel pretty, too?" Lily rested her hand on Ellen's shoulder.

"What good is pretty? Momma had lots of pretty hats, and she's gone."

"Ellen, let's not talk about that right now." Shocked by her outburst, Edward tried to silence her.

But Ellen's tirade wasn't finished. "If she hadn't been so worried about being pretty and having fancy things, maybe her and Pa could have stayed here and not left me." The girl dashed out of the door.

Lily stood with her hand over her mouth. She slowly turned to Edward. "I'm so sorry. I didn't mean to upset her." She lowered her hand to the base of her throat.

Edward silently scolded himself for noticing the delicate hand and the silkiness of golden hair draped across her shoulders. His niece had just run from the room after lashing out at Lily because she felt wounded anew by a reminder of the mother she felt had abandoned her.

Could he take away the hurt Ellen put in Lily's pain-filled eyes? That was a question he wasn't sure he wanted answered.

"I'm the one who should be apologizing. I'm sorry for Ellen's behavior." He looked through the window and watched as Ellen sat on the seat of the wagon and scrubbed tears from her cheeks with the back of her hand. He knew she hated to cry, especially in front of others.

He hoped he could explain. "You couldn't have known about my sister's dreams. When she was younger, all she wanted was to open a bakery. Cooking and serving others seemed to fulfill her. Then she married Wesley. Ellen was born the next year. Jane was so excited. She lived for Wesley and Ellen."

"She sounds like a lovely person."

"She was."

"I hope you aren't giving up on them." Lily's tone was almost pleading.

"I don't want to. I wish they'd never left."

"Why did they?"

Edward smirked a little at the memory. "Wesley wasn't the type to be content. Always wanted more. Got all dressed up in fancy clothes trying to impress people. At first, Jane didn't change. Then he had a small success with the hotel here in town. He convinced her they could make a real go of it in Santa Fe."

"Oh, my." Lily's voice was a faint whisper. "Poor Ellen." Pity filled her eyes.

He cleared his throat. As hard as he tried not to, he still choked up at the possibility that Jane might never come home. "I best get the rest of the stands off the wagon and get Ellen to school."

Lily gave him a sad smile, one that said she understood.

It took several trips to the wagon as he dug the stands out of the straw and brought them inside. Edward heard

Lily moving around in the stockroom while he unloaded the wagon. He set the last stand on the floor and called out a goodbye. Because she'd insisted, he placed a bill on the glass case. Her soft voice caused him to stop as he reached the door.

Lily looked everywhere in the room but at him. "Please explain to Ellen that I didn't mean to bring up bad memories for her."

"I will. She'll be fine. She's learning to be tough. Life deals you a lot of hard things. It's best to learn that when you're young. Keeps you from being disappointed later in life."

"Not always, Edward. Not always." A depth of sadness seemed to rise from her heart and fill the rich blue eyes. Lily picked up his bill. "If you'll give me a moment, I'll pay you." She disappeared into the storeroom again.

When Lily returned, Edward took the bills she offered and stuffed them into his pocket without counting them as she backed away from him.

"I guess I'll see you at supper." He hated the distance he sensed between them. They both wanted the best for Ellen, yet at every turn the child tried her hardest to rebuff Lily's efforts.

"I may be late. It depends on how busy I am today."

"I'll try to have the rest of the stands by the end of the week."

"That'll be fine." She was already moving toward the windows to arrange the hats in preparation for opening the shop.

He lifted his hat and opened the door. "And again, I'm sorry for Ellen's words. She was unkind."

"I understand." Lily stood still as he closed the door behind him.

Edward climbed into the wagon beside a silent Ellen. Lifting the reins, he released the brake and sent the horse forward.

Sad blue eyes threatened to haunt him for the rest of the day. As he and Ellen repaired the broken stand that afternoon, he saw visions of the gentle creature working in a shop, building a dream to succeed.

When Lily came home late that evening, Ellen was ready for bed. She had done her homework and chores and was playing quietly in her room.

"How was your day?" he asked when she closed the door.

"Long." He watched as she pulled off her gloves.

"Did you have a lot of trade?" He went to the stove and uncovered the bowl of soup he'd kept for her. He put it on a tray and added a cup of coffee.

"If you don't mind, I'm very tired. I'd like to go straight to bed." She looked toward Ellen's room. "Is there anything I can do to help with Ellen before I do?"

He wondered what had happened. This was not the response he expected after the excitement she'd shown over opening. "Ellen is ready for bed. Everything she needs is done."

She unbuttoned her coat, and he saw the slump of her shoulders.

"What about you, Lily? Is there anything I can do for you?" He indicated the tray. "I made some soup."

A tired smile did nothing to lift her face. "Thank you."

"You must be exhausted. Would you like me to carry the tray into the bedroom for you? I can put it on the table by the chair. You can relax and eat at your leisure."

"That would be perfect."

She stood in the center of the room while he took the

tray to her room. When he came out again, he stopped in front of her. "You know you can tell me anything."

Lily put a hand on his arm. Its lightness reminded him that though she was a strong woman, she was also a delicate creature. "I just need to rest right now."

"I'll say good night, then." He backed away so she could walk into her room. "Ellen, come say good-night to Aunt Lily."

The little girl came to the doorway of her bedroom. "Good night."

Lily's smile was genuine this time. "Good night, Ellen. I pray you will sleep well tonight."

Ellen stared after her as Lily went into the room and closed the door. "What's wrong with her? She looks sad."

"She does, doesn't she?" Edward watched the door, wondering what happened today to bring this normally cheerful—if not fiery—woman to such a melancholy state. "Let's get you tucked into bed. You can say a prayer for her tonight, too."

He led Ellen to her room, promising himself that he'd spend extra time in prayer for both of them. He'd put wings on those prayers tomorrow and try to find out what had gone wrong today. Maybe it would be something he could remedy.

Chapter Eight

No customers yesterday didn't mean today wouldn't be good. Last night she'd felt guilty going to bed without telling Edward about the day, but she didn't have the heart to expose her failure to anyone, especially him. After all he'd done to assure her success, it didn't seem right to tell him no one had entered the shop except for her sister. Daisy had dropped in for a brief visit and promised to come again later in the week.

Lily heard the bell and slid off her stool in the storeroom. She was determined to be hopeful.

Lord, please let this be a customer. I can't make a success of this business without Your help.

"It's me." Ellen stood just inside the front door, holding the display stand she'd broken.

"Oh. Hello, Ellen." Lily came around the display case.

"Uncle Edward made me bring you this." She held out the smallest of the stands Edward had made. "He said you prob'ly need it."

Lily reached out to receive the stand. "Thank you. It looks wonderful. You can't even tell it was ever broken." Lily placed the stand in the center of one of the front windows. She had hoped to have the stand today but had set one of the hats and a pair of gloves in the spot just in case it wasn't finished until the other stands were ready. She picked up the hat and set it on the stand, tying the ribbon in a loose bow.

"What do you think?" Lily asked Ellen, who still stood by the door. The little girl's eyes missed nothing as she took in the shop. Like her uncle, she was observant.

"Not too bad," she finally answered, "if you like all this frilly stuff." Ellen's answer may have been meant as a rebuff, but Lily caught a glimpse of wonder in her face.

"Most ladies do like pretty things." Lily held the gloves she wanted to display with the hat. "Would you like to hang these on the leaf? Your uncle's idea to make these stands hold more than one item was wonderful."

"No, thanks." Ellen gave a cursory perusal of the shop and turned on her heel. "Uncle Edward sent me over as soon as I finished my chores. I've got to get to school."

"I'll be sure to thank him when I get home." Lily moved to the doorway as Ellen walked out.

"He's just doing his job. That's how he makes money to take care of me."

"I know you must be proud of him. He's a good uncle." Lily tried again to speak to Ellen without the tension that seeped into their conversations.

"The best. He only has time for me. Nobody else." A stubborn tilt to her head made Ellen cuter than she knew. The fierce protection was precious but unnecessary. Lily had no interest in taking Edward's time from her. Luther Aarens had made certain that Lily had no interest in a man. Their failed engagement, the way he'd treated her, was the reason she was determined to keep her heart as her own.

Perhaps there was a way to put the child at ease.

"I'm sure you're right. I felt the same way about my father after my mother died when I was a little girl."

"Your momma died?" The anger seemed to drain out of Ellen. She wilted before Lily's eyes.

In a soft voice, Lily answered. "She did. I was just a little younger than you are. I still miss her."

"You do?" Ellen whispered when she looked up at Lily.

Time stood still as a little girl and a grown woman shared the pain only someone in their situations could understand, each remembering a love made more dear by its loss. Death had stolen one mother. A lust for life had taken the other.

Lily nodded her head softly. "I do." She bent at the waist so she could be face-to-face with Ellen. "The love of your momma stays with you forever. It's the part of her that lives in your heart. I think it's a way God lets us keep them close."

"I do feel it." Ellen's eyes were filled with tears now. A smile pulled at one corner of her mouth. "Especially when I'm playing with the doll she made me." She reached into the pocket of her pinafore and pulled out the worn doll Lily had seen so many times. "Momma said if I practiced with my doll, then I'd learn how to be a good momma, too. She said her momma made her a doll like this, and that's how she knew how to take care of me." Sobs broke from the child, and Lily wrapped her in tender arms.

She murmured softly. "What a wonderful gift she gave you. She taught you how to love."

Ellen sniffed and backed away. "But she left me. I must not be the kind of girl a momma can love. I don't think I know how to love nobody now. Except Uncle Edward." She wiped her sleeve across her face to dry her eyes.

"I've seen how you protect your doll." Lily pushed Ellen's hair away from her face and cradled the small cheeks in her palms. "Protection is one way to show love."

"It is?" Scrunched eyebrows formed a disbelieving frown.

"It is. I'm sure your mother trusts your uncle Edward to protect you. She showed how much she loves you when she picked him to take care of you. His protection is the way he shows you he loves you. It's the way you love your doll." Lily gave her a smile and winked. "It's also how you love him. That's why you've been trying to protect him from me."

"How'd you know?" Ellen backed up, surprised.

"Because I did it to my papa when I was a little girl. If ever a lady got close to my papa, I'd get between them and make sure she knew my papa was busy taking care of me and my sisters. That he didn't want another lady because there was no lady like my momma."

"Did you get in trouble like I do?" Ellen's childlike honesty spoke without reservation.

"I did." Lily stood to her full height again but kept a comforting hand on Ellen's shoulder.

"Did another woman get your papa?" Wide eyes seemed to fear the answer to this question.

"No, Ellen. No other woman did."

"So you protected him from all of them?"

"After a while I learned Papa didn't need me to protect him. He's a big strong man who would never do anything to harm me or my sisters. He loved us so much that he would protect us."

"Uncle Edward is strong. He's big and strong." Pride burst from her young face.

"That he is. So don't you worry about protecting him,

especially from me. I'm not going to try to take him from you. I understand how you feel. And I've learned enough about your uncle Edward to know he'll always protect you. You don't have to worry."

"But you married him. People get married 'cause they're in love. Uncle Edward must love you a lot more than me. He didn't even know you good, and he married you."

Did she dare to share the secret of her marriage with this child? "Your uncle did marry me for love. One of the reasons he married me was because he loves you."

The little face twisted in confusion. "I don't get it."

"He thought if he married me, you and I could be friends." She prayed she was helping by telling Ellen these things. "I was alone, and you have been missing your momma. He thought we could have each other while we wait to hear from your momma."

Lord, please bring Jane home. Don't let this be false hope I'm pouring into this little girl.

Ellen looked at the doll she clung to. Then she looked up at Lily. "I'm glad we talked."

"Me, too." Lily smiled.

"You're too pretty for me to stay mad at all the time. I was gettin' tired of having to say mean things to you."

"Thank you. I'm glad we got everything straight. Now we can be nice to each other." Lily stroked Ellen's hair, and her fingers caught in the knots that tangled the mass of brown waves. "You're very pretty, too, Ellen."

Pink tinted the girl's cheeks. "No, I'm not." She turned her face into one shoulder.

Lily reached under her chin and urged the child's small face to the front. "Yes. You are." The words were kind and soft-spoken. "I'm sure you're as pretty as your momma. You go home and ask your uncle." With another smile, Lily chucked Ellen under the chin and urged her on her way.

"Make sure and tell Uncle Edward thank you, if you see him before I do." She waved as Ellen bounced off the porch onto the dirt below.

"I will." She returned the wave and called over her shoulder. "See you later, Aunt Lily."

Aunt Lily? Without being prompted? Hmm. Lily smiled at the sound of that. Perhaps she and Ellen could be friends, after all. It was nice to think there would be no more incidents of taunting from the girl.

If only Ellen's uncle didn't set her nerves on edge. Maybe that would come in time.

Not that it mattered. Making a success of her shop before her father and Jasmine arrived demanded all of her attention. After the shop was established, she'd be so busy she wouldn't have time to remember Ellen's words. *Uncle Edward must love you a lot.* Ellen was too young to understand why Lily and Edward had married.

So why did the thought gnaw at her spirit? Did part of her still long to be truly loved? Her determination not to disappear into the background and be taken for granted had become a way to keep herself, and her heart, locked away from life.

Finding herself plunged into the middle of a new family had tilted her world on its axis. She had to be cautious to maintain her emotional equilibrium.

Edward nestled a small wooden horse in the straw-filled crate. He hadn't imagined his whittling would be an added source of income until Mrs. Croft had noticed one of the horses he'd carved for Ellen. Selling the toys to the general store kept him from feeling as though he was wasting the time he spent on his front porch. Time he used to think. The Lord knew he'd been doing a lot of that in recent days.

"Good morning, Stone." Edward turned to see Donald Croft in the open doorway.

"I was just on my way to see you." He put the last horse in the crate. "I got these done as quickly as I could. Thanks for letting me know you were running low."

Mr. Croft stepped into the blacksmith shop and picked up one of the horses. "Can't imagine how you do it. These are fast sellers. The kids love 'em." He moved the straw aside to survey the array of toys in the crate. "This oughta cover your tab and anything you may be needing for this week."

Liza Croft's shrill voice carried from the street outside. "Donald, where are you?"

"In here, Liza." The general store owner stepped nearer to the door and waved her inside.

"I declare, all I did was go into the bank for two minutes, and you disappeared." She came to stand beside her husband. "Well, aren't those the prettiest ones yet?" She picked up the smallest horse. "I'm going to put this one up for my niece. She'll love it."

With a swish of her ample skirt, she turned and went through the door into the street. She called over her shoulder. "Don't take too long, we're already late opening up today."

Mr. Croft shook his head. "It's a wonder I make a living at all. Some days she buys things faster than I can sell 'em."

Edward knew better than to comment. Mr. Croft might complain about his wife, but everyone in town knew it was a callous front to cover for the deep love he had for her.

Pulling the crate toward him, Mr. Croft spoke again. "I see your wife opened up shop yesterday."

Edward turned to look out the door at his building across the street. "I hope she's been busy."

Mr. Croft's face twisted into a frown. "I don't see how she can make a go of it with such a small selection. It's not like Milly Ledford's dress shop. Everybody wins in her case. I sell the fabric, and she makes the dresses. Hats and gloves don't seem to me to be a way to make a living." He looked out the doorway as a lady paused and looked at the hats in Lily's window before continuing on her way down the street. "See what I mean. I just don't think there's enough hat business in town to keep her open."

Edward straightened and took a step toward the door. "I hope she's successful. It's a help to me to have the place rented. And the town is growing."

Mr. Croft picked up Edward's crate. "Maybe. You never know. She'll need to offer a fine product is all I've got to say."

Edward grimaced inwardly. "Thanks for buying the horses."

"You're mighty welcome. Go ahead and work on some more carvings if you get the time. What about some kittens or puppies? The little girls might like those."

Edward nodded in agreement. "I'll see what I can do."

He walked to the front of the shop when Mr. Croft left and saw Mrs. Dismuke, the reverend's wife, look in the window of Lily's shop. He caught a glimpse of Lily watching hopefully through the window.

When Mrs. Dismuke walked away, Lily dropped her

head and stepped to the rear of the store. She looked back and saw him watching her just before she went into the storeroom. A shadow of disappointment crossed her face. Edward was not pleased at the way it made him feel. Her business was her responsibility, not his.

But her success would benefit him. At least that's what he told himself as he headed across the street.

The bell on the front door rang when he entered the shop.

"I'm coming," Lily called out as she stepped from the storeroom into the shop. "Welcome to Lily's Millinery and..."

The greeting died on her lips when she saw him in the doorway. He closed the door against the chill of the day and turned toward her, hat in hand.

"Oh, it's you." Disappointment rang in her voice.

"Good morning to you, too." Edward smiled to tease her.

"I'm sorry. I didn't mean to be rude." She looked past him through the windows. "I thought you were a customer."

"No need to apologize." His gaze took in her efforts. "You've done a fine job in preparing your shop." He nodded toward the hats in the window. "Quite a variety of colors and styles you've got there."

"Thank you." She adjusted the ribbon on the hat taking center stage on the tallest stand he'd made. "The display stands are wonderful. I'm certain they'll be a big boost to the reputation my shop will build as people discover I'm open for business." She shifted the gloves on the leaf below the hat. "They are sure to be a topic of discussion."

"I'm glad you're pleased." He pulled at his collar and

shifted his weight from one foot to the other. "So the customers like them, too?"

"No one has said anything yet." She looked to the street again.

"Oh." He moved to the glass case in the back of the store. "Have you had any customers yet?" Her answer could explain her sullen mood from the night before.

"Not yet, but it's early. I've seen several ladies looking in the windows." Lily talked faster than usual. "Ladies take a while to make decisions. They like to look and ponder before they decide if they're interested. I'm sure they'll be coming in soon."

"Have you placed an advertisement? Most folks in town read the paper. It comes out once a week."

"I have a notice coming out in tomorrow's edition." The small snort that followed the statement surprised him. What had he said to get her dander up so?

"Well, you don't have to get all snippy. I was only trying to help."

"I'm not snippy." Lily forced a delicate cough. "There's been so much dust to clean up. I still have a little tickle in my throat." Was she stretching the truth by trying to cover the fact that she'd snorted at him?

He reached a hand out to a small hat, then withdrew it before he touched the yellow ribbon.

"Do you like it?" Lily walked behind the counter and picked up the straw creation. "I made it to match this one." She gestured to the coordinating larger hat. "I thought a mother and daughter might enjoy the pair." What was she thinking? Why would she speak to him about a mother and daughter wearing matching hats, when she knew he hadn't heard from his sister? He didn't need to be reminded of all that Ellen was missing.

Edward took a step back. "You're probably right."

"I'm sorry, Edward. I didn't mean to bring up a painful subject." Lily laid a hand on his arm.

"It's not a problem. I'm sure some little girl and her mother will love them." Another step back and her hand fell away from him. It just wouldn't be Jane and Ellen unless God brought his sister home safely.

He glanced over his shoulder to the street. "Well, I've got to get back to work."

"Please forgive me. I often speak without thinking. It's my worst trait. I really do try to control it." In all fairness, he knew she hadn't intended the words to hurt.

Edward held up a hand and interrupted her. "There's nothing to forgive, Lily. You're offering your wares to ladies who like this sort of thing." He moved toward the door and put his hat on, jamming it down a little farther than necessary. He wouldn't let himself react to Lily. He needed to bury his frustration over the disappearance of his sister.

Lily placed a hand on his arm again. He stared at her hand for a moment and then turned his face to hers.

He saw remorse in her eyes. "I really am sorry. I don't know why I always manage to say something that makes you uncomfortable."

He smiled a little then. "We'll get it sorted out." Over time they would resolve all the uncomfortable feelings. She'd grow accustomed to his ways, and he'd learn to understand her. What then? Eventually Ellen would grow up and start a life of her own. Would they be two friends sharing a home?

The sunlight coming through the windows dimmed, and he looked over his shoulder to see Mrs. Dismuke reaching for the door. Milly Ledford, the local dressmaker, stood behind her. Lily dropped her hand from Edward's arm and backed away.

Was she embarrassed to be seen close to him? Perhaps concerned they might misinterpret her hand on his arm as affection? Her face turned the slightest shade of pink.

Her next words to him confirmed his thoughts. "Thanks for stopping in." It was as though she were dealing with a customer or tradesman.

Edward chuckled and tipped his hat to the prospective customers. "Ladies." He turned back to Lily. "Lily." Unable to stop himself, he reached up and ran a finger down her warm cheek. "I'll see you at home later."

Lily lifted a hand to cover the trail of his finger on her face. What on earth had possessed him to do that? And why was she so pleased that he had?

She had no time to ponder his amusement. Her first customers had arrived. Lily ushered the ladies into the shop. The glances the two ladies exchanged were obvious. It seemed the topic of their sudden marriage had not been forgotten. She set her mind not to care what anyone thought, as long as they bought hats.

"Good morning, Mrs. Dismuke. Mrs. Ledford." She lifted an arm to indicate the interior of the fresh space. "Please take a moment to look around."

"Call me Milly." The dressmaker smiled a warm greeting. "I've been dying to get in here and see what you have."

"Me, too. And call me Peggy. Your sister and I are dear friends." The reverend's wife held up a package. "I looked in the window earlier, but wanted to pick up this dress Milly made for me first. Do you think you might have a hat to match the color?"

"Let's open it up and see." As she untied the string

holding the brown paper together, the bell jangled on the front door. Two more ladies entered the shop. "Welcome to Lily's Millinery and Finery. If you'd like to take a look around, I'll be with you as soon as I can."

Lily's heart skipped a beat. In just a few short minutes, she'd gone from wondering if anyone would come to having more customers than she could help at one time. She glanced through the front window and caught sight of Edward as he tied on his apron. His eyes might be smiling, but the distance made it difficult to be sure.

"Oh, look, Milly. I think this one will be perfect." Peggy Dismuke's delighted voice brought Lily back to the moment.

Bustling through the rest of her busy day gave Lily no time to think about the handsome blacksmith. But when she flipped the sign to close the shop and pulled down the shade, his image seemed to float in the room behind her.

She turned to survey the space. The floors needed to be swept, and many of the items needed to be straightened. The sight of several empty display stands made her heart smile. With energy she hadn't known she possessed, Lily set to work pulling stock from the back room and arranging more of her original creations in the shop.

Lily forced herself to stop before she was finished. The shop would have to wait while she fulfilled her obligations to Edward and Ellen. There was supper to prepare and chores to do at home. She walked across the street, bundled against the brisk January evening.

"You're late." Edward sat at the table helping Ellen with her sums.

Not exactly a warm greeting. Lily shrugged out of her coat. "It was a busy afternoon. I've still got loads more work to do, but supper can't wait any longer."

Ellen dropped her pencil. "All done." She pushed her school things together in a stack and stood. "What's for supper?"

"I'm going to fry some slices of ham and boil some potatoes." Lily wrapped an apron around her skirt. "Would you like to help?"

"Sure!" Ellen carried her things to her room. "I'll be right back."

Edward watched Ellen leave. "What just happened?"

His surprise at Ellen's response almost made Lily laugh. "She's decided we can be friends."

"Oh, she did?" He added wood to the stove. "You'll have to tell me all about it."

Lily put a pot of water on to boil. "Not much to tell. We talked. Now she knows I understand her."

Ellen bounced back into the room. "What can I do? Fry the ham? Peel the potatoes?"

Lily chuckled at Ellen's eagerness. "Let's start with the basics and work up to knives and the stove on a night when I'm not in such a rush." Lily was peeling the potatoes. "You can set the table, and I'll let you pour the drinks. You can help me mix up the corn bread batter. I'll fry some small cakes on the stove."

The evening meal went without incident. It was refreshing to eat without wondering what might send Ellen into one of her moods. Lily admitted it was an added pleasure to watch Edward's disbelief at the change in the relationship between his niece and her.

"When we finish, I'll wash the dishes while you get ready for bed, Ellen." Lily needed to go back to the store for at least a couple of hours.

Edward pushed his chair away from the table. "That

was a wonderful meal. Thank you, Lily." He tousled Ellen's hair. "And thank you, too, Ellen."

Ellen glowed under his praise. "I'm gonna learn real quick. I wanna be a good cook, so when Momma and Papa come to get me I can show them what a big girl I am now."

Edward stilled. The pain on his face showed how much he wanted Ellen to be able to do just that. "We'll keep praying, Ellen." He turned to Lily.

"I need to do a bit more work tonight." He picked up his hat.

"Um, I need to work tonight." She hadn't thought he wouldn't be around to get Ellen to bed.

"Why? You've been there all day. Can't it wait until morning?" He put the hat on and reached for his coat. He was talking to her, but he was preparing to walk out the door.

"What about me?" Ellen came out of her room in her nightgown. She still wore her braids and socks.

"Aunt Lily will be here with you." Edward shrugged his shoulders. "I'm sorry, Lily, but I didn't know you'd need the time, and I already promised a delivery first thing in the morning. I've got to finish."

Lily looked at him. "It's time for bed, Ellen." She opened the door. "I'll be in to read with you in a minute."

She stepped onto the porch, and Edward followed. "You promised that marrying you wouldn't keep me from running my shop." She folded her arms across her chest, not sure if it was because of the chill in the air or the stress between the two of them.

Edward was calm. He towered over her but didn't move to intimidate her. "And you promised to do all the things a mother would do for Ellen."

"I am." She swung her arms wide now. "I came to cook supper when I had more work to do."

"I'm sorry I didn't realize the kind of time you'd need in the evenings." He looked remorseful. "I need to get this order ready." He scuffed his boot against the boards of the porch. "If you'll watch her tonight, I'll make breakfast tomorrow, and you can go to the shop early."

She had a lot of work to do to be ready to open again tomorrow, but it wasn't wise to leave the child alone.

Ellen called from her room. "I'm ready to read now."

Edward waited for Lily's response.

"Oh, all right. I'll go in early tomorrow." She put a hand on the door. "But we need to iron out some details of how we're both supposed to get all our work done and take care of Ellen."

The child's voice rang out again. "Are you coming, Aunt Lily? I've got a storybook that Momma gave me."

"Thank you." Edward stepped off the porch. "Don't wait up. Just make sure the door isn't bolted, so I won't have to wake you."

He walked into the darkness without looking back. Lily wondered how hard the fight would be to maintain her independence. The promises were falling apart, and they'd only been married a week.

She'd take care of Ellen. But she'd take care of her business, too.

Chapter Nine

Edward stood in the bank at the teller's window on Wednesday morning. He sensed Lily's arrival before he turned away, cash in hand. He saw her before she saw him. A becoming touch of pink lit her cheeks. But he refused to concentrate on her beauty.

"I didn't expect to see you here this morning, Lily. I thought you'd be busy preparing for another busy day."

"I finished getting everything ready and had a couple of errands to run."

"Well, I'm glad you were able take care of everything this morning." He'd been sorry to keep her from working the night before, but he'd had no choice.

Her small hand shot out and grasped his arm. The white glove was trimmed with tiny pearl buttons. He silently scolded himself for noticing the minute details.

"I was wondering if you could come by the shop later today." Lily's face was fresh and open as she waited for his reply.

"What is it you need?" Edward took a step back, and her hand fell. He folded his money and stuffed it into his shirt pocket.

"I have an idea for a sign for the shop." The feather on her hat danced near her eyes. It swooped forward from its perch and swept across the edge of her forehead. As soft as the feather looked, he knew her hair would be softer. If he kept being distracted like this, she'd visit him in his dreams tonight. What was the matter with him?

"I'm very busy today." His voice sounded gruff, but he didn't want everyone listening to their conversation. He could see the bank owner, Lester Bennett, watching from his desk behind the half wall separating the lobby from the rest of the bank.

Both gloves wrung the reticule she held. "Okay." Her voice was small compared to the exuberance it had held a moment earlier. "At your convenience." She looked toward the teller window. "I'll just be off, then. I've got to deposit the receipts from yesterday. I still have another errand before I open today." She reached into the reticule and pulled out a handful of bills.

"Lily, you shouldn't keep that kind of cash on hand overnight." Worried someone might realize she was alone in the shop and try to rob her, he felt it important to caution her.

The now-familiar stiffness of her posture returned. "I seem to remember it was your suggestion that I take care of the hat business and you would take care of the blacksmithing." With a slight lift of her chin she added, "I am willing to abide by your original suggestion. I'm quite capable of taking care of my business." With a sharp turn, her tiny feet tapped across the wooden floor to the teller window.

Edward lifted his eyebrows and pushed his hat farther down on his brow. What a stubborn woman. She frustrated and intrigued him at the same time. Her lips set together in determination were beautiful.

He spun around and headed outside. He stepped off the boards and onto the dust of the street and lifted a silent prayer.

Lord, she's a mite stubborn, but it'd be a shame for her to be hurt over it. If she won't listen to me, I hope You send someone she will listen to.

He walked across to his shop and swung the big front doors wide. When he turned to go inside, he saw Lily step out of the bank into the morning sunshine. She tugged her glove on and fastened the pearl button at her wrist. Pivoting toward the post office, she stumbled and almost lost her balance. He was on the point of going to her aid when Winston Ledford came out of the bank and caught her by the elbow.

Seeing that man with his hand on Lily's arm sent a flash of anger through Edward's chest. He'd give him one second to let go.

Then Lily turned to Ledford and started a conversation. Edward wasn't close enough to hear their words. He stood speechless when she grasped the man's arm and nodded. She lifted the hem of her skirt with her other hand. Ledford took her hand from his arm and placed it on his shoulder before squatting at her feet. He reached toward her foot and paused.

What was she thinking? How dare she stand in the street with the saloon owner! And lift her skirt like that. She leaned on Ledford's shoulder for what seemed like an eternity, and then she backed away from him.

A smug look crossed the man's face as he stood and brushed his hands together. More words were exchanged, and Ledford dipped his head at Lily. Edward caught the moment Ledford saw him watching the scene.

Mr. Ledford eyed her, and the two continued talking.

Lily put up a gloved hand and touched the feather at her brow. Was she flirting with a saloon owner? What good could he do as her husband trying to guard her reputation if she insisted on this sort of behavior?

He heard Ledford laugh. A slight movement and Lily turned her attention across to the blacksmith shop. Edward couldn't prevent the scowl that crossed his face. She turned back to her conversation. He was fuming. Enough was enough. Just as he moved to step across the street, Ledford nodded his head at her and walked away.

Edward ignored the hand the man lifted in greeting to him. He slapped his work gloves against his thigh and turned to march into his shop. He wasn't sure what had just happened. But he was certain he'd speak to her about, so it wouldn't happen again.

Just as soon as he calmed down enough to be civil.

After lunch, Lily sat in the workroom making yet another hat suitable for a lovely spring dress. Yellow daisies circled the ribbon she'd woven through the straw at the base of the hat just above the brim. She reached for a length of white ribbon with one hand as she turned the hat first one way and then another. The front bell rang.

"Coming," Lily called out and slid from her stool. Two young ladies waited inside the front door. She took in their dresses, such as they were—bare shoulders, and necklines plunged to places no lady would consider proper. The fabrics were sheer in places, and bows pulled up the fabric at intervals to make the short skirts even shorter, revealing a hint of colorful petticoats. The dresses weren't identical but were so much alike Lily knew they'd come from the same place. They hadn't been purchased locally.

She quickly recovered her composure. "How may I help you, ladies?"

Her customers looked at each other and grinned. The younger of the two spoke first. "Winston sent us to see you. Said you might have some things we'd be interested in." While she spoke, the lady's eyes perused the hats on the hall tree against the side wall. Lily didn't think she could be more than twenty years old. Her painted cheeks and lips made it hard to be sure.

The other lady looked toward the back of the store and the glass display case where Lily kept her most expensive offerings. The materials were too delicate to risk putting them out where customers and their children could handle them.

"I think I see just the thing for my new yellow dress." This lady was a little older than the first, perhaps closer to thirty. Her makeup creased in the lines around her eyes. Lily decided life must have treated the woman unkindly.

"Winston?" Lily asked.

"Winston Ledford." The young lady spoke again. "Said he met you outside the bank this morning." She picked up a black parasol from the stand in the hall tree and opened it. With a slight spin of her wrist, the parasol twirled in the afternoon sunlight coming through the front windows.

Lily looked outside just in time to see Liza Croft turn from her display window and march across the street in the direction of the general store. She looked like a woman on a mission.

"Oh, Mr. Ledford." The rather distasteful encounter

with the man came back to her. "He assisted me when my shoe became wedged in the sidewalk." Lily remembered him saying he'd send his girls by her shop.

He must have thought she wouldn't know how to handle these ladies. The smirk she'd seen in his eyes had been a challenge.

Lily walked behind the glass case and asked the older lady which hat she'd like to see.

"That one." She pointed to a hat Lily had made before her shop opened. It had turned out better than she'd imagined in the beginning. It was some of her best work, and she'd priced it accordingly. She pulled the white felt creation with organza and tiny roses from its place in the case. Several ladies had admired it, but no one had been willing to pay its price.

"Here you are." Lily smiled at the woman as she handed her the hat. "My name is Lily."

After a slight hesitation and a lifting of a brow, the lady responded. "I'm Virginia Jones. Most folks call me Ginger."

Lily adjusted a gilded mirror stand so Ginger could see her reflection. "Would you like to try it on?"

Ginger paused and leveled a frank stare at her. "You really want me to? Or are you just saying that because you're afraid to tell us to leave?"

Lily met the challenge from Ginger head-on. "Miss Jones, I'm in business to sell hats."

The young lady put down the parasol and laughed. "She's got you there, Ginger. I mean Miss Jones." She bowed in a mock curtsy.

"Be quiet, Lovey," Ginger snapped at her young companion. Then she turned back to Lily. "I think I would like to try this hat on, then." She reached up and removed the wisp of a hat she wore and set it on the case.

"If she's going to call you Miss Jones, I can be Lavinia Aiken, instead of Lovey. No sense in you being the only one treated like a lady." Lovey twisted her mouth in a smirk at Ginger.

"Of course, Miss Aiken. My goal is for all my customers to be treated well." Lily smiled at the younger woman before coming around the counter to help Ginger set the white hat on the crown of her head. "I have a splendid hat pin that would be perfect."

Ginger turned her head back and forth in front of the small mirror while holding the hat in place. "May as well do it up proper. Winston's buying today." She gave Lily a wink and spoke to Lovey. "You need to pick out something nice, too. No sense leaving empty-handed when we're being treated so well for a change."

Lily brought a cushion holding an array of hat pins from inside the case. She pulled one with a pearl-encrusted handle and laid it across her open palm to show Ginger. "What do you think?"

"It's right pretty. Is it expensive?" A smile crept into the dark eyes that had softened from cynicism to fun after Lily had made known her intention of selling her a hat.

Lily smiled back, enjoying the thought of Winston Ledford having to pay for his attempt at embarrassing her. "As a matter of fact, Miss Jones, it's one of my most expensive pieces."

"Then I think I'll just have to take it." Ginger accepted the pin and secured the hat to her head. She walked to the hall tree and took in her reflection from different angles. "What about you, Lovey? What has captured your fancy?"

Lily helped the two ladies choose several items. She followed them onto the sidewalk and thanked them for their patronage. "Please tell Mr. Ledford how much I appreciate him sending you by today." Ginger and Lovey laughed as they walked away, sharing the joke that, while Winston had attempted to intimidate Lily, all three ladies had benefited at his expense. The fancy hatboxes they carried were evidence of their success.

Turning to go back into her shop, Lily caught sight of Edward in the reflection of the display window. Liza Croft stood beside him wearing a deep frown. If Lily thought Edward looked unhappy this morning outside his shop, the expression he wore now would be considered thunderous. She stepped inside and closed the door, saying a prayer.

Lord, I don't know why some things happen, but thank You for the business. Please help Ginger and Lovey to know Your love and turn from the lives Mr. Ledford has made for them.

Lily set about straightening the merchandise that had been set in disarray by the two ladies. When the front bell rang, she put on a smile and turned to greet whoever was at the door.

Edward closed the door with unnecessary force and rounded to face her. "Just what do you think you're doing?"

Startled by his outburst, Lily didn't answer.

His brows came together in a deep crease that drew her into the depths of his brown eyes. It was like swimming in dark coffee. Hot and strong coffee. With a bite!

Edward pointed in the direction of the saloon without taking his eyes from her shocked face. "What are you doing entertaining those women?"

"Entertaining?" Lily fisted her hands and planted one on each hip. "Is that what you think I was doing?"

"I saw you laughing with them."

"We were laughing, but you have no idea what amused us, not that it's any of your business." Lily moved closer to him. She had to look up to see into his face. A storm lit her eyes. "I didn't come to Pine Haven to be bossed around by a man. If I'd wanted that, I could have stayed in East River and married Luther Aarens. At least he had better manners than to raise his voice to me."

"I heard you sending Mr. Ledford your thanks. That was quite a display you put on in front of the bank this morning, after my warning you to be careful. This town won't take kindly if you associate with the likes of the people from the saloon."

"Don't you come in here and tell me who I can and cannot associate with." Lily lifted a finger to poke his chest. He backed away as she stalked forward. "I opened this store to sell hats." Again she drove her finger into his chest. "I'll have you know those women spent enough money this afternoon to pay my rent to you for the next month." She took another step forward, and he was backed against the door. "And the laughter you heard was from three women who got the best of a man who tried to intimidate me."

"Intimidate you? How?" Edward couldn't move back, but she continued to move forward. She was straining her neck to look up at him now.

"Mr. Ledford told me this morning he'd send his girls around to my shop. Oh, he thought that was a fine joke. He had the nerve to laugh in my face. Sending them here was his way of provoking me."

"Why didn't you tell him no or send them on their way?" Edward reached up and captured her hand in his.

"Because I opened this shop to sell merchandise. They had money. His money. What better way to get back at him than to sell them my most expensive items?" She tried to tug her hand free, but he held it snugly. So she poked him again with the tip of her finger. "And what you saw this morning was me with my shoe stuck in the boards of the sidewalk. Mr. Ledford came out of the bank just in time to keep me from falling. He pulled my shoe loose from the planks. Nothing more." She suddenly deflated. Her head dropped, and her hand went limp in his.

Edward watched the color drain from her delicate face.

"Oh, no," she whispered. "If you think what you think…" Her voice trailed off to nothing. She raised her head to look at him. "What must everyone else think?"

Her eyes had turned violet with her temper. Now they swam in a blue sea of sorrow.

"I'm afraid they think what I thought." Edward released her hand. He didn't want to hurt her, but he couldn't send her a false message of support, either. This brave lady had come to town in a flourish of flowers and lace, but if she wasn't careful, her dream of success would die.

"I can't refuse to serve a customer because I don't agree with them. Those ladies were sent here to embarrass me. I thought I was being a good Christian to treat them with respect. If they don't see the value in themselves, shouldn't I show it to them by loving them? Jesus was always associating with people no one else would talk to."

"If you keep talking like that, Reverend Dismuke will

want you to give a testimony in church come Sunday."
He smiled at her and chuckled.

She giggled. "Do you think I should finish with the
Scripture in Proverbs about the wealth of the sinner being
laid up for the just, or do you think that would be too
much?"

He laughed with her. "You might want to save that
one for your second sermon."

Lily stopped and confessed, "I was pleased to take the
wretched man's money."

He tried to ease her anxiety. "My concern is for your
reputation. I know you're a good woman. Your father is
a fine Christian man. But people in a small town can be
unforgiving when they get the wrong impression."

"I couldn't help getting stuck in the sidewalk." Her
back straightened, and her face regained some of its color.

Edward held up both hands in an attempt to prevent
another stampede. He thought he might have a bruise
from where she'd poked his chest. "I know that. But people only see bits and pieces. They don't know you."

"I've certainly done a fine job so far—parading
through town in my nightclothes. Now I've been seen
cavorting with the saloon owner and selling hats to his
saloon girls. I'll be lucky to have a business at all by the
end of the month." An exasperated, gushing sigh punc-
tuated her words.

"It seems to me that none of it was your fault." Edward
thought about each statement. It painted a bleak picture
when she strung it all together like that. "'Cavorting' is
too strong a word. I'd say something like, 'consorting.'"
He tilted his head to one side, hoping she'd appreciate
his attempt at humor.

She shook her head and gave a slight groan. "You're

right. That sounds so much better." Her shoulders lifted as she took in a deep breath and lowered as she let it out. "There's not much I can do about it now."

"I'll try to help. I can make sure Reverend Dismuke knows why you welcomed those ladies into your shop. He can probably pass the word along to his wife, who can help by calming the fires of gossip started by Mrs. Croft."

Lily's eyes grew wide. "So that's where all this is coming from?"

Edward watched her, wondering what was in her mind. The emotions Lily had displayed in the past few minutes ranged from rage to sorrow to shame and back.

Resolve brought calm to her features. "Thank you for bringing these things to my attention. I assure you, I'll do everything in my power to make certain you are not embarrassed to have me as your wife."

"Lily, that's not what I meant." A new level of friend-ship had opened between them. Sharing spiritual truths and unpleasant facts, in an effort to come to a positive solution, was a difficult process for the best of friends. He thought they'd made progress by handling the events of the day. They'd ended the conversation with good humor, but in an instant she was all business again.

"But I saw you with Mrs. Croft before you came in here."

"Be reasonable, Lily." Edward captured her hand and turned it over in his. Today was the first day he'd noticed her hands without gloves. Calluses from the broom and pricks from her sewing needles and the tools of a milli-ner were scattered across her palm and fingers. He knew the other hand would be the same. This delicate-looking creature had an inner strength he hadn't seen until today. There was more to Lily Stone than the feminine surface she showed to the world. "Do you think I'd stand and talk to her without defending your honor?"

Her eyes were violet again, but he could see her fighting to believe him. She finally shook her head. "I guess not."

He dropped her hand and tipped his hat to her. "If you'll excuse me, Mrs. Stone, I have business with the reverend." He smiled at her, and the light that danced into her eyes ensured him of her gratitude.

"Thank you, Mr. Stone." She followed him outside. "Remember to come back when you have a few minutes so we can discuss the sign I want you to make."

The image foremost in his mind as he walked away was of her ashen face as she realized the situation she was in.

She was his wife now. It was his responsibility to protect her. He just hadn't known when he'd married her how often he'd have to protect her from herself.

Chapter Ten

Saturday dawned clear and cool. Lily dressed for the day with forced excitement for the first Saturday her business would be open. Surely she'd meet new people and have new customers today. Thursday and Friday had passed without a single sale. Oh, she'd seen several ladies on the sidewalk cast a look her way. In the end, they'd all gone away without stopping. Some had dared to come close enough to look in the window. She'd even heard one mother tell her young daughter they'd try to order her a hat from the general store because it wouldn't be right to shop at Lily's after what they'd heard.

Lily checked her reflection in the long mirror her father had given her on her sixteenth birthday. Edward had moved it over from her rooms a few days after their wedding.

She ran her hands down the front of her skirt to smooth the fabric. She wore blue again to match her eyes. The rich color always made her feel more feminine. After all, she was trying to sell stylish accessories to women who lived hard lives in the open country. Soft ruffles swooped up the side of the skirt and met in a large bow at the back of her dress. The bodice had small buttons and a lace collar. She knew just the hat she'd wear if she decided to venture out today. It was small with a tuft of blue organza nestled beneath a nosegay of tiny berries. She pulled it from its box and put it on the bed.

First, she had to prepare breakfast. A few minutes later, Ellen came from her room rubbing her eyes and moaning about being tired.

"It's Saturday. You should be excited about a day with no school." Lily put a plate of scrambled eggs in front of the child. "You can play and even come visit me at the shop later if you'd like."

Edward opened the door and came in from the outside. A cool wind whirled into the room before he could close the door. "It's a bit chilly this morning, ladies." He tousled Ellen's sleepy head and sat at the table.

"Here you go." Lily handed him a plate and joined them at the table.

Lily bowed her head while Edward gave thanks for their food. She prayed she'd have sales today that she could thank God for tonight.

Ellen perked up after a few bites of food. "Aunt Lily says I can go to the store today."

"She did?" Edward looked at Lily. "You can do that if you'd like." He grinned at Ellen. "Unless you want to help me with a special project."

"What?" Ellen was so excited she almost knocked over her milk when she waved her arms.

"Easy." He chuckled and moved the cup away from the edge of the table. "You'll have to choose without knowing." Lily watched the interaction between uncle and niece. The way he made little things fun for Ellen was sweet. He'd be a wonderful father.

Father? As his wife, if he had children, it would be with her. Lily choked on her biscuit. Edward thumped her on the back until she waved him off.

"Are you okay?" he asked.

"Fine." She sputtered again and took a drink of her coffee. "Thank you."

"What will it be, Ellen? A day in the hat shop or an adventure with me?"

"Hey!" Lily laughed. "Well, Ellen, do you want to try your hand at making a beautiful hat or work in a hot, smelly room and end up covered in soot?"

They all laughed then.

"I want to get dirty and smelly!" Ellen gave a strong nod of her head and speared another bite of eggs.

Edward smiled at Lily. "Nice try. But you just don't have my special touch for wooing her."

Lily stood and started to gather the dishes. "Next time I'll see about adding in a live toad or maybe a day of cleaning the stoves." Wrinkling her nose and scrunching her lips, she pulled a face at both of them. She still hadn't adjusted to sharing a house with the two of them. But on days like today, it didn't seem as difficult as she'd first thought it would be.

Everyone left the house in good spirits a few minutes later. Lily had just settled in to work on a new hat when the bell chimed. She bolted from the stool and stepped into the shop. "Good morning. Welcome to Lily's Millinery and Finery."

Daisy bustled into the shop. "Oh, Lily, how are you?" She hugged Lily.

Lily pulled away from her older sister without meeting her eyes. "I'm fine. Thank you." She looked out the window toward the street. "Did you come to town alone?"

"No. The boys are with Tucker at the livery. Then they're coming around to pick up the supplies I got from the general store. I dropped by Peggy's earlier, and she wanted me to leave the baby with her while we shopped." Daisy made her way to the hall tree against the side wall. "This is lovely." She pulled the spring hat with yellow daisies Lily had made earlier in the week. "I must try this on."

"Sit down and let me help you." Lily removed Daisy's modest bonnet and straightened her hair. She reached for the hat. "This will be just right for you, I think. It's perfect for spring."

Daisy eyed her reflection in the large mirror. "I love it. I just bought a length of yellow gingham to make a new dress. This is exactly what I need for the spring picnic at church." She rubbed her abdomen and met Lily's gaze in the mirror. "I'll be needing some new clothes with more room around the middle by then." A smile creased her face.

"Daisy! How wonderful!" Lily hugged her sister. Daisy's face was aglow with joy for the life that grew inside her.

"Isn't it? Tucker's happy. The boys are beside themselves. They love Rose, but I think they want a brother this time."

"What about you?"

"I'll be thrilled with whatever God decides to bless us with. A healthy child is my only prayer." Daisy loosened the ribbon from the hat and pulled it from her head. "I'll take this, ma'am. Will you please wrap it up for me?" Her sober voice made Lily laugh.

"Yes, Mrs. Barlow. Is there anything else I can get for

you today? Gloves, perhaps, or a parasol?" Lily wrapped the hat in tissue paper and put it in a hatbox.

"What do I owe you?"

Lily pushed the box across the glass case to her sister. "Not a thing. You and Tucker have been more help than I knew I would need. It's my gift to you."

Daisy frowned. "I can't accept it, Lily. I know what's going on." Her face grew serious.

"Whatever do you mean?"

"Peggy told me when I stopped at her house. What a horrid week it must have been for you." Daisy opened her reticule and pulled out some money.

"I won't take your money, Daisy. I did very well at the beginning of the week. Business will pick up. People just need to realize my shop is open." Lily nipped into the back room for a few seconds and returned with another hat. She went to the hall tree and put it in the spot that had held the hat Daisy had chosen.

"It's more than that, Lily." She came to stand near the hall tree. "Peggy said it didn't go well when she tried to talk to Mrs. Croft. She wasn't receptive to Peggy's explanations about your actions." At Lily's downcast look, she added, "I'm sorry. Because she's in the middle of town and most people do business at their store, she's developed a lot of influence. Which is sad, because most people know better than to hang on her every word."

Lily shrugged off her sister's sympathy. "Don't worry about it. People will see the truth. It may take time, but I came here to bring beauty to the ladies of this community. That's exactly what I'm going to do." She walked to the front display and watched two ladies come out of the post office next door. They looked in her window but scurried away when they saw her standing inside.

She turned back to Daisy. "When you and Peggy show up at church wearing my hats, ladies are going to want to come here, too. You're the prettiest way I know to drum up interest in my shop. So hurry up and make that pretty dress."

"I'm praying for you." Daisy hugged her tightly and retrieved her package.

"Thank you. I need it."

"How are you and Edward doing?"

"It's awkward, I guess." She pulled at the edge of her sleeve. "Ellen has decided to accept my presence. That's made things easier."

"But?"

"Daisy, you must know something of how I feel. You didn't expect to be married to Tucker when it happened."

"No, I didn't." Her sister put a hand on her arm. "It's not quite the same thing. I knew Tucker. We'd been dear friends."

Lily heaved a sigh. "Well, Edward wants to tell me what to do and how to run my business."

"Really? What has he said?"

She shrugged. "He thinks I should put my money in the bank every day when I close." It didn't sound horrible when she said it out loud. "He says I need to be careful who I choose to associate with."

Daisy made a small sound. "Hmm…that sounds like a husband trying to protect his wife." She gave Lily a serious look. "Try not to turn him away with your need for independence. God must have thought you two needed each other."

Lily shook her head. "I think God wanted Ellen to be safe." She opened the door for Daisy and found Edward on the porch.

"Edward." Lily put her hand at the base of her throat. "You startled me." Her hand went up to touch the hair at the base of her neck.

"I'm sorry." He took off his hat and held it in both hands. "I came to check with you about making a sign."

Daisy cleared her throat behind Lily. "How do you do, Edward?"

"Daisy." Edward dipped his head in a greeting. "I'm fine, thank you. Just saw your husband coming out of the livery. He said he's on his way to pick you up at the general store, if you're finished with your shopping."

Lily backed up to allow Daisy to pass through the door.

"Thank you." Daisy went onto the porch and turned back to Lily. "Tucker and I want you all to come to lunch tomorrow."

Lily started to refuse, but Edward accepted. "We'd like that. It'll be good for Ellen. Thank you."

"Come right after church," Daisy said.

She stepped outside and waved as Daisy left. "I'm looking forward to it. An afternoon in the countryside will do us all some good."

Daisy made her way across the street, and Lily turned to Edward.

"If you'll give me a moment, I've made a rough drawing of what I have in mind. I'll get it and show you where I'd like the sign to be mounted." Lily wrung her hands together as she spoke.

They stepped inside. "Has it been any better today?" His gaze dared her to deny she knew what he meant.

"No." She motioned for him to follow her into the workroom. "Peggy Dismuke came in and bought some handkerchiefs to send to her sister."

"It'll get better."

She opened her mouth to contradict him, but he held up a finger and tilted his head to one side. "I promise. Something else will happen. To someone else. And everyone will forget why you and I got married." He put the finger down and put his hat back on. "Now get your drawing, and let's see what you have in mind for a sign. Hopefully something to draw some positive attention in your direction." He smiled and leaned against the opening between the shop and the workroom.

A small smile caressed her lips and made its way to her eyes. Try as she might, she didn't understand how this man was such a comfort to her. He'd turned her life upside down.

She was grateful he was staying close by to help with the consequences of the upheaval.

On Sunday afternoon Edward entered Tucker and Daisy's cabin. Lily sat in the front room visiting with her sister. He and Tucker had been in the barn while the kids played outside after lunch.

"We need to load up and head back to town, Lily." He didn't like the looks of the sky.

"Surely you don't need to leave so soon?" Daisy put Rose back in her cradle and reached a hand to Tucker, who joined them.

Tucker put an arm around his wife and lifted a hand to point through the open door. "It seems there's a storm heading our way."

"Oh, my." Daisy went to the door and called to the kids to come quickly.

"How bad is it?" Lily moved to stand and Edward put a hand under her elbow to assist her from the chair. A trickle of heat trailed up the length of his arm. He saw she was not unaffected when she turned to him. He tried to focus on Ellen approaching with the twins.

"We better hurry, Uncle Edward. That looks like a mighty bad storm. I wanna get home now." Ellen's voice presented a brave front, but a slight tremble revealed her true anxiety.

Tucker closed the door against the growing wind. "You best hurry on."

"I want to be safe at home before the full force of this storm hits." Edward was concerned for his family. He wasn't accustomed to having a family to look after, but he wanted to do his best.

Lily turned back to him. "I hope the storm passes quickly so it won't hinder me from opening my shop tomorrow."

The quiet that met her words chilled more than the storm ever could. It was obvious no one here thought she'd have any customers tomorrow. He was doing everything he could think of to support her, but the fact was that people were avoiding her place.

"Oh, please, don't look at me like that." Lily implored Daisy to understand. "I simply must open. I can't let the gossip change me. Opening the store every day is the only way I know to combat the lies that have been spread about me."

"I don't think you'll have to worry about opening tomorrow." He didn't want to give her false hope.

"Why would you say that?" Lily grabbed her coat and rammed her arms into the sleeves. Try as he might, Edward couldn't match her speed. She was fastening the buttons before he could grasp the woolen collar to pull it straight. "How can I build a good name in Pine Haven if my own family and friends don't have faith in me?"

Daisy spoke up. "Lily, we have faith in you. I know your store will be a success. I heard more than one lady admire Peggy's new hat today. Rest assured she was singing your praises when they did."

Lily spun to look at him. "Why don't you think I need to worry about opening tomorrow, then?"

Edward put a hand on her shoulder. "It doesn't look to me like anyone will be going anywhere to shop tomorrow. This storm shows all the signs of keeping us tucked into our homes for several days."

Lily looked from one face to another. She lowered her head and reached for her reticule.

"Well, I need to be at home just in case." She peered through the window at the brooding gray sky. "Who knows? It may blow over without a whimper."

"Right. If you don't mind, I'd like to head on back just in case your optimism doesn't materialize." Edward shoved his hat down over his brow. "Ready, Ellen?"

"Yes, sir." The little girl tied her bonnet tight and pushed her hands deep into her pockets. "Bye, everybody!" Out the door she flew and clambered onto the wagon seat.

Edward offered his hand to Lily to help her into the wagon. In the rush to leave, she hadn't put on her ever-present gloves. When she put her hand in his, he felt the calluses on her palms he'd noticed once before. This woman he'd heard talking about frills and pampering wasn't taking the time to pamper herself. She appeared soft from a distance, but closer inspection showed the depth of strength and determination she possessed.

He walked around the front of the horses and checked

the harnesses before he stepped up to join them. He passed a heavy blanket for Ellen and Lily to tuck around their legs.

"Ellen, move over and give Lily more room on the seat." Edward shifted to the far edge of the seat to allow Ellen to slide closer to him. He'd have to drive the team hard to get home before the storm broke. The last thing he needed was for Lily to bounce right off the wagon. "We'll be going home in a hurry. It's gonna be a bumpy ride." He released the brake and signaled his team to head for home.

"Do you think we'll get home before it storms?" Ellen had to raise her voice to be heard above the sounds of the horses and wagon. Each bump sent the three passengers jostling against each other.

"I'm trying my best." Edward held the reins firm and drove the team as hard as he dared on the rough terrain.

They hit a deep rut in the road, and Ellen's small frame lifted off the seat. Edward and Lily reached for her at the same time.

"You handle the team, and I'll hold her." Lily pulled Ellen close and wrapped her tightly with both arms.

The trip to town dragged on for what seemed like ages. Edward thought they just might make it home before the storm hit. No sooner had town come into view than sheets of sleet began to pelt the trio as they huddled together on the seat. He looked over at Lily's flimsy hat and knew it was already ruined. Ellen's bonnet would dry by the fire, but the feathers and ribbon Lily preferred were beyond repair. Another reminder that such things might please the eye but the troubles of life could wreak havoc on them without warning.

"Push Ellen under the seat and slide next to me." Edward was shouting now over the fierce wind.

"I don't want to!" Ellen clung to him.

"Now, child." Edward's voice brooked no argument. Lily helped her slide under the seat and moved next to him.

"Pull the blanket over our heads. I'm afraid this will get worse before it gets better."

Lily fought the wind and worsening sleet, but managed to pull the blanket around him and then tuck herself close with the blanket over their heads.

Her small frame fit against him, invoking a strong desire to protect her. He began to wonder if they would have been better off staying at Daisy's cabin. It was too late to turn back now. They'd have to press on for home.

Ellen was directly beneath them. Edward felt her small arms wrap around one boot. She hated storms. The week her parents left her with him, they'd had terrible rain for days. The continuous thunder and lightning had buried fright deep in the child's soul. Why hadn't he seen this one coming earlier? He should have had her safe at home. It was his duty to protect Lily as much as Ellen, even if Lily insisted she could take care of herself.

Blinding snow fell with the frozen rain, stinging his hands and arms. His hat protected his head, but he knew Lily would be getting the worst of it. Ellen was safe under the bench. There was no refuge between them and town. They had no choice but to struggle on through the storm.

He shouted at Lily. "Put your head down!"

"I can't! If I do, I won't be able to hold the blanket over your head."

"I've got the blanket. Come here!" He lifted his arm and tucked her in close to his chest. He held the reins with one hand, snagged the far edge of the blanket with the other and pushed it into her hand. "Hang on to this!"

A streak of lightning lit the sky, and the team startled. It took all his strength to keep them from bolting. Ellen shrieked beneath the seat and tightened her hold on his boot. The echoing thunder rumbled low beneath the howling wind.

Edward narrowed his eyes, searching for the road that threatened to fade from view in the intensity of the storm. He pushed the horses as hard as he dared. "God, help us to get home safe."

"Amen!" Lily shouted from her cocoon beneath the edge of his elbow.

Edward didn't realize he'd prayed out loud. But right now they needed all the help they could get. He maneuvered the team around the last bend in the road before the edge of town and pulled on the reins. "Whoa, boys!"

He pulled the wagon to a stop under the roof that extended off the front of the livery. Icicles hung from the wagon. White puffs from the horses' nostrils floated up to be carried off by the wind.

"Make a run for the front porch." The sleet still pelted down. He had to raise his voice for Lily and Ellen to hear him. "I'm going to get the team inside the livery. Start the fire and get Ellen out of those wet clothes."

Chapter Eleven

"Let's go inside." Lily put a hand on Ellen's shoulder and urged her toward the front door of the cabin. The wind buffeted them on the porch.

"Don't!" The scream tore from Ellen. Her chin quivered, and she began to tremble. Melting snow dripped from her dress and coat. Black shoes pranced like a nervous horse in the middle of the frozen drift forming at her feet. Something just before terror emanated from the child's eyes.

Lily knelt before her and put a hand on each shoulder. "We're safe now, Ellen."

"Where's Uncle Edward? I want my uncle Edward!" The frightened voice rose to a fever pitch.

"He's putting the horses in the livery so they'll be safe, too." Lily spoke loud enough to be heard over the wind, but gently in an effort to calm the child.

"I want Uncle Edward." Sobs wrenched through Ellen. Lily pulled her close and pressed the child's wet face to her shoulder.

"He's coming, precious. Don't you worry. He's safe. He'll be right here." Lily swayed from side to side, rocking Ellen in her arms. "We're all safe." Lightning flashed and thunder followed before the light faded. The clap was deafening. Ellen and Lily both jumped and clutched each other more tightly. The child's scream was muffled by Lily's coat.

Edward ducked under the eave of the porch and knelt behind Ellen. "It's okay, baby girl. I'm here." He turned her to face him and wrapped his arms around her.

Lily immediately felt the chill of separation as Ellen's warmth pulled away from her. Snow blew onto the small porch with relentless force.

"I'll start the fire." She stood and skirted around the two as they clung to each other in the cold.

Lily searched in the dim cabin for matches near the hearth. Thankful he had laid the fire, she struck the match against the bricks and lit the kindling near the iron grate. She blew on the small flame, and the fire caught in earnest. She filled the kettle with water from a pitcher near the stove. Setting it to boil, she opened the front door again.

"Can you carry her in? The fire's going." Lily hoped Edward could hear her. The storm raged and blew its fury onto the porch, but the strength of it paled in comparison to the emotions she saw in the two shadowed figures. Ellen was curled against Edward, her tiny arms snaked around his neck. He held her close and spoke near her ear. Lily felt like an intruder in the scene. What tragedy racked their hearts and caused them to remain in a dangerous storm? Did the elements of nature dim in view of the heartache they nursed?

Edward rose at her words, lifting Ellen with him. He scooped her legs up and carried her like a baby in his arms. Lily backed into the room, holding the door wide for them to enter. He had to turn sideways to get through the doorway with Ellen.

Lily spread a blanket on the bench near the hearth, and Edward laid Ellen on it.

"Please get her some dry clothes and a towel."

She scurried to get the things he asked for, returning to find Ellen had stopped crying. Ellen sat on the bench facing the fire. Edward tugged at her coat and dropped it near his feet, in a wet heap with her shoes.

Lily pulled the shoes from the pile. "Edward, loosen the laces and put these on the hearth while I change her clothes." The kettle whistled. "Will you make tea?"

"Yes." He put the shoes down and went to the stove.

Minutes later Lily pulled a nightgown over Ellen's head and started to work on the long, thick hair with a towel.

Lily wrapped Ellen in a blanket and was pulling on her last sock when Edward handed Ellen the warm drink. "Be careful. It's very hot."

Lily smiled at the child, whose brown eyes reflected the flames.

"Thank you, Aunt Lily." Ellen's voice was a ragged whisper, her throat raw from crying in the storm.

Lily cupped her cheek in one hand. The fire had started to warm the tiny girl. "You're welcome, Ellen. Now let's see if I can find you something to eat."

"I'll take care of supper." Edward shrugged out of his coat. Water hit the floor, and rivulets traced the grain of the wood toward the fireplace. He hung the heavy garment on a hook near the fire's edge.

A smile teased Lily's face. "I'll do it."

"What about something simple and filling?" He sat on

the hearth and tugged off his boots. Water spilled onto the floor at his feet. He rolled thick socks down his calves.

"You are making a mess." Lily picked up a bucket from the corner of the kitchen and rushed to put it in front of him. It was unusual to be this close to him. The awkwardness of the past weeks faded in the urgency of the moment.

He wrung the water from his socks into the bucket and laid them across the edge of the hearth near Ellen's. "I'd say it's a bit late to worry about how much melting snow and ice is in here." He pointed to direct her attention to the floor beneath her feet.

Lily looked down to see a growing puddle. Water ran from the front edge of her coat. Her dress swished with moisture, and her shoes were worse than Ellen's had been. Warmth filled her face when she looked back to Edward, and she giggled.

"I see your point." She removed her coat, hoping the rest of the water would be contained in one area. She hung it next to his on another iron hook. "These hooks are handy here."

"Jane insisted on them." He picked up Ellen's dress and wrung the water from it into the bucket at his feet. "She didn't want me soaking the floor when it rained."

"Momma doesn't like a mess." Ellen's fingers laced around her tea. The color was returning to her face. "You'd be in trouble today, Uncle Edward."

With an endearing gentleness, he ruffled Ellen's damp hair, his hand so large it dwarfed the child's head. "You are right."

Lily sensed she was an interloper in their world. She wanted to be at ease with Edward like she was now with Ellen.

Or did she?

"Sit here." Edward stood and indicated his place on the bench next to Ellen. "You need to get out of those wet shoes."

In the glow of the firelight, the cabin closed in on her. "I'm fine. Thanks." She would have backed away, but he caught her by the elbow and tugged her toward the seat.

"Don't be silly. You'll catch your death if you don't get out of those wet things."

Lily dropped onto the bench beside Ellen.

"Can you help me unlace my shoes, Ellen? My feet are a bit damp." She smiled at the girl and winked. "But don't you worry. I never get sick."

"Never?" Ellen slid off the bench and squatted at Lily's feet.

"Absolutely never." Lily shook her head in slow, exaggerated seriousness. "Why, once I had to walk all the way home from town in the pouring rain. It's about five miles from East River to my papa's ranch. I didn't even sneeze once."

Edward attempted to follow her lead. "So, five miles? That's a long walk for a lady. You must be pretty tough." He had moved to the kitchen.

Lily smiled at Edward and spoke to Ellen. "I'm tough all right. Just not real pretty."

"That's not true. You're pretty as can be." Ellen pulled the first wet shoe from Lily with a swoosh of effort. She landed on her seat on the hearth, and everyone laughed.

"Thank you, Ellen, but you're too kind. I'm tough because I was always taking care of whoever was sick at my house. Kinda made me strong." The second shoe came off without resistance. "Don't you worry about me catching anything. I'm much too slow at running," Lily teased Ellen, and gave her a quick embrace.

"Thank you, child." She set the shoes on the hearth to dry. "My toes are already starting to thaw." She moved near the bucket and looked at Edward. "If you'll turn the other way, sir, I'll take care of getting rid of some of the water in my skirt."

He stared for a moment as if he was lost. His eyes were on her stocking feet, watching her toes wiggle in their new freedom.

"Edward," Lily prompted. "Please." With one finger and a twist of her wrist, she made a swirling pattern.

"Oh. Of course." He walked behind the screen in the back corner.

"I think a quick twist will work wonders on this old skirt." Lily talked to Ellen as she wrung the water from her clothes into the bucket at her feet. She heard Edward washing his hands in the basin. "What do you think you want for supper?"

"Can I come out now?"

"Just a minute." She squeezed the last of the water her strength could wrench from the heavy skirt. "Now is fine." Lily dropped the hem to hang limp at her feet. The fabric might be ruined. She'd try her best to clean and restore the shape of the garment later.

He came out wiping his hands on a small towel. "I'll help. What about scrambled eggs? Maybe we could fry a few potatoes." He flipped the towel over one shoulder and moved to the stove. In quick fashion he had lit the burner and started cutting the potatoes.

"I'll make coffee." Lily poked at the pins holding her hair. "I'm about to dry out here."

"Ellen, you can slice the bread." Edward dropped the

potatoes into the hot grease in the cast iron skillet. Then he pulled out a bowl and began to crack open eggs to scramble.

"You surprise me. You know, before, I never would have pictured you as an efficient cook." Lily filled the coffeepot with water from the pitcher and set it on the back burner.

"Oh, he ain't much of a cook. Pancakes and eggs is about all we ever ate before you came." Ellen tore the bread in her haste to slice it.

"Don't talk bad about my cooking, or you'll have to do it." Edward pointed a fork at Ellen as he teased her.

Lily put a hand over the child's and guided her as she sliced the next piece. "Saw it slowly and gently. Back and forth. Then you'll have a nice piece to cover with butter." She released Ellen's hand and watched her cut the next piece. "Very nice.

"Do you want to learn more about how to cook, Ellen?" Lily thought it might be another way for her to bond with the child.

Ellen shrugged one shoulder and slid the plate of bread to the middle of the table. "Mrs. Dismuke tried to give me some lessons. She said I'm too young."

"I was your age when Mrs. Beverly started letting me help in the kitchen." Lily watched curiosity cross Ellen's face.

"Who's Mrs. Beverly?"

"She's my papa's housekeeper. She took care of us after my momma passed on."

"And she let you cook when you were seven?"

"Not by myself. She let me watch her at first. I could help stir and mix things together. I had to learn how to be careful before she let me near the stove."

"Did it take long?"

"Only a few lessons. Then I got to start helping with basic chores and cooking."

"Could you teach me?" Ellen's face was free of the shadows the storm had brought. She glowed in the light of the hurricane lamp on the table. "I could cook for Uncle Edward when you have to work late."

Lily had struck a chord with Ellen she hadn't known was there. This little girl's desire to care for her uncle mirrored her own at that age. "If it's okay with your uncle. If you promise you'll still do little-girl things, too." She rested a hand on Ellen's shoulder. "Sometimes we get in such a big hurry to grow up that we forget to be a kid." She chucked the tip of Ellen's chin with her finger. "You have to promise."

"I will! I promise!" Ellen jumped from her chair and flung herself around Edward's midsection. "Please, Uncle Edward, can I? Can I?"

He dropped his spatula and pushed Ellen's hair away from the stove. He picked her up and set her farther from the hot surface. "Not until I see you're ready to be cautious. You very nearly set your hair on fire." Lily knew the harshness in his voice was born of fear from having to protect Ellen from the hot stove.

Ellen slumped in his arms, and her bottom lip slid out. "I'm sorry. I didn't mean to." She looked up at his face. "Don't be mad. I'll be careful." The pleading broke the tension that surrounded him in the instant of danger.

"I know you didn't mean to get too close, Ellen, but that's how accidents happen." He was eye level with her now. "You're not mature enough to learn to cook yet."

"But Aunt Lily said…"

"The matter is not open for discussion. You finish putting everything on the table now." Edward went back to the stove. Ellen put plates on the table, moping and murmuring under her breath.

"Mind your manners, Ellen." Edward kept his back to the room.

Did he think Lily would argue with him in front of his niece? Was he ashamed of his harsh reaction when Ellen got too close to the stove? Why did Edward marry her if he wasn't going to let her help with decisions like this for Ellen? Had he changed his mind?

Thunder sounded through the wind. Maybe the storm would blow over with the ferocity with which it arrived. Would they be able to navigate the changing climate of their lives? She wanted Edward to trust her with Ellen. She could make decisions that would help the little girl grow into a lovely young lady.

Would he learn to trust her to do that?

One could only hope.

"Ouch." Edward muttered under his breath when he nicked his hand for the second time. The small rabbit he was whittling would be stained with blood if he didn't slow down. He'd fussed at Ellen before supper for being careless, and now he was the one at risk.

Lily's soft voice floated across the room from behind him. She and Ellen had cleared away the dishes while he came to sit in front of the fire and whittle. Or escape. Lily's presence warmed the small cabin. The way she'd flittered across the space when they'd come home, helped get Ellen into dry clothes then scolded him for wetting the floor had made him smile.

If Ellen hadn't almost been hurt near the stove, he might still be in a pleasant mood. There was so much responsibility with the child. That's why he'd asked for Lily's help. And this evening, when she'd offered it, he'd turned her down. He couldn't explain why, even to himself.

Ellen's giggle joined Lily's airy laughter. He wouldn't look back again. The last time he dared to peek over his shoulder, Lily had caught him. Her smile told him she knew he wanted to be in the midst of the activity, but his pride prohibited it. The smell of burnt onions still hung in the damp air. He'd all but ruined their meal when he added onions to the frying potatoes and forgot to turn them in the skillet. He wouldn't stand around and risk the teasing he was sure he deserved.

Another stroke of his knife and the wooden rabbit's ear came off and landed in the pile of shavings at his feet. He threw the mangled animal into the fire and reached for a fresh piece of wood. Mr. Croft had asked him to create a variety of animals. The rabbit was his first attempt.

"Want some company?" Lily moved close to the fire and held her hands out to its warmth. He didn't look up at her. The tone in her voice warned him her cheeks would be rounded with a soft smile.

"Tired of being cooped up in here with the smell of burnt onions?" He chipped away large chunks of the wood to form the beginnings of a new rabbit.

"That could have happened to anyone. I daresay you wouldn't have done it if Ellen hadn't startled you so. Children can take away your focus quicker than anything else I know." She walked to the window near the front corner of the cabin and studied the sky. "The storm seems to have lost its fury. At least the sleeting has stopped."

Fresh shavings piled at his feet. He was being more

deliberate. Cutting his hand again would only embarrass him further.

Edward turned the wood in his hand. "I expect the snow to end within the hour."

"Ellen is tired. I sent her to prepare for bed." Lily stood near the window with her back to him.

"I'll go in and say her prayers with her when she's done."

"I best be getting ready to turn in, too." Lily pushed away from the window and stepped close to the hearth. It was her habit to go into her room when Ellen went to bed. It had prevented them from being alone together. They were both adjusting to the lack of privacy their hasty marriage had imposed on them.

Maybe he could soothe over his mistakes earlier by encouraging her friendship now. "Why don't you sit up awhile?" He sliced away a large corner of the wood he held and turned it in his hand.

"Are you sure?" At his nod, she continued. "I think I will. I want to mend a couple of Ellen's dresses. I could do that while you work." Lily spoke softly. "I'll just go and tell her good-night first." Lily knocked on Ellen's door and entered at the girl's quiet invitation.

Edward lowered his head and saw the sad beginnings of a bunny. He couldn't concentrate on it. He stood and moved to lean against the mantel and stare into the flames. Rushing back to town this afternoon, he'd thought only of their safety as he'd tucked Lily close and covered her with his bulk. The effect she had on him had set him reeling. The memory of the scent of her damp hair filled him. Sweet and fresh.

He hadn't been close to a woman like that since he'd danced with Eunice Hampton at the winter social just before Jane and Wesley left town. She'd been full of laughter and fun, but no emotion she stirred in him compared to the way he'd wanted to protect Lily today.

The door opened behind him. He didn't have to look to know it was Lily.

"Ellen said she's ready for you to come hear her prayers." Her heels clicked across the boards as she headed for his room.

He shook his head. He had to start thinking of it as *her* room.

When he came back into the front room, Lily sat snuggled in the corner of the settee she'd brought with her to Pine Haven. It was nicer than any furniture he had. It wasn't very big, so they'd been able to fit it into the room. There hadn't been room for everything she had, but they'd brought what they could to the cabin.

A small sewing basket stood open at her feet. She leaned into the corner of the settee so the light from the lamp on the table at her elbow spilled onto the dress she was mending.

He rocked his weight from one foot to the other. Never in his life had he entertained a lady in his home. He didn't count his sister. She'd entertained herself.

"Can I get you a cup of coffee?" He walked to the stove and poured a cup for himself.

"No, thank you." She tied a knot in the thread and used a small pair of scissors to cut it off close to the dress. "I don't want to risk spilling anything on Ellen's Sunday dress."

He set the pot back on the stove with a clink and sat in his chair by the fire. "Who taught you to sew?"

Lily must not have heard him. She looked up at him and said, "Hmm?"

He took a long drink of his coffee and set the cup on the hearth. "You told me your mother passed when you were a young girl. I was wondering who taught you to sew." He picked up the beginnings of the rabbit and started to whittle again. It would be easier to talk to her if he stayed busy. Maybe he wouldn't sound so nervous.

A smile crossed her face. "Mrs. Beverly, my father's housekeeper. She stepped in and did what she could with me and my sisters." She pulled a new length of thread through her needle and picked up another of Ellen's dresses. "I was the most interested in sewing and cooking. My oldest sister has been working the ranch for years, and Daisy moved here so long ago that I guess Mrs. Beverly had the most time to help me."

"I am indebted to her. As you can see from my attempts tonight, your cooking skills far surpass anything I could do."

She smiled at him. "Ellen told me your specialty is pancakes. Perhaps we should have them the next time you take over the cooking."

"The two of you seem to have come to some kind of agreement. How did you get her to stop being so defensive around you?" Ellen's animosity toward Lily had troubled him, but he didn't know what to do about it. He was relieved to see the drastic change in his niece's behavior. He picked up his cooling coffee and took a drink.

"She was worried I would steal your affections away from her."

He felt heat spill into his face as he sputtered and choked on the tepid liquid. "She thought that?"

"Yes, but you don't have to worry about Ellen imagining things that aren't happening. We talked about it, and she knows I'm not interested."

Not interested. What man wanted to hear his wife say she wasn't interested in his affections? In fairness, their marriage wasn't an affectionate arrangement, but her words stung nonetheless. He remembered her mentioning someone she'd planned to marry in East River.

"So, this Luther fellow still has your interest?"

Her mouth dropped open for just a moment. Then her face closed as all the progress they'd made in learning about each other disappeared. She rolled up the dress she was working on and stuffed it into the basket. She stood with an icy calm that was more powerful than the storm they'd endured on their way home.

"Wait, Lily." Edward stood. "I wasn't trying to imply anything."

"I heard no implication. I heard an accusation." She plucked up the basket and headed for her room. Now he could think of it as her room. She was using it to shut him out. He didn't know what else to think by her saying she wasn't interested in him.

Did he want her to be interested in him? He wanted her to be interested in Ellen. She'd done that. She'd built a bridge to his niece even after all the anger the child had aimed at her.

He slid between her and the bedroom door. "I didn't mean that." He put his hands on her arms. "Please forgive me."

She blew out a breath and squared her shoulders. "I am not interested in Luther Aarens. I haven't been since the moment I heard him tell his mother he only proposed to me so I could become a companion for her. That I was not someone he could ever love." No emotion accompanied her words. "I had been under the impression his attentions toward me were of a more personal nature. I was unaware he only wanted me for the service I could provide for his mother."

Edward didn't know what bothered him more—that her words were completely devoid of feeling, or the irony that after refusing to marry a man who wanted her to care for his mother, she'd married him to care for Ellen.

"I'm sorry." He didn't know what else to say.

"You've no need to be."

He didn't want to misunderstand her. "But you married me to care for Ellen." If she didn't want to care for Ellen, he needed to know now—before too much time passed. Ellen was beginning to show an attachment to Lily.

"You made no secret of the reasons for our marriage." She lifted her brows and let them fall again, her face a sad yet beautiful picture of resolve. "We can't always determine where we end up, can we, Edward? Or you wouldn't be a guardian to that precious girl, because you'd have kept her mother here. I would still be in East River happily married, but not to Luther Aarens. I might even have a child or two." She dropped her gaze to her hands. "Life isn't predictable. We have to stand up to whatever circumstances we're dealt and move forward."

"So you held no hope of romance or happiness when you came to Pine Haven?"

"I did not. I came here for independence and to start a life for myself."

"And I ruined that dream for you."

"I have a new life now. Just not the one I dreamed." Her words stung long after she stepped into the bedroom and closed the door.

Chapter Twelve

Ellen sneezed again. "Uncle Edward, I don't feel so good."

He pulled the skillet off the heat and bent down to look into her eyes. Glassy orbs in the depths of dark circles stared back at him. "Uh-oh." He put a hand to her forehead. The heat confirmed the suspicion of fever he got from her pink cheeks. "You go climb into bed. I'll bring some water before I go for the doc."

"I don't want Dr. Willis!" Panic struck her face.

He picked her up like a rag doll and carried her to her room. "You're going to be fine, pumpkin. I just want the doc to make sure you don't get any sicker." He pulled the quilt up to her chin and tucked it close around her. "I'll be right back with a cool drink of water."

When he returned, she sat up on top of the quilt he'd wrapped her in.

"Here you are." Edward held the cup for her.

Ellen drank deeply and lay back against the pillow. Her hair clung to the sides of her face in wet tendrils.

"You've got to stay covered up." He tucked the quilt around her again.

"It's too hot." She thrashed her head from one side to the other. "I don't want it."

"Leave the cover on. I'll be right back with the doc." He turned to peek at her before he closed her door. There was no way he'd wait to get help for her. Fever was a dangerous thing.

He grabbed his jacket from the peg by the door and tromped off the porch in the direction of the doctor's office. Lily came out of her shop as he rounded the corner. With a full head of steam, he couldn't stop.

Lily trotted to catch up to him. "What's wrong?"

"I need to get to the doc's office." He tried to sound calm, but the urgency of his mission came through in spite of his effort.

"Ellen?" Lily's face was serious in an instant.

"Yes. Fever. Sneezing. Achy." He picked up his pace.

"I'll stay with her until you get the doctor."

He pivoted on one heel. "I'll be there as fast as I can."

Lily stepped inside the cabin. When she'd left this morning, it had barely been light. Now the curtains were pulled back, and sunshine filled the room.

"Ellen?"

The sound of faint sobs came from the child's room. Lily tapped on the door and pushed it open a bit.

"I hear you're not feeling well." Lily smiled at the sliver of a girl hidden beneath the mound of a giant quilt.

"I'm so hot, Aunt Lily." Ellen didn't lift her head from the pillow, and her eyes barely opened.

"Let me help you." Lily pulled the cover back. She went to the small window and pushed it open slightly. A soft, cool breeze floated into the room.

"Uncle Edward said I had to stay under the quilt."

"My pa used to think that, too. Then we had a doctor who told us to cool him off when he had a fever." Lily picked up the cup by her bed. "I'll be right back with some water."

She dashed into the kitchen and poured water from the pitcher for the poor child.

"Drink this. Slowly." Lily slid her arm beneath Ellen's shoulders and lifted her enough to sip the cool liquid. Then Lily lowered Ellen to rest against the pillow.

Lily retrieved the washbowl from behind the screen in the main room and brought it with a cloth to Ellen's bedside. She wet the cloth and wrung it out gently over the bowl.

Rolling up the sleeves to Ellen's gown, Lily spoke soothing words to her while she wiped the girl's limbs, face and neck with the cool cloth. She dipped it into the water again and folded it to lie across Ellen's forehead.

"How's that? Better?" Lily stepped to the bedroom door at the sound of boots on the porch. "That'll be your uncle with the doctor."

"Ellen? Are you okay?" Edward came into the room.

An urgency raced across his features. He pulled the quilt over Ellen and banged the window shut. "I told you to stay under the quilt." He sat on the bedside and touched Ellen's face.

"Aunt Lily said it would help." Ellen spoke in a ragged whisper.

Edward turned to Lily. "I don't want her to catch a chill. That's how she got sick in the first place." He clutched Ellen's small hand in his.

Lily recognized the fear in his eyes. "We've got to get her fever down. When you bundle her up, it climbs."

"She made me feel better." Ellen coughed, her shoulders lifting from the pillow with the pain of exertion.

He pressed her gently onto the bed. "Try to take it easy. The doc said he'd be here as soon as he gets his bag."

Lily backed herself into a corner of Ellen's room. Her attempts to help the child had been seen as dangerous to her protective guardian. She hoped he wasn't right.

A knock sounded on the door, and Edward stood.

Lily held up a hand. "I'll let the doctor in. You can stay with Ellen."

She stepped out of the room and opened the front door for the doctor. "She's in the bedroom."

Dr. Willis wore a brown suit and carried a small black bag. "Thank you, Mrs. Stone." He moved at a brisk pace toward Ellen's room, never stopping as he spoke.

Lily put on some water to boil for broth. She went across the street and closed up her shop before coming back to help take care of Ellen.

Lord, please help this child. For all Edward's determination to be strong, he can't make her well. Let the fever break soon. Please.

Edward stepped out of the way so Dr. Willis could see Ellen.

"She got wet yesterday, Doc. We got caught in the storm on our way back to town. I got her home quick as I could. Warmed her up good by the fireplace and made her drink hot tea." He tried to keep the worry out of his tone.

"Did you go and get yourself sick, child?" The doctor laid a hand on her cheek. Then he lifted the cloth and touched her forehead.

"It was a good idea to put a cool cloth on her face." He dipped the cloth into the water and wrung it out again.

"Does it make you feel better?" He folded the cloth and draped it across her forehead again.

Ellen whispered, "Yes, Aunt Lily did it." Several deep coughs wrenched her chest. "Said it would cool the fever." The words took all her strength, and she seemed to melt into the pillow.

"Let's get you cooled off. Edward, fold the quilt back while I open this window a bit." Dr. Willis tugged the window open and backed up so the breeze would reach the bed.

A small smile touched Ellen's face. "That's better, Uncle Edward."

Edward stood on the opposite side of the bed from the doctor. "Are you sure, Doc? Her momma always bundled her up against a chill." He took Ellen's small hand again.

"I'm sure." Dr. Willis set his bag on the side of the bed. He pulled out the pieces of his stethoscope and assembled it. "I'm going to listen to your chest now, Ellen." He put the ivory tips in his ears and listened to her breathe through the wooden bell-shaped chest piece.

He took several minutes to examine Ellen. "I'm going to give you some medicine for the cough. It tastes bitter, but most medicine does." The doctor made her swallow the first dose.

Dr. Willis handed a small bottle to Edward. "Give her a spoonful three times a day." He began to pack up his instruments. "And keep her room cool. Not damp, but cool. If the fever gets worse, wipe her down with a cool cloth." He picked up his bag. "If it starts to rain, close the window, but don't pile the cover on until the fever breaks."

"Dr. Willis?" Ellen tried to prop herself up on one elbow but fell back against the pillow.

"Yes, Ellen?"

"Am I gonna die?"

Edward's heart clinched. No matter how he tried to protect her, there were things in life a body couldn't foresee. They should never have gone to the Barlows' after church. He should have felt the storm coming. Like his ma used to in her bones.

"Not if I have anything to say about it." Doc Willis gave a wink and patted the side of the bed. "You'll be up running all over the place in a few days. Your aunt and uncle will probably be wishing for the quiet again. Just stay in bed. Rest and drink lots of water. It's the best way I know to put out the fire of a fever."

Relief washed over Edward at the doctor's words. A smile covered his face, and he kissed Ellen's brow. He nestled Ellen's doll in the crook of her arm. "I'm gonna see the doctor to the door. I'll be right back." He stepped into the front room and closed the bedroom door behind him.

Lily was at the stove. "How is she, Doctor?" He could hear the concern in her voice. "I'm making her some broth."

"That's just what she needs." The doctor put on his coat. "Edward will fill you in. I've got another patient coming to the office."

She thanked him and turned back to the stove. Edward could see her lips moving in silent prayer as he opened the front door.

"Doc, thank you for coming so quickly." The men stepped onto the porch so their conversation wouldn't disturb Ellen. "How much do I owe you?"

Dr. Willis rested his bag on the porch rail and buttoned his coat. "Can you put a couple of shoes on my horse?" He retrieved the bag.

"Bring her by, and I'll fix you right up." Edward clapped a hand on the doctor's shoulder. "Will she really be okay, Doc?" He had to ask, in case the doctor had put on a brave face for Ellen's sake.

"She'll be fine. Don't you worry. Good thing your wife was here to help cool her off. It's important to get the fever down quick. You were smart to snatch her up when you did. A woman like that doesn't come along every day."

"I don't rightly know how to let go and let her help me yet. I've been running my business and taking care of Ellen alone for so long."

"Just let her do what comes natural to her. She's a good woman. She proved today she's got good maternal instincts."

"I'll try."

"Remember to keep Ellen cool and make sure she takes her medicine."

Now the relief was real. "Thank you. I will. I don't care how it tastes."

The doctor chuckled. "When she starts to complain about the taste of the medicine, you'll know she's feeling better." He set a small derby on his head and left Edward on the porch. "She seems to like your wife. Maybe let her sit with the child and read, or whatever it is women do to keep young ones quiet while they heal."

When the doctor disappeared around the corner, Edward collapsed onto his chair on the porch and stared into nothing. Fear had clutched his heart when Ellen had come to him with such a high fever. He couldn't lose her. Jane would never forgive him if something happened to her daughter while she was in his care.

Lord, please help Ellen. Thank You for the doctor's

help and the medicine. Please take the fever from her. And bring Jane and Wesley home.

When Edward lifted his head, regret swamped him. He remembered the tone he'd used with Lily. He'd all but accused her of endangering Ellen.

But she'd been right.

Lord, I need Your help, too. And forgiveness. From You. And from Lily.

He went back into the cabin to find Lily at Ellen's bedside, feeding her broth. He sat on the opposite side of the bed holding Ellen's hand. "Does that make your throat feel better?"

Ellen nodded, and Lily gave her another spoonful of the warm liquid. "That's enough for now. You close your eyes. I promise one of us will be here when you wake up." Lily put a hand on Ellen's cheek. "Rest well."

When Ellen fell asleep, he slipped into the front room for a cup of coffee. Lily was putting on her coat. "If you'll stay with her until lunch, I'll come back for the afternoon."

"You don't have to do that. I know you want to keep your shop open as much as possible." He didn't want to hinder her from working. And he didn't know how upset she was with him about disagreeing over Ellen's care.

"It's best for Ellen if she knows we're both here for her."

"You're right. I'll take the first shift. If I have time, I'll make us some lunch while she rests."

Lily smiled a knowing smile. "Do you think that's a good idea? She might not need that much excitement today." With a wave of her hand, she was gone, laughing at his cooking skills. Or the lack of them.

She filled his thoughts while he sat by Ellen's bed.

Doc Willis was right. Lily had proved herself today. Edward might not know why things happened as they did, but he was grateful to the Lord above for Lily's help. He needed to think of a way to show her.

Lily was surprised to see Ginger and Lavinia later that morning.

"I want a couple of your finest hankies," Ginger announced.

"I want a pair of gloves. Like a lady wears to church." Lavinia toyed with the lace on a white glove with pearl buttons.

"Those gloves would be perfect, Lavinia." Lily pulled the gloves from the display so the young woman could hold them.

Ginger was searching through an assortment of embroidered hankies from France. "She's got some idea she might want to go to church. Some fellow she met at the general store started up a conversation with her. Seems he's been looking for a wife but only wants a good church girl."

"I ain't wanting to get married yet, but he did make it seem like there might be more fellas in church than we've seen since we got to town." Lavinia handed the gloves back to Lily. "I might not have enough money for these. Mr. Winston said he won't pay for church gloves."

Lily smiled at Lavinia. "I'm running a special on church gloves today." She went to the glass display case and started to wrap the gloves for Lavinia. "Would you like a pair, too, Ginger?"

Ginger opened a colorful parasol and rested it on her shoulder. She tilted her head to one side while she studied her reflection in the hall tree mirror. "No, thank you,

Mrs. Lily." She lowered the parasol. "My first husband was a churchgoing man. I've been in saloons too long to be accepted back in a church now."

"God never turns His back on someone returning to His house." Lily hoped the people at Pine Haven Church would welcome Ginger and Lavinia if they came.

Ginger's smile was doubtful. "You know it wouldn't be just God to face if I went back to church. His people aren't always as welcoming. From what I've heard, they aren't too happy with you for being friendly to us. I can't think they'd been any happier to see us in their church."

"You're always welcome as my guest." Lily folded the hankies Ginger had selected into a length of paper and tied it securely with string. "Never mind what people think."

"Keep telling yourself that, honey." Ginger took her package and tucked it into the bend of her arm. "Maybe after a while it'll be true. For now, I'll be at the saloon. Everyone's welcome there."

Lavinia followed Ginger out of the shop with a wave over her shoulder. "Bye, Mrs. Lily. I might see you at church. It depends on whether the saloon opens this week."

A second visit so soon from Ginger and Lavinia was unexpected. Hopefully, they'd surprise everyone in town by coming to church.

Lord, please let me reach these ladies for You. And let others love them with Your love.

The best surprise she could wish for was that the ladies would be treated well if they did show up for services.

Lily returned in the middle of the day. They shared sandwiches, and Lily stayed with Ellen while Edward went to work.

He tried to do a full day's work in a few hours, but he couldn't concentrate. His mind swung like a pendulum between concern for Ellen and thoughts of Lily. One a helpless child in certain need of his care, the other an independent woman who fought to cover any sign of weakness or need.

He finally gave up on work and came home. He went straight to Ellen's room to relieve Lily, who left him to watch over the sleeping child.

Edward jolted upright. He must have fallen asleep in the chair beside Ellen's bed. The afternoon had faded to evening.

He put a hand up to rub at the soreness in his neck. Ellen's breathing was raspy but even. He headed toward the front room to find Lily sitting at the table reading her Bible.

He ran a hand through his tousled hair and squinted to see her in the twilight. "I didn't mean to fall asleep."

"It's tiring to tend to the sick. I prepared supper." She stood and walked to the stove. "Is she better?"

"She's still sleeping."

Her eyes darted a glance over his shoulder to the open door to Ellen's room. "I want to make sure she has a good meal."

A moan came from Ellen's room, followed by a deep coughing spell. Edward rushed into the room and put an arm under Ellen's shoulders to help her sit up.

The child settled and sent a smile beyond him to the doorway. "Lily." The whisper cost her another coughing spasm.

"Don't try to talk. You need to rest your voice." Lily's soft tone seemed to caress Ellen as she lay back against the pillow. Lily entered the room.

Edward offered her a chair. "Will you sit with Ellen while I dish up the food?" When she didn't move to answer, he reiterated, "Please? You must be tired, too."

"Okay. It will be good to sit a spell." Lily dipped her head in agreement.

From the front room Edward could hear Lily's hushed voice, but he couldn't make out the words. Once Ellen chuckled, only to end up coughing. He picked up the tray laden with fresh bread and stew and went back into Ellen's room.

"Ladies, you must take it easy for our patient to get well. No laughing or carrying on until the fever is gone." He hoped his lighthearted tone contradicted the seriousness of his words. Lily's presence was having a healing influence on Ellen. He could see it in the girl's face.

"We're being good. Aunt Lily was just telling me about one time when her papa was sick. He coughed and coughed until he tore his nightshirt. She had to sew it up again." Merriment played in Ellen's eyes.

Edward set the tray on the bed after Lily helped Ellen to sit up. He draped a napkin across the front of Ellen's nightdress and reached for the bowl of stew. "Want me to feed you?"

"I want Aunt Lily. She can tell me more stories."

Edward turned to look at Lily, his eyebrows raised. "Would you mind?" He offered her the bowl and spoon.

"I'd be glad to entertain the patient." She nodded toward the door. "You may take a break, if you'd like. We girls will be fine on our own for a bit."

Edward released the stew to her, careful not to brush her fingers with his. The heat of the bowl wouldn't move him like the warmth of her touch. He left the door ajar and headed for the stove.

He sat in front of the fire with a bowl of hearty stew. Dipping the bread into thick gravy, he savored Lily's cooking skills. She had spoiled them with her delicious meals.

From the sounds of giggling and laughter in the bedroom, it seemed she was also adept at nurturing children, despite his earlier belief to the contrary. Did she know she possessed so many talents? Her hats were beautiful, for sure, but the food and caring were natural. Care for her fellow man came easily to her.

That caring was the reason she wanted for customers. It was one thing to reach out to people. It was another thing entirely to do it to one's own detriment. Sacrificial caring was a strong Christian principle. He hated how it had marred her reputation among the good people of Pine Haven. When they got to know her as he and Ellen did, her true heart would be evident to all.

If only they'd give her time.

Deep in thought, he didn't hear Lily enter the room.

"She wants to rest now." Her voice drew him to its warmth. "It seems she's a little better. She was able to eat most of the stew."

A final swoop of his spoon around the inside of his bowl gathered the last bits of potatoes and gravy. He retraced the spoon's path with his last bite of bread and popped it into his mouth. He stood with the bowl in one hand and wiped his chin with the wrist of his sleeve.

"Who can blame her? This is the best stew we've had in this house in...well, in longer than I can remember." He set his bowl on the table and took Ellen's dishes from her. "Are you going to eat?"

"Yes." Lily ladled stew into a bowl and looked over her shoulder toward the bedroom. "Maybe we can get her to eat a little more after a while. She hasn't eaten much today."

"I'm glad she's been able to sleep." Edward stacked the bowls in the basin to wash later.

Lily examined her fingers, touching the nails, then turned her hands palm up and looked at him. "I'm sorry for upsetting you earlier."

Edward saw sorrow and hope in her eyes. "I wasn't upset with you." They stood with the table separating them. "I was worried about Ellen."

"I overstepped my bounds. I do that. I do or say something without thinking it through first." A nervous laugh bubbled in her throat. "Papa says it puts people off. He's forever scolding me for it."

Edward moved around the table. "You were right, you know." He reached a hand toward her, but the right to touch her wasn't his. He dropped it to his side. "Doc says cooling the fever was helpful. Thank you."

Blond waves framed her face, and relief turned her blue eyes to violet. Such beautiful eyes. This time she reached to rest a hand on his sleeve. It was as though a bird rested on his arm. The weight of it was so light he had to look to confirm its presence, but the wonder of it paralyzed him.

The air stilled. Peace settled between the two of them.

"I'm so glad. I don't think I could have stood it if I'd caused Ellen more suffering. I know that was your concern."

He laid his hand over hers. "Thank you for understanding. Please forgive me for my harshness."

"If you'll forgive me."

A tug beneath his hand beckoned him to release her. A rightness in the comfort of her touch told him to resist. Sparks flew from the fireplace as a log crackled and shifted. He wrapped his fingers around her hand and rubbed his thumb across her knuckles. The violet eyes widened.

"Uncle Edward?"

Coughing and whimpers dragged him back to reality.

"Coming, Ellen." He released Lily's hand. "There's fresh coffee on the stove."

The violet faded to blue, and the moment was over. Had it really happened?

Lily picked up her bowl. "I'll see to the dishes after I eat."

"Thank you for the supper."

Lily waved off his thanks. "Let me know if I can help."

"I will."

More coughing made him realize it was time for Ellen's medicine. He went into her room to tend to her. While he soothed the child back to sleep, he wondered if he could soothe his heart back to its normal rhythm.

How could the touch of a callused hand bring comfort? Was it wise for him to allow himself to be comforted by her? He rubbed his sleeve at the memory of her hand under his.

The more he learned about his wife, the more he liked her. He'd have to be careful. She'd been faithful in her promise to help him with Ellen. He couldn't risk making Lily uncomfortable in their relationship by letting himself fall for her. She'd made it plain she wasn't interested in him. Ellen would suffer if he made Lily uneasy around him.

He didn't know who would suffer more. Ellen? Or him?

Chapter Thirteen

"What is that caterwauling?" Lily threw back the quilt, slid her feet into slippers and tied on her robe. "How's a body supposed to sleep with all that racket?" It had taken her hours to fall asleep. Thinking about her reaction to being so close to Edward had kept her awake. It wasn't only the closeness they'd felt, but the sudden backing away that had hindered her rest. This middle-of-the-night screeching was not a welcome sound.

She crept quietly through the front room of the cabin. Edward lay on his back, stretched out near the fire, snoring lightly.

The moon was high in the sky when she opened the front door to find a yowling kitten on the step. A tiny paw wedged between two boards was the apparent reason for its distress. She pulled the door closed behind her to keep from waking Edward or Ellen.

"You poor baby. No wonder you're crying so." She stooped to extricate the paw and landed on her seat on the porch when the freed animal launched itself at her.

"Oh, my. You are upset, aren't you, little one?" Lily pulled the kitten from its perch on her shoulder and cradled it in her hands. Tiny claws nipped at her flesh. Then a pink tongue dragged roughly across the knuckles on her thumbs. The crying turned to mews and nuzzling.

"You're trembling." Lily pulled the kitten into the lapel of her robe. She took the orange-and-black ball of fur to her room and wrapped it in a towel.

"I'm guessing you're just old enough to be away from your mother, but not quite confident." She rubbed the tiny head with the towel and promised her help to the lost animal.

By the time the sun came up, Lily had a plan. She hoped Edward would consent.

After breakfast, Lily and Edward assessed Ellen's improvement. They decided to leave her to rest. Edward would work and check in on her frequently. Lily would open the shop and come home for lunch.

Lily bundled the cat into a basket and covered it with a towel, praying it would be silent until she got it out of the cabin. She wanted to make sure it was healthy before telling Edward about it or giving it to Ellen.

She crossed the street and stepped onto the walk in front of her shop. She set the basket on the boardwalk and unlocked the door, humming a chipper tune at the thought of Ellen's reaction to her idea.

"Mrs. Stone." Winston Ledford's voice startled her when she reached to pick up the basket.

"Mr. Ledford." Lily's breath caught. She was forced to stop when he blocked her path.

"How is business?"

"Everything is well." She leaned to look beyond his shoulder.

"Looking for your Mr. Stone, are you?" Cold eyes awaited her reaction.

Lily stretched to her full height. "Not that it's any of your business, but I'm concerned about our niece. She's been ill."

"I'm sure you'll take good care of her." Cynicism dripped from every word. "I hear you've gone out of your way to be helpful to my girls."

"I make it my practice to be helpful to all my customers."

"Just be careful not to discourage my girls. I don't mind if you sell them hats and such, but I won't tolerate you interfering with their work." A serious weight filled his tone.

Lily caught sight of Edward opening the doors to his shop. He stopped to study her for a moment. She turned her attention back to the saloon owner.

"Mr. Ledford, any conversation I have with Mrs. Jones or Miss Aiken is entirely my business. I won't let you, or anyone else for that matter, tell me what to do." She hiked the basket up higher on her arm and took a step toward him. "So don't bother trying to threaten me again. I don't threaten."

He chuckled. What on earth could cause the man to chuckle when she was giving him such a solemn speech? She turned to follow his gaze toward the bank. Mrs. Croft was coming through the doorway, towing her reluctant husband by the sleeve. Exasperated, Lily pivoted in the direction of Edward's shop. His retreating back told her he'd seen and disapproved of her. Again.

"I think you may be correct, Mrs. Stone. I don't see you as a threat at all. I don't have to worry about you affecting my business. All I had to do was stand in the middle of town and engage you in conversation. You've affected your business by associating with me. I give it two weeks, at the most three, before you won't be an issue for anyone in Pine Haven." He touched the brim of his hat. "Good day to you."

The spiteful man left her standing on the sidewalk. Behind her was her shop, empty of customers for days on end, save for the preacher's wife and Mr. Ledford's employees. Behind her stood a nosy woman who chose to believe the worst of her without giving her an opportunity to prove her true Christian character. But the most painful of all was seeing the back of the husband she'd married to protect her name as he walked into his shop.

Why did it hurt so badly to be rejected? She'd come here to escape the confines of being at someone else's beck and call. To be on her own. But she was caught in the middle of a town in transition. She'd fooled herself to believe she could bridge the gaps between the old and new. She'd wanted to be left alone. Not to be alone.

A rumbling purr and the rustle of the towel covering the kitten drew her attention. Did Edward really believe she'd be consorting with the saloon owner? Had he opened the doors of his business a moment earlier, he'd have known it was a random encounter.

Why hadn't anyone been close enough to hear her rebuff him? If only she had a witness to her resistance to the man's attentions.

Lily stepped into her shop and closed the door. The little girl in bed with a fever needed the cheer a tiny kitten could bring. The cleaning and grooming of the small animal must be done before she approached Edward. She was certain the frightened animal would scratch and resist. But putting a smile on Ellen's pale face would make it worth the effort.

Edward may be angry with her, but surely he wouldn't refuse Ellen the joy of a warm, furry friend.

Edward tied on his leather apron. He refused to look at Lily standing in the open doorway of his shop. "Ellen is resting and I'm busy."

In spite of his frustration at her continued association with Winston Ledford, it took all his focus to keep from welcoming her. He wanted her here. He'd tried to help her. Her determined refusal to control her behavior in public was an obstacle not just to her business but to their relationship, as well.

A nagging voice in his head reminded him of her honorable goals. Of her caring nature. His angry mood silenced the voice. Seeing her on the street with the saloon owner rankled him for reasons he wasn't willing to explore.

He picked up a shovel and scooped coal into the forge in preparation for the morning's work.

"I've brought her something." She held the basket out for him to see.

Edward blew out a long sigh and turned to her. He had to put as much effort into this arrangement as he expected from her. He dropped the shovel back into the hopper, causing black dust to float in the air between them.

"I think God sent us a little help for her to pass the time while she has to rest." She took a step toward him.

The towel in the basket moved. Now he was curious. "What is it?"

"See for yourself." She held the basket closer.

A purring sound greeted him as he lifted the towel. The kitten looked to be about two months old. "Where did you get such a critter?" He dropped the towel back into the basket but left the cat uncovered. Button eyes of green watched his every move.

"He came to me in the middle of the night." The teasing chuckle in her throat chipped away at his ill humor.

"He did, did he?" Edward dropped the metal shank he'd need for his first project on the edge of the forge near the growing heat of the fire. "What did you do? Sleep with your window open?"

"No." Lily smiled at him in earnest. "He woke me from a sound sleep, crying because his paw was caught in the boards of the porch steps."

"You know, if you fed him, he'll never leave."

"Oh, I know. That's why I made sure to feed him right away."

Edward eyed the tiny creature. "How did you get him without me hearing you?"

She smiled, a slight lifting of the corner of her lips. "It might be hard for you to hear over your snoring."

"Well, you may as well give him a name, then. He's yours for life."

"I think Ellen will love him." She placed the basket on his workbench and lifted the tiny pet with her gloved hands.

Edward backed away from her. "I think he'll be a great cat for your shop."

Lily moved closer, petting the speckled fur with one hand while she cradled the kitten against her coat with the other. "But isn't he cute?"

"Not to me." A hand went up, palm out, to emphasize his disagreement with any notion that the cat should stay with Ellen.

"He's adorable. I know Ellen will think so."

"Nope. Not for one minute." He shook his head back

and forth while she continued to pursue him with the animal.

She leaned in close and offered the cat to him, tripping over the corner of the coal hopper. The shovel slipped to the floor with a metallic crash.

Startled, the cat launched itself from Lily's hands to the front of his shirt. Lily stumbled backward and lost her balance. Flailing in an effort to stay on her feet was useless. She landed on her seat in the mound of coal. A cloud of dust rose around her. Before he could help, she pressed both hands on the sides of the hopper and pushed herself up.

Lily clapped her gloves together. A shower of powdered coal drifted to the ground, leaving a fine layer on the front of her pale blue skirt.

It didn't escape his notice that her clothes and hats complemented the color of her hair and eyes. Even covered in soot, she was as fine a lady as he'd ever seen.

"Are you all right?" Edward hoped she wasn't hurt. He extricated the tiny claws from his shirt and dropped the kitten into the basket.

"Perfectly fine, thank you." Without looking away from him, she rubbed her skirt smooth and tugged at the hem of her coat, leaving a streak of black wherever her ruined gloves touched.

He dared not laugh at her. The flash of light in her violet eyes warned him. But the rumble of humor bubbled in his chest as he fought back a grin.

She picked her chin up, stretching her spine to reach all of the height God had given her.

Certain the top of her head would nest pleasantly under his chin, he smiled.

"Is there something you find amusing?" Lily put a hand to her hair, and he chuckled. Her eyebrows shot up.

An unsuccessful attempt to compose himself was followed by outright laughter when she brushed a knuckle across the tip of her nose, leaving another streak of coal.

"Really, Edward, I do not see why you are so amused. You may be big and strong and handsome, but your manners are sorely lacking." Lily's eyes grew wide. "What I mean is…"

"I heard you. You don't need to explain." She'd called him handsome. Something in her voice when she said it made him wish it could be true.

"May I offer an apology for my lack of manners? It's not every day I see someone so prim and proper in such a state." He stepped to a bench on the far side of the shop and retrieved a clean rag. "There's some water in the rain barrel outside the front door. Feel free to freshen up, if you'd like." He held the rag out like a peace offering.

Lily reached for the rag and saw her sleeve. Then she peered down at the front of her skirt. "Oh, my. Is it everywhere?" She looked to him for the confirmation she knew was coming.

"Afraid it is." A smile threatened to crease his face.

"I must be a sight."

"I'd say you are." He grinned then. "Please forgive me. I didn't mean to laugh at your misfortune."

"Really?" She touched the rag to her nose and pulled it away. His face let her know she'd only made it worse. "I discern no end to your mirth at my expense."

"It's just amazing to me how you can manage to look so pretty all covered in soot like you are."

Lily felt her cheeks flame. He probably only called

her pretty because she'd foolishly said he was handsome. "Now you're just being silly. There is nothing pretty about my present state."

He stepped close and took the rag from her. With a gentle hand he dabbed at her nose and cheek. "That's better." His eyes locked on hers and dared her to breathe. "Just as I expected. Still as pretty as ever." One corner of his mouth lifted.

Lily's head reeled. He was too close…and tall…his muscular build imposing. Was she leaning toward him? Could she stop herself? Did she want to?

She'd been around strong men every day at her father's ranch, but this man was different. By not moving, without a word he asked her permission to stay near her. Was he asking to come nearer still? As her husband, did he think she should welcome his closeness?

The space of his workshop seemed to shrink. The heat from the fire in the forge seemed to grow hotter even though the bellows was still. She fought the urge to step back.

Dredging up new strength, she spoke. "Edward, I…" The whisper died in her throat.

"Uncle Edward?" Ellen's voice called from behind her. "How come I don't hear any hammerin'?" A disheveled head poked around the corner of the forge. She must have entered through a back door.

Lily took a step back. Edward pushed the end of the metal piece into the fire and pumped the bellows.

"Lily! I thought you were going to stay at your shop all morning." Ellen stepped toward Lily with outstretched arms.

Lily caught the child's arms before the anticipated hug. "I'm all dirty. Don't let it get on you."

"Why did you come here instead of to the house?" Curious eyes lifted to quiz her.

"I needed to see your uncle first."

"Why?" Ellen flung a glance over her shoulder at Edward. "He ain't sick."

"Speaking of sick, why are you out of bed?" Edward's face bore disapproval and compassion at the same time.

"I'm tired of being in bed. And my fever is better. You said so."

"You still have to stay in bed until you're completely recovered. Doc's orders."

Lily sought Edward's permission with her eyes to share the kitten. Surely he was too kind to deny the child this small comfort.

The kitten meowed in his basket on the bench.

Ellen's brows climbed her tiny forehead. "Uncle Edward?" She tucked her handkerchief doll into the pocket of her pinafore and reached for the cat.

"No, Ellen." Edward picked up his bellows and frowned at Lily.

"Oh, please." Ellen's voice was muffled as her nose nuzzled the fur of the tiny kitten. She lifted her pale face. "Has he got a name? Is he yours? Where did you get him?"

Lily chuckled at the string of questions. "He showed up on the porch steps last night. He doesn't have a name, and we were just discussing who will keep him." She gave a nod to Edward. "You'll have to ask him."

"Can I keep him, Uncle Edward?"

"No." Edward set the bellows aside and turned the metal in the fire.

"Please, Edward." She added her pleas to the little girl's.

"Can we call him Speckles? He's got so many speckles." The calico kitten licked at Ellen's hands.

"That's a wonderful name, Ellen." Lily was triumphant.

His shaking head marked the end of Edward's argument against the cat. "It appears I am outnumbered. But there will be conditions."

Lily laughed at his expression of mock defeat.

Ellen gave a weak laugh. "Can he take a nap with me? I'm supposed to stay in bed, but I get lonely."

"I think Speckles would like that very much." Lily touched the small animal's head.

"Aunt Lily, you're all speckled, too. Maybe I should call you Sparkles instead of Aunt Lily. You're all covered in shiny coal dust."

It was Edward's turn to laugh. "It sounds fitting to me."

"Very funny." She smiled at the two of them laughing and happy. It was a relief after the stress of Ellen's fever. "Ellen, I've got just enough time to tuck you back in bed before I have to go back to the shop."

"Thank you, Uncle Edward." Ellen snuggled the kitten close, and Lily retrieved the basket.

"Don't thank me. It was Aunt Lily's idea." He crouched in front of her. "It's only for while you're sick. Speckles goes back to her shop when you're well again."

The little girl put on a brave face and turned to Lily. "Can I come visit him there?"

"You certainly may."

"Back to bed with you, young lady." Edward dropped a kiss on Ellen's head as he stood. "I'll be over in a few minutes to give you your medicine."

"You go on ahead. I'll be right along in a minute."

Lily watched Ellen snuggle the kitten high into the curve of her neck. The little girl whispered to Speckles as she walked back the way she'd come.

"Edward?" A new idea formed in her active mind. Why hadn't she thought of this in the first place?

Edward pulled on thick gloves and picked up his hammer. "What is it now, Lily? I can see your mind churning away behind your eyes. I am certain this can't bode well for me." He checked the tip of the metal and pushed it back into the glowing coals.

"Actually…" She drew out the word, trying to decide the best way to broach this new subject.

"See. There it is. The plotting and planning I suspected." A smile pulled his lips into a thin line and dimples creased his cheeks.

"This idea would make it easier for you while Ellen is recovering. And it would keep her from being lonely."

"I thought Speckles was going to take care of that problem."

"He will, for the most part." Lily shifted from one foot to the other on her tiny heels. The hem of her skirt stirred the dust at her feet.

"I'm waiting." Edward's smile turned to a suspicious grin.

"What if Ellen stays with me through the day? I can make her a place in the workroom to rest. You can work without interruption, and she can keep me company."

The grin faded. "That's very kind of you, Lily, but she'll be fine at home."

"I know you're busy. You've got to shoe a horse for Dr. Willis, and you've still got to finish the other hat stands for me. And the sign."

"What about your work? Ellen needs her medicine,

and she'll have to eat. Not to mention the cat will have needs, too." He stood between the forge and the anvil shaking his head.

"I don't know why I didn't think of it before." Lily took a tentative step and placed a hand on his arm. The strength she drew from the touch was more for herself than to assure his attention. "I'm offering. And if we're being honest here, we both know I probably won't be very busy today." She tried to keep the disappointment from her voice.

Was it just a couple of weeks ago she hoped to be busy with customers, making new friends and living a life independent of the responsibility of tending the needs of others? How quickly Ellen had made her way into Lily's heart. The thought of the child alone in bed for the day was sad.

"Please let me do this. For Ellen. It's why you married me."

"I married you so she would have a motherly influence in her life."

"If she was my own flesh and blood, I'd want her close by while she is sick." She saw his resolve waver. "It's what we agreed to."

Chapter Fourteen

The January sun was setting, and a cool breeze had threatened from the west as he'd walked across the street to Lily's place. Without having to worry about Ellen, he'd been able to shoe Doc's horse and make good progress on the remaining stands for Lily. The drawing for the sign was complete, too.

The bell rang as he entered the shop. Lily must have seen him coming across the street. "We're in the workroom."

Ellen was perched in the middle of the makeshift cot Lily had made for her in the corner of the workroom, the kitten nestled asleep in her lap. "Uncle Edward, I was good today. I took a nap this morning and again after lunch." She rubbed the kitten's ears. "Two, if you count that short one before you came."

Lily stood near the cot. "I'd say she'll recover quicker than we first thought. Dr. Willis stopped in and was pleased with her progress. He thinks if we keep her quiet and restful for a few more days, she'll be as good as new."

"When he brought his horse by this morning, I told him she was here."

Edward had noticed the pristine shop when he arrived.

The floors shone, and every hat was displayed with care. Lily must have worked while Ellen slept. Not one trace of a customer could be found.

"Are you ladies ready to go home?"

"I am." Ellen climbed off the cot and put the kitten in its basket.

"You two go ahead. I'll close up shop and be there in a few minutes." Lily bolted the back door and straightened the cot before following them into the front of the shop.

Edward lifted Ellen, and she wrapped her legs around his middle, the cat and basket hanging from her arm. "Don't be too long." He adjusted the child while Lily tucked a quilt around her small frame to keep her warm for the short trip across the street.

"Just a few minutes." She closed the door behind them.

By the time he had Ellen tucked into her bed with the kitten on the blanket, he heard Lily come into the cabin. He sat with Ellen, half listening to her ramble on about her day, never losing track of Lily's movements in the cabin. First she'd gone to her room and hung her coat in the wardrobe. Then she washed her hands in the bowl in her room. He strained to hear her light steps as she went to the stove to start their supper.

"I had fun with Speckles. He likes me. You really do need to let him stay with me all the time. He'll be lonely at night at Aunt Lily's shop." Ellen stopped petting the animal and looked up. "Are you listening to me, Uncle Edward?"

"Hmm?" He sat up in the chair and leaned his elbows on his knees. "Sure. You don't want the cat to be lonely."

"Yay!" She jumped from the bed and flung herself at him, kissing his cheek. "Thank you, Uncle Edward! Thank you!"

Lily came up behind him. How he heard her over the noise Ellen was making, he wasn't sure.

"What has happened in here?" Lily smiled and waited to hear what the commotion was all about.

"Uncle Edward said Speckles can stay here with me. Even after I'm well."

He didn't. "What?" He looked from Ellen to Lily. "I didn't say that."

"Yes, you did. You said 'sure.'"

Oh, no. He'd have to pay more attention, or these two would have his life turned upside down.

"I said, 'sure, I heard you,' not 'sure, you can have a cat.'"

"I'll leave you two to sort this out." Lily laughed. "I need to get the corn bread into the oven."

Upside down? It was too late. In the past few months, he'd gone from being a contented bachelor to full-time uncle, and now to guardian and husband. His world was more than upside down. It was topsy-turvy. Strangely, it wasn't as unsettling as he'd thought it might be.

When he tucked Ellen into bed later that night, she insisted on recounting her day to him, saying he wasn't paying attention before supper, so she'd tell it all again. She loved the hats Lily made. Did he think she could make pretty things when she grew up? On and on, she rattled about things Lily said and did. When she finally settled against the pillows after another dose of the dreaded medicine, she sighed and pulled the kitten into the circle of her arms.

"Uncle Edward?" Her words were whisper soft, weak with fatigue and the remains of the illness.

"Yes, sweetheart?" He touched her forehead and was glad to note her fever wasn't as high as it had been the previous day.

"Do you like Aunt Lily?"

Her eyes were closed. Could he save his answer in hopes she'd fall asleep?

Ellen turned onto her side and snuggled into the pillow. "Do you?" she asked again.

"Yes, I do." He straightened the blanket and extinguished the wick in the lamp on the bedside table. The shadows in her room danced in the glow of the moonbeams shimmering through the barren trees outside her window.

"Good. Me, too." Eyes closed, a yawn settled Ellen deeper into the night. "I know she's pretty. But I think she's strong, too."

"I think you're right, little one." He kissed her forehead.

"Thank you for letting me keep Speckles." Her words were barely a whisper as slumber pulled at her.

"You rest now. I love you." He turned in the doorway and took one last look at her sleeping form. She was right. Lily was pretty and strong. Unlike any woman he'd ever known. She was grounded in her faith, even when putting it into practice put her reputation at risk. She was beautiful. There was no denying that. In fact, Lily was disproving a lot of his long-held beliefs about women. And life in general.

If only he could shake the image of her engaged in conversation with the saloon owner. Why did she continue to jeopardize her standing in the community by associating with Winston Ledford?

He closed the door to Ellen's room and turned to see Lily on the settee, one of Ellen's dresses in her lap and her sewing basket at her feet.

"Is she all settled in?" Lily concentrated on the needle she was threading.

Edward looked over his shoulder. "Yes. She was asleep before I left the room." He went to the stove and poured himself a cup of coffee. "Can I get you a cup?"

Lily looked up from her mending with a small smile and a shake of her head. "No, thank you."

She was the picture of solace. How had this woman never married before she came to Pine Haven? Were the men in her hometown daft? Lily should be sitting in a home full of love and children of her own, not in front of his fire, mending Ellen's clothes after having cooked them a meal. She deserved to be loved. Just like Ellen deserved her mother and father.

Then Winston Ledford's face came back to him, smiling at Lily in the street. Had Lily allowed her charitable heart to cast her in a negative light in her home community, too? People could be persnickety creatures when it came to what they considered appropriate behavior of a young lady.

He drank a large gulp of his coffee and strangled on its heat. He sputtered and lowered himself into his chair near the fire.

"Are you okay?" Lily looked up again.

"Fine. Just drank it too fast."

"You better be careful." She spoke absentmindedly, but it was just the opening he needed.

"Speaking of being careful." He paused and considered his next words. "There's something I need to say."

"You sound serious." Her hands stilled. "What is it?"

"I saw you this morning." He cleared his throat. "Talking to Winston Ledford again."

The slow intake of breath and slight rise in her head warned of her dismay. "Again?" Her even tone was taut with tension and the effort to control it.

"Well, you have talked to him before."

"I have." She wasn't making this easy.

"It's just that I married you to protect your reputation, and…"

The calm left her. "And what? Do you honestly think I'd risk my reputation after paying so dearly to restore it? You aren't the only one who gave up something for this marriage."

She was right. He was benefiting from her relationship with Ellen. Her world had turned upside down in a much shorter time than his. She was probably reeling from the spin of it.

He started over. "What I mean to say is, I think it would be easier to protect yourself in the future if you avoid the likes of Winston Ledford. He can only hurt you."

"He came up to me on the street. What was I to do? Short of being rude, I had to at least speak to the man." She tilted her neck back and looked at the ceiling. "And the irony of it all is that he's as upset by my kindness to Mrs. Jones and Miss Aiken as everyone else in town."

"He's upset? Was he unkind to you?" He was out of his chair before he realized it. It was one thing for him to caution Lily, but another thing entirely for that snake of a man to treat his wife in a manner unbecoming of a gentleman.

"He warned me not to upset his girls, as he calls them."

"Did he threaten you?" He sat on the settee beside her and reached for her hand. It trembled in his. "What did he say?" If he harmed Lily in any way… He forced himself to listen to her answer rather than marching out the front door and into the saloon to confront the man.

"Not exactly. He just told me not to discourage them. He doesn't want them to be tempted away from the life he's offered them." She sighed. "In the end he said he didn't have to do anything to me. He said I'd destroy myself just by being kind to them." She looked up into Edward's eyes. "And to him." She shook her head. "But I wasn't kind to him. I told him not to threaten me. I told him he couldn't tell me who to talk to and not talk to."

Edward put his other hand over hers and held it snug until the trembling stopped. "I'm sorry."

She squinted her pretty blue eyes at him. "You're sorry? You didn't do anything."

"I did exactly what Winston Ledford did. I tried to tell you what to do and who to associate yourself with."

"But you're trying to protect me." Her eyes softened when she said the words. "And he was trying to protect himself."

"I'm not that good with explaining myself, but I really do want to protect you."

Lily laid her other hand on top of his. Its warmth and gentleness were welcome.

"You know, Edward, we want the same things. I want my business to succeed for me, but also for Ellen and for you. I don't want to do anything to put that at risk."

"I realize that. I knew it before, but Winston Ledford has a knack for infuriating me."

"Are you jealous?" She started to smirk. Then, as if she heard the words after she said them, she pulled her hands away. Her voice lost all its mirth. "There's no need to be."

He tugged her hands back into his. "I know." He gave her hands a light squeeze and released them before going to stoke the fire.

They had reached a new understanding of one another tonight. He knew it would help them as they cared for Ellen. But he was beginning to wonder how much they could help each other.

Before they turned in for the night, Lily convinced him to let Ellen spend the day with her again tomorrow and every day until Doc said she could return to school.

Morning would bring a new day. Filled with what, he did not know. But he was eager to find out.

"You need to stay on the cot. I promised your uncle Edward."

"I just want to go outside for a minute." Ellen juggled the kitten and her doll in her small hands.

"It's time to rest. You've been up a bit more today. I don't want you to overdo it and relapse."

"What's relasp?" Ellen squinted at Lily and dropped her doll. Speckles wriggled free and swatted at the edges of the doll's hem.

"Relapse." Lily picked up the doll. "It means to go backward. The time you've spent resting has made you stronger. If you try to do too much too soon, you'll get worse instead of better." The doll was worn and dirty. She unfurled the wrinkled edges of its dress.

"I don't want to get sicker." Ellen harrumphed and leaned back against the pillows. She pulled at the kitten's ears. "But I'm tired of resting. I thought all this resting was gonna make me not be tired."

Lily laughed. "It will. It just takes time. Remember, Dr. Willis said the hard part would be resting when you started to feel better."

"Well, this must be the hard part then. 'Cause I'm ready to get up."

"I think I know something we can do that won't tire you."

Hope stirred in Ellen's eyes. The fever had left her sockets sunken and dull. The color had started to come back into her cheeks, but fatigue washed it away again in a matter of minutes if she exerted herself.

"What can we do?"

"I can get a basin of warm water and some soap. You can give your doll a bath."

"It won't hurt her?"

"No, of course not, silly girl. No more than it hurts when you take a bath." Lily chucked Ellen under the chin and gave her the doll.

"Sometimes, Momma had to scrub mighty hard behind my ears and under my fingernails." Ellen giggled.

Lily set the basin on her workbench and helped the child onto her stool.

Together they worked to clean the doll. Endless play had soiled the handkerchief but not beyond repair. When they set the doll on the bench to dry, Ellen went back to her cot without argument.

"Do you think my momma misses me as much as I miss her?" Ellen lay back and pulled Speckles close.

Lily didn't want to give Ellen false hope about the return of her parents, but she didn't think Edward wanted her to make the child think they were never coming back. She answered the only way she knew how. "I'm sure she does." Lily pulled a quilt over the child. "Didn't she tell you so in her letters?"

"The letters stopped coming." A tear slid down one cheek, and Lily sat down to draw Ellen into her arms.

"Oh, honey, they were too sick to write." They rocked back and forth, Ellen sobbing and Lily crying in silence. Lily remembered the pain of realizing her mother was gone.

"I wish they'd come back." Ellen lifted her head and gulped in air, then collapsed against Lily and wailed.

"Hush, baby. It's okay." There were no words to ease

the pain in Ellen's heart. Lily knew she wasn't qualified to help her, but Edward wouldn't be back for hours. "Don't wear yourself out with crying."

"I can't stop. My heart hurts. And I want my momma!" Her voice climbed in hopeless desperation with each word.

Lily tried her best to comfort Ellen. What did one say to a child who didn't know if her parents were coming back for her? The weeping spell and Lily's rocking motion lulled the sad girl to sleep. She was gently snoring when Lily went into the front of the shop.

One look out the window confirmed that hers was the only shop void of business again today. How long could she stay open without regular customers? If it weren't for the trickle of lady passengers who stopped in while the train took on water, she wouldn't have sold more than two hats this week. Thankfully, those ladies were generally pleasant and happy to spend their money.

Maybe she should write a letter to her father and let him know what was happening in Pine Haven. She didn't want him to be taken by surprise by her lack of steady business when he came to town.

The train whistle blew, announcing the arrival of new passengers.

She could write tomorrow. If no one came today. Or maybe next week. Maybe this lull would blow over and she'd never have to share her struggles with him. It would be enough to convince him she was content in her marriage— failing as a shop owner was something she hoped to avoid.

"How was your afternoon?" Edward ruffled Ellen's hair and scratched the cat behind the ears. He'd had a long day's work and was looking forward to a good meal. Lily keeping Ellen with her for the day had allowed him to catch up on several small projects.

"Better than the morning," Lily said. "The trade from the train was better than yesterday afternoon."

"What have you two been up to?" He took off his jacket and hung it on a peg by the door.

"I helped with the corn bread." Ellen was excited. She was still a bit pale, but he was glad to see her feeling better.

"She worked hard." Lily put plates on the table. "As hard as someone can when they're resting."

Again Lily had helped Ellen and made her feel special. He was tired from having lost sleep while Ellen was so ill. Tonight nothing would make him happier than sitting around the table with this beautiful woman who gave so freely of herself without expectation of reward.

"It smells delicious." Edward looked at Ellen. "You better make sure there's plenty of butter on the table for me."

"Yes, sir!" A happy girl put the butter on the table and went to her room.

"Thank you for all you've done for her." He caught Lily's hand in his when she turned back to the stove. It was delicate and warm. Soft and strong at the same time. "You've really made her life better."

"She wanted to learn." Lily didn't look at him.

"She's wanted a lot of things I couldn't give her." He hoped he wasn't making her uncomfortable, but he couldn't resist reaching out to her. "You're the first person who's taken the time with her."

"Ellen is a delightful child. Anyone would be blessed by spending time with her."

A chuckle escaped his chest. "We both know she did her best to run you off in the beginning."

"Only because she was afraid." Her quick response was serious. He had to lean in to hear Lily's whispered words. "Afraid I'd take you away from her."

He gave her hand a slight squeeze. Lily tugged to pull her hand away.

Edward didn't release her. "Instead, she brought us together." He didn't blink for fear he'd miss her reaction to his words.

She slid her hand from beneath his. "She knows she'll never have to worry about you leaving her."

Ellen's voice interrupted them. "Are you coming? It'll all be cold if you don't come now." She slid into her chair at the table and put her doll on the seat by her.

Lily untied her apron and hung it by the back door. She smoothed the front of her dress and came to the table. He watched her every move from his seat opposite her. She unfolded her napkin and laid it in her lap before reaching for Ellen's hand and bowing her head so he could say grace. Everything about this woman was refined and beautiful.

As he thanked God for the meal, he wondered what she must think of him. Or if she thought of him at all.

In true Texas fashion, Sunday morning the wind howled outside his window. Last Sunday's snowstorm had blown in with a fury and was gone in hours. Most of the week had been sunny with mild weather. Today promised to be another blast of winter.

Edward was grateful he didn't live where the weather stayed cold and brutal for months on end. Enduring the scattered days of cold was enough for him.

"I'm ready." Ellen came from her room.

"The wind is a mite rough. We could stay home today."

He touched the glass on the window with the back of his hand to gauge the outside temperature.

"Uncle Edward, I'm well. Doc Willis said so when he came by yesterday." She pulled her new hat to adjust the angle.

"He said your fever is gone. He didn't say for you to go out in the wind." Why must everything be an argument with this child?

Lily came out of her room wearing her blue coat and pulling on her gloves. "Why, Ellen, you look fetching today."

Lily was fetching, too. The blue of her coat matched her eyes. Her golden hair glimmered in the morning light spilling through the windows.

"Thank you, Aunt Lily." Ellen tugged at the ribbon. "I did the bow like you showed me." Lily had given Ellen the hat on Friday after supper. It was stouter than anything she owned, but very pretty at the same time. The new hat seemed to make Ellen glow. He fought back his sadness at the thought of what her parents were missing by not being part of her life.

Edward forced his attention back to deciding whether or not Ellen should go out today. "She wants to go to church, but I'm not sure about the weather."

"I promise to bundle up and stay warm. I won't even ask to play outside."

Lily asked Ellen, "Are you certain you'll be able to sit still while everyone else is playing?"

A solemn expression accompanied the child's response. "I will." She turned to Edward. "Please, can I go? Aunt Lily said she made my new hat so even bad, cold weather couldn't hurt me." She swiveled back and forth without moving her feet. The bottom edges of her coat caught on the motion and swished like the church bell he heard ringing in the distance.

"I don't know." He opened the door to gauge the wind.

"Please, Uncle Edward. I miss my friends. You already made me miss Bible class."

Lily added, "I think she'll be okay."

"Well, if you promise no argument about dawdling outside in the weather, I guess we can risk it."

"Oh, boy!" Ellen skipped to the front door.

"Whoa, there. No running and getting all excited. I don't want you to overdo it."

"I won't. I don't want to relasp." Ellen grabbed his hand and tugged him out the door. Lily followed them down the steps. "Let's hurry so I don't get cold."

Edward laughed and caught her up to put her on the wagon seat. "Cover up with that blanket."

Lily took his hand, and he helped her into the wagon.

"Thank you, Edward." Her voice was quiet as she tucked the blanket close around her legs. He climbed aboard, and they made their way to the church.

"I'm afraid we might be in for some more cold weather, the way the wind's blowing."

"As long as it doesn't snow and storm like it did last week, I'll be fine." Lily put her arm around Ellen and pulled the child close.

"I just hope it holds off till after the service. The thought of being caught out like that again doesn't appeal to me." Edward pulled up close to the church door and set the brake. He swung his weight off the side of the wagon, boots stirring up the dirt as he landed.

"Ellen." He took his niece by the waist and set her down. He turned back to the wagon. "Lily."

"Thank you." Lily held out her hand to him.

Instead of taking her hand, he encircled Lily's waist with his hands and lowered her to the ground. Heat spilled into her cheeks as he released her.

"Hold a seat for me." He gave her a wink and climbed back into the wagon. "I'll be right in." He didn't know why he had the sudden urge to flirt with his wife like a schoolboy, but he did.

Lily stood frozen on the spot where he had set her down. Had he winked at her? Her eyes saw it, but her mind wasn't sure.

Ellen called from the church doorway. "Come on, Aunt Lily."

Just inside the front door, Lavinia Aiken stood wringing her hands and making a valiant effort to blend into the wall. Mrs. Croft entered and gave a small snort as she made her way to her customary seat.

"Lavinia, you came." Relief at Lavinia's presence pushed all thoughts for herself from Lily's mind. "Do you see the gentleman who invited you?"

"No. Mr. Ledford was right. I don't belong here." She probably would have backed away, but Lily took her by the hand.

"You do, too. Church is for everyone." Lily smiled. "I see you wore the gloves."

A smile turned to a smirk. "Ginger told me it wouldn't matter. Said I could dress like a lady, but I wouldn't be welcome here."

Lily faced the front of the church and tucked Lavinia's hand inside her elbow. "Yes, you are. Come sit with me." The drag against her progress as she headed toward an open bench made her wonder if she'd be able to convince Lavinia to stay.

A small gust of cool air stirred the hair at the nape of Lily's neck as the door opened and closed behind her. In an instant Edward was at Lavinia's other side. "Good morning. Welcome to Pine Haven Church."

Lily could have kissed him for his kindness. She released Lavinia and introduced them. "Edward, this is Lavinia Aiken. Miss Aiken, Edward Stone, my husband." She didn't know how long before she'd grow accustomed to referring to him in such a way.

Edward said, "Pleased to meet you, Miss Aiken." A slight smile lifted Lavinia's face.

"Uncle Edward, sit here." Ellen pulled Edward's hand, and he slid onto the bench beside her. "Is she your friend, Aunt Lily?"

"Yes, Ellen. This is Miss Aiken. Miss Aiken, this is Ellen Sanford, my niece."

"I like your gloves. Did you get 'em at Aunt Lily's shop? That's where I got my hat." Ellen tugged at the bow.

"Yes, thank you." The quiver in Lavinia's voice diminished with each passing minute. "Your hat is quite lovely."

Reverend Dismuke stepped up to the lectern, drawing everyone's attention to the front of the church.

"Please sit with us." Lily indicated the seat beside Edward and Ellen. She stepped in next to Edward. Lavinia sat on the end of the bench.

Joy at having Lavinia in church beside her filled Lily's heart. She could forget all the empty days in her shop and the gossip she'd endured. She'd shared the love God had for her, and Lavinia had responded to it. Nothing else mattered.

The deep voice that sang beside her during the opening hymn held a higher place of esteem to her. Edward had shown kindness, not just to her but to Lavinia, as well. He was a respected member of the community and the church. His acceptance of someone new in their midst would carry a lot of weight.

Lily treasured his acceptance of her as his friend and not just someone to help with Ellen. All the more so, as she learned his character. Living in the same home with Edward and Ellen had given her the opportunity to see how genuine his goodness was. This close to him in church, where every time he shifted in the seat he bumped her shoulder, was proving to be a serious distraction. She might have to spend extra time in Bible study this week to make up for missing most of the sermon.

Somehow they were making this arrangement work. The only time she'd seen him upset or angry was when there was danger, like the night of the fire, or a potential problem, like trying to protect her reputation.

She had grown to love Ellen. And now she was beginning to enjoy Edward's company. If his actions and demeanor today were an indication of his feelings, he wasn't unhappy, either.

Did she dare to hope they were building a lasting relationship?

Chapter Fifteen

Immediately after the closing prayer, Lily found herself pulled into a hug by Daisy. "Good morning, little sister."

"Hello, Daisy. This is my friend, Lavinia Aiken."

"I'm Daisy Barlow. It's so nice to meet you."

Certain Daisy knew who Lavinia was and why she'd come to Pine Haven, Lily appreciated the enthusiastic greeting.

"Won't you join us for lunch?" Daisy asked.

"Oh, I couldn't possibly." Lavinia was shying away.

"I'm concerned about the weather." Lily turned to Lavinia. "Why don't you come to lunch at our home? I prepared a stew this morning. The cold creeping through the walls last night made me want something hearty today." She leaned in close and lowered her voice. "I even made a cake. Just because it's Sunday, of course."

Edward buttoned his coat. "You ladies make your plans. I'm going to get Ellen wrapped up in the wagon. I'm ready for some of that stew. I hope you'll join us, Miss Aiken."

Daisy patted Lily on the arm. "Well, maybe next week the weather won't be so chilly. I hope you will make plans to attend the Winter Social. It's only a couple of weeks away."

Lily nodded her agreement. "I'm looking forward to the opportunity to get to know more of the ladies in town."

"Harold and Minnie Willis have offered their barn for the event. It's one of the biggest in the county and close to town. You should come, too, Miss Aiken. It'll be great fun." Daisy smiled and said her goodbyes.

When lunch was over, Ellen was sent to bed for a nap. Edward excused himself to work in his shop. Lily knew he was going to whittle and only left the house to give her time to visit with Lavinia. His thoughtfulness pleased her, but it was no longer a surprise. If she stopped to think on it, he was always doing something for someone else.

Lily pulled her fork across the plate, gathering the last of the crumbs and icing. "Thank you for staying for dessert, Lavinia. A cake always makes it feel more like Sunday to me."

"I haven't had a meal like this since I came to Pine Haven." Lavinia took a sip of hot tea.

"Did you enjoy the church service this morning?" Lily had waited to broach the subject, not sure Lavinia would want to talk about it.

"To be honest, I was a little surprised."

"How so?" She hoped it was a good surprise.

"Everyone was so nice." Lavinia stared into the fire. "Well, almost everyone."

Lily knew she was referring to Mrs. Croft. "The church is a haven for everyone in a community. A place where you can be loved and helped. Most everyone tries to live up to that purpose."

Lavinia turned to her. "Do you think they would

accept me every week?" Wariness caused her voice to wobble.

"I'm sure of it."

Lavinia looked back into the flames. "The part where the preacher man talked about all things being new…" Her voice trailed into silence.

"That's one of my favorite verses in the Bible. I love knowing God will help me start over." Lily spoke softly. She was hoping to encourage Lavinia, but the words were true for her, too. The new start God had given her in Pine Haven came at a time when she needed hope.

Please give me the right words, Lord. Help Lavinia to see how much You love her.

"Is that for anybody, or just people in the church?" Lavinia's questions were sincere.

"It's for anyone. God gives us all the opportunity to start our lives over with His care and direction. He removes the effect our past has on our future. He gives us new direction and purpose."

"I'd like that." Moisture filled Lavinia's eyes as she looked back at Lily. "Ever since I got to Pine Haven I've felt I was disappointing my family. None of them ever worked in a saloon. They were all honest, God-fearing folks." She hung her head. "I think they'd be ashamed of me."

Lily chose her words with care. "Sometimes in life we find ourselves in difficult circumstances. We don't always see the choices God has put before us. We can choose what looks like the only path and discover later our true purpose is in a much different direction." Lily paused.

That's what she'd done when she agreed to marry Luther. How grateful she was that God revealed a new choice by allowing her to come to Pine Haven. She couldn't imagine going back to a life where she didn't count. Where all that mattered was what she did for someone else, and no one saw her for who she was and the value she had as a person.

Finding herself married to Edward, a virtual stranger when they'd pledged themselves to each other, had changed her life. In her heart she realized God had given her a better future with Edward and Ellen than she'd have had with Luther. She was beginning to think it was better than her plan to be alone, too.

"Is it too late for me to change paths?" Lavinia's breath caught on a sigh. "The more I think about spending every night of the week dancing with strange men, the more scared I get. I don't want to be someone men only see as a way to forget their troubles and have a good time."

"It's never too late." Lily leaned back in her chair. "I'm proof of that."

"You?"

"Yes, me." It was her turn to stare into the fire. "I spent years caring for my sick father, while all my friends married and started families of their own. After a while, people stopped seeing me as Lily, and I became Mr. Warren's daughter. I was the girl who served the punch at social events, never the one who got asked to dance."

"But you're so pretty. How could anyone overlook you?"

"My duties to my father kept me busy. Over time, I grew comfortable. Then I withdrew from any opportunity. The withdrawal threatened to become bitterness. I began to feel trapped, but I knew a good daughter wouldn't abandon her father in his time of need."

The memories of Luther's first attempts to woo her

flooded her mind. In hindsight she saw his unabashed efforts to pawn her off on his mother. She remembered the evenings she talked with the older lady over coffee while Luther begged off to work in his office. How had she been so blind?

"It was so bad that when my father regained his health, I jumped at the first—and only—suitor who presented himself. I came to my senses the night I heard him telling his mother he'd never really love me, but I would be a good companion. For both of them."

"No wonder you wanted to come here. I'd rather work on my own than have a heartless man take care of me." Lavinia gasped. Her eyes widened as the weight of her words sank in.

"We aren't so different after all. In my situation, it was a suitor. In your case, it's Winston Ledford." Lily smiled at her. "At least you've realized it before you're as old as I am."

"But you had your faith in God. What can I do? I've come all this way because I didn't have anyone or anything left at home."

"God has given us all a measure of faith. All we have to do is believe."

Lavinia thought for a few moments. "I'd like to change paths like the preacher said today. I don't want the old things in my life to continue. I want a new life, but I don't know how."

"It's simple. Like Reverend Dismuke said, just pray and ask God to guide you. He will."

"Will you pray with me?"

"Gladly." Lily took Lavinia's hand and prayed for her new friend. She thanked God for their friendship and prayed for God to show Lavinia the path He had for her life—and for Lavinia to have the strength and determination to follow it.

"Thank you." A new light of hope shone in her eyes when Lavinia spoke again. "I know I don't want to be a part of the saloon. But I don't know what kind of work I can get in Pine Haven. The saloon was my only means of support. Mr. Ledford won't take kindly to me deciding I don't want to work for him."

"We'll think of something." Lily was so pleased Lavinia wouldn't be working at the saloon when it opened in a few weeks—so glad she spoke without thinking. "In the meantime, you can stay in the rooms above my shop."

Shock covered Lavinia's face. "I can? Won't the landlord mind if you take in a boarder?"

It was more important for her friend to be away from the saloon than for Edward to give his permission first. "I'll settle everything with my husband." Another thought came to Lily. "And I'll write a letter to my father to see if he can make a place for you at the hotel."

"Oh, Lily, I don't have money to stay in the hotel." Worry drew her brows together.

"Not as a patron. To work there. My father is buying the hotel in town. He and my sister and his housekeeper are moving to Pine Haven soon."

"Really? A respectable job?" Surprise lit Lavinia's features. "I'll do anything. Scrub floors, wash clothes, cook. Whatever they need."

Lily laughed at her giddiness. "It's settled, then. You can stay over the shop until we hear from my father or you find another job and a place of your own."

Edward came in the front door, a cold wind blowing behind him.

Lily rose from her place on the settee. "I need to step

over to the shop with Lavinia. We may be a while." She decided it would be best to talk to Edward about Lavinia's plans when the two of them were alone.

He stood in front of the fire warming his hands. "That's fine. If you're late, I'll give Ellen a light supper and turn in. I've got a busy week ahead."

Lily and Lavinia worked in the rooms above the shop to prepare it for Lavinia. With no extra room in the cabin, Lily had left her bed when she moved into Edward's home.

By the time Lily got home, Edward was stretched out before the fire asleep. Watching the moonlight as the wind howled outside her window that night, she pondered the best way to approach Edward. Would he care that Lavinia was staying over the shop? Surely not, if it was just a short stay.

She smiled at the peace that had flooded Lavinia after they prayed. Lily's Millinery and Finery might not be doing as well as she hoped, but it was worth every penny she'd lost in business to see a young woman choose a better life.

Lord, keep her safe and help her find a job.

It was easier to pray for Lavinia than it was to deal with her own situation. Would her business continue to suffer? How would people view her now that Lavinia was staying in her rooms?

Tomorrow they would set the place in proper order for Lavinia's stay. Rearranging her former home was the easy part.

A cloud danced across the face of the moon. She'd have to talk to Edward in the morning.

Edward awoke with a start. He had a busy day and would need to drive Ellen to school to keep her out of the cold. He could hear Lily moving around in her room.

He rapped on her door.

Lily called softly. "Just a minute."

He spoke through the door. "I just wanted to let you know I'm going to get the wagon. I've got deliveries to make today and want to drive Ellen to school."

Her muffled voice came to him. "Okay, but I need to talk to you."

"Can it wait? I need to load the wagon, too."

"Sure. I'll wake Ellen and make some breakfast."

Loading the orders took longer than he anticipated. When he came back inside, Lily was on her way out the door. "I've got to run. Can you come by the shop today to talk?"

"I'll try, but I can't promise today."

"I left breakfast on the table for you."

"Thank you." He closed the door against the brisk morning.

He turned to see Ellen almost ready. "Let's get going so you're not late."

He dropped Ellen at school and headed to make his first delivery. As he crossed the intersection in the middle of town, he looked to see if the road was clear. He was dumbfounded to see Lily follow Miss Aiken into the saloon.

What was she thinking? Had she given up on ever having a successful business? She had promised him that she understood why he wanted her to avoid Winston Ledford.

"Whoa!" Edward pulled the reins and made a hard left turn. He set the brake and jumped from the wagon in front of the saloon. Disbelief that he was about to push open the swinging doors of a saloon caused him to shudder. He'd vowed never to darken the door of this establishment. Why did this woman have the power to draw him into situations? Could he save her from herself? Did she want to be saved?

"We're not open." Winston Ledford stood at the end of a magnificent hand-carved bar. A crate of whiskey being unpacked by a man behind the counter evidenced the future ugliness that would, no doubt, take place in the room.

"I'm not here for business. I've come for my wife." Come to get her. And to leave. All as quickly as possible.

A smirk stretched across Winston's face. "The ladies in the saloon are not available for gentlemen until we open next month."

Edward clenched his fists at his side, willing himself to stay calm. This man was as slick as any snake he'd ever seen. "My wife is not one of your ladies."

"You saw her come in here, didn't you?" The smirk became a grin.

A door opened near the top of the stairs running along the wall opposite the bar. Both men turned at the sound.

"Edward, what are you doing here?" Lily started down the steps, a valise in one hand. Lavinia followed her, carrying another bag.

"We'll talk about that outside." He met her at the foot of the steps. "Let me take that." He took both valises and followed the ladies to the front door.

"Come back anytime." Winston leaned against the bar, arms folded across his chest. His suit was pressed and clean, the tailoring exact, the very picture of arrogance. "You're always welcome."

The ladies left without acknowledging his words.

Edward leveled a glare at the man. "You'll be doing yourself a favor if you stay away from my wife."

"I'll do as I please, Stone. I always do."

"Don't say I didn't warn you." The saloon doors swung wildly behind him.

He dropped the valises into the back of the wagon.

"Would you care to tell me what's going on here?" He struggled to control the grit in his tone. He looked from Miss Aiken to Lily.

Lily smiled and laid a gloved hand on his sleeve. "It's awfully cold. Can we tell you after we get back to the shop?"

Edward extended a hand to help them into the wagon. It took all his restraint to remain quiet as he climbed aboard and turned the wagon around for the short drive to Lily's shop.

Once the ladies were inside and he'd unloaded the valises, Edward closed the door against the wind.

"Now, if you don't mind, I'd like to know exactly what you were thinking going into a saloon. Especially after all that has happened since you've been in Pine Haven." Try as he did to prevent it, his words rang with acidity. Miss Aiken was in the background when he directed his indignation at Lily.

"You were asleep last night when I got home. I tried to talk to you this morning, but you didn't have time. That's why I asked you to come by the shop today." She had the audacity to look hurt. "Surely you know me well enough by now not to question my actions or motives." Pain filled her voice.

He'd hurt her again. Would he ever get it right with this woman?

Lord, You know she gets the better of me. Give me wisdom.

"Please don't be angry with Lily. It was my fault." Lavinia took a step toward him. "She was helping me get my things." She pointed to the valises at his feet.

He'd carried the bags for them. Blinded by his anger, he'd gone through the motions of helping them without considering the implications of the heavy bags. And how quickly they must have packed them.

Edward turned to Lily.

She finished Miss Aiken's explanation. "Lavinia has decided she doesn't want to work or live in the saloon." Her eyes begged him to understand.

Miss Aiken spoke again. "Lily offered to help me. I didn't think about how it would look for her to go with me, or I'd have gone alone."

Lily broke in, "I didn't want to risk Winston Ledford trying to manipulate her or force her to stay."

"I see." He pulled his hat off and spun it in his hands. The anger was replaced with regret. "Will you forgive me, Lily?" Once again he'd misjudged her. She was always helping someone. And it seemed all she got for it was grief. From him and everyone else.

"I shouldn't." One side of her mouth pulled up. "You've got to learn to trust me."

"You're right. Again." Lost in the blue depths of her eyes, he found himself swimming in emotions unfamiliar to him. A sensation of falling caught him off balance. So much so, he had to adjust his footing.

"I'm so sorry for causing this misunderstanding." Miss Aiken's voice came to him.

He cleared his throat. "It's not your fault."

"Since you're here, I have some business I'd like to discuss with you." Lily's straightforward manner effectively closed the subject.

"If you'll both excuse me, I'll head upstairs." Miss

Aiken eyed her valises before disappearing into the workroom.

The stairs creaked with her ascent before Lily spoke again.

"There's more to tell you about Lavinia."

"What?" The hair on his arms and neck bristled. If Winston Ledford had harmed that poor girl, he'd be paying another visit to the saloon. Twice in one day, after a pledge to never go, would be unavoidable.

"Oh, Edward, it's the most wonderful news." She reached her gloved hand to his sleeve. It was a habit of hers that gave him pleasure.

Lily lowered her voice and leaned close to him. The scent of honeysuckle filled his next breath. "After lunch yesterday, Lavinia talked to me about the sermon. She's prayed and asked God to redirect her life according to His plan." Beautiful blue eyes turned to violet as he watched joy overwhelm her.

"That is wonderful news."

"It complicates matters to a certain degree."

"How do you mean?"

"Now she doesn't have a job or anywhere to stay. If it's not a problem for you, I've offered for her to stay here in the rooms over the shop."

Edward saw her big heart expanding to include another person in need. Since he'd met her, she'd married him for Ellen's sake, offered friendship to ladies who were shunned by everyone else in town and now she was willing to take in someone with nowhere to go. Was there no end to her generosity? Did she see the potential for continued harm to her business if she followed through with this plan? "Are you sure this is a good idea?"

Hopeful eyes pleaded with him. "As the landlord, you have final say."

"Have you considered what people will think?" He hated the words, but they had to be said.

Lily smiled. "Edward, don't you see? Now people will see how important it is to reach out in love to others."

"Some may, but others will gossip. What if Miss Aiken changes her mind and wants to return to the saloon?"

"Without a safe place to start a new life, that's exactly what could happen. I know with friends and time, she can make a go of it."

"I wish everyone had your optimism." He huffed out a sigh. "If you really want to do this, I have no objection as the landlord."

"Thank you, Edward!" Lily stepped up on her toes and brushed her lips across his cheek.

The air stilled, and she froze in place, pink staining her face. Their eyes locked as she lowered herself onto her heels, hand still resting on his arm. Surprise at her kiss turned to pleasure. He put a hand over hers. "You're most welcome, Lily. I'm glad I can do something to make you happy." The gravel in his voice was beyond his control. "Very happy."

Her other hand went up to cover her mouth. He took a step back and set his hat low over his brow. With a smile he said, "Let me know if you need my help arranging the furniture upstairs."

He sat on the seat of his wagon, knowing he had a full day's work ahead of him. No amount of work would take his mind off the wife he'd left rescuing a friend.

God, help me to understand her motives and see her heart before I jump to protect her. I want to be a good husband.

He lifted the reins and let them fall to signal his team it was time to go. What would it be like to be Lily's true husband? Not just her protector and friend, but the person she turned to for comfort and support—because she loved him. He left town behind and headed to a nearby ranch to make his first delivery, the memory of her kiss fresh on his mind. Could they build a true marriage on a foundation of convenience?

"What have you done?" Lily spoke to herself.

Lavinia appeared in the doorway to the workroom. "Do I need to find somewhere else to go?"

Watching Edward leave without a backward glance, Lily soaked in the stupidity of her actions. How could she kiss him? Their marriage wasn't one of love or affection. They'd both agreed to that before the ceremony.

But his eyes—the surprise she'd seen in them. Was it filled with pleasure? Or was she completely out of her mind? How could she face him tonight?

She turned to answer Lavinia, but her mind was on the blacksmith. Tonight couldn't come soon enough. Nor could she dread its coming more.

That evening, when Lily walked into the cabin, Ellen met her at the door wearing her Sunday best.

"Uncle Edward is taking us to the hotel for supper. He says it's time we had a treat." Her young face glowed with anticipation.

"He did, did he?" Lily removed her hat.

"Yep, and I can eat dessert, too."

Edward came out of her bedroom. "I'm guessing Ellen has shared the news." He was also wearing clothes he usually reserved for church services. They'd agreed to keep his things in her room for Ellen's sake. Careful scheduling allowed them to change clothes without raising suspicions in the child's mind about their marriage. Ellen was always in bed before them, and Edward rose in the mornings before she awoke.

"Yes, she seems to be excited about a special dinner."

"I hope you don't mind. I thought you'd enjoy a rest from cooking." He paused before adding, "You work so hard all day, and then in the evenings, too."

She smiled, pleased at the kind gesture. "I look forward to it."

At the restaurant, Lily sat in the chair Edward held for her. "This is lovely. No wonder Papa is so happy with his purchase." She put the linen napkin in her lap and took in the beauty of her surroundings. They sat at a table near the fireplace. Sconces glowed against the floral wallpaper.

"My momma picked the colors." Ellen wiggled in her chair. "She said eating in a pretty room makes the food taste better."

"Did she now?" Edward winked at his niece. "Did she also tell you that little girls in pretty rooms must be still?"

Ellen drew in a fanciful breath, inhaling the atmosphere. "I know. It's just been such a long time since we came here." She stilled and dropped both hands into her lap. "It kinda makes me miss Momma and Pa."

"I think being in this lovely room your mother decorated should make you feel close to her." Lily put a hand under Ellen's chin. "It's okay to be happy and remember happy times."

A strong sniff preceded agreement. "I'll try."

Edward used the leather-bound menu to hide much of his face, but she knew he was fighting the same memories Ellen fought.

"We don't have to eat here. I have plenty of ham for sandwiches at home. I can bake a batch of cookies while we eat them." She reached for her reticule.

The menu lowered slowly, and Edward caught Ellen's eye. "Do you wish to leave?"

"No, Uncle Edward. I'm starting to like it. We just didn't come for such a long time. I forgot how it makes me think of Momma."

"It's settled, then." He turned to Lily and gave her a dimpled smile. "You've cooked for us every night. Tonight we would like to treat you. This is the best place we know to do that."

"If you're certain." Lily placed her reticule back on the corner of the table and picked up a menu. "The smell of fresh bread has given me an appetite."

"If I'd tried to cook for you at home, the only smell would be bacon frying to go with flapjacks." Edward chuckled. "Or maybe some burning onions."

"I love the smell of bacon." She laughed with him.

"Me, too," Ellen chimed in and laughed with them. "But I want fried chicken tonight." She looked at Lily. "Uncle Edward can't fry chicken. He tried one time. There was a fire!"

Edward's face turned red. "It was a small grease fire. Contained in the skillet. No one was hurt." The volume of his voice lowered with each defensive word as though he recognized their futility.

Lily smiled at his protest and thought of the fire that brought them together. The smile faded. That fire hadn't been contained. Only the future would tell if anyone would be hurt by the consequences of that night.

They ordered their food and sat talking while they waited for it to come.

"Miss Aiken seems to be happier." Edward took a long drink from his water glass.

Was he as nervous as she was? The way he tugged at the collar of his best shirt made her think so. Was he remembering how she had kissed him?

Thinking it best to keep the conversation on safe topics, she answered, "She is. It's as if the weight of the world has lifted from her shoulders. I've written to my father inquiring about the possibility of her working for him."

"You've been a true friend to her."

"We all need friends." She couldn't stop the smile from covering her face. "I'm grateful for you and Ellen."

He raised his glass. "We are the ones who are grateful for you."

The food arrived. Ellen's hearty appetite overrode her manners, and Edward cautioned her to eat slowly.

The meal was delicious, and Lily found herself relaxing in Edward's company. Ellen's childish banter made them both laugh. Could they settle into being a friendly family that shared in special occasions and enjoyed being together?

Edward took a roll from the bowl in the center of the table and buttered it. "You've certainly had a hand in spoiling her to good food."

"Aunt Lily, could you teach Uncle Edward to make biscuits like yours?" Ellen spoke around a mouthful of potatoes. "That way, when you have to work late, he can make supper."

Edward raised an eyebrow and waited for her answer. Could she work in close proximity to a man who set her on edge? Would she make a complete fool of herself by falling at his feet or spilling flour all over the kitchen?

"I'm not much of a teacher, Ellen."

"You taught me stuff." The child reached for her glass of milk and drank deeply.

"Children are easier." No, she didn't think she could teach Edward. The way his eyes penetrated hers. Searching. What would he find there?

A few weeks ago it would have been a lonely woman no longer seeking companionship, someone convinced she'd rather be alone than used or taken for granted again.

Tonight he would find someone who surprised even her. The days and weeks in Pine Haven had brought a myriad of changes to her life. For the first time she had lived alone. That hadn't gone as she'd anticipated. The rejection she faced and the likelihood her shop would fail before her father arrived had surprised her. The confidence that dared her to try this adventure had shifted. Her marriage to Edward, finding herself as a wife and substitute mother, had shifted her heart.

Living in Pine Haven was not about being her own person anymore. It was about finding peace. Knowing she was living her life in a way that pleased God. Knowing Lavinia was waiting for her at the shop was more important than a hat sale or a shipment of parasols.

In seeking a place to belong, Lily had found a new person inside herself. Someone who was willing to risk everything if it meant another human being would be better for the effort.

Sitting in this hotel, having supper with two people she'd grown very fond of, Lily realized the seeking was over. She'd found what was missing from her life. Acceptance.

Chapter Sixteen

Edward put his silverware on his empty plate. He watched Lily savor the food and thought about the night he'd brought her here after their wedding.

He put up a hand and pulled at his collar. The strangling sensation was something he remembered from being a lad trying to work up the nerve to speak to a girl at school. "Have you decided if you want to go to the church social?"

"That would be such fun!" Ellen pushed the last of her roll into her already full mouth.

"Ellen, remember your manners."

"Yes, sir." The little girl speared green beans and waited.

The interruption had kept Lily from answering him. "I'd like to take you."

"I think we should all go." Lily smiled at Ellen but didn't look at him.

Edward leaned forward. "Ellen will be there."

Lily turned to him.

"I'm asking if you'd consider letting me take you to

the Winter Social like a social call." There, he'd said it. Now he could breathe.

Well, maybe after she answered.

Pink lit Lily's cheeks, and she worried her bottom lip with her teeth. Then he saw it. A glimmer of light. Replaced in an instant by caution. Had her sudden kiss given him false hope? Part of him wanted a real marriage. Would Lily be willing to try to build that with him? Was courting her after they were married the right way to approach her?

"I'd be honored to accompany you."

"But…" He waited for the withdrawal of her reluctant consent.

"What about Lavinia? I can't leave her on her own so soon. It's important for her to feel she's part of the church family."

Swoosh. Air filled his eager lungs. "She may come along with us."

"Are you sure?"

"As long as you are saying yes, I'm sure." An excitement bubbled inside his chest. For a minute he imagined himself not unlike Ellen. So happy he couldn't be still.

"That's settled, then." Lily's smile was demure. And beautiful. Her voice soft. "Now, Ellen, tell me. How is Speckles doing today?"

Lily's blue eyes lingered on his face while she listened to the latest adventures of the mischievous kitten.

This would be the best Winter Social in years. He was certain of it.

Edward flipped the last pancake onto a plate and set it on the table just as Lily opened the bedroom door. "Good morning."

"Good morning to you, Edward. What has you up and about so early?" She came to the stove and poured a cup of coffee. The skirt of her dress brushed against his leg. It was a dress he hadn't seen. The ruffles on the cuffs were white against the pale green of the sleeves. Everything she wore was feminine and beautiful. Just like her.

But this morning he had a different young lady on his mind. "I wanted to talk to you for a few minutes before Ellen wakes." He indicated the table, and they both sat down. Ellen's reaction to the hotel dining room had him concerned about how the child was handling her parents' absence.

"This looks wonderful. Two meals in a row where I didn't have to cook?" Lily thanked him for cooking and said grace over the food. "What do you want to talk to me about?"

"What did you think about Ellen's mood last night at the hotel?" He speared a piece of ham and added it to the pancakes on his plate. "I think she's trying very hard to be patient about Jane and Wesley not being here, but I don't know if it's time we started planting the seed in her mind that they may not return."

Lily put her fork down. "Do you think that's necessary? Is there no hope?"

"I wish I knew. I've contacted the town doctor again and the sheriff. Neither of them has heard anything more than they were able to tell me before we married." He looked toward Ellen's room. "I just don't want her to have false hope and be crushed later."

"That's one way to look at it." Lily focused on some unseen place. "What would you tell her?"

"At this point, just that we can't find them." He shook his head, hating that he was in the position of breaking his niece's heart. "She might take it better if we tell her what we know in stages."

Lily dropped her voice to almost a whisper. "I remember when my mother passed, how I felt. I don't know how hard it would have been to not know what happened. It was tragic to know my mother was gone from this life, but to wonder if she was sick and couldn't get to me... I don't know how I'd have felt about that. Especially at Ellen's age. She's too young to have so much put on her."

"That's what I'm afraid of. If we don't tell her anything, will she go on talking of Jane and Wesley as if they'll be home in a few weeks? If we start to hint at the possibility that they might not return, it may help ease the blow."

"I'd like to give her hope." Lily's blue eyes darkened with sorrow.

"She's going to have to adjust to the idea that we may be her parents from this time forward."

"I think having an uncle and aunt who love her is keeping her from feeling abandoned."

"I do, too, but I won't give her false hope. I can't pretend, when the sheriff and the doctor have all but said they're gone."

"But they haven't said it." She reached across the table and put her hand on his. "If you won't give it more time, at least give her hope."

A thump from Ellen's room let them know she was awake. "I'll give it two weeks. I'll contact the sheriff again." He lowered his voice. "Then we'll have to tell her."

"I pray you hear good news." Lily pulled her hand back as Ellen opened her door.

Edward couldn't help but notice the extra care Lily

showered on Ellen during breakfast, coaxing a smile more than once with her antics. Ellen's doll was transformed by their imagination into a lovely princess dining in a palace by the time he got up from the table. He stood behind Ellen's chair and mouthed *Thank you* to Lily.

Lily had been good for Ellen. No matter what happened, he knew he'd done the right thing by marrying her.

Only God knew who would benefit more from having her in their lives—Ellen or Edward.

"You haven't been here two weeks, and you've learned more about making hats than I did in three months under the milliner at home in East River." Lily put one of Lavinia's creations on a stand in the front window.

"Do you really think it's good enough to put in the window?"

Lavinia's timidity was surprising. How did this sweet young girl ever imagine herself as a saloon girl? And why did Winston Ledford think she was up for the job? Once again, Lily offered a silent prayer of thanks that Lavinia had responded to God's love for her.

"I do." Lily tied the ribbon and turned the angle just so. "It's a good thing Edward finished these extra stands and brought them. We've been busier in the last week than I was the first week I opened."

Lavinia dropped her head. "I feel so badly for causing you all that trouble."

Lily dismissed her concern with a heartfelt smile. "The trouble was all but forgotten when you walked away from the saloon. I told you the church folks and people in town would see the change in your life."

"I'm glad people have realized your kindness and friendship to me was the reason I was brave enough to turn to God for a new life." She dabbed at a tear threatening to fall from her lashes. "I can't imagine if I had to be at the saloon when they open tomorrow evening."

"Thankfully, you'll never have to worry about that again." Lily handed her a feather duster. "If you'll dust in here, I'll bring out the other hats we made last night."

"Yes, ma'am." Lavinia gave a playful bow and took the duster. She became serious when she straightened. "Thank you again for letting me help you here until your father arrives. I know my room and board are costing you."

"The sales of the hats you've made are more than covering the costs. I think Ginger must be telling people to come here, too." Lily reached into the cash box and pulled out an envelope. "As a matter of fact, I've got something for you. Here is your commission on the things you've sold."

"Lily, you can't pay me. We agreed I would help out."

"That was before you revealed your God-given talents." She pressed the envelope into Lavinia's hand. "After you finish the dusting, why don't you see if Mrs. Croft has a ready-made dress you can purchase to wear to the Winter Social on Sunday?"

The clothes Mr. Ledford had purchased for Lavinia had been left at the saloon. She wore the few things she'd brought with her when she'd moved to Pine Haven. Lily knew she needed more.

"Are you sure she wants to see the likes of me in her store?"

"Yes. She spoke to me after Bible study on Wednesday evening." Lily put her hands on Lavinia's shoulders. "Nothing too flowery, mind you, but kindly just the same. Something about noticing what a good worker you are."

They both laughed.

"I guess seeing me sweep the sidewalk every morning when she goes to the bank and post office has made us friends of a sort." Lavinia tucked the envelope in her skirt pocket. "Thank you. I'll go as long as we aren't busy."

Lily went to look out the front window. The Winter Social was in two days. Since their supper at the hotel, Edward had been kind and attentive. They'd even shared a cooking lesson. She noticed he laughed more readily. She made it a habit to sit in front of the fire after Ellen went to bed at night. They'd talked about everything from their childhood to their favorite Bible verses.

He made one excuse after another to come to her shop. He'd made two trips with her orders—first the additional stands, then the sign. Yesterday he'd come back to mount the sign on its hinges in the window sill. She pulled at the loose tendrils hanging at the base of her neck and looked through the glass, wondering if he'd come again today. A smile betrayed her hopes to anyone who might see.

Lost in thought, she didn't notice Winston Ledford until he stood facing her on the opposite side of the glass. She started and backed away. He opened the door and entered.

"Ladies." He removed his hat.

"Mr. Ledford." Lily noticed Lavinia backing into the workroom and stepped to block his line of sight. "What can I do for you?"

"You've done more than enough, Mrs. Stone." He peered over her shoulder.

"If you're not interested in making a purchase, I'm rather busy." She refused to be frightened of this man or his threats.

"I warned you not to interfere in my business."

"I have not." God had successfully drawn Lavinia away from his business. She trusted the Lord to protect her from Winston's anger.

"Lovey's presence here speaks to the fact that you have, indeed."

"Miss Aiken is not your business."

"She is the reason I am short on workers for my new establishment. I've come to speak with her."

"She does not wish to speak with you." Lily had known he wouldn't settle so easily when Lavinia left. They'd discussed how they would handle any attempts he might make to contact her.

Ignoring Lily, he called out, "Lovey, come here."

Lily heard the rustling of Lavinia's skirts. "There's no need, Miss Aiken. I'll take care of this." She opened the door and gestured for him to leave.

Taking advantage of her leaving a clear path, Winston stepped toward the workroom.

"I believe my wife has asked you to vacate the premises, Ledford." Edward's voice resonated from behind her. With her back to the door she hadn't seen him approach, but she'd never been more glad to see him. "As her landlord—and husband—I'm going to insist you comply with her wishes at once."

Lily could see the wheels of the saloon owner's mind turning, deciding how likely it would be for him to come out ahead in a confrontation with Edward. Wisely, he opted to leave.

"This is not over, Lovey. You can't hide in this hat shop forever." Winston turned to Lily. "You leave me little choice today, but whether you like it or not, I am a merchant in this town now. I will make a success of it. And I will not allow you, or anyone else, to get in my way."

"Careful, Ledford. I'm restraining myself. If anything were to happen to these little ladies, or if they became concerned something might happen to them, I'd be forced to protect them. You don't want to be the cause for that concern," Edward said.

"You misunderstand, Stone. My purpose is to offer viable employment to ladies in this town. Making more money in a month than this hat shop will see in six." He was tall enough to look down on Edward as he passed him to leave.

Unintimidated, Edward turned to fill the doorway. "Your presence isn't welcome here. Remember that."

He closed the door and turned to Lily. "Are you all right?"

"We're fine. Thank you for showing up when you did."

Lavinia came from the workroom. "I'm so sorry. I can find another place to stay. Do you think there's a possibility I could start working at the hotel before your father arrives?"

"It's not your fault, Miss Aiken." Edward watched out the window as Mr. Ledford walked toward the center of town.

Lily gave her a brief hug. "You're not going anywhere. I've grown accustomed to having you here."

"I can't believe he came here looking for me. I told him when I left that I wouldn't be back." Lavinia began to dust the shop.

"Try to stay out of his way as much as you can. He'll get the point soon enough." Edward turned to Lily. "I'll be watching him. If either of you feels threatened at any time, let me know."

She was determined not to be intimidated. "Thank you, Edward. I pray it doesn't come to that."

Lavinia moved to the other side of the shop with the duster, and Edward leaned closer to Lily.

"Are we still on for the Winter Social?"

She smiled at him. "Yes. Ellen asked when she brought Speckles to visit this morning. She said he would be lonely while she was in school." She indicated the basket in the corner. "Poor little thing had been crying before she got here. It might have something to do with an incident she said involved an ash bin at the edge of the hearth." Lily giggled at the thought of Edward cleaning up after a kitten he hadn't wanted in the first place.

"That cat should be grateful to be inside." A mock snarl crossed his face. "I've spent more time cleaning up after the little rascal than I can spare. Be warned. He's not as cute as he looks."

"Like you?" She giggled until she heard Lavinia excuse herself from the room.

"Looks like you've gone and said it now." Edward gave her a wink.

"Oh, my. I'll have to be more careful. You might go getting the wrong idea." Enjoyment in his presence filled her with satisfaction. Taunting him was one of her new favorite things to do. That strong masculine face turning pink pleased her to no end.

"I best be going." Edward opened the door, ducked his head a bit and walked onto the sidewalk.

"I'm glad you came." She wiggled her fingers at him and held her breath until the door closed.

The Winter Social couldn't come soon enough. For the first time in her adult life, she was excited about attending a social event. No one would expect her to serve the punch or wash up when everything was over. She would go as Edward's wife and enjoy the afternoon and evening.

Yes, this new life suited her just fine. New friends, a successful business—now that everyone realized the positive results of her association with Lavinia and Ginger—and a husband who winked at her when he came to her rescue.

Rescue? Did she really need Edward to rescue her from Winston?

No.

Was it nice to know he was there if she did?

Absolutely.

Edward laughed and picked his hat up off the ground. He beat it against his leg to remove the layer of dust it had collected when it was knocked off the table by his worthy opponent in the final arm-wrestling match. It was the one event at the Winter Social all the men enjoyed.

Doc Willis clapped him on the back. "Wouldn'a thought I could beat a man who swings a hammer all day long."

"To be honest, that's probably how you won. I didn't think you could, either." Edward laughed and turned to look for Ellen. He found her among the children eating cookies in the corner. The barn had been set up with sections for each activity. A smaller place than the Willis ranch couldn't hold a crowd this size. The food was along one wall, the games for kids were in one corner, and the men were testing one another's strength in the opposite corner. The ladies were gathered at the tables visiting, the meal long since passed.

"If I can have everyone's attention…" Reverend Dismuke stepped onto a makeshift platform fashioned of hay bales with planks of wood across the top. "It's time for the pie auction."

The men cheered and gathered around the preacher. Someone off to one side held up the first pie.

"Remember, you'll be sharing the pie with the baker, so bid carefully. This pie was made by my wife. I thought we best auction it first, so there's no fighting over it at the end." Several people chuckled, and Reverend Dismuke smiled at Peggy. Not wanting to miss out on the excitement, the ladies had come to stand behind the men. "You all know the money we raise tonight goes to help fund the school for the rest of the year, so bid like the providers you are."

A sporting round of bids followed as several pies were sold to the husbands of the women who baked them. Laughter and teasing filled the atmosphere as the bids went higher and higher.

"This next pie is from a newcomer." Lavinia's pie was held in the air. "It smells mighty fine. You can't see it from where you're standing, but these look like some of the finest pecans of the crop. Miss Aiken, where are you?"

Lavinia tried to hide her face, but Lily pointed her out.

"Who'll start the bidding for this pie?" For a few seconds Lily was afraid no one would bid. She watched Lavinia withdraw into herself. Her arms folded across her chest, and her head hung as she clinched her jaw.

Then a quiet voice came from the opposite side of the barn with a substantial bid. Lily tried to see the bidder, but she was too short. Lavinia peeked up at her.

"Do you know the bidder?" Lily could see her friend's face brighten with relief.

"It's the young man from the general store who invited me to church." Lavinia spoke in hushed tones. "I've seen him in service a couple of times since I started attending, but he hasn't spoken to me."

The reverend called for more bids. After a short round of back and forth, Lavinia's pie sold for a good sum. She put her hand over her mouth to catch a bubbling giggle that threatened to draw attention to her.

Lily smiled and hugged her friend. "You've done it, Lavinia. You've made a place for yourself among the good people of Pine Haven."

"Thank you, Lily. I couldn't have dreamed it without your friendship and encouragement."

A shy cowhand approached holding his newly purchased pie. "Miss Aiken, would you please join me for some pie?"

The two walked toward the tables where everyone had eaten the meal earlier.

"You should be very pleased with yourself." Edward's voice came from behind Lily. "That young lady's life is forever changed for the better because of you."

"God made the difference for her." Lily dashed a happy tear from her lashes. "I just got to be a witness to the transformation."

Edward threw one hand into the air and called out a price. Lily turned to see her pie was up for bids.

An ominous bid came from a spot near the back of the barn. Unnoticed until this moment, Winston Ledford had entered the barn. Lily's mouth dropped open. Several ladies gasped. A low rumble from some of the men signaled their agreement with the ladies.

Lily heard Mrs. Croft's voice above the others. "The nerve of that man! What is he doing here?"

Edward looked at Winston. He held his hand up and topped Winston's bid.

Winston doubled Edward's bid.

The crowd no longer masked their curiosity.

Edward did not look away from Winston. He raised his price again.

Winston countered with another doubling of the offer.

Lily knew it was more than anyone had paid for a pie that night. Not even the wealthiest of ranchers had offered so much money. She leaned in close to Edward and whispered. "It's too much money. He's trying to provoke you."

Edward turned to Reverend Dismuke. "I will pay three times his offer."

"Going, going, gone! Sold to Edward Stone. Thank you for your contribution to the school fund." The crowd applauded. Lily knew it wasn't just for the amount of money raised, but the show of wills they'd witnessed between the two men.

Without hesitation, the preacher asked for the next pie, and everyone's attention moved to the bidding.

"Edward, you didn't have to do that. It's so much money." Lily put her hand on his arm.

He covered it with one of his own and lowered his head so their eyes were level. "There was no way I would let that man buy your pie. You are not for sale." He gave her hand a squeeze. "Would you care to join me for dessert?"

A smile of relief and gratitude crossed her face. "I'd like that. May I ask Ellen to share it with us?"

"You may." Edward released her and went to collect his pie. "I'll be right with you."

Lily saw him head in the direction of Winston Ledford. Somehow she imagined the saloon owner wasn't accustomed to anyone getting the better of him. To see her husband win their contest of wills pleased her immensely. Pleased and excited her. For the first time in her life she hadn't been at the punch bowl. She'd been at the center of attention.

The attention hadn't been fun for her. But the victory Edward claimed meant she was no longer a wallflower. And the sweetness of the pie wouldn't be the only memory her mind would savor when the night ended.

After he confirmed that some of the men were watching Winston Ledford leave the property, Edward started to relax. He paid his bid and collected his pie. Lily and Ellen sat with punch cups when he came to the table.

"Aunt Lily's pie is the best one ever!" Ellen picked up her fork while he cut wedges for everyone.

"Looks like it to me. I've never seen such a fancy crust." He winked at his niece and gave her the first piece.

The three of them laughed and ate their treat in relative privacy, nestled as they were in the corner of a barn filled with people.

Edward had reached for a second slice when Ellen's demeanor started to change.

"Did you eat too fast, Ellen?" Lily must have noticed it, too.

"No." Ellen sniffed, and her eyes swam in fresh tears.

In an instant Edward was beside her, squatting to be level with his niece as she sat on the bench. He touched her forehead with the back of his hand. No fever. "Do you hurt somewhere?"

"Here." She pulled her doll from her pocket and held it to her chest. She sniffled, and the tears fell onto her cheeks.

"Does your tummy hurt? Or has someone hurt your feelings?" Lily asked softly.

"I miss Momma and Papa." She sobbed in earnest now. "Momma loves the socials." Ellen buried her head in his shoulder. "And Papa always buys her pie."

He folded her into his arms and rocked her. Tears soaked his shirt. "Honey, I know. I miss them, too."

Lily reached a hand to rub Ellen's back while he held the child close.

He put his hands on Ellen's shoulders and pushed her back just enough to see her reddened face. "Let's get you home." He'd been afraid this was coming. The child couldn't continue to wonder and wait on her parents. He had to tell her what he knew.

The background noise of others eating pie and laughing had faded away when Ellen started to cry. Now it crashed into his mind like a maddening wave of chaos. He had to get Ellen home. To console her. To protect her. To tell her the truth.

Edward stood, bringing Ellen into his arms like a babe cradled against its mother. "Please see to a ride for Miss Aiken while I get Ellen to the wagon."

He carried Ellen into the night and wrapped her in a blanket on the front seat of the wagon.

Lily joined them, and he leaned to speak softly in her ear. "We need to tell her."

Lily exhaled and her soft, warm breath teased his neck above the collar of his shirt. Her whisper was more faint than his. "Must we? Now?"

He took her hand and gave it a reassuring squeeze. "She'll only get more distraught later if we don't face this."

He felt the answering pressure of her gloved hand in

his as she said, "May God give us the words." He turned to Ellen, where she sat on the edge of the seat.

"Ellen, we need to talk about your momma and papa." He held the child's hands in his and looked up into her tearstained face.

"I don't want to, Uncle Edward." She sniffed big and stuck out her bottom lip. "You don't look happy. I don't want to hear anything about them that's not happy."

Lily moved in close beside him and put a hand over his on Ellen's. "Uncle Edward wants to help you understand."

Ellen swallowed a gulp of air. "I'm afraid you're gonna tell me Momma won't come back. Her or Papa."

Edward cleared his throat. "They've been gone a long time, Ellen. Sometimes things happen that can't be helped. If your momma and papa could be here, you know they would."

"They're coming back for me!" Ellen's voice rose in desperation.

Suddenly, Edward couldn't believe his ears.

"I'm here, baby girl."

Ellen squealed and threw her arms wide. Edward caught her as she lunged from the wagon. He set her down, and she ran into her mother's open arms.

Edward was speechless. Jane was crying and kissing Ellen's face. He put an arm around Jane, thrilled at the sight of his sister. And worried by Wesley's absence.

"How? When?" Surprise at her sudden appearance left him befuddled.

Jane laughed through her tears and spoke to him over the top of Ellen's head. The child had become lodged in her embrace. "I just arrived. I came by wagon with friends. I'll explain it all to you."

He leaned close and asked quietly, hoping Ellen wouldn't hear, "Where's Wesley?"

Ellen leaned back and looked up into her mother's face. "Where's Papa?"

Jane squatted in front of Ellen and put a hand on each of the girl's shoulders. "Honey, Papa wanted so much to come home to you."

"Where is he?" Ellen looked around, searching the shadows of the moonlit night.

Edward's heart broke at the pain he saw on his sister's face. He could only imagine what she'd been through. He put a hand on her shoulder to reassure her.

Jane looked up at Edward and then back to Ellen. "I got very sick. That's why my letters stopped. I was too sick to write, but Papa took good care of me."

"He's a good papa." Ellen's lips trembled. Edward knew her mind was trying to prepare her for what her heart didn't want to hear.

Jane continued, "Yes, he was. No one could have loved you or me more than he did." She took a deep breath. "That's why he never left me while I was sick. But then he got sick, too."

A tear slid down his sister's face. He'd do anything to take from her the sorrow he saw in her eyes.

"Your papa was sicker than I was. He helped me get better, but…" Her words halted. Finally she was able to finish. "Papa couldn't get better. He was just too sick. I'm so sorry, Ellen, but he passed. Last week."

Ellen cried, "No, Momma!" The little girl fell against her mother's shoulder and wailed.

Edward went down on one knee and wrapped the two of them in a hug. He held them while they wept. He sensed Lily behind him and knew she was praying for them. Had it only been minutes before that he'd tried to find the words to prepare Ellen for this possibility?

When Jane was able to calm Ellen to a point that he felt it was best to go home, Edward helped his sister and niece into the back of the wagon. Jane's friends had their wagon nearby, and he arranged for them to bring Jane's things by his home the next day.

He covered Jane and Ellen with a blanket and helped Lily onto the seat beside him. Ellen, worn-out from her tears, fell asleep with her head in her mother's lap.

Lily hadn't said a word since Jane had come upon them while they talked to Ellen. He knew she'd worried over Ellen's reaction, should anything have happened to her parents. Now, they were facing it.

Chapter Seventeen

Edward carried Ellen into the cabin and laid her on her bed. When he came back into the front room, Jane and Lily were introducing themselves.

"His wife?" Jane turned when he came into the room. "I thought you were never getting married."

He looked from his sister to his wife. "A lot happened while you were gone."

"I can see that," Jane said. "It's lovely to meet you, Lily. I wish I'd been here for your wedding."

Lily began, "If you'd been here—"

"I wish you could have been here, too," Edward interrupted. He'd come to stand by Jane and tried to shake his head without Jane noticing. "It was a simple church ceremony. Just after the first of the year." He didn't want Lily to tell Jane the circumstances of their marriage. He didn't want Lily to seem less than a real wife to his sister. Where the need to protect her came from, he couldn't say. Over the time they'd been together, it had just become part of who he was.

Jane looked to Lily. "I'm glad to have a sister."

Lily acknowledged her words with a forced smile.

Edward didn't know what was going on in Lily's mind, but he could see the storm brewing in her violet eyes.

Their whole world had changed tonight. Again.

Having Jane home was a blessing he'd begun to think would never happen. Losing Wesley was a burden he hated for his sister and niece to bear.

Lily finally spoke. "Have you eaten?"

Jane tugged her gloves off. "Not since breakfast, but you don't have to bother. I can grab some bread and a slice of cheese."

"It's no bother. You must be famished from traveling so far." Lily tied on her apron. Edward watched her now-familiar movements as she broke eggs into a bowl.

He took Jane's coat and hung it by the door. "Come sit at the table. I'll get you a cup of coffee, and you can tell me everything."

Sadness filled Jane's face. She sat in Ellen's chair at the table and told them all that had happened since she and Wesley had left Pine Haven. They'd established their business and had hopes of doing well. They made preparation to come for Ellen just before they took ill.

"But the sickness...that was the worst of all." She hung her head. "So many people. Most of our neighbors. It struck our area of the city, and in a matter of days people were sick and dying. The doctor was overwhelmed, though I guess it wasn't as bad as it could have been. They were able to keep people from coming into our part of town. In a matter of weeks, it had died away. It hit the young and old worst. The doctor said because Wesley tended me so long, he was weaker when he got sick." A tear dropped from her lashes. "He died because he was taking care of me."

Edward's heart broke for her. As displeased as he'd been by their decision to leave Ellen behind, he now realized that to take her would have put her at risk of death. He thanked the Lord for letting her be safe with him.

"I'm so sorry for the loss of your husband." Lily put a plate of scrambled eggs and toast in front of Jane. "He must have loved you dearly."

Jane smiled up at Lily. "He did. The doctor tried to get him to send me to the hospital, but he didn't want me to get worse. He thought being around others would make me sicker. The hospital in our area filled up with patients. In the end, we had to be taken to another hospital."

"How did you have the strength to come after all of that? Why didn't you wire? I would have come for you." Edward hated the thought of her suffering alone.

"I know. That's why I didn't send a telegram." She asked Lily, "Isn't that just like our Edward? He'd drop everything and dash off to help someone else."

Lily turned to him. Her eyes were solemn. "That's one of the first things I learned about him."

Jane continued, "By the time Wesley passed, we'd spent all our money on hospital bills. Wesley had borrowed against the business. I sold it to have the money to pay the undertaker and settle the mortgage."

"Jane, I'm so sorry about Wesley, but don't you worry about you and Ellen." He didn't know what else to say. His sister had gone away dreaming of a better life only to find herself back in the same place, but without her husband and practically without funds.

"We'll get through this." He put a hand on her shoulder. "We always do."

Lily listened to Jane's heart-wrenching story. Watching Edward's compassion for her grief, Lily remembered how kind he'd been to her the night of the fire. He'd rushed into a burning building to save her. And after risking his life for her, he'd pledged himself to her to protect her reputation—and for the sake of his niece. She'd never known anyone more selfless.

He sat at the table listening to his sister's plight, and Lily knew he'd never leave Jane or Ellen without his support and care. Without Wesley to provide for Jane and Ellen, he would take responsibility for them.

Would Jane want to open the bakery now? If she did, what was to become of Lily's Millinery and Finery? There were a couple of vacant buildings in town, but until her father arrived, Lily had no way of securing another location.

Jane and Ellen could sleep in Ellen's room tonight, but that would never do for a permanent arrangement. And Edward couldn't continue to sleep on the floor in front of the fire. He deserved a bed and the privacy of a bedroom in a cabin filled with women.

There were so many questions. And no answers.

Lily's mind swirled with it all. "If you don't mind, I'm going to turn in for the night."

"Thank you for cooking for me, Lily. You'll have to let me return the favor." Jane was a picture of kindness, a woman anyone would love for a sister-in-law.

"She's an amazing cook, Jane. You're in for a real treat." Edward beamed as if he was proud of her. Was he?

"Jane, if you'd like, I think I have something you could use to sleep in for the night." Lily stepped into her room. She pulled a nightgown and robe from her wardrobe. Jane was a bit taller than her, but it would do for a night. When she turned around, Jane was at the bedroom door.

"This is so thoughtful." She accepted the clothes. "I'm sorry for barging into your home like this."

Edward came to stand behind Jane. "You're always welcome in my home."

My home. Did he not consider it to be her home, too? Lily watched them and wondered what her role in his life would be after tonight. Nothing was happening like either of them expected.

Edward asked, "Jane, why don't you sleep with Ellen? We'll figure out something more permanent over the next few days."

"Thank you, Edward. I knew I could count on you." Jane turned and slipped into Ellen's bedroom, closing the door quietly behind her.

"I think I'll say good-night." Lily moved to close the door.

Edward put a hand on the door. "Would you mind sitting up a bit? There's a lot to talk about." He grinned at her. "Please."

This was the playful expression he'd begun to wear over the past few days. He seemed to be inviting her out of her shell and into his life. But all that had changed now.

"For a little while." She went to the stove and poured them each a cup of coffee. They sat at the table, and she cut him another piece of the pie he'd won at the auction. She cringed when she thought of the price he'd paid. "Was it only a few hours ago that we were at a pie auction?"

He used the side of his fork to cut a large bite. "It seems like days instead of hours."

Lily ate a bite of her pie while he polished off most of his piece.

She put her fork on the plate. "What will you do about caring for Jane and Ellen?"

"I guess it depends on what Jane wants to do." He took a drink of coffee. "I'll talk to her about that in the morning."

"It's all so sudden for her. Losing her husband and

having a child to raise without a father. It's a lot for any woman."

"I'll be there to help her. She won't be alone like a lot of widows." He pushed his plate toward the center of the table.

"You're very reliable. That must be why she trusted you to care for Ellen while they were gone." She couldn't bring herself to look at him but stared into her coffee. "I'm so heartbroken for that dear child over the loss of her father, but so relieved that her mother is home to care for her."

"Because we thought they were both gone, it is a blessing for Jane to be back."

"I'll help you do whatever you decide is best." He no longer needed her. With Jane home, Ellen had her mother. And with her husband dead, Edward had the added burden of Jane on him. It wasn't fair for him to have to care for her, as well.

"Thank you. You've been a tremendous help with Ellen." He went to put his plate and cup in the basin. "She'll need us all now to help her adjust to her pa being gone."

"I'll pray for her. God knew what He was doing by establishing such a strong relationship between you and Ellen. She'll turn to you more now than ever before." She put her dishes in the basin. "If you don't mind, I'd like to turn in."

He reached for her hand. Had he reached for her this afternoon, she'd have expected a warmth and tenderness at his touch. Tonight, her heart was cold with confusion. Her future once again lay before her, clouded by situations beyond her control.

"The pie was delicious. Worth every penny." He touched her cheek with the back of his other hand, the knuckles rough from hard work. Work he'd have to increase to keep up with his new responsibilities.

Lily had forgotten all about Winston Ledford and his challenge. The music in the barn and the sounds of laughter had faded from her mind. Tonight she heard the echo of her heart as it cried out to be loved by a man who had only married her to care for a child who no longer needed her.

She loved him. More than anyone or anything she'd ever loved in her life. In a way she'd never loved before. Why did her heart spill this truth to her now? When the one she needed didn't need her anymore.

Tomorrow might hold unwelcome changes in her life. She wouldn't let her heart lead her this time. Luther had tempted her with the idea of love. A love he never had for her. Edward had never offered her love. Only his name in exchange for nurturing Ellen.

She stepped out of his reach. "I'm glad you liked the pie. It was for a good cause. The school is important to the community."

Edward put his hand in his pocket. "I see. So you think I bought the pie for the school?"

"No." She twisted her hands together in front of her. She didn't want to hurt him, but if she opened herself to him, only to be rejected later, she didn't think she'd have the courage to move beyond it. "I know you bought the pie to protect me. The same way you married me to protect me."

The grin he'd used to entice her into sharing pie with him moments before was gone.

She finished her thought before she lost her courage. "It's the same way you'll protect Jane and Ellen." She fought back tears. "You're a good man, Edward Stone."

"Lily, are you upset with me? Have I done something wrong?"

"No. You've done everything right." She couldn't bear it if she broke down in front of him. Realizing she loved him had tilted her world on its axis. She needed time to sort it all out. Before she said or did anything to make herself look foolish or needy. The last thing she wanted was for him to take care of her because he had to.

Why didn't she see it before?

All that time when she'd resisted helping others because she faded into the background of life, she'd wanted to be appreciated for who she was—not what she did for others.

She'd done the same thing to Edward. Unknowingly. She couldn't use him. It would make her no different than Luther. Was that how he saw her? Did she look to him like someone who had only accepted his offer of marriage for what she would benefit from it?

Her love for him poured over every thought she had. Nothing was the same anymore. Not the way she felt about him. Not even the way he looked to her was the same. He'd always been handsome. Through the filter of love she saw him for who he really was. Inside. A loving champion. A brave protector.

Used by everyone who could benefit from him.

She wouldn't do that to him. Not anymore. She needed time alone to pray and think.

"I need to go to bed. Please forgive me. I'll do the dishes in the morning." She opened the door and looked back at him. "Good night, Edward."

He stood silent, perplexed by her retreat.

Inside her room, she leaned against the closed door, eyes lifted in prayer.

Lord, help me. I never thought to love him, but I do. What do I do? If he still needed me, we might be able to

*make something of our marriage. As it is, I can't risk de-
stroying our friendship by letting him know how I feel.*

If Jane and Ellen moved out, their marriage would
change. Hiding her newly discovered feelings without
Ellen acting as a buffer between them would make their
marriage more challenging. She could move into Ellen's
room and treat him like the friend he had become. Could
her heart bear it?

Lily was up early the next morning. Spending the night
in anxious prayer had yielded no answers. The only positive thought was Ellen in the arms of her mother. In the
end that was the thing that mattered most.

Hoping to avoid questions from Jane, Lily dressed
quickly and went to wake Edward. His reaction to Jane's
questions about their sudden marriage let her know he
didn't want his sister to know the details of their relationship.

She knelt to lean over his sleeping form and wished he
loved her. He lay on his back. The steady rise and fall of
his chest, coupled with the peaceful expression, made her
want to let him rest. Unable to help herself, she reached
to move a wisp of hair that fell across his forehead. He
stirred, and she snatched her hand away.

"Good morning, Edward," she whispered and put a
hand on his shoulder to nudge him a bit. "I thought you'd
want to be up before Jane wakes."

He drew in a deep breath and opened his eyes. The
cloud of sleep in them cleared to a smile like none he'd
ever given her. Light shone in their depths. Without the
guard of wakefulness, did he harbor feelings for her, too?
"Lily." He lifted his hand and caressed her cheek.

The door to Ellen's room opened, and Jane came into

the room. Lily jerked to her feet. Edward leaned up on one elbow.

Jane spoke first. "I'm sorry, I didn't mean to interrupt..." She left the rest of her thought to hang in the tense air.

"You've no need to apologize." Lily tried to think of something else to say. What would her sister-in-law think of her? Edward sleeping on the floor, and his wife sneaking around in the early morning to wake him didn't portray an image of a happy newlywed couple.

Edward lumbered to his feet. "You're not interrupting, Jane." He folded the quilt and tossed it onto the settee. "Lily was just..."

He looked to her for help, but she didn't know what to say. "I was just deciding what to make for breakfast." She hurried to the stove. "How about oatmeal? It's a chilly morning."

The three of them set about their morning routine. No one mentioned the awkwardness of Jane discovering Edward in the front room. Ellen woke while Lily cooked. She came to the table without brushing her hair. Her doll hung over from the crook in her elbow.

Lily tousled her hair. "You need to brush your hair."

"Momma does it for me." Ellen backed away from her touch.

Jane turned from stoking the fire. "Ellen, did Aunt Lily teach you to brush your hair?"

Ellen shot a glance from Lily to her mother. "She did, but you always did it before. I like it when you do it."

Lily turned back to the stove and ladled oatmeal into bowls. Edward didn't need her help with Ellen now that Jane was back. It appeared Ellen didn't need her, either.

Jane spoke to Ellen. "I'll brush your hair tonight before bed as a treat. This morning you will do as your aunt

Lily said." Ellen tromped into the bedroom and closed the door. Jane smiled at Lily. "She has always been a mite stubborn. Thank you for teaching her. She has such thick hair, I always found it quicker to do it myself. You've saved me much work in the future."

"Ellen is a sweet child. She likes to have her own way, but she is a dear."

"What a gracious description of my little one." Jane chuckled and came to pour milk for Ellen and coffee for the adults.

Lily liked Jane. She admired the way she spoke to Ellen. She appreciated that Jane hadn't belabored the situation this morning by insisting on knowing why Edward wasn't in the bedroom with his new wife. Jane was considerate, someone Lily would choose for a friend. She hoped Jane wouldn't think less of her if she found out that Edward hadn't wanted to marry her.

Edward came in the front door carrying an armload of firewood. He put the wood on the hearth. "I hope you two are getting to know one another." He brushed his gloves together and pulled them off.

"We are, brother dear." Jane set the platter of ham Lily had cooked on the table. "You've married quite a nice person. Ellen told me Lily has even taught her to brush her own hair."

He came to the table. "Lily has taught us all a lot. Even taught me and Ellen a bit about cooking." He caught Lily's attention and winked at her again. If he didn't stop this open flirtation, how was she to rein in her heart?

Ellen came out of her room dressed for school with her hair neatly brushed. Jane pulled her into a hug.

"Momma, do I gotta go to school today?" Ellen's eyes

were filled with hope for a day at home. She dropped into her seat at the table.

"Not today, moppet. I want to spend every minute of today with you." Jane sat beside her daughter.

Edward prayed and the food was passed around the table. "Jane, we need to make some arrangements for your future."

A pall settled over the table. "I've been thinking about that all the way home from Santa Fe." Jane put her fork down and looked at Ellen. "How would you like to help me open the bakery and run it? We're going to need to earn money, and I could use a good helper."

Ellen swallowed big. "Do you mean it? I can help?" Her eyes filled with tears as her young heart tried again to digest the loss of her father. "But how will we do it without Papa?" She dashed the back of her hand across her eyes. "And Lily has her shop in the bakery now."

Jane looked at Edward and then back to Ellen. "You let the adults work out the details. You just be ready to become a baker." Jane put a hand on Ellen's on the table. "Without Papa here, we'll have to take care of ourselves." Sadness washed over Ellen at the words.

Edward cleared his throat. "I'm going to make certain you're both taken care of."

Lily listened like a stranger in the place she'd come to think of as home. She'd allowed herself to become the mistress of this house, and now she sat listening to Edward pledge himself as provider to his sister and her daughter. Where would she fit in the scheme of things? Did she?

As soon as she could, Lily excused herself and headed to the shop, leaving Edward and his family to plan a future that might not include her. She couldn't sit and listen.

Edward would have to tell her later. If Jane was going to take over the building, Lily didn't know what would happen to her business.

With a deep love for Edward filling her heart and mind, she knew the shop wasn't important. Not when her marriage was on the brink. Would he want her out of his life, the same way his sister was about to say she wanted Lily out of her building?

Edward and Jane walked into Lily's shop to the sound of the clanging bell. He rubbed his hands together in the warmth of the room.

Jane looked everywhere at once and spoke softly to herself, "Oh, my. This is lovely."

Lily came through the doorway that led to the workroom. "Good after…noon…" The words died on her lips when she saw him and Jane. Her face was pale, and her eyes were the lightest blue he'd ever seen them.

"We wanted to come by and let you know what we've worked out." He hoped Lily would be as pleased with their decision as he and Jane were.

Lily stopped beside the glass display case that held her most valuable merchandise and put a steadying hand on the heavy piece of furniture. "I'm ready." She looked as if she was braced for bad news.

Jane burst out with their plans. "I'm going to open my bakery!" She looked around the shop with a smile as big as Texas. He'd wanted Jane to do this before. Watching her excitement confirmed his belief that her own bakery would go a long way toward making her happy again.

Lily balled the hand that held the side of the display case into a fist. Her knuckles grew white. "I'm very happy for you. You deserve a fresh start after all you've been through."

Edward grinned at Lily. "I knew you'd agree. That's what I think, too. It will be something positive that she and Ellen can do together. It's not the life we all hoped they'd have." He put a hand on Jane's shoulder. She smiled in acknowledgment of his sympathy. "But I think it's the best way to move on with their lives."

Lily wrung her hands in front of her skirt. "When do you plan to open?"

Jane had moved to the front window. "Almost immediately. Ellen and I will move in this afternoon."

"That soon?" Lily looked surprised.

"I don't want to put you and Edward out any more than I already have. You've been so gracious to care for Ellen, but I think the sooner she and I get settled into our new life, the sooner she'll accept her father's passing and begin to heal."

Lily paled. "Do you think she's ready for such a big adjustment so soon?"

Edward answered her. "I think it will give her something to keep her mind on. Give her hope." He added, "Plus, she's been telling her mother about the things you've taught her."

"Where is she?" Lily looked through the front glass as if expecting to see Ellen outside the shop window.

"She's packing her things. She promised to have everything together before Edward and I return, so she can scurry on over," Jane answered. "Edward was kind enough to come along so I could satisfy my curiosity about what you've done with this place. Everything is lovely. Much nicer than I'd imagined it could be."

"I did my best." Lily's voice wavered. "It's a lovely building."

Jane nodded. "The windows were what caught my eye. Beautiful displays are so important for drawing the customers in."

The door opened with a flourish, and the bell announced Ellen's arrival. She flung her arms around her mother. "I'm all finished." She gave Lily a giant smile. "Isn't it wonderful, Aunt Lily? Me and Momma are going to open the bakery at last. She's even gonna let me help name it." She took a deep breath and asked her mother, "Can I start bringing my stuff across the street? It's not too heavy."

Edward laughed. "I'll carry everything over this afternoon." Seeing these three ladies safe and happy was more than he'd dared to dream. His heart still contracted a bit when he looked at Jane with Ellen. He was so grateful God had seen fit to spare Jane. Ellen wouldn't grow up without her loving mother in her life. Edward would do everything he could as her uncle to make up for the void left by her father's passing.

"I'm very happy for you, Ellen." Lily's love for his niece was apparent. "You'll have to let me know which name you decide on. I want to be one of your first customers." Lily looked at him then. He saw the brewing storm in her eyes as they darkened.

He wanted to speak to Lily alone. "Now that you've shared your news, Ellen, why don't you and your mother have lunch at the hotel? I imagine she might even let you have dessert today."

"Can we, Momma? Just the two of us?" Ellen tugged on Jane's hand.

Jane laughed at her daughter's excitement. "If you

promise to be on your best manners." She put a hand on Edward's sleeve. "Thank you for all your help. I don't know what I'd have done without you at the bank today. And thank you, Lily, for being so kind. I know my arrival has unsettled your world. I'm grateful for all you've done for Ellen and Edward."

"It has been my joy to spend time with Ellen."

Ellen left her mother's side and went to hug Lily. "I had fun with you, too, Aunt Lily." She released her and went with Jane out of the shop.

Edward watched them go and turned to see Lily wipe a finger under one eye. "Are you crying?" He went to her side.

"I'm fine." She took a step back. "If you'll excuse me, I've quite a lot to think about." She pivoted to go into the workroom. He put a hand on her elbow.

"Lily, tell me what's wrong. I know the news about Wesley isn't what we'd hoped for, but it's almost like a miracle that Jane is home with Ellen."

She kept her back to him. "God was merciful. I know that my father was a rock to me and my sisters after our mother passed. Jane and Ellen will help each other heal. It's good they have the bakery to give them something to look forward to." Her voice caught, and he tugged her elbow until she turned to him.

"What's wrong then?"

"Don't you know?" Lily spread her hands out and spun to the left and right. "All of this. How am I supposed to close my shop in one afternoon? Where will I store everything until I can figure out what to do? And there's the question of Lavinia. Where will she go?" She almost didn't breathe for talking so fast. "I guess she could sleep in Ellen's room tonight, but she can't stay there. I'm sure you'll want me to move my things in there." She stopped and looked at him, despair in her eyes. "Or do you want me to do that this afternoon?" She gasped and choked back a sob. "Or do you want me there at all?"

Her words spun in his ears like a twister. Where had the torrent come from? "Why would you close your shop? And why can't Lavinia stay here?"

"There isn't room upstairs for three people. It's just big enough for Jane and Ellen. And if she wants to open the bakery immediately, I'll have to have my merchandise out of the way." She sighed and looked over his shoulder. "And the sign." Tears filled her eyes, but she didn't let them fall. "It fits so perfectly in this window. I don't know if I can find somewhere new and use it. It's exactly what I wanted. You captured the heart of my designs when you made it." She turned to him. "Do you think you could alter it?" She sniffled on the last words.

"Alter it?" He reached for her hands. "It's fine right where it is."

"But it's going to be a bakery now." Her frown was full of sorrow, not anger.

"Oh, Lily, did you think Jane was going to come in here and run you out?"

"She said she wanted to move in this afternoon. She talked about the display windows and Ellen said she could carry her things across the street."

"All of that is true. Jane loved those windows from the first time we looked at this building. And she is moving this afternoon."

"That's why I've got to figure out what I'm going to do with everything." She stopped crying and stared at him. The strength she'd shown in every situation came to the fore again. "Lavinia will help me." She pulled her hands, but he didn't let her go. He would never let her go.

"Lily, Jane is buying the building between the post office and the bank. I went with her to the bank to arrange a loan to help her until your father arrives and buys the hotel."

A cloud crossed her face. "Two doors down from here?" Her voice was very soft, wary even.

"Yes. It was actually built by the same man who built this place." He leaned close to her. "It has the same display windows."

"It does?" Confusion still filled her face.

"It does." He put a hand on her cheek. "So you don't need to close your shop. Jane is going to start fresh in a new location. She'll still be across the street from me, so I can keep an eye on her and Ellen."

"But what about us?" There was a plea in her words that gave his heart hope. Hope he never thought he'd experience. After a lifetime of working and doing good for others, he'd given up hope of having something wonderful for himself. Somewhere along the way, he'd become content to muddle through life without thinking about all he was missing by being alone.

Since he'd married Lily for the sake of Ellen, he thought this was just a new chapter in the story of his life—with the same ending. He'd solve someone else's problem with little to no thought or benefit for himself.

But his life had changed forever the day he'd married her. When he'd brushed that kiss across her gentle cheek after Reverend Dismuke had spoken the ceremonial words over them, his heart had awakened. Like a new morning with just a twinge of light breaking through the darkness of a long night, the changes had been gradual.

The darkness gave way to shadows that were banished in the full light of a new day. Today. The day he knew he loved Lily with every part of who he was.

God, please don't let her dash my hope. I never dreamed You'd bring someone as amazing as Lily into my life. Please let her love me as much as I love her. If not, please let her stay long enough for me to show her how I feel.

Lily didn't know what to think. Or how to feel. She'd gone from contentment with Edward and Ellen the day before to realizing she loved him. Then his sister, a woman who truly needed him, had come into their lives and turned everything upside down.

That wasn't fair. Lily's life had turned upside down when Edward swept her into his arms the night of the fire. No matter how she'd dismissed his kindnesses and attention, he'd won her heart. But did he want it?

Edward squeezed her hands in his. "What about us?" His handsome face crinkled into a smile. "You and me?" The smile grew.

She couldn't hide her biggest fear. "You don't need me anymore."

He pulled her hands together and pressed his lips to her knuckles. "You don't think I need you?"

Her head spun. She couldn't think straight if he kissed her. And those eyes. They drew her into the brown depths. She could see her reflection in the dark center. "You married me for Ellen."

He grew serious. "I did."

Lily didn't realize she was holding her breath. "You didn't lie to me about why you wanted us to marry, but

I've grown to believe you would be a part of my life forever. And now you don't need me anymore."

A twinkle danced in his eyes. "What do you intend to do?" He released her hands.

"I guess I could move into Ellen's room, unless you want me to move here with Lavinia." She hadn't had time to think.

"I don't want you to do that."

"But with Jane here, you don't need me." She braced herself for his response. How could she survive without him? He'd gotten inside her thoughts. Her prayers. Her dreams.

Edward leaned back a bit. "Do I need you? Will I be able to take my next breath without you?"

Lily stumbled a step away from him. Catching one hand in his, he righted her. She didn't speak.

"I will. But I can guarantee you, that breath won't be as sweet. I'll get hungry tomorrow, and I'll eat. But I won't be satisfied."

He tugged on her hand. "I can still see, but without you, nothing is as beautiful."

Lily's mind reeled with a dance she never thought she'd dance when she'd watched life pass her by from behind a punch bowl in East River. She seemed to melt in front of him. An aching, slow dissolving of the fear of his rejection.

He took advantage of this rare moment of her silence. "When you offered friendship to Miss Aiken and Mrs. Jones, I thought you were taking too much of a risk." His smile was so distracting. The words tumbled from his lips. She must concentrate. In the space of just a few minutes, her world spun around. The nuances still unclear, she forced her focus on his words.

"You proved me wrong." He smiled and dropped his hand to her waist. "When you didn't want to tell Ellen that her parents were probably not coming back, I thought you were refusing to face reality and trying to protect Ellen from the inevitable truth. To be honest, I'd given up hope of Jane coming home again. The letters had stopped. Then the telegraph came saying they'd been gravely ill and couldn't be found."

She wanted to stanch the flow. His heart had been evident from the first day they met, from the minute she felt it beating in his chest when he carried her out of the fire. Only a selfless man would care like he did. For Ellen. For the church. Even for Mrs. Croft in all her orneriness.

"Edward."

He shook his head to silence her. "I didn't think they were coming back. Over and again you've shown hope and faith." He released her and stepped back.

She tried to breathe. To take in every word. To embrace the hope he was talking about. Hope she'd relinquished in the dark of last night.

He took her hand and stared into her eyes. "You taught me by example. So much so, I'm going to take a big step for me." He reached to tuck a strand of hair behind her ear, the touch gentle and full of caring. "I'm going to have faith you'll be willing to risk your happiness with someone who's settled with contentment for too long. I don't just need you. I love you." He pulled her hand back to his lips and brushed the knuckles with a promise.

She found her voice. "I was so weary of helping others all the time. That's why I made the needlework of the verse in the workroom. I had to remember to care for others more than I care for myself. I got lost taking care of others before." She put her other hand in his and pulled them together between the two of them as she leaned closer. "But I've learned that when I help others, I'm becoming a better person. You've shown me the joy of helping others. You sacrificed your life to take care of Ellen—and then to marry me and save my reputation in this town. When I took care of my father, I was happy to do it, but I got tired. Taking care of Ellen was a joy. Taking care of you will be my life's delight. I love you."

She leaned away from him and warned, "I'm never going to be able to avoid controversy. If I see someone in need, it doesn't matter to me what people will think if I help them."

Edward gathered her into his arms. He kissed her temple. "That's one of my favorite things about you."

All the breath swooshed from her when he dropped to one knee, taking both her hands in his. "Will you stay married to me, so we can spend our days loving and caring for each other?"

His eyebrows wrinkled his forehead as he waited.

"On one condition." Lily couldn't believe this was happening. How did the loneliest woman in East River become the happiest woman in Pine Haven?

"What would that condition be?" Dimples came into view, teasing her for an answer.

"Only if you promise to catch me when I fall."

"I promise." And he proved his word by pulling her off balance into his waiting arms.

Epilogue

◜◞

March 1881

The day was finally here. The morning train would arrive soon.

Edward reached to help Lily from the wagon. The feel of her waist in his hands as he set her to the ground never grew old. How had he managed to snare such a lovely woman?

"You can let go now." Lily tapped him on the shoulder.

"I don't want to." He winked and grinned.

Ellen ran up the sidewalk with Speckles in his basket. The kitten dug his claws into the wicker, seemingly accustomed to her boisterous ways. Ellen had convinced her mother that Speckles should live with them.

"I can't wait to meet your papa." The child gave Lily a hug. "Uncle Edward says he's real nice."

Laughter bubbled in Lily's throat. "He is. I think your uncle Edward might be just a bit nervous to meet him again today."

"He might be nervous, but Uncle Edward ain't never

scared." Ellen skipped over to a nearby bench and sat playing with Speckles.

Edward covered the hand Lily tucked into his elbow with one of his own. "I know God brought you here. The letters your father and I have exchanged since our marriage have been pleasant. I see no reason to be nervous." Funny how tight his collar felt as he said the words. Mr. Warren had agreed for them to marry, but it was the first time he'd meet the man as his son-in-law.

Winston Ledford stepped through the door of the depot onto the platform.

"Ledford." Edward greeted the man, trying to follow Lily's example of being hopeful that people could change.

Edward felt Lily's reassuring squeeze on his arm. "Hello, Mr. Ledford."

"Stone, Mrs. Stone." Winston touched the brim of his hat with two fingers.

"I hear you two are the guests of honor at a big shindig today."

"We are," Lily answered for them. "My father is hosting a celebration of our marriage. You're welcome to come. We want to share how God has blessed us with all our friends and neighbors."

"No, thank you, Mrs. Stone. You may have won Lovey over to your Bible ways, but not me."

"You'll be in our prayers," Lily countered in her true Christian fashion, loving people who didn't know they needed to be loved.

"Don't know as I can stop you from praying, but don't expect to see me in your church." Winston Ledford made his way to the edge of the building and disappeared around the corner.

"Some people take longer than others to realize God

loves them." Edward pulled her close. "Don't give up. You won me over."

"You didn't need winning over." She smiled at him. "You just needed to remember how big God's love is."

Jane joined them on the platform. "Ellen insisted we be here for your reunion with your family." His sister embraced Lily. "I think reunions are wonderful." She smiled at Ellen as she bounded up to them.

"I'm especially pleased to meet the man who made it possible for me to stay in Pine Haven. Because of his purchase of the hotel, I had the funds to open the bakery." She kissed Ellen on the top of her head.

"Momma lets me work in the bakery, too. Momma's Bakery will be mine when I grow up."

Lily smiled at Ellen. "Tell me again how you chose the name for the bakery." She knew her niece loved to share the story.

"I always called it Momma's Bakery. She makes the best bread and cakes I ever ate, and everybody loves her cooking. Your store has your name on it, so Momma should have her name on the bakery."

Edward rubbed Speckles behind the ears. "I'm relieved to have you back in town, Jane, and to know you're staying. Don't know what I'd do without Ellen to make me smile."

Lily added, "I'm glad you found a good location. My shop is doing so well, with Lavinia's promise to stay on and help, I'm able to keep up. I wasn't sure how I'd handle having to move."

A whistle blew in the distance. The train would arrive in minutes.

Edward pulled Lily aside.

"I love you." He whispered the words to her. "Are you ready?"

The violet of her eyes told him she was. "Yes." She lifted a gloved hand to touch the side of his face. "Lavinia is closing the shop now. Daisy and her family will meet us at the hotel. They thought Papa would want a moment to greet his new son-in-law before the celebration. Daisy can hardly wait to tell him and Jasmine about their coming addition. She didn't want to take away from our moment. So much joy for Papa in one day."

He put an arm around her shoulders. The sweet scent of her hair filled his senses. "I've been thinking about something."

She turned to look at him, their faces almost touching. "What would that be?"

"With Jane and Ellen moving into their new home over the bakery, it's been awfully quiet at our house."

"It has been." She leaned against his shoulder, and he put his other arm around her.

"Maybe we need to give Ellen a cousin or two." She jerked her face to his. Pink flooded her cheeks.

"I'd like that very much." She stepped up to kiss his cheek.

"Is that so?" He grinned at her. "Before I met you, I thought I'd spend the rest of my days alone or with Ellen."

Lily took a step back and stumbled. He caught her by the elbows and settled her onto her feet.

"God always puts someone in your life to love you." The softness of her answer pulled him in. "And someone for you to love."

* * * * *

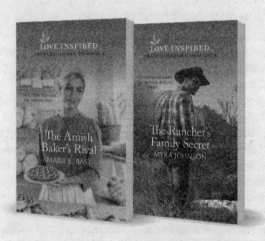

SPECIAL EXCERPT FROM

LOVE INSPIRED
INSPIRATIONAL ROMANCE

With the help of her service dog, she's finally living her life, but is she healed enough to help her past bully care for two orphaned little girls?

Read on for a sneak preview of
Earning Her Trust *by Brenda Minton*
available May 2022 from Love Inspired.

The brick building that housed the county Division of Family Services always brought back a myriad of emotions for Emery Guthrie. As she stood on the sidewalk on a too-warm day in May, the memories came back stronger than ever.

Absently, she reached to pet her service dog, Zeb. The chocolate-brown labradoodle understood that touch and he moved close to her side. He grounded her to reality, to the present. She'd been rescued.

Rescued. She drew on that word. She'd been rescued. By this place, this building and the people inside. They'd seen her father jailed for the abuse that had left her physically and emotionally broken. They'd placed her with a foster mother, Nan Guthrie, the woman who had adopted her as a teen, giving her a new last name and a new life.

But today wasn't about Emery. It was about the two young girls whom Nan had been caring for the past few weeks. They'd lost their parents in a terrible, violent tragedy. They'd been uprooted from their home, their lives and all they'd ever known, brought to Pleasant, Missouri, and placed with Nan until their new guardian could be found.

That man was Beau Wilde. A grade ahead of Emery, Beau had spent their school years making her life even more miserable with his bullying.

He'd taunted, teased and humiliated her.

She shook her head, as if freeing herself from the thoughts she'd not allowed to see the light of day in many years. Those memories belonged in the past.

Just then, a truck pulled off the road and circled the parking lot.

Emery hesitated a moment too long. Beau was out of his truck and heading in her direction. He nodded as he closed in on her.

"Please, let me." He opened the door and stepped back to allow her to go first. "Nice dog."

"Thank you," she whispered. She cleared her throat. "His name is Zeb."

Don't miss
Earning Her Trust *by Brenda Minton*
wherever Love Inspired books and ebooks are sold.

LoveInspired.com

LOVE INSPIRED

Stories to uplift and inspire

Fall in love with Love Inspired—
inspirational and uplifting stories of faith
and hope. Find strength and comfort in
the bonds of friendship and community.
Revel in the warmth of possibility and the
promise of new beginnings.

Sign up for the Love Inspired newsletter
at **LoveInspired.com** to be the first
to find out about upcoming titles,
special promotions and exclusive content.

CONNECT WITH US AT:

Facebook.com/LoveInspiredBooks

Twitter.com/LoveInspiredBks

LISOCIAL2021